INTO THE SUFFERING CITY

A NOVEL OF BALTIMORE

BILL LEFURGY

Front cover image: Baltimore, MD, looking west from 400 block East Baltimore Street, 1910. Back cover: Baltimore, MD, looking north from Federal Hill, ca. 1900-1906. Both images from Library of Congress, Prints and Photographs Division (accessed March 6, 2020).

ISBN (Paperback): 978-0-578-61878-4
ISBN (Kindle): 978-0-578-62545-4
LCCN (Paperback): 2019920495

This novel's story and characters are either products of the author's imagination or used fictitiously. Baltimore is, of course, a real city and the author has worked to frame the novel in an accurate physical and historical context. Any resemblance to actual events, organizations, or persons, living or dead, is entirely coincidental.

First edition: April 15, 2020

High Kicker Books

Takoma Park, MD

www.billlefurgy.com

TITLES BY BILL LEFURGY

Sarah Kennecott and Jack Harden Mystery Series

INTO THE SUFFERING CITY: A NOVEL OF BALTIMORE (BOOK 1)

MURDER IN THE HAUNTED CHAMBER (BOOK 2)

Non-Fiction

CRIMINAL SLANG: ANNOTATED EDITION OF THE 1908 DICTIONARY OF THE VERNACULAR OF THE UNDERWORLD

PROSTITUTION AND ILLICIT SEX IN BALTIMORE: COMMERCIALIZED VICE, REPORT OF THE MARYLAND VICE COMMISSION, 1916

For Lisa, with love for Russell, Eileen, Tristan, and Violet

"Through me the way into the suffering city,
Through me the way to the eternal pain,
Through me the way that runs among the lost.
Justice urged on my high artificer;
My maker was divine authority,
The highest wisdom, and the primal love.
Before me nothing but eternal things
Were made, and I endure eternally
Abandon every hope, who enter here."
These words—their aspect was obscure—
I read inscribed above a gateway . . .
—Dante Alighieri, Inferno, Canto III, 1–11

All marriages between a white person and a negro [sic] or between
a white person and a person of negro [sic] descent to the third
generation inclusive are forever prohibited and shall be void and
any person violating the provisions of this section shall be deemed
guilty of an infamous crime and punished by imprisonment in the
penitentiary not less than eighteen months nor more than ten years.
—The Maryland Code, 1904, Article XLV, Sec. 305—Miscegenation
[Repealed 1967]

CHAPTER 1

SARAH—MONDAY, OCTOBER 11, 1909, 9:00 A.M.

*D*r. Sarah Kennecott scanned the dead girl's naked body. The corpse had a small bullet wound near the heart. The right side of the forehead had a one-inch gash over a swollen, purplish bruise, and dark material clustered under fingernails of the right hand. A shallow quarter-inch cut marked the top knuckle of the left index finger. The upper lip had a slight bulge.

Sarah knew exactly how to proceed with the postmortem examination—if she were in charge. Which she most definitely was not.

With difficulty, she broadened her awareness to include the three men also standing around the autopsy table. *Do make eye contact,* she told herself as her pulse sprinted. *Do control the tics. Do not offend the men. Stay out of trouble.*

Bare electric bulbs lit the body chamber of the Baltimore city morgue with brutal efficiency. The dead girl's blue-black lips contrasted with the bright white autopsy table, which had rust spots from where tools had chipped the enameled surface down to the iron base. Saws, drills, chisels, and knives lay ready on a scratched steel counter below shelves of organs floating in

1

murky glass jars. A harsh chemical stink mixed with the odor the dead hung in the dank air. None of the sights or smells disturbed Sarah's focus.

"Old Horace Shaw went and killed himself this pretty little high-kicker," rasped the coroner with a blast of whiskey breath. He was an older man with broken capillaries exploding across ruddy cheeks. A fine thread of what looked like maple syrup ran down one side of his chin whiskers and over his cravat.

"Just another day in Baltimore," said the medical examiner, whose gray handlebar mustache dominated his gaunt face. "Shaw and the rest of those damn politicians have let our city become a playground for fallen women. Every slattern south of New York has flocked here to make a dirty dollar." He shot a sharp look at the scribbling male attendant. "Don't put that in the notes!"

The attendant jumped. "I-I-I was only j-j-jotting the time and date, sir."

"Why can't we get a clerk who can speak right?" The medical examiner turned his cold gaze on Sarah. "And to top it off, we're forced to have this twitchy little girl standing in our way. Things are going to hell in a handcart around here."

Unlike with the dead, Sarah was uncomfortable with the living. Experience had taught her the best way to cope with people was to concentrate on the work at hand. She picked up a nearby clipboard holding the police report along with four photographic prints. One print was of the dead girl lying naked on her back in a bed against a wall. Someone had placed a towel over her chest and groin. The gain in modesty came at the expense of concealing how much blood was on or under the body.

Another photograph showed the whole room, which was in an extreme state of disorder. The final two photographs showed both sides of a small pistol; one side had "H. Shaw" engraved in bold lettering. The weapon was also covered with dark, swirly markings—the police had processed the gun for finger marks.

"There's no mystery here," said the coroner. "Police Commissioner Lipp wants us to work fast and get Shaw arrested. That will also have the benefit of knocking the commissioner's main competitor out of the mayor's race."

"Amen to that," said the medical examiner. "Commissioner Lipp is a godly man and the only one tough enough to clean up this city—he's got to be elected. All right, then. Let's get started."

"Her name is Lizzie Sullivan, a showgirl, nineteen years of age." Sarah read aloud from the report. "Police found the body in the deceased's boardinghouse room, along with a discharged pistol. A feather pillow with powder burns and a bullet hole was also found." The only sounds were the coroner's wheezy breathing and the drip of melted water from the corpse iceboxes. Sarah lowered the clipboard. "Where are the bedsheets from the crime scene?"

The medical examiner flicked a speck of dust off his white medical gown. "You're here, missy, strictly to observe. Stop your annoying prattle."

Sarah pressed the clipboard to her chest. "You must address me as 'Doctor.'" She forced herself to stop rocking back and forth on her feet. "You know my qualifications. I graduated from the Johns Hopkins School of Medicine this spring with a specialty in pathology. And let me remind you I am here at the request of the mayor to learn the truth behind this murder. That is my job with the Pinkerton National Detective Agency."

The two men rolled their eyes. "Political shenanigans," said the medical examiner. "The mayor must be in the pocket of the Pinkertons for him to send you instead of someone who knows what they're doing. What kind of physician works for a gumshoe firm?"

Sarah hesitated. He had a point—the Pinkerton Agency was

not her preferred employer. She should be working as a pathologist.

"No sheets. All we have is the body," said the coroner. "The report says there was blood on the bed. It's safe to assume she bled out."

"The report fails to specify how much spilled blood was present at the scene. We are missing a key piece of information." Sarah looked at the girl's body. "The victim is not, however, drained of blood."

The coroner's jaw tightened. "How do you know that, *Doctor*? We haven't even opened her up."

"Observe the lividity pattern." Sarah pointed to the pronounced purple patches along the visible edges of the girl's back, rear end, and thighs.

"Lividity is present even after severe blood loss," said the medical examiner with a deep sigh. "Guess your fancy school didn't teach you that."

"If she suffered severe blood loss, the lividity would be much reduced and would present as more pink than purple," said Sarah. "Also, let us consider the cut on the right side of the head. Surely it occurred before death." Sarah was swaying again, and her extended finger moved closer to, then farther away from the girl's head as she spoke. "The area is swollen and discolored, indicating the blood vessels had time to expand. There are signs of healing."

The coroner and the medical examiner glowered in silence. Sarah's shoulders clenched tighter and a bead of sweat rolled down her spine as she struggled to assess their reaction. It was reasonable to suspect they viewed her behavior as difficult. And, for unknown reasons, they were ignoring her valid points.

The men turned the body over on its side. "No sign of a bullet exit wound or any other trauma to the back," said the medical examiner. He rolled the body back and sliced into the abdomen. After a quick check of the stomach and other organs, he cut open the chest, using long-handled cutters to snip the ribs. Dipping his hands into the cavity, he conducted a perfunctory examination of the heart and lungs, splattering fluid onto his apron.

"Right. Here's the bugger." The medical examiner plunged forceps deep into the chest and pulled out a small bullet. "I say this is a homicide with death due to a twenty-five-caliber gunshot wound to the heart. That's consistent with the discharged pistol and the hole in the pillow. Will that make the commissioner happy, Mr. Coroner?"

"Yes," said the coroner. "It's the perfect finding."

"I disagree about the cause of death." Sarah blurted the words out. "The gunshot wound must have occurred after she died. The bullet pierced a coronary artery. If alive when shot, she would have bled internally and perhaps even jetted blood externally. Yet there is little internal hemorrhaging, and from the crime scene photograph it is apparent there was no blood spray on the bed or adjacent wall." Sarah forcefully gestured at the photo on the clipboard.

"Lower your damn voice, girl." The coroner snatched the report from her hand and flung it onto the nearby counter. The clipboard skittered over the slick surface and fell onto the floor, coming to rest under a cadaver ice chest in a puddle of water.

"Why are you unwilling to acknowledge obvious evidence? And you have not even examined the brain. This is not a competent examination," she said, small hands slashing the air.

"That's enough sass out of you." The coroner pointed a sausage-like finger at the door. "Get out."

"Ah, she's not worth your breath," said the medical examiner. "Let's get out of here and leave her to the sputtering clerk." The men laughed coarsely as they ambled off to the dressing room.

"Miss—I-I-I mean, Doctor—do you wish me to enter your

comments into the notes?" The morgue attendant stood poised with his pencil.

She slammed her palm on the workbench. "Do not mock me." He shrank away, Adam's apple bobbing. A pang of regret hit her for browbeating the man, who must have truly meant what he had said. She tried to relax the discomfort in her shoulders as she stared at a cockroach scuttling across the greasy tile floor. "No. Nothing I said is official, but I offer my gratitude to you for inquiring."

"You're more than welcome, Doctor. I have a daughter who's interested in nursing. She's a good student and sometimes has notions about becoming a physician. We tell her to be realistic. Still, it's wonderful to see a woman working in the health field."

"Your daughter's ambition is the most encouraging thing I have heard in days." Sarah stepped to within inches of the man. "There is a book your daughter must read. I will bring it to you."

"That's very kind, but please do not trouble yourself." The clerk took a step back as he spoke. "I-I-I can't be asking you to come back to this unpleasant place on my account."

"It is an excellent book in memory of Mary Putnam Jacobi. Dr. Jacobi won a Harvard University prize for her essay 'The Question of Rest for Women during Menstruation,' which refuted the notion that women had to rest during their monthlies to avoid damaging their reproductive organs." The clerk took another step back as Sarah kept talking. "Dr. Jacobi is a wonderful model for any girl considering medicine. And it is no bother for me to come back. I am at ease around the dead. We can understand with precision why they are, in fact, dead. I—"

"Thank you, Doctor. If you will excuse me, I-I-I need to suture the corpse and finish my report."

After washing, Sarah removed the white gown, ignoring the lint adhering to her jacket. She lifted her broad-brimmed hat, piled high with lace and silk flowers, from the coatrack and, with a complete absence of fuss, plopped the millinery on her head and anchored it with a single long pin.

Stepping outside, she put her hands over her eyes to escape the midmorning sunshine. She was at the edge of the harbor and engulfed with the smell of brackish water, raw sewage, and dead fish. An occasional warm breeze carried the smell of rotting oysters dumped outside a nearby packing plant, causing her to gag.

Harsh sounds came from everywhere—steamboat whistles, longshoremen shouts, sawmill shrieks. The noise forced her to clap her hands over her ears. Slowly Sarah adjusted to the full sensory experience and began walking.

The cabdriver who had brought her said he would wait at the nearby President Street Railroad Station, but she wanted to avoid the man at all costs. His crude sexual comments had been the worst she had endured in days.

She headed up East Falls Avenue toward Pratt Street, where she could find another cab. The fetid stream known as Jones Falls ran along her left. A silent procession of worn men shuffled by on the right, all bent under massive loads of freshly cut lumber.

As she walked, Sarah thought about her difficult time in the morgue, which was just the latest in a long line of confusing, often frustrating, encounters. She could never grasp why some people appreciated her ability while other people held it against her. At school, the instructors were fond of the girl they called "little miss professor" for her habit of talking in detail about a few favorite subjects. Classmates, on the other hand, called her a teacher's pet and relentlessly teased her social awkwardness.

She had excelled academically at Vassar and Hopkins, and then won a prestigious postgraduate internship in pathology at a major out-of-town hospital. But the internship supervisor, citing disobedience, had forced her out just last month. Somehow, she must find a way to fulfill the promise, made over the side-by-side graves of her father and older sister Grace, to focus her life on catching murderers.

Sarah's most immediate concern was getting back to the Pinkerton office as quickly as possible to write a report on Lizzie Sullivan's autopsy. Her boss would complain the report was too long and complicated. No matter—her only care was uncovering the truth.

A motorcar roared past and splashed foul liquid across her skirt from ankle to thigh. She looked at the stains in disbelief. Everything was so hard. She wanted to do good, but things kept going wrong.

Looking out over the sludge-brown Jones Falls, she saw mottled seagulls screeching and squawking as they jockeyed for bits of bobbing offal. Across the muddy flow, her eye went to a great blue heron standing in a shallow spot, elegantly dipping its beak and pulling out one waggling fish after another. She watched until the bird had its fill and took flight toward the harbor, and beyond that, the open waters of the Chesapeake Bay.

She continued walking and reached a spot where the entire width of the street was covered by a pool of water so big the breeze stood up little waves on its surface. Sarah hitched her long skirts and kept going. At the halfway point the pool was two inches deep. Just then, the breeze stopped and an oily rainbow spread on the water before her.

She remembered how her dear sister Grace used to say that seeing a rainbow meant happiness was coming. As much as Sarah wanted a change for the better, there was absolutely no valid reason to think that colors on a puddle promised her anything.

CHAPTER 2

JACK—MONDAY, OCTOBER 11, 1909, 9:00 A.M.

*T*he Monumental Lunchroom was all about location. Near the intersection of Baltimore and Charles Streets, the joint sat in the heart of the city, wedged between the business and government districts.

It was the perfect spot for a guy with a load of bad beef to pass cash to a health inspector over a plate of scrambled eggs, or for a city councilman blocking expansion of a burlesque hall to share a cup of coffee with the hall owner and discuss what a showgirl could do to solve the problem. It was also the ideal place for a private dick to snag clients driven by the typical mix of fear, desperation, greed, and revenge.

Jack stood on the sidewalk in front of the beanery, wincing at the sudden clack and screech of a passing streetcar. People glanced at him as they came and went. They saw a tall, clean-shaven man in his late twenties, lean as a wolf, a battered derby pulled low over his eyes. Despite his threadbare suit, frayed shirt, and scruffy necktie, his black leather shoes gleamed.

Nobody looked at him closely enough to detect the paralyzing dread that made it hard for him to take a breath. And he had good reason to be afraid. He owed Jimmy "Knuckles" Vogel

9

nine hundred dollars, plus the 20 percent vig, with no way to start paying the marker when it came due Saturday. If he didn't come up with a two-hundred-dollar payment, Vogel's gorillas would come visiting. But that wasn't driving Jack's panic.

He forced himself to go inside and find a table with a view of the front door. Black coffee showed up, but as the burned, bitter liquid hit his lips more of it slopped onto the saucer than into his mouth. He poured the brew back into the cup, willing his hand steady as the homey smell of hot grease stirred a faint interest in breakfast. Looking back to the door, his stomach flopped and his fists clenched. These were the kind of people he was truly scared of—thankfully he saw them first.

The man was big, with a neatly trimmed dark beard. Pulling at the guy's hand was a boy about three years old. The child looked calm but could start bawling any second. A week ago, the last time he was in this place, a squawking brat had conjured Jack's ghosts and sent him into one of his violent blackout fits. He could only hope today's kid would keep his yap shut.

"Should I be mad or glad to see you, hon?" The waitress, unlike himself, remembered all the details from his last visit.

"Be happy as a June bug, darling. I've got nothing but joy in my heart."

"And nothing in your wallet." She was an older woman with a humped back and a mass of wrinkles framing deep-set eyes. "Mr. Top Hat was in a couple of days ago looking for you about a job of work he needed doing. He's given up on you, I reckon."

Lady Fortune was really giving him the cold shoulder. The man with the top hat had paid top-dollar last month to cover up a congressman's habit of cheating at high-stakes poker. Jack delivered a payoff to the cardsharp, who was threatening to blab. But the guy was greedy and wanted more. Jack countered with a threat to spread word about the sharp's ring with the hidden pin used to mark cards. That shut him up. "Sorry to have missed the man. I was showing some visiting English nobility the sights."

"Flapdoodle. The only dukes you know are your two ignorant fists." Her eyes narrowed to slits. "Joke if you want, but everybody knows you've got real bad nervous trouble. Get both your oars in the water, boy, or nobody's going to hire you to get a cat out of a tree."

"Doing great. Honestly, I've spent the last week strolling around our fine community." That was true if walking feverishly twelve hours a day counted as strolling.

He took the same path every time, about twenty miles, from his room near the Fells Point waterfront out Dundalk Avenue past the eastern city line to the smoke-belching steelworks at Sparrows Point, then back along North Point Boulevard and west all the way to the seven-furlong oval of Pimlico race track, then back through Druid Hill Park and along the Baltimore and Ohio Railroad tracks to his starting point. It was the only way to manage his relentless agitation and tortured thoughts. And dodge his ghosts.

"Get ahold of yourself." She punched his arm, leaving it numb. "Where's the man who understands people like nobody's business? There've been times when you're more like one of those clairvoyant mind-reader types than a private detective. Like when you figured out where they hid that kidnapped boy."

"That was almost a year ago."

"Sure. But you saved a kid. Some soft-headed types went all swoony and thought you were a hero."

"Yeah, and it did make me all warm inside. Too bad it didn't make me any money." The family had hired him to get the kid back, promising a fat bonus. He'd quickly tracked one of the kidnappers to a speakeasy over in the Canton neighborhood. The guy loved to blab, and three rounds of whiskey later, he let slip where the boy was.

Jack got lucky later that night when he found the kid's two minders drunk. He was less lucky when one of them managed to grind a broken bottle into his calf, but the kid got home safe. He ended up with no luck at all when the family stiffed him on the bonus.

After that, he drifted toward fixing problems for a certain kind of rich man. The type who would pay well for hushing up a scorned mistress, shutting down an extortionist, or paying off a cop to dismiss this or that charge. Stuff that Jack justified to himself as only borderline crooked.

The work centered on assessing two things about the person who could make the client's problem go away. First was sensing an emotional soft spot—such as the mistress's lingering affection, the extortionist's secret fear, or the cop's particular greed. Second was knowing how much cash it would take to leverage the sentiment to his employer's advantage. He had no shortage of work. When he could do it.

The waitress shook her head. "Do you have a nickel for some apple pie? Might as well make some money off you before you don't have a feather to fly with. Or get killed."

"Yes, ma'am, please. And another cup of your best black misery." She ambled off with her skewed gait. He glanced around again to size up the crowd. The bearded man and the kid were busy with big dishes of steaming grits. Good.

Jack had come to Baltimore two years ago, fresh out of the army. The seventh-largest city in the country with half a million people offered anonymity—and the place was alive with money.

Baltimore's harbor, on the Atlantic Ocean, generated cash from shipping everything from fresh seafood, to chemical fertilizer, to manufactured goods. The city was a railroad hub, and steel rails moved freight practically everywhere. Streams of travelers packed luxurious new hotels and fleabag flophouses every day of the year. Cash lubricated local politics, and there was the bonus of even more government-related dough flowing just forty miles down the road in Washington, DC.

He'd also come to appreciate Baltimore's mad energy. People poured in from the countryside to make more money, grab more freedom, and have more fun than they ever could have dreamed of back on the farm. A supercharged culture carried everyone along on a current of change that left the old days and the old ways in the dust. The relentless focus on the hustle-rush, brand-new, right-now sometimes helped him forget about the past.

"Copper's here looking for you about a murder." The waitress approached with her veiny hands shooing. "I don't know what you've gone and done, but get yourself out the back fast as you can."

Jack had no memory of a murder, but it didn't pay to take chances. The cops might just be in the mood to knock him around for the heck of it. Give any set of men uniforms and badges, and it was a sure bet they'd push people around just because they could. He ran into the alley behind the lunchroom. It was blocked at both ends. Men were rolling barrels off a freight wagon to the left, and two cops stood in front of a patrol wagon to the right, their tall leather helmets making them look like big bullets.

"Harden," said a beefy sergeant with a patchy red face and drippy mustache. "You must think we're galoots." The man yawned extravagantly and smacked his lips. It was as if he'd just woken from a nap, which maybe he had. Cops were notorious for cooping—bedding down during their shifts in the cozy back room of some cooperative store owner or saloon keeper.

"Thought never crossed my mind," said Jack, walking toward them. "Just trying to get away from a gal with a bone to pick. You know how that goes, right? If you'll excuse me, I'll be on my way."

"You're coming with us."

"Why should I, boys?" Jack heard the blood pounding in his ears as he looked at the cops in their long blue coats with the shiny brass buttons and the gleaming badges, slouching with the easy arrogance that comes from authority.

The sergeant spit a long stream of tobacco juice at Jack's feet.

"Listen, lowlife, if you know what's good for you, just do what I say. Or we'll let the locust wood do the talking." The other cop, his pointy nose veering brokenly off to one side, walked up and poked Jack with a nightstick.

Jack turned to the guy. "Lay off." He tried to keep his voice level, but there was an edge to his words.

The cop took a step closer. He smelled of cabbage and beer. "Aw, that weren't a good poke. This is." The nightstick rammed into Jack's ribs and almost knocked him over. Time slowed as he staggered and then straightened up. Jack looked at the cop and saw it would be duck soup to throw a right cross into that bent nose. He imagined the satisfying feel of the impact flowing up his arm as the cop went down. Satisfying but stupid.

"Come on now before we beat you like a darkie," said the sergeant. "And hand over that Colt you got."

Jack was fond of the Colt Army Artillery revolver, but not so much to get knocked around over it. He presented the piece butt-first. Twisty-nosed cop looked so disappointed Jack almost smiled before they hustled him into the Black Maria, slammed the wagon door, and threw the bolt.

Today's roll of the dice was a crap-out, which was nothing new; he was on an endless losing streak. *For they have sown the wind, and they shall reap the whirlwind: it hath no stalk; the bud shall yield no meal: if so be it yield, the strangers shall swallow it up.*

The voice in his head spouting scripture was a new problem. Jack banged his skull against the wall for a few seconds before the voice quit. The wagon rattled and rumbled for a while and stopped. Then—nothing. Thirty minutes—an hour? —dragged by. He sat in the dark listening to the passing thump of hooves and grumble of metal wheels on the granite paving stones. The street whir was almost soothing.

With no warning the rear doors flew open and the cop sergeant grabbed Jack's arm to hustle him along the sidewalk. They were on Baltimore Street, outside the Continental Building. At sixteen stories, the place was the tallest skyscraper in the city. They went into the grand entrance under the spread wings of two huge black brass birds—eagles, or maybe falcons— perched on columns four stories up. The cop stopped in the middle of the marble-clad lobby, plush with Turkish carpets and potted palms. A well-dressed gent with an upturned collar and silk cravat took a wide arc around them on his path to the door.

"Sarge, how about letting go of my arm? Promise not to run away. And it's the least you can do for making me cool my heels for so long in your club car."

"Shut your trap. Someone's meeting us."

A small, plain young woman approached them. Tendrils of mousy hair hung carelessly down from her upswept coiffure. Her well-cut clothes, erect carriage, and deliberate stride led Jack to peg her as high-class. But after noticing the lint, stains, and chemical reek on her long navy skirt and gray tailored jacket, he wasn't quite sure what to make of her.

"Is this the guest for the Pinkerton Agency?" she asked the space between the two men.

"Yes, miss," said the sergeant. "You got something for me?" She handed him an envelope. He opened it and riffled through a wad of cash. "Good day, miss." The policeman tipped his helmet and turned to leave.

"Forgetting something, aren't you, Sarge?" Jack stuck out his hand. The cop pulled the Army Colt, shoved it at him, and stomped off. Jack stuffed the pistol into his waistband and turned to the woman.

She looked past Jack's left shoulder as she spoke to him. "Mr. Jack Harden. My name is Sarah Kennecott. I am to escort you to the Pinkerton offices." Her flat voice struck him as snooty and stuck up.

"Sorry to be a bother, Lady Pinkerton, but I don't trust people who shanghai me."

The only change in her impassive expression was a slight

15

twitch of her left eyebrow. "My name is not Lady Pinkerton. My name is Sarah Kennecott, as I informed you previously. I do not understand your reference to a city in China."

"Come on. You paid that cop to kidnap me." Jack glared at her while she stared off into the distance. "Forget it. 'Bye." He turned to leave.

"Mr. Jack Harden. Wait." He turned around. Her hands were fluttering and flapping in front of her like little birds. "We need you to investigate a murder. I must bring you up to the office." She spoke quickly, her unblinking brown eyes skittering away from his gaze.

He'd worked with the Pinkertons in the past, although they had never dragged him into a meeting like this. Still, they paid well. "All right. But only if you call me Jack. And I'll call you Sarah. I prefer that to Lady Pinkerton."

"No. We are not nearly well acquainted for such informality."

"The only time I get called 'Mr. Jack Harden' is when I'm hauled in front of a judge. It's plain Jack or nothing, Sarah."

Her hands jerked even faster as she pondered his demand. "Very well . . . Jack. Let us go to the elevator."

"Hell, no. I don't ride in those death traps." He broke into a sweat. "Let's take the stairs."

"The office is on the top floor. It is a time-consuming climb."

Jack spotted a placard mounted on an easel:

Attention all Guests! We wish you to know the Results of the latest test of our Safety Air Cushion Elevator System! Bobo, a Circus Monkey, was dropped from the sixteenth floor in our Elevator Car. Bobo is fine!

He pointed at the sign. "You think that if this elevator contraption is safe for a monkey it's safe enough for me, right? Nuts to that."

"What you say does not make sense in my ears." Her face remained an immobile mask.

An elevator car opened with an emphatic ding. "Going up," called the operator.

She stepped toward the car and turned around. "You must come with me."

Frenzy had him by the throat. He wanted to run out of the place and was ready to knock down anyone in his way. Instead, he reached out to her with a nervous laugh. "Listen, lady, I don't like those things." She shrank away, resting flat against the marble wall. The elevator closed and whooshed off without them. "I wasn't being fresh, honest," he said, rubbing the back of his neck. "I just hate elevators. They spook me."

She stared at the floor. "I cannot stand to be touched."

"Touched by the likes of me, you mean."

"My senses are keenly susceptible to stimuli from all individuals." Sarah stepped away from the wall. "You should have stated initially that you fear riding in elevators."

"Jeez, read between the lines. You can't expect a guy just to admit being scared."

She stared past his right shoulder. Jack weighed the need for a job against the difficulty of dealing with this odd gal, and the job was losing. He was also still real sore about how the cops had dragged him here. Screw the Pinkertons for making his life even harder—he'd take a chance at getting work elsewhere.

"I will take your arm, which may reduce your anxiety concerning the elevator car." Sarah was now standing uncomfortably close.

The offer was so charmingly sincere that Jack's fear and irritation ebbed just as a new car opened. "Okay, I'm game."

She took his elbow firmly and led him into the car. He gave a tight smile, amused that she was fine with touching if she was the one doing it. Jack thought about making a joke about how the princess had to kiss the frog rather than the other way around but terror blotted out everything as the operator slammed the metal safety gate shut.

A scream began crawling up from his belly as the car shot skyward. Then something close to miraculous happened—Sarah gave his arm one squeeze and he stopped shaking. He remained terrified, but no longer felt like he was jumping out of his skin. "You must be an expert stenographer to work for the Pinkertons," he said as they walked into the sixteenth-floor hallway. "They hire men for all their secretarial positions. Maybe it's your skill getting guests up to the office."

"I am not trained as a stenographer."

She's got no business working for this outfit, thought Jack. *Probably just a peculiar girl parked here as a favor to her family. Maybe her only talent is handling a nutty uncle.* After a short walk they were in the office of the Pinkerton superintendent.

"Sarah." The superintendent had a thin mustache curled at the tips and a stripe of whiskers down his chin. His manner was one of oily overconfidence, much like a second-rate magician. "I told you to have one of the men bring Harden up."

"It was more efficient to escort him myself." It dawned on Jack that she used the same voice—a monotone without emotion or inflection—all the time, regardless of whom she was addressing.

The superintendent gripped his forehead and swept his arm down in a show of irritation. "Remember, darling, you're here to take notes. I'll tell you if you need to contribute to the conversation." He turned and pressed a moist palm into Jack's hand. "Harden, glad to see you. Sorry for the abrupt invitation, but we have an emergency, and I figured the police could find you quicker than anyone. Meet my close friend Horace Shaw. He owns a big oyster packing plant on Henderson's Wharf down in Fells Point and is a sure bet to be our next mayor."

A brawny man of about forty-five stepped forward. His meaty face was sunburned and scarred. A carefully groomed mustache sat awkwardly out of place between a lumpy nose and thick, tobacco-stained lips. The suit was new and expensive, the fine cloth straining against his bulk. A diamond stickpin glittered from a pricey necktie, and a chunky gold ring hung off his right pinky finger. Despite the clothes and jewelry, the man came off as seedy. Jack knew the type. Born dirt poor, the guy had brawled and hustled his way to success. And while Shaw wasn't entirely comfortable fitting into his elevated station in life, he had no intention of sliding back down.

"I'm told you're just the man I need." Shaw spoke with a politician's phony warmth.

Jack shook the offered hand, which was rough as a rasp. "Need for what?"

"Let's everybody sit down," said the superintendent. Jack avoided the plush sofa in favor of a hard-backed chair. He noticed Sarah sit in a matching chair, back straight and shoulders pulled back like a cadet at drill. "Horace is a fine man with deep interest in local politics. He'll be an excellent, excellent mayor."

The superintendent's reverential tone shifted to one of mild distress. "He has a problem that demands your special skill, Harden. The police have the absurd notion that Horace was involved with the death of a dancing girl. She was killed late last night or early this morning. Name's Lizzie Sullivan."

"Why do the cops suspect him?"

Jack kept his eyes on Shaw, whose stuffed armchair groaned as he shifted his bulk before speaking. "Shot with my pistol. Thing has my name engraved on it. Someone's trying to frame me."

"A pickpocket stole the pistol from Horace," said the superintendent. Shaw gazed silently off into space, looking as if he wanted to be anywhere other than here—even clinging to a capsized boat in the middle of the Patapsco River.

In Jack's experience, the less a guy talked in this kind of situation, the more trouble he was in. "Can I assume Shaw knew the girl and that he doesn't have a respectable alibi for the time of the murder?"

"I didn't know the little slut." Shaw's voice was now devoid of bonhomie.

Sarah looked up while still scribbling notes. "What is your alibi?"

"I'm not going to be grilled by a girl who smells like an undertaker." Shaw waved her off with a thick hand.

"I cannot possibly smell like an undertaker. Morticians use arsenic-based embalming fluid. I have just come from the city morgue, which uses liquid formaldehyde to preserve bodily organs. Each chemical has a distinct odor."

The superintendent shot Sarah a dark look. "Horace, the girl is a doctor, believe it or not. I pulled in a big favor from the mayor to have her observe Lizzie Sullivan's autopsy for anything useful."

Jack glanced back at Sarah with a mix of dread and curiosity. He hated doctors but had never seen one of the lady variety, even though he knew they were around. Her work for the Pinkertons made even less sense than before. Surely she could earn a lot more money pretending to patch people up—and deal with a better sort than the three men in this room to boot.

"What the hell good does it do to have her involved?" asked Shaw.

"While the coroner has listed the cause of death as a gunshot, I have some doubt," said Sarah.

"You have some doubt, do you now?" Shaw tromped his foot. "Who's going to believe you? I'd look like a weak fool having a woman bang the drum for me. Anyway, there's no need for that. I'm innocent."

"We should insist upon a reexamination of the body—"

"That's enough out of you, Sarah. Be quiet." The superintendent turned to Shaw with an apologetic look. "Horace, let's get back to giving Harden what he needs to know."

"I get the picture," said Jack. "Shaw's the prime suspect. When's the coroner's inquest?"

"Tomorrow," said the superintendent.

"What inquest?" Shaw sloshed a wad of chewing tobacco from one cheek to the other.

"Coroner has to get a jury to look at evidence about a suspicious death," said Jack. "If the jury decides it was homicide, the cops make an arrest. Mostly the jury does what the coroner wants them to do. If you've got anyone to vouch for your whereabouts last night and early this morning, you'd better have them testify at the inquest."

"Let them talk to my real good pal the governor. I was with him and a gaggle of associates on a steamboat excursion down to Newport News. Got back Sunday morning in time for church and spent the whole rest of the day canvassing for votes in Ward Three—probably where I got pickpocketed."

"I assume the governor wasn't with you when the cops think you killed that girl," said Jack.

Shaw stared at the floor sullenly. "Told you I didn't do it."

"You need someone to vouch for you or—"

The superintendent interrupted. "Harden, you're making Horace uncomfortable. He says he didn't do it, and that's good enough for me. I'm sure there's a way to resolve this matter without accounting for every second of the man's time."

"A good resolution depends on who needs what kind of compensation. And if the cops don't have any more evidence against Shaw other than that gun."

"We're counting on you to persuade the authorities to leave Horace alone. He's in a spirited election and doesn't need any distraction." The superintendent offered an envelope. "Here's fifty dollars to get started. If you can help Horace out of this jam, there's a lot more in it for you. He's offering a five-hundred-dollar bonus."

"My, my," said Jack. "That's a lot of money. But it should be, considering you're counting on me to swing a big-time bribe."

"Don't put it so crudely," said the superintendent.

"Whatever you say." Jack took the envelope and tucked it into his jacket. He wasn't eager to help a murderer get away with it. Still, five hundred iron men would go a ways toward covering his gambling marker. "Shaw, I need to ask you a couple more questions."

Shaw made his chair creak for its life as he crossed and then uncrossed his tree-trunk legs. "What for?"

"If you didn't kill the girl, who did?"

"Who cares? Just get me cleared."

"That's not so easy. Cash doesn't always make the police forget about a murder. It might also be necessary to point the cops to a handy suspect, like someone who might want to set you up. Who's your worst enemy?"

"Police Commissioner Adolph Lipp. My main opponent in the mayor's election." Shaw heaved himself up, walked over to a brass spittoon near the door, and let loose a long squirt of dark brown tobacco juice. He ran the back of his hand across his lips and then across the seat of his trousers.

"I know Lipp," said Jack. "He's the Bible pounder who raids Sunday liquor sales with a pistol in one hand and a hymnal in the other. Loves to see his name in the paper." Lipp was a sanctimonious sort who was, even by Baltimore standards, a raging bigot. His campaign slogan was something like, "The saloon ruins righteous character, while the Negro and the immigrant ruin racial purity."

"He's the bastard who's lined up most everyone who hates me," said Shaw as he crashed back into his chair. "Pardon my French, miss, but I'm in a state. Lipp's got all the teetotalers, immigrant-haters, and churchgoing types locked up. There's more of them than you might think. Lipp's meaner than a snake and wants his boot on my neck. But I've got the votes to smash him like a bug." Shaw pounded his fist into his palm like a sledgehammer hitting steel.

"If Lipp's out to railroad you, it's a problem." Jack saw that Shaw was in more trouble than the man was willing to accept.

The superintendent sniffed. "I'm told the commissioner is a man of integrity who lets his men do their jobs without undue interference."

"In other words, the superintendent believes the cops will put their money hunger ahead of whatever the commissioner wants," said Jack. "Who's the lead detective on the case?"

"A cop named O'Toole questioned me," said Shaw.

Jack smiled broadly. "Snake Eyes O'Toole. The dirtiest city dick there is. That's good news for you. But we need a patsy other than Lipp. Who else has it in for you?"

"There's a third man running in the election—he hates me, too. Name's Lucas Patterson. A joke of a candidate. Soft rich boy." Shaw gave a rude snort. "He's called the millionaire social-ist. A real radical dynamiter that hardly nobody's going to vote for—just the good-government bleeding hearts. Patterson supports all sorts of goo-goo nonsense. Coddling bums. Giving coloreds special rights and women the vote. Putting child labor rules on the backs of businessmen. I can't run my oyster packing business without using kids. Patterson don't care that families would starve without their kids' wages. He thinks those ignorant brats should waste everybody's time going to school. Patterson's a traitor to his class and his race. He's only running as a gadfly."

"A rich man isn't a useful suspect," said Jack. "Who else can you give me?"

"That's enough for now." Shaw scowled and looked at his watch. "I know I'm in deep horse—forgive me, miss." He stood up. "Superintendent, Harden, I'm counting on you to do whatever it takes to keep me out of jail." He looked at Sarah with a frown. "Don't want anyone to know the girl's done anything for me, hear? I'd never live it down. I want her off the case."

"Oh, yes, yes," said the superintendent in his butteriest tone. "You can count on that."

"Good. I know how this kind of thing gets fixed. Just tell me who I got to pay and how much." He put on his ten-dollar hat and left.

"Harden," said the superintendent as he waved a sheet of paper, "here's the Sullivan girl's boardinghouse address. The only other thing we know is that she worked as a dancer at different theaters around the city."

Jack stood and took the paper. "Anything else?"

"We need you to keep a clear head, so don't blow what I just gave you on a wild bender. Save the loony, liquored-up brawling until after you finish things. Got it?"

"I don't drink."

"Sure, sure." The superintendent gave a tired wave. "Just keep your focus on the assigned task. Don't make me regret doing you a favor by giving you this job rather than using one of my own operatives." He picked up the telephone receiver. "I'll call someone to escort you down to the lobby."

Jack bridled, knowing that he was the one taking the risk. The Pinkerton Agency contracted out dirty work that might besmirch the firm's well-crafted reputation for ruthlessness that stopped just short of breaking the law. If Jack landed in hot water for offering a bribe, the superintendent would claim astonished innocence and disavow any role in the matter. Jack was easily expendable, unlike a regular Pinkerton dick. "Forget it," he said. "I want Sarah. She knows how to handle the elevator."

"No," said the superintendent with a forceful shake of his head.

"I do not object," said Sarah. "I helped him cope with his

morbid fear of elevators earlier. It is logical to assume he needs additional help to return to the lobby."

"Let's go, Sarah," said Jack, striding for the door with the superintendent guffawing behind him. Jack turned to her in the hallway. "Why'd you embarrass me like that? Now he thinks I'm chicken-livered as well as a boozy nutcase."

"It was not my intent to cause embarrassment. I merely mentioned what I learned from you earlier." She abruptly veered her gaze past one side of his head to the other while both her hands wagged.

Sarah tested Jack's ability to size people up. She was willful and blunt, as well as brainy. But her behavior was beyond stiff—she didn't seem to know how to deal with people in a natural or even normal manner. And what was the deal with that poker face and those fluttery hand gestures? He had never run across anyone remotely like her. "Let's go down to the lobby," he said. "I want to talk with you."

Once again she took his arm and held it just the right way to keep him from coming apart as the elevator dropped to street level. She let go as soon as they stepped into the lobby. "Where'd you learn that arm trick?"

"I worked with nervously disposed invalids in a lunatic asylum. Some patients were victims of an inherited disorder, others suffered from a shock or mental trauma. Patients responded well to touch—it relieved their anxiety." There was no hint of bragging.

"So—even crazy people can't avoid doctors these days."

"At Johns Hopkins Medical School I studied all aspects of the medical sciences, including psychology, anatomy, surgery, and obstetrics. I had a particular interest in medico-legal pathology, which covers toxicology—"

Jack held up his hand to stop the torrent of words, most of which meant nothing to him. "You said you doubted Lizzie

Sullivan died from a gunshot wound. How can we get that checked into before the coroner's inquest?"

"A second autopsy is difficult to obtain. The authorities require a compelling reason."

Jack was in a hurry to go see the person in the best position to kill the case against Shaw, but it was always good to have another angle to play. "Can you get the superintendent to talk with his pal the mayor? Seems like you can provide a good enough excuse."

"I can provide an excellent rationale. The bullet hit a coronary artery, but there is no evidence of extensive bleeding. That almost certainly means the gunshot occurred postmortem. If administered prior to death, the wound might even have caused exsanguination, as the heart would continue pumping at pressure adequate to—"

"Sarah. You've convinced me. You need to talk to your boss."

One of her eyebrows jerked faintly. "The superintendent has instructed me not to annoy him with verbal details. I am to communicate with him in writing only."

"Shaw made it pretty clear that he doesn't want you involved, but maybe you'll just have to make the boss listen about how best to help the client. Look, I've got to run. Let me take you to dinner tonight, and we can discuss how to handle this."

She held up a hand. "No."

"What? Why not?"

"I have three reasons. First, accepting a male escort may lead to a misunderstanding on his part with regard to physical intimacy. Second, I must write my report. Third, I do not approve of your mercenary role in this case. You are willing to subvert justice to collect your fee. I find that offensive."

"Wait a minute. We both work for The Eye."

"Who or what are you referring to by that term?"

"Those creeps." He jerked his thumb up. "You know, 'The

Eye that never sleeps.' Same devil that pays you. How come I'm
a mercenary and you aren't?"

"My only goal is to pursue the truth. I will stay here
tonight to write a thorough report for the superintendent
about what I observed during the autopsy. Lizzie Sullivan
deserves justice."

He noticed that the more she talked, the louder her voice
became. It was as if she were unaware of the need to regulate
her volume in the course of a conversation. "You're kidding
yourself, sister, if you think your hands are clean as long as
you're working for the Pinkertons. Or that your little report is
going to amount to a hill of beans in terms of getting that girl
justice."

Sarah looked at the backs of her white-gloved hands and
then the palms as her cheeks turned bright pink. "I want this
conversation to end," she said.

Jack jammed on his derby and walked out of the Continental
Building into the rainy afternoon bustle. No one had ever called
him a mercenary, although the word had floated through his
head a time or two. Truth and justice—she seemed to believe
they were real. *The path of the just is as the shining light, that shineth
more and more unto the perfect day.* Jack pressed both fists over his
eyes until the voice faded.

He needed to work off some agitation and didn't mind
walking in the rain. As he strode east on Baltimore Street, fat
raindrops pounded his hat and jacket.

The rain brought out different smells as it gurgled in the
gutter. There was a mineral tang from the paving stones and a
pleasant animal-plant scent from the manure and vegetable
waste scattered everywhere. He liked how the clip-clop of the
passing horses was different in the rain—the sound was clearer
and richer. After a few blocks he came to the awareness that
he'd be chilled to the bone by the time he got to the Silverstrike
Hotel at High and East Fayette Streets. He dug in his pocket and

was glad to find the change needed for the streetcar that groaned to a stop just ahead.

Jack jumped on the trolley, and as he dropped onto a bench, the Colt poked into his ribs. Maybe it was a warning. The guy he was going to meet was a violent brute with a badge that let him get away with anything. Jack gazed at his hand and saw that the tremor, while bad, was less than it had been at the lunchroom.

CHAPTER 3

SARAH—MONDAY, OCTOBER 11, 1909, 2:00 P.M.

*S*ixteen favorite books lined up precisely on her desk at the Pinkerton Agency provided a welcome distraction from a blinding headache. She arranged the books alphabetically by title, then rearranged them from thinnest to thickest. As she worked, she stroked their pebbly, reassuring covers and fanned creamy pages to release a soothing inky scent. Handling the books reminded her of joyful childhood memories.

She had been born into a world of overwhelming sensory anguish. Everything was too vivid, too intense. People especially terrified her with their big, alarming faces and loud voices. Her panicky tantrums eased only after she'd managed to shut down her emotional reactions and withdraw into a private world.

She eventually grew tolerant enough of her environment to appreciate select surfaces, such as the cool smoothness of her blanket's satin edging and the faint woven feel of the wallpaper in her room. Certain people—her father, her sister—gradually seemed less scary. After learning to walk, she discovered her father's library. Her favorite activity after that was pulling books off the lower shelves and exploring their wonderful smells and textures.

29

When she was three and a half, she found a colorful piece of paper haphazardly folded into a series of uneven squares. Her sense was that the object needed fixing, and she presented it to her father.

He smoothed the paper open to reveal an outline divided into shapes of different colors. Great black lines ran across the shapes. Her father told her it was a map of the United States, with railroad lines connecting cities. He pointed his finger at the text while sounding out the title of the map: "The Eastern Span of the Baltimore and Ohio Railroad Highway of the Continent, from Great Rivers and Lakes, across Prairies, over the Alleghenies, down the Valley of the Potomac to the Sea." In the days that followed, she loved sitting in his lap as he named the cities and towns along the rail lines. Within a few weeks she was able to read everything herself.

On her fourth birthday, her father gave her *Alice's Adventures in Wonderland*. He read it to her and Grace many times while they snuggled close. Sarah began to read other books on her own, and by the time she was seven, she had devoured dozens, including *Black Beauty*, *On the Origin of Species*, and *The History of the Decline and Fall of the Roman Empire*.

Sarah forced her attention back to the present and found herself calmer. A small knot of pain remained behind the center of her forehead—lingering tension no doubt arising from Jack Harden's statement that her work would not reveal the truth about Lizzie Sullivan's murder. It was true that the Pinkerton Agency's role in the case did not center on justice. Still, she would finish her report tonight and press it upon the superintendent. Helping their client surely was his paramount interest.

She needed more evidence for the report, compelling facts that would force people to understand how Lizzie really died. The best way to get those facts was to examine the dead girl's body as soon as possible—right now, in fact.

Sarah glanced back down at her books and pulled out *In*

Memory of Mary Putnam Jacobi. It was the slimmest volume in the row, with a marvelous ribbed cloth binding. She had intended to buy another copy for the morgue clerk's daughter. Gently stroking the book's cover, she decided giving it up was worth the loss.

THE TWO-STORY red brick morgue perched at the very edge of the harbor, as if to keep the dead as far away from the living as possible. Near the side loading dock, a man struggled to drag an oblong form wrapped in dirty canvas from the morgue's dead wagon. Two men, dressed in white, watched idly from the dock. A steam-powered saw obliterated every other sound as it screeched somewhere in the vast commercial lumberyard that surrounded the place. Sarah stood outside the front door, gathering her courage.

Saying anything untrue was nearly impossible for her. But, through experience, she had learned that people often preferred to skirt or obscure the truth. If someone appeared worn and tired, you were supposed to say "You are looking well." If someone asked how you were doing, you were supposed to say "Fine, thank you," even if you felt horrible. If she absolutely had to lie or overlook some rules to examine Lizzie's body, so be it.

The morgue reception area was a stark, unwelcoming space that smelled of mildew with a hint of acrid cleaning solution. Yellow paint peeled from the dirty walls. A single electric light in a chipped green metal reflector dangled from the ceiling next to a curled strip of adhesive flypaper dotted with small bodies.

The clerk Sarah had met earlier in the day sat behind a large desk piled high with papers and boxes of equipment. A calendar advertising "Stafford's Rib Cutters, Skull Chisels, and Bone Saws: We Open Up a Whole New World for You" hung behind him.

"I am interrupting your lunch."

"It's no problem at all, Dr. Kennecott." The clerk stood and came around to the front of the desk. "How can I help you?"

"I have brought you the book we discussed this morning. For your daughter. It has some of the most positive words ever written about a woman physician. I want to give it to her—to encourage her studies."

His eyes bulged at the proffered volume. "I-I-I don't know what to say." His Adam's apple did its vigorous dance again.

"You could say 'I will give it to her.'" The clerk dropped his gaze to the floor and attempted to speak, but the only sound he made was a string of puffs. "Sir," she asked, "are you feeling well?"

He shifted his weight from side to side. "I-I-I am ashamed to have offended you with my impolite response, Doctor."

"Do not concern yourself." She took a step toward him. "I require no expression of gratitude. All I want is you to take the book from my hand."

The clerk took the book as if it were a rare volume. "Thank you so much, Doctor. It is so very, very kind of you. My daughter will read it with interest."

"Yes. That is what books are for." She stepped closer. "I wish to take another look at the body we examined this morning. I need some additional information for my report."

"That's a bit unusual, Doctor." The clerk was now bent backward over his desk, with Sarah about a foot away from him. "The coroner usually decides who can view the bodies."

Sarah tilted her head forward to stare at a dark blue stain on the right lapel of the man's dingy white lab coat while trying to think of what to say. She needed to construct a lie to the effect that the coroner had given her his permission, but forming the words was a mighty struggle.

"I-I suppose just this once will be fine," said the clerk with a jittery laugh. "I'll get the porters to retrieve the body from the icebox." He slipped quickly out of the room, leaving the book on his desk. Sarah took off her gloves and lovingly stroked the book's cover. She felt tightness in her throat and pushed away the rising grief. This was a worthy sacrifice. The clerk returned with two big men. "We'll lay the body out while you get ready, Doctor."

After hanging her hat and getting into a gown and apron, she went back into the body chamber. Lizzie Sullivan was again stretched out on the table. Sarah lifted the right hand and peered closely to see strands of dark fibers clotted with blood under the nails. She used fine tweezers to remove the material. "Do you have a small paper sack?"

The clerk cleared his throat nervously. "I'm not sure y-y-you should take anything, Doctor. It's against the rules."

"The coroner is finished with his examination. And the body will be washed soon for burial. Think of me cleaning her finger-nails for that purpose." Stars and shimmers floated through her vision. Sarah willed her legs firm to counter a profound urge to start rocking.

Muttering to himself, the clerk found a paper bag and gave it to her. She placed the fibers from under the nails into the sack. Looking at the girl's face, Sarah again noticed that the upper lip appeared unusual.

She pried open the mouth, revealing decayed teeth and irri-tated gums. Peeling back the upper lip revealed a narrow strip of what looked like wadded paper molded around the upper gum line. Some gentle tweezing was enough to lift the slightly damp paper away, revealing badly recessed gum tissue—the mottled roots of the front teeth peeped between bits of swollen, inflamed flesh. Lizzie Sullivan was not a practitioner of good oral hygiene. The bit of paper joined the clotted fibers in the bag.

Sarah looked again at the cut on the girl's forehead. It appeared to have come from a straight-edged object. She glanced at the floor where the clipboard had fallen earlier—it was still there, lying in a puddle of ice melt. She picked up the clipboard and glanced at the dripping-wet contents.

The photographic prints were badly curled but still clear and sharp. The photo of the girl splayed on the bed showed no sign of anything that could have caused the head trauma.

Sarah grabbed a scalpel and quickly cut away the flesh around the bruise on the corpse's upper right forehead. Next, she used a drill and bone-cutting forceps to cut a two-inch-square in the girl's skull. This was not the typical procedure, but there was no time to saw open the skull to do a proper examination of the brain. Most of her anxiety fell away as she focused on using the instruments.

"Wait! You can't do that!" The clerk rushed to her side and raised his arms up and down frantically. Sarah ignored him and lifted the cut piece of bone to reveal a large mass of clotted blood under the first layer of tissue beneath the skull. It had the appearance of an acute subdural hematoma—the blow to the head had caused internal bleeding, which in turn placed great pressure on the brain. That, more than likely, was what had killed Lizzie Sullivan.

"I am finished." She replaced the piece of cut bone and stepped away from the table.

"I'll say you are. I'm reporting this right now." The clerk rushed off, white coat flying behind him. Sarah put the bag with the newsprint and fingernail scrapings in her purse, then glanced at the police photographs. She stuffed them into her purse as well, then hurried to wash her hands and get out of the gown and apron.

As she walked through the reception area, she heard the clerk shouting into the telephone about how some crazy woman had hacked open a skull. Sarah was offended—she did not like her technique referred to so crudely.

She walked quickly to the President Street station, hailed a cab, and set off to Johns Hopkins Hospital. The evidence presented a clear picture, but it was good practice to seek another opinion.

"GOOD DAY, DR. KENNECOTT."

Sarah froze on the sidewalk outside the Pathological Building on the grounds of Johns Hopkins Hospital. She was in a rush to consult with someone other than the professor of psychiatry who stood smiling before her on the building's steps. He was a muscular man with a neatly trimmed Vandyke beard, Homburg hat, red necktie, and dove-gray suit jacket. "Dr. Norbert Macdonald, I do not have time to converse."

Macdonald nodded. "Aye, we'll talk this afternoon." He spoke with a thick Scottish burr.

"I must cancel our appointment. Something urgent has arisen."

"That is disappointing."

"Excuse me."

Macdonald clicked his heels and stepped aside, still smiling. "Remember that I hope to cure your mental issues and to write a case study."

Sarah wordlessly walked past him up the stairs and into the building, knowing she had violated a social rule by abruptly abandoning the doctor. That was unfortunate because she did not object to his company.

Recently returned from work with world-renowned figures in psychology, he had been hired to head a new psychiatric hospital the university was building. Macdonald had advance word about Sarah and invited her to meet soon after settling into his temporary office in the Pathological Building two weeks ago. She willingly accepted his invitation, drawn by the man's fluent German.

During their meeting, Macdonald produced photographs of individual faces and asked her to identify the emotion each person displayed. It had been a difficult, painful task. She always had trouble looking at faces—eyes, in particular—as they broadcast overwhelming emotional signals. She could only bear to examine each photograph for a few seconds.

She was not surprised to hear that nearly all her guesses at the emotional state shown in each photograph were wrong. She was, however, nettled when Macdonald described her in passing as cold and unfeeling. The opposite was true. Sarah felt joy, anger, fear, and more with great intensity. But she had concluded that, in addition to having difficulty identifying the emotions of others, she had at least as much trouble communicating her own.

Macdonald had offered to provide psychoanalysis to help improve what he called her "psychopathic emotional disorder." The doctor recounted his own success with analysis and explained that he kept a detailed journal about his thoughts and actions to help him dig into his subconscious. He also wanted to explore Sarah's personality as the basis for a published case study. She wanted nothing to do with what he proposed, but had agreed to meet with him again as a courtesy.

Hurrying down the hallway, she rounded a corner, and nearly collided with the man she had come to see.

"Sarah, hello."

"Greetings to you as well, Dr. Frederick Anson." Her pathology mentor was short and bald but for a three-inch tuft of hair rising from the top of his head. His thick spectacles greatly magnified his eyes. The man was also extremely fond of brightly colored clothing. Some unkind students called him "the horned chameleon," although she failed to grasp why.

"I hear you are . . . consulting with the Pinkerton Agency," he said.

Sarah was mildly infatuated with the man. Not a romantic

desire—it was more a longing to ease her isolation. More than once she'd wondered if she could tolerate having his arms around her like her father had done, but had never considered testing the idea. "Yes, that is correct. I wish to confer about a recent murder and discuss my reasoning as to the cause of death."

He pulled a watch from his scarlet waistcoat with a bandaged left hand. "I can give you a few minutes."

Sarah quickly explained how she came to make two trips to the morgue and gave a rapid overview of what she had observed. Anson removed his glasses and wiped them on his shirtfront.

"What is the dead girl's name?" He squinted at her.

Sarah hastily skated her gaze across Anson's unfocused eyes, curious that he would ask such a question. "Her name is Lizzie Sullivan."

Anson put his glasses back on. "When do you estimate the time of death?"

"I had hoped to consult with you about that. Based on my observations, I estimate that she died late last night or early this morning. But I believe she received the fatal head injury many hours prior, given that the tissues had time to bruise and begin to heal."

"Do the police have a suspect?"

"Doctor, given your limited time, I wish to discuss the condition of the body rather than review the broader facts of the case."

He looked at her closely. "Was there a fracture of the victim's skull?"

"No. The modest appearance of the cut and the lack of a fracture drew attention away from the head injury during the initial autopsy. I learned more during my return to the morgue."

"Going back without authorization to examine the body was wrong. You could face serious consequences." Anson spoke softly, but it was unlike him to show such deference to bureau-cratic rules.

"Truth is what matters, not protocol," she said.

"I say this as your friend, Sarah. You absolutely must—*must* —learn to obey the men in charge. If the coroner has ruled the gunshot wound as the cause of death, then you have to accept his opinion. I'm sorry to speak to you this way . . . ." He rubbed his hands together before holding them out limply, palms up.

She stared at his hands silently for some moments before reaching into her purse. "The head trauma has the appearance of a subdural hematoma. Enough blood accumulated over a period of time to cause fatal pressure on the brain. The source of the injury is unknown. There is also the question of where and when both the trauma and the gunshot took place. I have pictures of the crime scene. Tell me what you see."

He took the pictures and held them inches from his eyes. "I see the room is a mess, as if it had been torn apart during a search. The head injury looks minor."

"The body is in a naturally supine pose on the bed—it is as if she were sleeping just before death," said Sarah. "Or engaging in sexual intercourse."

"Perhaps."

"There were feathers embedded in the gunshot wound. That is consistent with a close-range shot through the pillow, which presumably was used to muffle the sound. It appears she was shot while laying as pictured."

"So, the gunshot did kill her."

Sarah stamped her foot hard enough for the sound to echo off the paneled wall and make Anson jump. "I have already told you about the lack of bleeding from the gunshot wound—she was dead before the shot." She began rocking vigorously, her long skirts swishing. "Hours or days can pass before a hematoma may cause enough bleeding in the brain to cause death. In this case, I witnessed relatively fresh clotting over the brain consistent with the injury occurring approximately forty-eight hours prior to death. A more precise calculation would be possible with a full inspection of the brain."

He handed back the pictures and peered at her with his hugely magnified eyes. "Leave this alone, Sarah, or you will get yourself into big trouble. Again."

"I am conducting this work on behalf of a Pinkerton client. I will document everything in my report, which I am eager to have turned over to the proper authorities."

Anson clasped his hands and blinked slowly. "I know that once you take the bit in your teeth, there is no stopping you."

"I do not understand that statement."

"I mean that when you decide to take something on you refuse to let it go until the matter is resolved."

"Yes, that is my nature. May I have use of laboratory space over the next several days?"

He hesitated. "Maybe." He glanced at his watch. "I must go. Meet me in the main hospital administrative office tomorrow morning at ten a.m. so that I can let you know for sure."

"I shall meet you at that precise hour." She turned on her heel and quickly walked away.

SARAH KNEW she would be yelled at for returning to the morgue. The superintendent would fuss and refuse to listen to any explanation. He probably would rant again about how impossible she was and order her to attend to the filing backlog.

Once, when he'd been especially angry, he declared that she never would have been hired if not for the fine reputation of her late father. Sarah knew the real reason the agency had hired her was her close friendship with Margaret Bonifant.

Riding up the Continental Building elevator, she was confident that, however much her boss scolded her, the new evidence about Lizzie Sullivan's death would prevail over everything else. Once he calmed down and listened to what she had to say, the superintendent would know she had done the right thing. The details she uncovered would help Horace Shaw, their client who had promised a bonus. Most importantly, the police would have crucial evidence for their investigation.

All the typing and chattering stopped as soon as she stepped into the office. Sarah normally did not pay attention to her colleagues, yet it was evident that everyone was staring at her. She remembered the stain on her skirt. Once she had gone most of the day with a big rip down the side of her jacket that she would never have noticed if a coworker had not pointed it out.

"Sarah," said the superintendent from his doorway, "come into my office. Right away."

She walked inside, and he closed the door with a bang. Sitting in front of her—and making no effort to rise—was a hatchet-faced man of about fifty, with long side-whiskers and small, dark eyes. The shoulders of his black frock coat were dusted with dandruff, and his shirt collar was starched but well worn.

"Sarah. Police Commissioner Lipp says that you went to the morgue and chopped open a skull." The superintendent sat woodenly behind his desk. "You're in serious trouble."

A cold panic seized her. "I reexamined the body of Lizzie Sullivan using medical techniques that should have been employed initially as part of a proper medico-legal examination. No chopping occurred. I used a Burr drill and DeVilbiss forceps to open the frontal bone to inspect the dura—"

Commissioner Lipp pounded the floor with his walking stick. "Good gracious, girly, I don't care if you pricked her with a sewing needle. You had no business even seeing the body. I'm ready to have you arrested for tampering with remains." He jabbed his finger at her while speaking in a high, scratchy voice.

A sense of overwhelming chaos rendered her weightless. Language fled as she swayed from one foot to the other.

"Sarah, pay attention," said the superintendent sternly. "Remain still."

She forced herself motionless and, with a great act of will, recovered her ability to speak. "I am giving you my complete attention," she said, looking at the wall behind the superintendent's head. She took a deep breath. "You should know I have additional evidence about Lizzie Sullivan's death. The gunshot did not kill her."

"Superintendent, this is outrageous." Lipp slammed his walking stick down so hard Sarah flung her arms out as she jumped. "I know that villain Shaw hired you to help him evade justice. That in itself is terrible. But if your organization is attempting to falsify the obvious fact that Shaw shot that girl with his very own gun—sir, you will pay."

"Commissioner, I'm mortified." The superintendent wrung his hands. "She had no instruction from me or this agency to meddle with the investigation. The girl is headstrong and has her own ideas, regrettably. Rest assured that we will not let news of this unfortunate incident leave the room. And I will drop Shaw as a client immediately."

Sarah struggled to comprehend what was happening. Why was the superintendent so eager to disavow their client? And why was the police commissioner rejecting important new evidence about a murder? Confusion jostled with anxiety for dominance in her mind.

"See to it. I've already got too many difficulties." Lipp smoothed first one of his sideburns and then the other, raising faint clouds of dried skin. "I'm working night and day on the purity voting amendment to the state constitution. We must eliminate the Negro and the immigrant from politics to safeguard our great race. Praise God for giving me strength to carry out His will." Lipp set his walking stick against a knee and raised his arms heavenward. Then he gave the superintendent a hard look. "You need to do more to fix this, sir."

The superintendent looked at the top of his desk. "Sarah, your services are no longer required."

She heard the words without processing them. "Which services? Do you want me to concentrate on filing?"

"You're fired, Sarah. Pack your things and leave the office immediately." The superintendent kept his eyes down.

"One other thing, dearie." Commissioner Lipp leaned forward and pointed a bony finger at her. "Keep your mouth shut about Lizzie Sullivan. Go stay with some auntie and make sure you never cause me any trouble again. If you do, I'll have you thrown in jail. You got it?" His little eyes glinted with a dark light.

Sarah focused on the tip of Lipp's chin as her entire body trembled. "You should wish to learn the truth behind this murder. I have pointed you to crucial evidence, but you reject it. I must conclude that you are not interested in conducting an unbiased investigation. That runs counter to your official responsibility."

The superintendent stood and gestured to the door. "Sarah. Let's go."

Lipp gave a long, brittle laugh. "This is priceless. I'd heard you weren't right in the head, and it's true. Who do you think you are, girl? You're nothing but a spastic little freak who's been overeducated beyond any practical use. You should be locked in an attic instead of running around causing decent people trouble." He leaned over on his stick. "You are a walking disaster. I heard about what happened during your internship after Hopkins—dismissed by your supervisor for insubordination. Then the Pinkerton Agency took pity on you, and you repay their kindness with an unforgivable misdeed. Such a sorry creature. Sad." He flicked a hand at her as if she were a mosquito.

Sarah went back to her desk. As a child, she used to fling

herself down and bang her head on the floor when negative emotion overwhelmed her. Now all she could do when upset was let the great gobs of fear, anger, and frustration surge within her. The experience was so powerful that she wanted to tear herself into a pile of tiny pieces and spontaneously combust.

Here she was again, suffering the consequences of her limited knowledge of—and weak appreciation for—the proper way to interact with people. Should she not have ventured to reexamine Lizzie's body? Should she not have screamed when her internship supervisor removed his trousers, pinned her against a wall, and demanded sexual intercourse? Both actions on her part seemed entirely justified, but both actions also got her fired. She forced her numb hands to put her precious books into a canvas bag, desperate to get home. But the bag was too heavy to budge.

The edges of her vision grew cloudy as tremors ran through her body. Studying murder victims and identifying their killers— the sole focus of her life—might never be possible. If so, she had no idea what would become of her. Bad things could happen— maybe even a return to the horrible place she had escaped from seven years ago.

She would rather die than accept that fate.

CHAPTER 4

JACK—MONDAY, OCTOBER 11, 1909, 2:30 P.M.

*N*o joint in Baltimore could beat the ragtime piano players at the Silverstrike Hotel. Bob Foster, the best middleweight boxer ever and Baltimore's native son, ran the place. He'd opened it with money won in a forty-one-round title fight in Silverstrike, Colorado, against Nils Karlsson, "The Slugging Swede." Foster was famous citywide, cheered on even by most whites.

The hotel was dead center in the neighborhood known as The Pot—short, so it was said, for The Cauldron of Sin. Pimps, punks, pickpockets, and hop peddlers loitered on the sidewalk, along with the occasional upstanding citizen slumming for a thrill. A cocaine hustler, rain dripping from his expensive fedora, sidled up to Jack.

"Hey, bud." The guy was taking short, nervous puffs on a cigarette. "You're looking for some burny to blow, right? Some snow in October? Got the real thing, right here."

"I'll bet you sling more of that dope than Carter does Little Liver Pills. Wasting your time with me, though. Not a whiffer."

"That's hard to believe." The man turned his head and gave

Jack a sidelong stare. "You sure got the jumpy look of a big-time coke fiend."

Jack waved the guy off. If only there was a drug that would make him forget, that would block out the pain. . . . He'd drunk whiskey nonstop for a stretch after getting kicked out of the army with a bobtail discharge, but boozing had only put him in a place where the ghosts pressed in closer and cried louder. Alcohol also turned him into a raging terror who got into fights, tore up barrooms, and otherwise unleashed pain on everything and everyone. It was safer to suffer sober.

The Silverstrike's bouncer, a massive six-foot-six specimen, called out a greeting. "Last I heard you were Jack-in-the-jail-box a week ago after getting crack-brained drunk and mixing it up with the coppers," he said. "Surprised that pretty mug of yours isn't all bashed in."

"Wasn't true about being drunk. I hate the blue boys enough to fight them dry."

"I stand corrected. You're a plain old lunatic. What, cops let you out of the stir because they were tired of hearing you yelling about being the king of England?" The bouncer's chuckle rumbled like a far-off thunderstorm.

Jack gave him a pained smile. It was good to have a reputation as crazy, but only up to a point. "That's a real screamer. I'm working on a job. Snake Eyes around?"

The man stopped laughing. "Detective's wearing out his welcome. How much police protection can one place stand?" Worry lines crinkled his brow. "He's at his usual table. Hey— what I said? Keep that between you and me."

Jack nodded and went into the barroom. The place was a quarter full and smelled of unwashed bodies, cheapo hair pomade, and stale tobacco smoke.

As his eyes adjusted to the dull light, the first person he saw was a piano player talking a smooth hanky-pank to an indifferent audience. "Yes, sir, I'm playing all the raggedy tunes you

45

love. I'll be syncopating while you're intoxicating." He played a little riff to highlight the joke but no one laughed. "Say, now, it's the top of the oyster season, right? Let's celebrate with this little number called 'I Don't Care About the Rest of the World Because Baltimore's My Oyster.'" He started pounding the piano with a springy up-and-down melody. The guy was good.

Jack scanned the crowd, mostly single men sitting with their shoulders hunched while staring into their drinks. A painted gal at a nearby table looked bored as a fading prospect jabbered on with some hard-luck story. Snake Eyes O'Toole was alone at his table in the back, working on a plate of pig's feet, hands shiny with grease.

When Jack came to Baltimore, a friend warned him that Terrance "Snake Eyes" O'Toole was bad news. The detective was said to have started out as a smart, hard-nosed cop devoted to his mother. He'd lived with her into his thirties, and she would often telephone the station to lecture him. Sometimes she was hot about things her son hadn't done right, such as not properly washing the dishes or leaving the trash bins in the wrong place. Other times she was angry because she felt her only child didn't care enough about her. His fellow bulls had fun listening to the tough guy meekly apologizing over and over again.

A couple of years back, the story goes, Snake Eyes didn't show up to work for a few days. Cops went to his house and found him, bedraggled and out of his head, telling the festering corpse of his mother that he would be a good boy from now on if she would just wake up.

Afterwards, he'd seemed to pull himself together and was back to work right away. But now his brutality and corruption knew no limits. There wasn't a saloon or whorehouse in town that he wasn't squeezing for graft. Despite his blatant crookedness, O'Toole was even more infamous for his savagery. He took pride in clobbering at least one person every shift—often a Negro because that was easy to get away with. Still, skin color wasn't a crucial factor, and the detective delivered his beat-downs with a fair-minded enthusiasm.

Jack knew that O'Toole was a Detroit Tigers baseball fan, which figured. Ty Cobb, the meanest cuss in the game, played for the Tigers. Jack's favorite player was Honus Wagner, who was just as good as Cobb—maybe better—and a decent man as well. It so happened that Wagner's Pittsburgh Pirates were playing the Tigers in game three of the World Series that afternoon.

He walked up to the man's table. "Detroit got great pitching on Saturday from Wild Bill Donovan, Snake. Nice job tying the Series." O'Toole said nothing as he leisurely fished into his pocket for a pack of cigarettes. He picked up a matchbook with a cover advertising Peruvian Wine of Coca and lit up a stick. "Let me know if you get a pack of smokes with the Honus Wagner baseball card," said Jack. "Know you haven't got any use for it."

O'Toole turned his blank, dead eyes on Jack. The man's face was a ghastly landscape of pits, bumps, and fissures. A spongy growth abutted his left nostril, and pig grease glistened on his chin and wispy mustache. "Wagner makes zero dollars off those cards. Sucker." He took a drag and blew a perfect smoke ring. "What?"

"Join you? Pinkertons hired me to help out Horace Shaw."

O'Toole kept his creepy stare going for so long that Jack wondered if the guy was trying to work some sort of hoodoo spell. "Sit," he finally said.

Jack sat on the edge of a chair. "Heard you got some evidence tying Shaw to that dead showgirl. Poor old Shaw just can't figure how that happened." Jack steeled himself for another hypnotizing-the-prey stare, but the other man spoke right up.

"Tell Shaw he's wasting his money on your bag of guts. Man's getting arrested after the inquest. He ain't got a China-man's chance of dodging it."

"Shaw's got the long green. He'd be more than happy to

show his gratitude to someone who could put an end to this misunderstanding."

"You trying to bribe a Baltimore city detective?" O'Toole spoke in a bored tone as he poured a drink from a bottle. "Have to arrest your ass." He downed the glass in one quick motion. Then he put his cig on the edge of the table, picked up a pig's foot, and chewed off the last shred of flesh sticking to the knuckle. He wasn't even interested in considering a bribe, which had to be a first. Somebody had promised the guy something big to keep Shaw in Dutch.

"It was just an innocent question. Here's one more: What do you know about Lizzie Sullivan?"

The lawman tossed the pig bone on the floor and then casually sucked his fingers. "Like what?"

"Like anything. Tell me: Was she close to her mother?"

O'Toole curled his upper lip, revealing a snaggly bunch of yellow teeth. A front tooth was chipped like a jagged pane of glass in a broken window. "Get lost, mope. Now."

Jack got up and walked to the bar. He'd played that badly. Chances were slim that O'Toole would have told him anything, but the wiseass question guaranteed the brush-off. Jack needed information. He had to be smarter about getting it.

"Branch water," he told the unenthusiastic barkeep. When the glass finally appeared, Jack found his hands were shaking worse than ever.

He looked at the line of men next to him as he sipped. Barflies and spreesters trying to dull their troubles. A paperhanger smart enough not to try to pass his phony sawbuck bills in this place. A sharp-eyed bunk artist on the make for a pigeon. Too bad for the gullible Jasper who wandered in here or, for that matter, just about any other saloon in the city—the yokel would get big-citied in a hurry.

Prints of boxers covered the walls. There were pictures of Bob Foster along with others. Paddy Ryan, with his beer gut hanging over his white tights; "Gentleman Jim" Corbett, proudly flashing his handsome mug; Jack Johnson, with his long, muscular arms and legs. Two young women were pictured slugging it out in what looked like a fancy drawing room complete with an elaborate hutch full of bone china. One dame had thrown a left jab wide, and the other looked ready to unload a killer uppercut. "Hey, Bob around?"

The bottle jockey didn't look up from polishing a glass. "Left word not to be disturbed."

"Send a bottle of Pikesville Rye back to him now."

"Two bottles would get his attention faster."

Jack tossed a ten-spot on the mahogany. "Okay; keep the change. Tell him Jack Harden wants a few minutes of his time." The guy snatched the cash and disappeared through a back door. Jack drained his water and wished he had ordered another before sending the barman away.

"Mister, give a girl a light?" Jack turned to see a drawn woman in a low-cut dress leaning over with an unlit cigarette. He was getting a great view of her overflowing cleavage and a snootful of bargain counter perfume. The woman was so worn out, it was hard to tell if she was twenty-five or forty. The face paint didn't do much to hide a black eye.

"Don't smoke."

"Sweet man, worried about my morals. For two dollars I'll show you my full appreciation upstairs." She stepped closer and touched his jacket arm. Her fingernails were filthy and the back of her hand covered with shiny white scars.

"I mean I don't smoke," said Jack. "And I'm not in the mood for company."

"Gosh, things are slow today," she said, leaning on the bar and gently rubbing the mouse under her eye. "Bound to pick up tonight, right?" Hope and regret twisted around each other in her voice like strands on a frayed rope.

"How old's your baby?"

The woman jerked her head up to look at him. "How'd you know I have a kid?"

"Your tits are big for your body."

She tossed her head back and laughed. "Thank God for nature's bounty, brother." She tugged down at her neckline. "This gets a man's attention every time, but congratulations. You're the first one to notice with your brain rather than your Johnson." The mirth faded quickly, and she stared quietly at the floor. "My boy's three months old."

The barkeep gestured from the rear door. Jack peeled off a ten-dollar bill from the Pinkerton money and handed it to the woman. "Go home. And quit smoking." He made for the door, ignoring the woman's cries of gratitude. He didn't deserve thanks—all he'd done was throw a sop to his guilt.

Bob Foster was sitting with his chair tilted back and feet propped up on his desk. Jack always wondered how, after dozens of fights, Foster had kept his handsome face, with its smooth skin and straight nose. Unlike many seasoned fighters, his eyebrows were nearly scar-free and his ears showed no sign of deformation. He wore a fancy pink-striped shirt and a dotted red silk necktie, complete with a black pearl stickpin that cost more than Jack had made in the previous year. A bottle of Pikesville was open in front of him next to a half-full glass.

"Only thing I like more than drinking this stuff is drinking it for free," said Foster as he poured an extra glass.

"It's all yours," said Jack, pushing the glass away.

Foster tossed both glasses back, one right after the other. "Fine. I'm happy to pour it down my neck for a bit and then tell you to leave."

"Heard about Lizzie Sullivan?"

"White girl who got murdered. Awful shame. Terrible."

"You knew her."

Foster poured another glass. "She was a sweet kid. The kind you want to help get away from a real bad man."

"Who?"

"One of my piano players, Nick Monkton. She thought it was love. He saw it as a business opportunity."

"He pimped her out. Nice guy."

Foster shot him a look that had probably terrified more than a few of his ring opponents. "Nick's trouble. Knew it soon as I laid eyes on him—all swagger and big talk. Only kept him around because he's a fine player and a great ragtime song-writer. I got to know Lizzie through him."

"Think he killed her?"

"Possibly." Foster took a long pull from his glass. "If so, you can be sure it was about money. That's the only thing the man cares about. Always has some racket going, some angle to play. I warned Lizzie that he was a nasty, conning heel."

"Where's he now?"

"All I know is that he was hauled off to the Irish clubhouse around eleven last night. Good riddance. He better not show his face in my joint again. Could be bad for his health."

"The cops took him to the station—what for?" Jack pushed the derby up his forehead.

"Could be any number of things. Vice. Fraud. Wrong race."

"Nick's colored?"

"You'd think he was white."

Jack scratched his head and stared back at Bob.

"A classy preacher came by last week to tell Nick his great-granny died. Nick wasn't here so he asked me to pass on the message along with some old books of hers. The reverend was a boxing fan and excited to meet me. He jabbered and jabbered and let loose something about how the old gal overcame the pain of slavery through prayer. Guy got upset and said that was a secret—made me promise to say nix. I'm only telling you because you're so generous with the Pikesville." He poured another glass.

"One slave great-granny is enough to consider someone black?"

"Yep." Foster snorted and took a drink. "Law says if you have one black great-grandparent you can't marry a white person."

"Don't politicians have better things to do than put stuff like that on the books?"

"Don't play the high-minded white boy with me. This is Baltimore." Foster's feet came off the desk as his chair slammed to the floor. "You know damn well how worked up your people get about race. Crazy afraid that all any colored guy wants to do is slit their throats and take their women. I've been all around the country—all around the world—and there's more hatred of Negroes in Baltimore than just about anyplace else."

"Then why do you still live here?"

"Same reason you do, man. Baltimore has bully style—it's jumping with energy and action you don't find in another city."

"A place where a guy like Nick could meet up with a girl like Lizzie."

"As if you got a clue what a black man has to worry about if he's with a white girl." He curled his big hands into fists and slowly relaxed them. "Associating with Lizzie Sullivan could get a colored guy in deep trouble. Arrested—hell, even killed."

"You think the cops hauled Nick off for that reason?"

"Maybe. They also tore apart his room here looking for something. Could be they were after his compositions." Some of Foster's ferocity faded. "Man may be trash, but he sure can write good songs. Making a name for himself. Guess who likes to come listen to him play?"

"Teddy Roosevelt?"

Foster clapped once and laughed. "Not far off. Lucas Patterson, the millionaire socialist himself. Patterson's a fine judge of piano players. He's also known to be friendly to good-looking young men."

"You mean that Patterson's—"

"Yeah. Nick is too, when the money's right. If Nick had any sense he'd use the situation to get his songs published and promoted. Patterson's more than happy to help him out. There's just one problem. Well, two."

"Nick isn't happy being Patterson's pet."

"That's one. The other's that Patterson is the only person I know who didn't like Lizzie. Really, truly hated her. I guess the man figured she stood between him and Nick."

"Could Patterson have killed her?"

Foster lifted his glass and twirled the golden liquid. "Don't want to speculate on that."

"What more can you say about Lizzie?"

"Danced at the Gayety when Nick didn't have her otherwise engaged."

"Like with Horace Shaw?"

"That's who people are saying killed her. Wouldn't surprise me in the least."

"Any other ideas about who else other than Shaw might have killed her?"

"I see. Shaw hired you to get him off. The man's looking guiltier all the time." Foster pulled out a big gold watch but didn't bother looking at it. "Time's up, gumshoe."

"That's a quick few minutes." Jack got up to leave, aware that Bob knew more than he'd let on about both Nick and Lizzie.

"Harden." Jack looked back. "Heard you can't pay a sizable marker that's due shortly. Going to have trouble fingering a killer if a bunch of strong-arm men jolly you up. Could even end up floating face-down in the harbor basin."

"I got time. Mind if I look at Nick's room?"

"Sure—it's number twenty-six. One more thing, pal. All I said? You didn't hear it from me."

"Not like you to be scared, Bob."

53

"The good book." Foster looked solemn. "Psalm one forty, three to four."

"Don't know it," said Jack before walking out and closing the door. In the hall, he leaned against the wall with his hands pressed over his ears as the voice thundered in his head. *They have sharpened their tongues like a serpent; adders' poison is under their lips. Keep me, O Lord, from the hands of the wicked; preserve me from the violent man; who have purposed to overthrow my goings.*

The voice still had him shaking as he went upstairs to number twenty-six. The door was smashed and hung open crookedly on one hinge. The room was torn apart, with dresser drawers dumped on the floor and the mattress flipped and shredded against the wall. Pages of sheet music were scattered everywhere.

A couple of well-worn hymnals lay open on the floor. He picked one up and fanned its pages, finding an inscription on the flyleaf: "For Annie Monkton, whose trying life has served to strengthen her belief in Our Lord. Thank you for sharing your story of bondage, struggle, and faith with me." It was signed "Rev. Charles Lombard, Baltimore." Annie Monkton—Nick's great-granny?

Jack gave the room a last look. If there had been anything valuable in this place, it was gone.

THE EASTERN DISTRICT police station was a squat brick building on Bank Street downwind from a vinegar factory. The pungent smell made Jack's eyes water as he climbed the cophouse steps. As if visiting this dump weren't awful enough.

The one good thing was that a desk sergeant here owed him a favor. When a major bookie got killed two months ago, a city councilman hired Jack to find his policy sheets before the cops did. When Jack found the papers, he spotted a big-time debt sheet for the sergeant. Figuring one good turn deserves another, he grabbed it and passed it on to the cop.

Stepping into the lobby, he noticed that electric lights had replaced the old gas lamps. The new lighting revealed exactly how dirty and beat up everything was. The floorboards were worn down below the nails and filthy with cigarette butts, squashed bugs, and balls of hair and dust. Sooty ridges stood out in relief on the hastily slopped plaster walls. The bench seats were worn smooth from countless brawlers, drunks, pick-pockets, stick-up artists, and more than a few innocents dragged in off the street. The place smelled like stale sweat and dried blood.

A raised wooden desk ran the length of the rear wall. Two cops were sitting behind the desk. One was asleep, his head thrown back and snoring with his mouth open. The other—Jack's sergeant buddy—was leaning over and wearily explaining something to a redheaded woman wringing a handkerchief. Jack gave a wide berth to the full cuspidor and waited at the waist-high baluster railing in front of the desk.

"Miss, I've told you all I know. Don't do no good to keep on pestering me." The sergeant saw Jack, and a look of relief flashed across his face. "You need to move on, miss. Another's waiting behind you."

"Yinz all got to tell me something. How can someone get killed and the police not know nothing?" The sound of the woman's hick accent jolted Jack back to his childhood on a remote farm in western Pennsylvania. A shiver spilled through his gut. More bad memories.

"Sorry, miss. Next."

The woman spun around and walked past. Even in the harsh glare of the electric light she was beautiful. She was in her mid-twenties with huge green eyes and a shiny mass of flaming red hair that hopelessly outshone an old straw hat with its faded ribbons. A faint spray of freckles dotted her peaches and cream complexion. Even though her lips were pursed with worry, they still seemed to invite kissing. The body under the faded calico dress was curvy.

"Harden, how's the hammer hanging?" said the cop as Jack stepped up to the desk.

"Tough one, huh, Sarge?" asked Jack with a man-to-man grin. The woman must have been badgering the cop pretty bad—most men would fall all over themselves to get next to a dame like that.

"You got no idea, brother." He put his hands together and flexed them out, cracking his knuckles like firecrackers. "People always think the cops are holding out on them," he said. "It ain't true."

"You mean it ain't always true."

"What you want, snooper?"

"Need to know about Nick Monkton. He was carted in last night from the Silverstrike Hotel."

The cop rubbed his rheumy eyes. "I tell you, are we square?"

"You bet."

"O'Toole brought him in. Sweated the guy in the back room for a while. Then some big muck-a-muck lawyer showed up and got the guy sprung."

"Nick's not the type to have that kind of representation. Who sent the mouthpiece?"

"He was Lucas Patterson's personal lawyer. Threatened holy hell if we didn't leave sweet Nicky alone. Really gave it hot to O'Toole and got him to back off, if you can believe that."

"What time was Nick let go?"

"Late—like two a.m."

"What was O'Toole after?"

"Monkton had something Snake wanted bad. Not sure what. That's it—we're done here."

"Does the name Lizzie Sullivan mean anything to you?"

The cop looked like no name could have irritated him more.

"Beat it, or I'll come around this desk and club you good." He picked up a newspaper and leaned back in his seat.

Jack walked around the railing and was about to the front door when the redhead rushed up from behind. "Stop, mister, please stop." He turned to see those enormous eyes pleading up at him. Jack was in a hurry, but she was hard to ignore. "Sorry, I done heard you mention Lizzie Sullivan. She's my sister. She—she got murdered last night. I found her body." The woman gasped and pressed the handkerchief to her lips.

"What's your name, miss?"

"Clara. Clara Sullivan."

"Miss Sullivan, you have my condolences."

She dropped the handkerchief to reveal a trembling chin. Tears rolled down her cheeks. "This is so horrible. I come to town to fetch Lizzie back home. Found her"—she paused to utter a sob—"dead in her room this morning. I been setting in this station trying to learn something for hours. I can't just go tell Ma and Pa she got killed and nothing else. They'll be wanting to know who did it and that they got caught."

What kind of parents would let a young woman travel alone into the big city to bring back a scandalous sister? This gal was in a pickle. But Jack, as a rule, steered clear of damsels in distress—he had too many troubles of his own to deal with. "Sorry again, miss. I got to go."

"Why were you asking about Lizzie?" Her eyebrows sprang into gleaming copper arcs. "Are you a detective? What's your name?"

"I'm a private detective checking into Lizzie's death. Name's Jack. Now—"

"Jack, I think my sister was up to something with Nick Monkton that got her killed."

"Such as what?"

"Such as, if I tell will you help me?" Her voice was throaty and her long, pale eyelashes fluttered.

"We can maybe work something out." The possibility of that was definitely growing.

"Please." She tilted her head down with her eyes glued on him in a perfect look of girlish vulnerability.

She made his knees knock. And she might have dope that could help unravel Lizzie's murder. The only thing pulling him away from her was an urgent sense that another woman was in a better position to help wrap up the case and get him the bonus he dearly needed.

"Okay. Can you meet me at the Monumental Lunchroom tomorrow morning, eight o'clock? Then I can give you my full attention."

Her face brightened just a little but it was enough to hit him like a big, soft punch. "Thank you so, so much. You're the first person who's been nice to me in this big, awful city." She gave him a fragile grin.

"You'll find that I'm one heck of a nice guy." He flashed his most winning smile.

"Golly, that's wonderful—'bye." She gave him a wave. He strode out of the place with the back of his neck tingling in a strange way.

Outside, the light was fading and the sharp vinegar smell now had a sickeningly fruity undertone. The factory was preparing another fresh vat. Jack's head throbbed as his stomach did somersaults. He looked for a distraction and flagged down a bootblack lounging under a gas streetlight, which was already sputtering and hissing in the early twilight.

"Yes, sir. Get the best shine in Baltimore right here for a nickel." The kid was about eight years old and wore a dirty jacket over torn pants.

"I want the rag and the brush twice. Do it double time and I'll give you a dime. I'm seeing a lady."

"You got it, mister." He dropped to his knees and pulled the tools of his trade from a wooden box. The kid's little hands were stained black from the fingertips to the wrists. He worked fast, with rag snapping and brush flying. The shoes soon gleamed with an almost unnatural glow.

"Kid, you got talent." Jack flipped him a dime. "Happen to know who won the Series game?"

"Pirates, eight to six. Wagner had three hits, three runs batted in, and three stolen bases."

Jack hailed a cab and headed back downtown. Since Snake Eyes wouldn't take a bribe, the best bet to collect on this job was to get a second official opinion on Lizzie's cause of death—if someone with sway said the gunshot didn't kill her, there might be enough doubt to keep Shaw out of the slammer. He needed to get another autopsy scheduled right quick. Otherwise, case closed.

His best shot was getting that lady doctor who talked like a book to prove that Shaw's pistol wasn't the murder weapon. They hadn't parted on great terms, but Jack was usually able to sweet-talk women into liking him. True, he had no experience charming a proper lady. Especially one as quirky as she was. But it would be tough for Shaw if he got collared, and far tougher for Jack if he missed out on the chance to put a dent in his debt.

CHAPTER 5

SARAH—MONDAY, OCTOBER 11, 1909, 6:30 P.M.

"*G*lad you're still here. I'd hate to have killed myself climbing those stairs for nothing."

Sarah whirled to see Jack, hat off and panting for breath, standing in the office doorway. She did not want to deal with anyone right now, especially not this unethical hireling. She stared at the wall behind the visitor while standing rigidly next to the bag of books on the desk. "What's with the bag? Been shopping?"

He was not going to leave her alone. She had to say something. "I have been dismissed and must leave immediately." An unbearable situation had gotten even worse. She yanked off her right glove and started chewing her thumbnail with vigorous little bites.

"What—they gave you the gate? They're even stupider than I thought. Here, let me help you with your bag."

"No. I will ask someone else. Go away."

"I don't see anyone else handy. Besides, you helped me in the elevator. Least I can do is return the favor." He stepped close and grabbed the bag's handle.

She noticed a complex mix of odors. The strongest was a

pleasant leathery smell with a metallic edge—it brought to mind a horse harness hanging in the sun. But there were also two other unpleasant scents—a vinegary tang and the sweet reek of whiskey. She stepped back and waved a hand in front of her face.

"Do I smell that bad?"

"Yes. I do not like the odor of whiskey or the odor of vinegar, and mixed they are hard for me to have in my nose. I insist that you leave me alone. Do so immediately." If not for the books, she would run away as fast as possible.

"You really are delicate, like you said. I promise not to stand too close." He lifted the bag and headed for the hallway. "What do you got in here—a rock collection?"

He had remembered her refined senses. She followed and caught up with him at the elevator. Why the speculation about a rock collection in the bag? There was no logical basis for assuming that, which probably meant his question was not literal. Was he using one of those non-sensical figures of speech that people were so unaccountably fond of? Or perhaps he was attempting to use humor to interact with her. In any event, she was in no mood to try and interpret whatever he was saying. "I have books in the bag. They are important to me." She pressed the elevator call button.

"I may still need your help going down," he said. "Guess I'm delicate about some things, too."

"I will take your arm again. After that, you will leave the bag by the curb and depart. I will have the driver boost my bag into the cab." The elevator door opened and she reached for his arm, realizing too late she had forgotten to put her glove back on, which made the experience of touching him difficult.

His arm tightened as the car dropped with a hiss. One squeeze from her and the tension in his arm lessened, as it had before. When they reached the lobby, he lugged the bag out the entrance and stood next to the building, making no move toward the waiting cabs. "Your assistance is appreciated, but I insist that you leave me alone. Otherwise I will call for a policeman."

Jack transferred the bag to his other hand. "Oh, I see. You're afraid I'm going to steal your bag of gold bars. Don't worry—I might be a mercenary, but I'm no thief."

She stamped her foot. "I told you I have books in the bag."

"Listen, Sarah, I want to talk about how Lizzie died, about getting a second autopsy before the inquest tomorrow. Let me buy you dinner. It'll help take you mind off those idiots." He nodded toward the building behind him.

She tried to find the right words amid her clashing thoughts. This man gave no indication of relinquishing her bag. She glanced around and saw no policeman. There were only two options: screaming for help or agreeing to his request. If she called out, he might drop the bag and damage one or more books. And there was no guarantee that anyone would come to her assistance quickly. "Very well. Note I am not prepared to converse at length. And if you make any romantic overtures I shall cry out."

Jack smiled. "I'll control myself. I know a restaurant right up the street."

As they walked toward Monument Square, Sarah felt a prick of pleasure to be among the couples strolling in the gathering dusk. She thought of herself as alone in the world, and most of the time that was fine. It meant she had freedom to do as she pleased without the distraction of having anyone impose any more rules or limits. But loneliness did cause her pain from time to time.

They were about to cross Fayette Street when a hackney carriage came racing toward them, the driver screaming curses over the clattering of hooves. The carriage came to a halt, iron-rimmed wheels skidding and shrieking against the Belgian block paving stones. The horse was white-eyed and snorting with fear.

"You miserable piece of crow bait!" A whip cracked against the horse's back, causing it to rear with a terrified cry.

Jack froze for a second before dropping the bag and grabbing the mare's bridle. The animal tried to pull away as Jack spoke to it in a soothing voice. It calmed, only to rear again when the driver cracked his whip on the beast. Jack went to the driver and pulled him down from the wagon to the street. The man threw a powerful punch that Jack dodged and countered with a blow to the man's face. The driver fell, and Jack jumped on him in a frenzy.

Sarah stepped behind Jack and squeezed his shoulder firmly, causing him to stop in mid-swing. "Stop," she said. "You prefer not to act this way." The tension lessened in his muscles, and breathing raggedly, he got off the man.

"Crap, pal. You're cuckoo." The driver got to his feet unsteadily, hand over his bleeding nose.

"Your horse got scared by a rat or something. You don't whip a panicked animal, idiot."

The driver wasted no time getting back into his carriage and trotting away. Sarah stepped back by her books. It was a mistake to be with this man.

"It's okay. I'm fine," Jack said, taking off his derby and fanning himself. "Sorry. I was in the cavalry and can't stand to see horses mistreated." Sarah bounced on her toes, unsure what to do. She hated unpredictability, and it was jarring to see this big man switch from apparent normality to brutishness in moments. She observed him with darting glances. He was still agitated, although less so than before. "Thanks for stopping me. Sorry to drop your bag." He bent down and carefully put a volume that had slipped halfway out back into the bag.

"Everything okay here, miss?" Two well-dressed young men approached.

Jack stood quickly. "Clear off, clowns, or I'll chew you both up good."

"Let the lady answer for herself, chum," said the taller of the men as he reached into his jacket pocket.

Sarah stared at the sidewalk. "I do not require your assistance," she said. "This man is no longer dangerously violent."

"Suit yourself, honey." The men walked off.

"That's not exactly a ringing vote of confidence," said Jack as he lifted the bag. "Maybe I did go kind of buggy. Don't quite remember."

"I have worked with the insane and know their habits. You, however, took a rational action to resolve an instance of cruelty. Your rapid escalation of anger was aberrant, although it appeared to stem from an altruistic impulse—"

"All that fancy talk's wasted on me." He walked across the intersection while she stayed on the other side of the street.

Jack gestured for her to cross, and after a moment, she did. "I'm not making fun of you, Sarah, but you're the first woman I've ever seen who marches when she walks." Jack was grinning. "There's none of that mincing that makes a gal look like she's stepping on eggshells."

"I would step more carefully if eggs were in my path."

"That's a good one. Here's our restaurant." He opened the door for her, and soon they were seated at a small table for two.

The freshly starched tablecloth pleased her greatly, and she ran her fingertips over its crisp whiteness several times while also appreciating the warm, waxy scent of the candles burning in the small candelabra at the center of the table. It was a quiet place, with only a low hum of voices and the faint clink of silver on china. From an initial sensory standpoint, this was acceptable. It was just a matter of getting this encounter over with as quickly as possible.

"Do you want something to drink?" he asked.

"I will have half a glass of red Burgundy. Please insist upon a superior vintage. Inferior years have far too much tannin."

Soon after, the waiter appeared with a bottle and two glasses. Jack waved away his glass. "I don't want any. Let the lady see if she likes it."

The waiter stared at Jack, then turned slowly to Sarah, sighed, and poured a small bit into her glass. She stared at the deep red-purple shimmer for a long moment. Matters of etiquette were essential. They served as a rule-based framework to guide her social behavior. This was unprecedented—she had never judged the fitness of wine with a man at the table. The waiter cleared his throat. There was nothing to do but lift the glass and taste. She was pleased as the velvety liquid slid across her tongue—this was an excellent vintage.

"Well?" asked the waiter.

"The wine is satisfactory." She set the glass down, and the waiter filled it halfway with another sigh before leaving. "You do not drink wine yet I noticed the smell of whiskey on your person. That is contradictory."

He laughed. "What's weird is that I spend a lot of time in saloons as part of my job and don't drink booze. Been thinking I should carry a flask of tea around with me to dump in a glass so that I fit in with everyone else. What's your pleasure for eats?"

The menu was rich with foods that she liked, and soon she was enjoying a hot bowl of terrapin soup followed by a filet of sole. Jack refilled her wineglass just as she was taking a bite and unable to say no. A warm glow began to replace the knot of tension in the center of her chest. When she finished the second glass of wine, she felt something close to relaxed.

"Tell me why you think the shot didn't kill Lizzie Sullivan." Jack belched, having just dispatched a plate of oysters with crude, lip-smacking energy.

She put her hands over her ears, lowered her head, and stared at the table.

He tapped the edge of her plate with his knife. "Sarah— what's the matter?"

She uncovered her ears. "Your awful table manners upset me."

"That so." He put his knife down. "I'll sit still, then."

"I have already told you about the lack of bleeding from the gunshot, which is inconsistent with receiving that type of wound while alive. Since our prior meeting, I went back to the morgue, opened Lizzie's skull, and discovered a major hemorrhage. The bleeding inside the skull means the injury happened while she was alive. Based on what I saw, I would say the injury took roughly forty-eight hours to kill her. That means Mr. Shaw could not have murdered her Sunday night or Monday morning."

Jack toyed with an empty oyster shell. "You opened her skull?"

"That should have been done during the initial autopsy."

"How did she get hit in the head? Did someone whack her? Maybe she tripped on a carpet?"

"That is as yet undetermined. What matters is that the delayed fatality of the head injury, along with evidence supporting the gunshot as occurring after Lizzie died, should allow Mr. Horace Shaw to present a credible alibi, assuming he was traveling with companions out of town as he claimed."

"What can be done about getting the official results changed?"

"As I said before, that requires a major effort. A high-level city official would have to request the action. I would think Mr. Shaw would have an interest in pursuing that course. He has refused to take that step."

"What about a family member of the dead girl—say, a sister?" The waiter plunked down plates piled high with crab, succotash, and boiled potatoes. "If the sister demanded another look would the big shots have to do it?"

"In all probability, yes. Does Lizzie have a sister in the city?"

"Seems to. I'm talking with her tomorrow."

"She will have to act quickly. Once the body is washed and embalmed, evidence is lost and the courts are less inclined to accept results. You must press her to act."

"I'll do my best. She's a country bumpkin and might not go for having her relation sliced and diced."

"I never have understood the opposition people have to dissection of the human body. It is no different than cutting into a pig or cow. Humans do, in fact, share remarkable similarities with those animals in terms of musculature and internal organs. Why are so many eager to eat animal flesh while also remaining resistant to autopsy?"

Jack pushed away a plate of rare steak the waiter had just brought.

"If you fail to convince the sister to ask for a second autopsy rest assured that I have obtained pieces of evidence from the body."

"You cut off pieces of the body? Doctors. Cripes."

"I accept that you do not like me, but do not accuse me of macabre and unprofessional behavior. I merely removed objects from the body, including fibers from under her fingernails."

"It's nothing personal—I just don't like medical types." He poked at a small plate of cooked carrots. "I got wounded while in the army over in the Philippines and the sawbones did more harm than good."

"Tell me what happened to you."

"I was with two other soldiers in town when this Moro native attacked us. They call it 'running amok,' and it's about a guy getting possessed by a tiger spirit—or just going crazy—to kill people. White devils like us were popular targets. My two buddies got chopped up and I got a Kris knife stuck through my left arm before I shot the guy dead. Then I get hauled to a field hospital where a stumblebum doctor put his foot on my arm and yanks the knife out. I'm screaming in pain and bleeding all over the place but all the guy does is tell me to shut up while he looks at the knife, his dandy new souvenir. Then some other medico staggers over, puts a dirty bandage on me, and offers me the dregs from his whiskey bottle. A bit later my arm gets all red and swollen and the two quacks tell me they need to amputate. No way I'm going for that, so I drag myself back to my unit. After a while I healed up."

"That is a dreadful story. I must tell you, however, that not all medical—"

"Sure. You're going to say I just got dealt a lousy hand that one time. Okay, let's talk about Lizzie." Jack leaned back, head cocked. "What's the big deal about that stuff you took from under her fingernails?"

"It is possible that Lizzie received the blow to her head during a struggle. If so, she may have scratched her attacker through an article of clothing. I can examine the fibers under a microscope to identify them. There may be traces of blood on the fibers, which, if true, could mean the killer has scratches on their body. Perhaps I should turn what I have over to the police. Even though I no longer have a connection with the case, I want justice served."

Jack speared a potato and gobbled it down whole. Sarah turned her head and looked down at the shiny wooden floor. "You just decided to do all that stuff—with the skull and the fingernails—on your own," said Jack with his mouth full. "I'm starting to see why the Pinkertons let you go."

She stood. "I want to go home now."

"If you care about the truth," said Jack, "please sit down."

Sarah swayed for a moment and sat. Her place setting was perfectly arranged except for a teaspoon, which the waiter had brushed to one side. She lifted the spoon to put it where it belonged.

"Listen—the cops don't care about justice. They've already decided Shaw did it. He's getting arrested tomorrow. I've got to get him off."

Sarah smacked the spoon onto the table with a sound like a pistol shot. "No one cares about the truth, least of all you. Your only interest is in collecting money."

Jack refilled her wineglass as she breathed rapidly, hands clenched. "Right. I get my hands dirty to earn my dough. You're a do-good idealist with your head in the clouds. Let's consider the possibility that our interests overlap."

"Have you no ethics? Lizzie Sullivan's killer must be caught. If Horace Shaw is guilty of the murder then he must be held accountable, regardless of how much money he is willing to pay you. That is the law." She took a large gulp of wine as awareness dawned that she was perhaps behaving in an aggressive, confrontational manner.

"Hey, no need to yell. I just—"

"And how dare you patronize me as an idealist. I acted to have the killer of my father and sister arrested and convicted. I have a more personal investment in seeking justice than you can begin to understand." She almost did not care about the reprimand that was surely coming from Jack in response to her unladylike behavior.

"I'm sorry for not giving you enough credit. Tell me about your father and sister."

"No." Sarah was now furious with herself for mentioning what had happened to her family, having never before said anything about it to anyone who did not already know. How had this man gotten her to reveal the most painful episode of her life? She had been so stupid in agreeing to this dinner. She sipped more wine, despite knowing she had already had too much.

"I understand if you don't want to talk about it." Jack slurped his water. "Let me just say that I lost faith in justice because of what happened to me in the Philippines. Innocent people were killed and nobody got called to account. Probably why I'm a little nuts." He hung his head for a second before

69

snapping it back up. "And I don't want to talk about that, either."

Sarah remembered the altercation in the street. "That event involving the native attacker still lingers in your mind. Tell me more about its impact on you."

"You just keep on coming, don't you?"

"Psychological trauma is a topic of great interest to me." Her brain came alive with all the medical information she had consumed on the subject. Jack, along with the rest of her surroundings, faded away to faint shadows in the background.

"It wasn't the amok guy. That didn't bother me much. But something else did. My unit cornered a thousand natives and we got orders to wipe them out. I refused when I saw they were mostly women and children. All of them got killed—I couldn't stop a damn thing. I haven't been able to get what I saw, what I heard, out of my head. Satisfied?"

Situations triggered extreme distress for the man—such as riding in an elevator or witnessing the mistreatment of a horse. She recalled writings of Dr. Sigmund Freud about individuals with memories of trauma trapped in their subconscious that caused them recurring episodes of intense emotional pain. Jack must suffer terribly, at the edge of what a human being could bear. She felt the physical sensation of her heart warming as it experienced his pain.

"Sarah." He tapped the tabletop. "Sarah? You drifted off again."

She gave a start as her attention returned to the restaurant. "A doctor should have insight into the problem and relieve your suffering." She stole a quick look at him.

"Yeah, right. You quacks are all the same—you pretend to know stuff but you don't." He snorted. "Men got killed over there. Others were crippled and worse. They're the ones people need to care about. My loony spells don't deserve any regard."

"Do you hallucinate? I assume you have troubled thoughts

and agitation. You may have an ailment known as soldier's
heart. Some Civil War veterans appeared changed by their military experience, with mixed physical and psychological symp-
toms. They presented with fatigue, overuse of drugs and
alcohol, nervous disorders, intense irritability, and cardiac
weakness."

"I'm not weak. Why are we still talking about this? You're
really on a jag—keep your voice down."

"We must also consider railroad spine. People of all types
who have survived terrible railroad accidents without apparent
injury have been found to suffer serious nervous conditions,
sleeplessness, and diminished health. Speculation is that
concussion of the spine during the accident is the cause,
although others—myself included—believe the cause is neurological. Can you give me more details about your experience?"

"Forget it. Why do you care? Nobody else ever has."

"I am a physician. I aim to understand the specific causes of
ill health, both physical and mental. I want to help you."

"Hah—you sure talk a good game, Doc, I'll give you that."
He squirmed in his seat for a long while. "You got a cure for
ghosts?" he finally asked.

She looked up and saw that he was giving her an intense
glare. Her eyes flicked back down to her tidy place setting. "The
role of psychological trauma in causing mental distress deserves
more study. I wonder about the impact of guilt upon people who
survive horrific episodes where others die. You may experience
hallucinations as a symptom of your guilt."

"The ghosts of those dead natives haunt me, I swear. I see
them all the time—sometimes just a few, sometimes dozens.
Mostly women and children. Babies. They're all bloody. They
cry and scream, babble at me in some strange language. They
want my help, but I can't do anything, just like I couldn't do
anything during the massacre. Drives me completely around
the bend. I tell you, the spirits are as real as you sitting across

from me now. I've never told anyone before because it sounds crazy."

"What you describe as ghosts are nothing more than a product of your mental anguish." She focused intently on moving her water glass and bread plate one-quarter inch to the right. "There is no rational basis for spirits or the supernatural."

"I'm not so sure. Lots of smart people believe in spirits. There's stuff in the paper all the time about it and I've heard about people called sensitives—they can talk with the dead and deliver messages to and from the living. Sometimes I think I should find a good sensitive and try to settle things with all my dead people."

"That is nonsense." Sarah chopped the air with a stiff hand.

"Come on." Jack pointed a finger at her. "Wouldn't you like to talk with certain dead people? Like your father and sister?"

"The spirit world does not exist. I do not wish to discuss this topic any further." Sarah swept her hand over the table, knocking over her water glass. She barely noticed the water dripping onto her lap.

"I guess the deal here is that I have to spill my guts and you don't." Jack used his napkin to mop the tabletop while she sat still. "I've never met a gal like you before," he said with a smile. "You want to talk about facts rather than how you feel—even though you feel plenty." He tried to catch her eye but she refused. "You've had a rough day, Sarah. I'll try to be nicer to you."

No one had ever been so calm and kind after she knocked over a glass. She had a long history of toppling things while dining, and the act always drew exasperated cries and rebukes from her dining companions. Jack treated the event as an unintentional accident. His insight into her personality was even more astounding. Warmth spread from the center of her chest to her hands and face. "How much money can one earn as a detective?" she asked with a hurried glance.

"Are you knocking me again? Yeah, okay. I'm a soulless hired gun. I admit it."

"I am genuinely interested in the earning potential. As you know, I no longer have a job."

"What, it's not enough being a lady doctor? You want to be a lady detective, too?" He laughed. "The pay varies from little to less than little. Got five hundred bucks riding on this one, though. Probably what a doctor makes every month for a whole lot less trouble."

"You said that earning money and pursuing the truth can coincide. I find that concept appealing. We should work as a team to solve Lizzie's murder." She blurted out the words in a tumbling rush before clapping a hand over her mouth. This impetuous behavior would only set her up for a rebuff. No man would put up with her if he had any choice in the matter.

"I'd say you were joking, but I get the idea that you don't kid around. Hey, you can take your hand off your mouth—nothing you could say would bother me too much."

She dropped her hand to the table with force. "Because you do not take me seriously. Do not underestimate me because of my sex."

"Sarah, I really admire your brains. Still, I can think of two reasons right off the bat why we can't work together. First, I'm obligated to do what I can for Shaw, guilty or not. I gave my word. Second, there are some dangerous characters mixed up in this case. Too dangerous for a lady like you."

"I will not take no for an answer," she said with a gesture that bumped and rocked the candelabra. "I insist we meet again tomorrow to talk further." The room was slightly off center, and she was pleasantly light-headed. "I will visit my mentor at Johns Hopkins Medical School tomorrow at ten a.m. Tell me where to meet you at eight thirty a.m."

"Okay, let's meet at the Monumental Lunchroom tomorrow

morning. Once you see me in the clear light of day you may change your mind."

Sarah felt strangely relaxed, almost buoyant. All her cares and worries were still there, but now a big, fuzzy blanket rested on top of them. "Let me see your shoes."

"My shoes?" Jack yanked at his shirt collar, then stuck his feet out from under the table.

"I glimpsed them earlier. I love how well-polished leather looks. Not patent leather. Real leather. Your shoes have a remarkable sheen." She leaned down to get a better look and had to tell herself not to touch his shoes. They were hypnotically lustrous.

"Okay, show me yours."

"My what?"

"Your shoes."

"Mine are not so shiny." She extended her feet and hiked her skirt and petticoat to reveal her sad-looking footwear. "I got them wet this morning and ruined them." She banged her toes together playfully before appreciating that she was flashing her thin legs with shocking immodesty. The skirts came back down, and her legs shot back under the table. A furious blush heated her face. *Stop behaving like a perfect fool*, she told herself. *Get yourself under control.*

Jack laughed. "Sarah, it's okay. I promised no romantic overtures, remember?"

"Correct." She began rocking in her chair.

"What's with the swaying? And that thing with your hands?"

"They are tics. Nervous habits. I have a variety of them."

"Know what? I do like you. You're a hundred percent sincere all the time. That's rare."

Sincere. Could he be referring to her complete inability to adjust her manner to suit different people in different circumstances? That aspect of her personality had caused her much trouble socially—was he now praising her for it? Or maybe he was taunting her in an especially cruel way. As he counted out the cash for the bill, she saw his hands were trembling.

Outside, he hailed a motorized taxicab and put her bag of books inside. "Maybe I should ride with you to your residence. A woman out alone at night—it's not safe."

"Any woman out alone at night in the city is considered a prostitute, I know." She was wobbly on her feet. "That is yet another barrier to contend with. I am quite used to traveling alone in carriages—or auto machines—during the evening."

She turned away from him, got her feet tangled, and stumbled. Jack caught her arm and held it. She looked up at him. "I am," she said, "uncomfortable with you touching me."

Jack let go and backed away with a grin. "Good night, Sarah."

She climbed into the cab with her heart pounding. As they motored off, she gazed at a series of electric shop lights demanding attention with their blinking garishness. She ignored them, wondering instead if her high spirits were justified. Jack could end up disappointing her—as most people did.

Enough of that. Pursuing this case would require gathering and analyzing much evidence. She would start reviewing the physical clues tomorrow. But there was a way for her to obtain some new information tonight.

Sarah knocked on the glass partition and told the driver to go to an address in the exclusive Mount Vernon Place neighborhood. To anyone but her, this was a most unlikely place to collect information about a potential murderer.

CHAPTER 6

JACK—MONDAY, OCTOBER 11, 1909,
9:00 P.M.

With Sarah canned from the Pinkertons, Jack knew the odds of getting another autopsy for Lizzie were long. Lucky about running into the sister. He had to get her to demand a second look at the body. Otherwise this case would stall and leave him where he started: dead broke.

Jack hotfooted it west on Fayette Street on the way to Lizzie's boardinghouse, which was down by the harbor basin steamship piers. The city courthouse filled the view off to his right, with banks and fancy stores on the other side.

Turning left on Light Street took him past buildings named after fat cats. He walked by the Carrol Building, the Crane Building, and the Lanahan Building. All new, built after the great 1904 fire that burned everything for blocks around. Those guys with their names in spiffy new brick and stone were enjoying a brief moment in the sun until the next fire, the next wave of construction, the next version of Baltimore appeared. The constant churn was something he liked about the city. It kept him on his toes and reminded him that everything changes.

He came to the intersection with Pratt Street, which was a dividing line. South of Pratt was grittier—a place where people worked the docks, bottling plants, machine shops, and the wholesale produce trade.

The harbor was off to the left, and the lighted hulks of side-wheel paddlers were floating like constellations on a watery horizon. One boat, farther out in the water, was shooting a spray of orange sparks from its smokestack. Streetcars rumbled by and knots of people were coming and going to the saloons, bordellos, pool halls, duckpin bowling alleys, assignation rooms, and other distractions offered in this part of town.

A right off Light Street on Conway took him down a brick canyon formed by the hulking state tobacco warehouses on either side of the street. The sweet, earthy smell of the plant was so strong he could taste it.

The next block gave over to fresh baking smells wafting from the nearby National Biscuit factory. The address he was looking for was at the end of the street, just across from the retaining wall for the Baltimore and Ohio Railroad underground tunnel. Beyond the wall were a succession of huge wooden train sheds lined up against a five-story, thousand-foot-long brick ware-house. Locomotives groaned and hissed like fitfully sleeping dragons.

Lizzie's boardinghouse was a narrow three-story row job identical to others flanking it up and down the block. Its only distinction was a working streetlamp opposite the entrance that lit the front steps like a stage. He rapped on the door. A white-haired man appeared with a smoking oil lantern.

"You want the room?" he asked.

"I'm here about Lizzie Sullivan. Private detective."

The man shot out his lower lip until it almost touched his nose. It wasn't a happy face. "Already talked to the cops. I want people to forget about that girl so's I can get a new boarder. Get on out of here." He tried to close the door, but Jack had his foot stuck against the jamb.

"It'll just take a minute, pops. Then I'll leave you in peace."

The man backed inside with a grunt and started up a listing staircase. Jack closed the door and followed. The place smelled of greasy boiled meat. At the top of the stairs, the man threw open a door and went inside. The room was dreary with beat-up furniture and a bed with a sagging mattress. "Here it is. A nice, first-class room." The guy swung the lamp around, hoping to prove his point.

Jack looked at the door lock. The paint over it was undisturbed. He went to the window. Its lock was also in place. "There a fire escape?" He pointed outside.

"Nope. Ain't no law calling for one neither."

"When was the last time you saw the girl alive?"

"Like I told the cops, she knocked on my door late Sunday night, close to midnight. Lost her key while out. Heard she was dead around six the next morning. That brick-top sister of hers found the body and told me to call the coppers."

"How'd the sister seem?"

"Angry. No tears—tough moll."

"What happened to the dead girl's stuff?"

"Put it all in there." He pointed to a steamer trunk at the foot of the bed. "The sister pawed through it but didn't want nothing."

Jack opened it. Lizzie's belongings were sparse—a few dresses and other clothes, hairbrush and toiletries, ceramic figurines. Two things were out of the ordinary. One was a carpenter's chisel, its wooden handle stained with something dark, maybe blood. The other was a piece of sheet music titled "Oh! The Suffragettes" with a picture of a cop arresting a well-dressed woman. He picked it up and a piece of paper with handwriting on it peeped out from the edges of two pages.

"What did she do with that chisel? Whack rats?"

"Got no rats in my rooms, bub."

"Mind if I take the tool and music?"

"Go ahead—if you get on out of here."

JACK WALKED to a saloon on Light Street where cops hung out. He stepped inside just as the piano player finished pounding out a mushy version of "Come Along, My Mandy." A red-faced copper threw a meaty arm around the ivory hustler and demanded to hear "Cuddle Up a Little Closer, Lovey Mine." At the sound of the opening notes, the cop started a clumsy dance with a lavishly mustachioed colleague, much to the delight of the crowd. Cute. These guys were more fun than a crate of monkeys.

Men and the occasional woman lined up hip to hip at the bar. The only empty space was near the end. Jack took his place and noticed an open door on the wall behind the bar, which meant the joint had a separate room for black patrons. Sure enough, he heard a red-hot tune pulsing through the opening. The beer might be staler and the whiskey weaker on the colored side, but the music was guaranteed to be a whole lot better.

"What you having, chum?" The barkeep was a beanpole of a man with a mug only a mother could—maybe—love. He had a weak chin; hooked beak nose; and rough, red patches of skin splashed on his cheeks and forehead. With his shock of orange hair and long white apron wrapped around his scrawny body, he looked like a smoldering cigarette.

"Branch water. In a clean glass." He put a foot on the rail.

"You look way too serious. This is a saloon, not a church." A woman stood next to him, her red lips forming an inviting grin. She leaned over and crooned softly into his ear: "'I'm so lonesome / I tell you what is more, my heart is feeling mighty sore.'"

"Maybe this *is* a church," said Jack as he put a hand on her back. "And you're a canary that's fluttered straight down from heaven."

"Can you get me out of this, honeybunch?" She tilted her head to the other side where a rough-looking guy with one of those newfangled toothbrush mustaches was leaning over and oafishly badgering the barkeep over the quality of his liquor.

Jack dropped his hand and edged away from the woman. He didn't have time to mess around with her, much less punch out the boyfriend and draw the attention of the dozen or more cops nearby.

"Hey now, it's Balt-ti-more's battiest sleuth." A man stepped into the new space next to him at the bar. It was the guy Jack had hoped to find in the joint—the one city detective with whom he was on good terms. "I keep expecting to find you dead in some alley with your face half chewed off by rats."

He was about Jack's age, but already had a double chin and a set of jowls. Too bad the current fashion for younger men limited him to a mustache—the guy would have looked a lot better with a full beard. He had a Horse's Neck cocktail tight in his grasp.

"Didn't know a bull could get away with knocking back those sissy drinks in public," said Jack.

The detective pointed at the water glass and snorted. "Who ever heard of a detective who don't booze? It ain't nowhere close to natural. Tell me why I should bother talking to a queer mug like you."

"Stay on my good side—I'll put in a word for your wretched soul at the pearly gates."

"It'll take a lot more than abstaining for you to make it to heaven, hoss." The detective chuckled. "Hey, I hear you're raking in cash from the Big Man."

"Then you won't be surprised when I ask about the Lizzie Sullivan murder." The detective looked around and rubbed the fingers of one hand together. Jack reached into a pocket, pulled out eight bucks, and decorated the mahogany with the bills. "Take it. That's my bang-up Pinkerton dough."

The detective scooped up the cash. "Shaw did it, no question. We found a gun engraved with his name on it by the body. Coroner will swear the gun killed her."

"What else you got?"

"Looks like Shaw was unhappy with the service she was providing. He shot her and got dressed in a big hurry. So quick he left his monogrammed drawers and overcoat behind along with his pistol. Not only that, we got a cabbie who says he picked up a real agitated Shaw down near the girl's place around one a.m. last night. Cut and dried. Shaw's got big-time friends, but all the dough and connections in the world won't keep him from landing in the clink after the coroner's inquest tomorrow. Lipp's made it clear he wants Shaw arrested, and the coroner's happy to play ball. It's a lead pipe cinch."

Jack brushed away a fly that was lazily buzzing around his head. "What's the connection with Nick Monkton? He was the murdered girl's pimp. Heard that Snake Eyes picked Nick up last night and gave him the third degree."

"Yeah. That colored pimp apparently has something real important." The detective lowered his voice to a whisper. "O'Toole didn't get what he needed before Patterson's big Injun lawyer showed up. Snake had to turn Monkton loose—can't bluff a swell mouthpiece about holding someone without a solid charge."

"What was Snake after?"

"Let's just say that the order came down direct from the main squash in the front office."

"Commissioner Lipp. How does Lizzie fit in?"

"Dunno."

"Tell me on the level: Was what happened between Snake and Nick connected with Lizzie getting kicked? Maybe you guys have something linking Nick to her murder? Or anything else that could help me out here?"

"I ain't telling you nothing more about the case. You know how O'Toole is."

"Come on."

The detective looked away with a frown. "I gave you good dope, babe. Don't stretch your luck. Hey, I got to see a man about a dog." He left to join a group at the other end of the place.

Jack stepped away from the bar and pushed his way outside into the cold, wet mist. Two men staggered into the street, arms draped around each other. One guy tossed his head back and let out a loony howl, causing something in his mouth to glint in the light of the guttering streetlamp. The other man stuck a hand in his companion's mouth and yanked out a shiny prize. "I got them gold choppers!" he said, doing a clumsy jig.

The first guy windmilled his arms, reaching for his lost tombstones. "Give it," he mumbled. "Them's only gold-plated."

The holder of the stolen teeth flashed in bright silhouette, a dumbfounded look on his slab face. A speeding automobile, its kerosene lamps blazing, knocked him to the street and accelerated away. The man staggered to his feet while waving both arms and yelling curses at the receding machine. The other guy stumbled around, head down and arms out, searching the dank roadway.

Jack moved on into the damp chill. His old overcoat had given up the ghost last winter, and he couldn't afford another. Turning up his jacket collar, he walked east along the harbor, watching the night's grip on the city fade away.

The air smelled of the sea; the Fells Point docks were close enough to hear barges groaning against the piers. It was weirdly quiet. During the day, the place was jammed with people, including sailors, oyster shuckers, and canning factory workers. When the sun went down, there were speakeasies and plenty of other places to seek pleasure or vent pain. The roughness of the place suited him. Plus it was cheap to live down here—the closer the water, the lower the rent.

Getting to his boardinghouse on Aliceanna Street was just

dangerous enough to make things interesting. The dim, hissing glow from the gas streetlights did little to reveal the craters in the sidewalk, the ruts in the street, or the splayed mess of rotten fruit and other garbage. Slick spots from overflowing drains and privy vaults blended with the murk.

A false step could cause a slip and snap an ankle. That would mean lying on the street with the rats and dogs before some early riser came within shouting distance. A sudden sweet, grassy odor reminded him of another hazard: the big piles of horse manure from yesterday's traffic. He'd heard the tens of thousands of horses in the city each produced twenty pounds of manure a day, which was easy enough to believe.

With the first pink light of dawn, the Bible voice came to life in his head. *The night is far spent, the day is at hand: let us therefore cast off the works of darkness, and let us put on the armor of light.*

Jack put his hands on either side of his skull and tried to crush the voice. It went quiet. A week or so later, he'd conclude the voice was trying to tell him something important. Right now, though, it was nothing but a haunting reminder from long ago about his cowardly father, sickly mother, and powerfully unhinged sister.

CHAPTER 7

SARAH—MONDAY, OCTOBER 11, 1909, 9:00 P.M.

*N*ever had Sarah appeared so late at this door. She hesitated before ringing the bell but then gave it a firm push, reminding herself that the occupants of this house had always been glad to see her.

The butler received her coolly before withdrawing to notify his employers, both of whom quickly appeared. Margaret Bonifant was a handsome middle-aged woman; Blaine Bonifant was a head taller than his wife, with piercing blue eyes he used to great effect as the city's most successful lawyer. A former star wrestler at Yale, he was known as "Night Train" Blaine for running over courtroom opponents with powerful arguments they never saw coming. Despite the late hour husband and wife were still dressed in formal evening wear.

"My dear, how lovely to see you." Margaret directed the butler to take Sarah's book bag and embraced her with a maternal hug.

She had a long-standing fondness for Sarah. Her beloved only child had shown no interest in other people and never learned to speak. His sole interest had been toy soldiers, and he covered the floor of a large bedroom with hundreds of lead figures. He followed a strict daily routine of breakfast, flipping through the same few illustrated military history books before lunch, tending to his soldiers all afternoon, dinner, returning to the soldiers until 10:00 p.m., and then bed. Margaret had doted on the young man until his death from tuberculosis at age twelve, shortly after Sarah's birth.

"What have you been up to, traveling around late at night?" asked Margaret. "My word—have you been drinking?"

As was her habit, Sarah resisted slightly as the other woman stepped away from the embrace. Margaret was the only person whose touch brought her pleasure. "I consumed wine during dinner with a private detective, Jack Harden. And before that, I was dismissed from the Pinkerton Agency. That is not a problem because I, with potential assistance from Jack, am investigating a murder."

"The Pinkertons fired you?" Blaine scowled darkly. "I'll take care of that."

"I always regarded that position as temporary until I found a pathology position."

"This will not stand. I will call the superintendent right now."

"You will not, my dear." Margaret eyed her husband steadily. "I had doubts about a proper young woman spending any time near private detectives. It is high time that Sarah turn her talents to something more suitable."

Blaine stood still for a moment before nodding once, very slowly. "As you wish."

Margaret held a tight smile as she placed her hand on Sarah's forehead. "You are a little flushed, dear. Sit down. Blaine, darling, you may withdraw."

"Sarah, you are witness to the only person in creation who has the ability to dismiss me out of hand." Blaine smiled, then laughed. "If Margaret were a man, she would be president, at the very least. Good night, ladies."

The two women sat in elaborately upholstered armchairs as the butler reappeared with a silver tea service. He filled their cups and silently padded away. Sarah closed her eyes to focus on the exquisite feeling of the thin porcelain edge on her lips and the sudden hot, tannic flow of the black tea into her mouth. The experience was soothing and stimulating at the same time.

"Don't fret, Sarah. I'll make some calls to secure you another position."

"I remain committed to pathology."

Margaret leaned forward and stroked Sarah's arm. "Poor dear, still obsessed with your notion of justice. I can see why—you had such an unjust childhood, starting when your insane mother decided to cavort with charlatans and ghosts rather than take care of her family. Which dead poet talked her into leaving? Byron? Shelley?"

"She claimed the spirit of Henry Wadsworth Longfellow instructed her to travel to Boston to bring messages from the dead to the living. She was, and remains, in the grip of a highly subjective mental state that she believes allows communication with the spirit world." The dull ache in Sarah's lower back flared into a sharp pinch. "I do not excuse that she abandoned her family. And, as you know, I reject the practice of spiritualism."

"Sarah, dear, please lower your voice."

"I apologize."

"No need. Your mother always had her way with everything, including your father's willingness to give her a divorce. I wonder, do you think she ever blames herself for the deaths of your father and sister—or anything?"

Sarah set her teacup down with a forceful clonk.

"I'm sorry for raising all of this, dear. I admire that you do not bear a grudge against the adults who failed you as a child. Let's change the subject. I recently met the new president of Johns Hopkins University. I will ask him to get you a hospital position."

"At present I am conducting my detective investigation."

Margaret's jaw tightened. "I was hoping I'd misheard what you said about that folly. It is preposterous for a well-bred young woman to conduct such an inquiry. And it is unacceptable for you to have anything to do with a private detective. They are men of appallingly low character. You were supposed to avoid them at the Pinkertons."

"Jack is rough and uneducated. Yet he is not insensitive nor unintelligent. Thus far, I find him kind and accommodating. We are both looking into the death of a young showgirl."

"This is outrageous. When we arranged for that job for you I told the superintendent to restrict your work to reviewing files and preparing documents. And to hear that this man—this *detective*—took you to dinner and plied you with wine. He had your virtue at his mercy."

"My manner does not offend Jack. He stated appreciation for my sincerity and intelligence. I enjoyed conversing with him."

"Sarah, you have no idea what can happen. The world is full of men looking to take advantage of young women. As a member of the lower class, this person no doubt sees you as a victim who will provide money under the cover of romance. I demand that you never see him again."

"Romance is out of the question. It would be strictly a business arrangement."

"Don't be so sure. You are completely innocent when it comes to dealing with men."

"I am not a child. I request that you not treat me as one."

Margaret's lips formed a thin white line as she firmly set her teacup and saucer on the tray and then stood. "Sarah. You will put an end to this foolishness. Immediately."

"I wish to know more about three men who may have some connection with the showgirl's murder. I believe you know them. Horace Shaw is suspected of the murder but claims innocence. He provided the names of two men who may have falsely implicated him: Adolph Lipp and Lucas Patterson. The three men are running against each other in the election for mayor. You may begin with a discussion of Horace Shaw." She had a notepad and pencil ready.

Margaret put a hand over her heart and looked away while drawing deep breaths. A nearby clock ticked away the silence. "Well, I take some small comfort in that you are interested in living people rather than corpses." She sat back in her chair. "The Shaw family has an interesting history. The great-grandfather ran a prosperous tobacco plantation on Maryland's Eastern Shore before the War of Northern Aggression but the place failed. Horace was born under very humble circumstances—as a young man, he worked as a waterman, gathering oysters and other sea creatures from the Chesapeake. Then he moved to Baltimore, got into politics as a street tough, and built the city's most powerful political machine. Now Horace wants to be mayor—no doubt he wishes to further enrich himself through graft and corruption."

"Does he have a habit of consorting with prostitutes?"

Margaret gasped. "Such language." She took a sip of tea. "I will say that Horace is known as a man with crude appetites. I am not surprised that he has gotten himself into trouble."

"Is he capable of violence?"

"Most certainly."

"Please now inform me about Police Commissioner Adolph Lipp." Sarah spoke without looking up from her notebook.

"The Lipp family is one of the oldest in Maryland. At one time, they owned much land, which they lost after the war. The family, like that of Horace Shaw, fell into reduced circumstances. The father had a brewery that went bankrupt. Adolph took to moralistic preaching. I've lost track of all the evils he rails against. The press turned him into a sensation when he and Carry Nation smashed up a big saloon downtown a year or so ago. That was just after a scandal in the police department, and he was appointed commissioner as something of an antidote."

Sarah took a break from her furious scribbling. "I spoke with Adolph Lipp today. He was more interested in damaging Horace Shaw than in pursuing justice."

"Commissioner Lipp is careful to be seen as virtuous, but you are correct—he's filled with hatred, most especially toward Negroes and immigrants."

"If Adolph Lipp's views are abhorrent, why is he popular?"

Margaret slowly shook her head. "Part of the answer is the nature of Baltimore itself. Slavery flourished here. And the town was infamous for its violent anti-immigrant gangs. I'm sad to say our fair city is still referred to across the country as Mobtown."

She rang for the butler and told him to take away the tea service. "Sarah, it's late. I will have a room prepared for you."

"No. I cannot stay, as I have things I must do at home. I need a cab." Sarah had a cherished evening ritual involving her sister's dolls that she absolutely had to perform each night before bed. After the servant had left with instructions to call a hansom, Margaret prepared to stand. "You may now tell me about Lucas Patterson." Sarah had her pencil poised above her notebook.

"Ah, yes, Lucas. A curious fellow." Margaret tapped the arm of her chair with a finger as she gathered her thoughts. "His great-grandfather made a fortune in guano—bird droppings from ocean islands that is prized as fertilizer. He bought a big parcel of land near the city and fancied himself a southern gentleman, complete with slaves. Lucas's father collaborated with the northern occupiers and saved much of his fortune. Lucas is quite well off and is now the leading voice of political progressivism in the city. He is known for establishing the Children's Benevolent and Protective Society, which helps provide for hundreds of poor and orphaned youngsters every year."

"Can he win the election for mayor?"

"He is a radical, and his chances of winning are slim. Still, he is supremely dedicated. Perhaps that's why he has yet to marry. He is the most eligible bachelor in the city—every society mother with a marriageable daughter has circled him for years. He's rich, of course, as well as handsome and charming."

"Is he above reproach?"

"There is a strange quality about the man. He is a bohemian who frequents disreputable establishments to listen to degenerate colored music." Margaret shifted in her chair. "Lucas also can be a bit too zealous in promoting his social and political interests."

"Has he wronged anyone? Does he engage in corrupt practices?"

"No, dear, nothing like that." Margaret stood and stroked Sarah's arm. "If you wish to learn more, I can arrange a meeting for you with Lucas tomorrow. You and he may like each other. You share a certain intensity of mind."

"Yes. Such a meeting will be of great assistance."

"His office is in a very bad part of town—I'll arrange for a chaperone to escort you."

"No. I am quite used to visiting places all over the city by myself."

"The dregs of society are unlikely to be put off by that modern woman attitude of yours." Margaret stood. "I'll arrange a meeting, but please consider gathering information in a better setting this coming Thursday."

Sarah tried to remember what was happening on that day.

"I'm referring to the annual Daughters of the Confederacy Oyster Banquet at the Belvedere Hotel," said Margaret. "Plenty of men will be there—including the three you have been asking about."

Sarah fumbled with her pencil and notebook and quickly stood. "I have not returned my RSVP."

"Don't worry about that. You can come with us. I can help you get the right dress and accessories. I know you are less than fond of such events, but it would be healthy for you to mingle with others."

"No." Sarah dropped her notebook, stooped quickly to pick it up, only to drop her pencil. "My displeasure in attending far outweighs any reasonable expectation of obtaining useful information." She retrieved her pencil and jammed it, along with her notebook, into her purse.

"I know you are uncomfortable with people. How, then, are you going to do this investigation of yours?"

"A detective solves mysteries. As a scientist, I do the same." The butler entered and announced the cab had arrived. "Good night, Margaret."

"Sarah—"

"I will admit my task is challenging. I am resolute in undertaking it."

Margaret enveloped Sarah in a warm embrace. "My dear. Please be careful."

Bouncing over the rough streets on the way home, Sarah's attention flitted between her wine-induced headache and the known details about Lizzie Sullivan's murder and its aftermath. Horace Shaw was likely more involved than he claimed—but to what extent? Commissioner Lipp had influenced the autopsy to direct sole blame toward Shaw. Was Lipp's motivation solely political, or did he also have a relationship with the girl? And how did Lizzie get the head injury that killed her?

Sarah was accustomed to working alone and perhaps that was just as well in this case. Margaret and Dr. Anson, her two most steadfast allies, were both less than enthusiastic about the investigation. The only person who could help was Jack, whom she barely knew—and a man of questionable integrity with signs of emotional disturbance.

She chewed her pinky and thought hard. She was the only

person with the desire and the capability to rigorously analyze the evidence in this case. But, reluctant as she was to admit, she could not work out the problem alone. It was necessary to obtain additional information, and that required interacting with people—not her strength. Jack, on the other hand, related to various individuals with apparent ease.

The truth was that she and Jack, working together, were the only people in Baltimore who could solve Lizzies' murder.

CHAPTER 8

JACK—TUESDAY, OCTOBER 12, 1909, 7:30 A.M.

*T*he third cup of black coffee was doing its muddy best on him as he collected his thoughts at the Monumental Lunchroom.

He'd woken that morning to find his shoes covered with mud and worse—a hazard of walking at night. The holes in both soles were now the size of silver dollars. He didn't have the money or the time to get them fixed, so folded hunks of newspaper would have to do for now.

This was going to be a full day of chasing down leads and grubbing around for any information that could help Horace Shaw. Swinging that would be tough, as the guy was looking more like a murderer all the time. The cops were going to collar him, and a jury would eat up how he ran away from a dead girl while leaving his gun and drawers behind. What a mess-up.

Speaking of messes, Jack had gotten himself into a bad one with his gambling debt. He had been in an awful state of mind at Pimlico racetrack when he placed that idiot bet with Knucks Vogel. An hour earlier, Jack had been walking over the Cedar Avenue bridge toward Druid Hill Park when the blast of a locomotive whistle on the tracks below stopped him dead.

A dozen ghosts showed up on the bridge—a few brown-skinned women and a bunch of writhing, bloody children. One woman, shot through the eye and wailing gibberish, kept pushing a bawling baby at him. When they disappeared, Jack found himself astride the bridge rail, staring at a jumble of sharp rocks seventy feet down. He backed off the rail and slapped one side of his face and then the other until he could move himself through the park and up Park Heights Avenue.

He was still in a daze when Vogel buttonholed him outside the track. The guy needled him about a horse named Happy Jack going off at ninety-nine to one in the next race. "Happy Jack! You got to lay a bet on that nag, right?" Jack went in for nine hundred to win. Vogel blanched, asked if he was serious, and reluctantly took the action.

When the race began Jack didn't even bother to watch—he knew the bangtail would finish out of the money.

What in blazes was he thinking? Now here he was, trying halfheartedly to scrimp on expenses, with burned black coffee for breakfast. The stuff sat in his stomach like tannery acid. Maybe he should just splurge and enjoy his last few days of decent health before Knucks unleashed the inevitable beating. Give up, roll over. The reflection in his cup was shaking its head no.

"Don't you look thoughtful this morning." The Pinkerton superintendent sat down uninvited, gesturing for Jack to lean over the table toward him. "We have to drop the Shaw case," he said in a low voice. "Too hot politically." He shoved an envelope across the table. "Here's your termination fee."

The envelope held forty dollars in bills. "Hush money," said Jack.

"Call it what you like, man." The superintendent snorted and lifted his chin. "Just remember I'm the man who picked you out of all the low wretches fit for the job. Keep quiet and I'll throw you another bone sometime."

"Playing both sides of the fence, aren't you?" Jack shot out his hand and held the man in place as he tried to rise. "First you want me to get Shaw off the hook, even if he's guilty. Then Lipp steps in, and you don't care if your good friend Shaw hangs— even if he's innocent."

"Stop pretending your morals aren't for sale, chump." He wrested his arm free and left.

Jack motioned for the waitress to fill his cup. She complied with a menacing grimace. He tried to shoot her a smile but found his jaw clamped so tight that he couldn't move his lips. Instead he pulled out a five-dollar bill from the envelope and shoved it at her.

"What's this?" she asked. "You need change or you trying to make me like you?"

"Just feeling generous today. Take it."

She put her hands on her hips. "Fool. You know you need to be careful with money."

"What's the fun in that?"

"Fun." She flexed her left hand as if preparing for a jaw-twisting slap. "Suppose you think it's fun to act all strange."

"Way I see it, we're all kind of strange."

"The way I see it, you're a dumbbell." Her face showed something like concern before she moved to the next table.

Jack looked down into the tarry blackness of the cup, his mind a blank until the Bible voice came booming: *My confusion is continually before me, and the shame of my face hath covered me.*

He squeezed his eyes shut and leaned forward, his head inches over the table. The superintendent was right—they both swam in the same dirty pool of corruption. A vision came to him of the inner harbor after a hard rain had washed all kinds of disgusting stuff into it—garbage, human waste, rotting animal carcasses.

"Hello. I'm so sorry to bother you. Is this a good time?"

Clara Sullivan stood hesitantly in front of him, radiating a shy loveliness.

Jack jumped to his feet, sending the chair tumbling backward. "Miss Sullivan. Please have a seat."

Last night she had been simply beautiful. This morning she was an absolute knockout. A faint dusting of face powder hid her freckles, and her lips were set in a pouty little smile. Gone was the frumpy straw hat and farm girl shift. Now she was wearing a big hat dripping with ribbons and a showy pink dress with a high lace collar. The outfit was a cut above the typical farm girl's Sunday-go-to-meeting best. The back of his neck tingled like it did when he met her the night before, only stronger.

She sat daintily as he held her chair. "Gosh, you're such a gentleman and all. You got to call me Clara." She cleared her throat timidly. "I won't pester you too long. I was just really, really hoping we could talk about the men maybe connected with Lizzie. She mentioned some names—can't hardly recollect. If I hear some suggestions it might help me remember. And maybe that can help you catch the man who hurt Lizzie."

"You said yesterday that Nick and Lizzie were up to something. What did you mean?" Jack gave her a big smile. In addition to being a feast for the eyes, this fine gal might pay to keep him on the case.

Clara folded her hands on the table. "She said Nick had something worth a ton of money. They were fixing to cash in on it real soon."

Jack drummed his fingers. "What did they have? You must have some idea—was it something shady?"

She turned her big green eyes directly on him. "Don't think it was legal. She was already getting money from . . . selling herself. Got a feeling she was thinking about blackmailing someone. Don't know who—it's got to be someone with money." She pulled out a handkerchief from her sleeve and began crying softly. "This is so terrible. My poor little sister—first ruined, then gone crooked, then killed."

"I only know about one guy who paid for the pleasure of your sister's company. Name's Horace Shaw. Ring a bell?"

"It sounds kind of familiar." She looked up from her handkerchief expectantly. There were no blotches or puffy spots on her gorgeous face—just a slight redness in her eyes. Jack remembered a woman friend telling him that every girl should know exactly how long she can cry and still look her best. "Tell me something about him."

"He's a businessman running for mayor. Runs an oyster packing business and is a heavy hitter in local politics."

"Hmm . . . he got money?"

"Yeah, plenty. Got two other names for you, both guys also in the mayor's race. What about Adolph Lipp? He's a puffed-up reverend who's made a career off other people's sins." From her reaction, Jack knew he had hit pay dirt.

"Adolph Lipp." She scrunched her face. "Yes, I think she mentioned him. Tell me more about the man."

Jack scratched his chin. Plenty of Bible thumpers allowed themselves adulterous romps, but would Lipp be so careless during an election? Then again, sex could turn any man stupid. "He's the Baltimore police commissioner. Wants to be mayor."

"Can't hardly believe someone like that would do something so horrible." Clara shot her hands up to either side of her face as her eyebrows raised. "Does he have a lot of money? Enough to make Lizzie take the risk of blackmailing him?"

"He hasn't got much dough. What do you know about Lizzie and Lipp?"

She presented him with a coy little smile. "Don't expect me to tell everything that Lizzie said. Sisters tell each other things that no man should hear."

"If you want to help me catch the killer, you'd better spill it."

"Lizzie was scared of the police. Probably because of what

Nick forced her to do. She was so afraid of getting arrested as a . . . fallen woman. That's when she mentioned Mr. Lipp. Poor thing. Yes, I'm sure of it."

"The commissioner doesn't put the collar on prostitutes personally. Why would she worry about Lipp?"

"You said he was an enemy of vice. I reckon many other wayward girls feel that way." She dabbed an eye with her handkerchief and drew in a breath as if to gather strength to continue a difficult conversation. "You mentioned a third man. What's his name?"

"Lucas Patterson. A rich bleeding heart who's a long-shot candidate for mayor," said Jack. She opened her mouth to speak. "You want to know about his money," said Jack, cutting her off. "Well, he's got a bale of kale—millions." He looked at Clara closely and could sense wheels turning in her head. "Think Lizzie and Nick were trying to cash in on some crooked deal with Patterson?"

"I never heard about Mr. Patterson until now." She shook her head. "Golly, I'm so useless. I can't help you none at all."

"Tell me exactly what Lizzie told you about what she and Nick were up to."

"She just dropped some hints, that's all. About how smart Nick was and how he could turn screws to make people bleed money. When I begged her to give up her life of sin, she told me not to worry—that Nick had hooked a big fish. Big enough so they could move to New York and go respectable. I warned her that Nick was a bad man. Lizzie was so trusting. You know?" Clara's chin trembled.

"What about Nick? Could he have killed Lizzie?" Jack watched her carefully.

"Sure. The man's evil and violent. I told that to the police. Are they going to arrest him?"

"Right now, Shaw's the prime suspect. The cops have some

evidence against him, but it's possible they have the wrong man. Even so, I'd recommend you steer clear of Nick."

"This is all too much for me." Tears welled again in her eyes. "To think I have to stay in this awful city for another couple of days before I'm allowed to take Lizzie back home. You say the police know who killed her? I'm so thankful. At least I can tell Ma and Pa that."

"Like I say, the cops might have made a mistake with Shaw. Nick or somebody else might be the real killer. I'd like to keep looking into it but I'm off the case."

"Oh, dear. Why is that?"

"Detective agency cut me loose. This case is all tangled up in politics. If you can pay my fee I'll keep working to find out for sure who killed your sister. We've got to act fast—the coroner's inquest is later today and the authorities are moving ahead without all the evidence."

"That's very kind, but I have no money to spare." She dropped her eyes and twisted her handkerchief. "And I've been raised to trust the people in charge. I can't see how the police could arrest the wrong person for such a bad, bad crime."

She slowly raised her head with a shy look. "I have no right to ask you this—I'd like to talk with you again before I leave. I'll be at my cousin's place today and most of tomorrow." She clutched her handkerchief into a tight ball and shot him a bashful little smile. "Can we have supper tomorrow night and talk again? I understand if you have more important things to do. You're just the nicest man —you've helped me feel a little bit better during this terrible time."

Jack knew he should beg off—he had to keep a tight rein on his time and money.

"Please." She moved so close that the arm of her luxuriously soft dress brushed against his wrist. Then she put her gloved hand on top of his. "I'm so alone." She was giving him that adorable head-down, eyes-up look again.

"I'll swing by your place at six o'clock tomorrow evening," he heard himself say. This woman was impossible to resist. "Where does your cousin live?"

Clara leaned in closer, smiling with a perfect set of little white teeth. "Gee willikers, thanks so much. I'm staying at the Hotel Kernan."

Jack's brow shot up. "That's a ritzy joint. Expensive as anything."

"I know, way more than we can afford." She rolled her eyes. "Pa made me promise to stay someplace big and safe. It's the fanciest thing I've ever seen. Got flush toilets and ceilings taller than a barn. I had to buy this outfit before I had the gumption to register."

It didn't square that a rube like her with a cousin in town would end up in one of the best hotels in the city and buy a fancy set of duds on top of it. "Where'd your Pa get that kind of dough? And why did he let you come here all by yourself?"

"He sold off his two best heifers. And he'd have come himself if he weren't sick bad with consumption. And Ma's lame. My cousin's supposed to keep an eye on me but she's got to work." Tears formed in her eyes again.

"Jack. We had an appointment at eight thirty a.m. It is now eight thirty-two a.m."

Sarah. This must be the day for everybody in the world to sneak up on him. Jack pulled his hand from under Clara's and stumbled to his feet. "Dr. Sarah Kennecott, meet Clara Sullivan, Lizzie's sister. We were discussing the case. Please join us."

Jack held her chair as Sarah sat and looked over the top of Clara's big hat. "Clara Sullivan. We need you to request a second autopsy before today's inquest. The first autopsy missed the actual cause of death, which I believe came from a hemorrhage precipitated by a blow to the head."

An impish smile played across Clara's lips for half a second before her face shifted to a look of utter confusion. "What—I beg your pardon?" Jack noticed how the corners of the woman's eyes turned down to show off feathery eyelashes that shined like pale orange flames.

Sarah's expression remained blank. "I am trained as a physician with a specialty in pathology. Jack and I are working to learn about persons associated with Lizzie and discover the truth behind her murder."

"Actually, the Pinkertons have dropped the case," said Jack. "And Clara has no money to spare to hire us."

"Regardless," said Sarah, "as the victim's sister you have the right and the obligation to demand a thorough autopsy. A second postmortem is necessary to gather the evidence needed to ensure justice."

Clara laughed nervously. "I'm sorry, that's awful, just awful. Enough bad stuff has already happened to poor Lizzie. I can't bear to think of her being . . . whatever it is they do during those autopsy things. Let's just let her rest in peace. Please, please."

"You do not understand," said Sarah as her hands fluttered and bounced on the table in front of her. "The only way to obtain conclusive evidence is to saw open the skull and remove the brain for careful examination. In lieu of standard procedure, I made a small opening through the frontal bone and found evidence of a subdural hematoma, which means—"

"Sarah," said Jack as he took in Clara's horrified expression, "let's forget it."

"No. We must convince her to press for another postmortem—"

"I'm sorry, Doctor," said Clara in a small voice, "I can't hardly do that. Doctor—Sarah—what's your official role in the case?"

"I have no official role."

"I see. Jack mentioned the three men running for mayor and said they might have—an association with Lizzie. Do you know of any others who might be involved, apart from that horrible, awful Nick Monkton?"

"Not at this time."

Clara reached over to pat a hand as Sarah yanked both hers off the table. "Oh, good gracious me—I'm sorry," said Clara. "I just wanted to thank you, Sarah, for caring about what happened to Lizzie and all. You're such a good person. Bless you."

Clara turned to Jack. "I best be going, Jack. I'll see you for supper tomorrow night." Her voice had just a hint of throaty seduction. She rose from the chair with an animal grace he hadn't noticed before—like a tigress coming up from a crouch. "Good morning, all." She offered a sweet smile, waved, and walked off. Jack saw a city detective get up from his table and follow Clara out the door.

He turned back to Sarah. "I'm sorry I didn't have a chance to tell you about Pinkerton dropping me. It just happened this morning."

Sarah was looking intently at the tabletop. "Do you plan to fornicate with that woman?"

"What? Heck, no. We were talking about the murder."

"Does she expect to fornicate with you?"

He leaned back in his chair and eyeballed Sarah with a grin. She was the rare woman who paid little attention to her appearance. Her face didn't have a speck of paint or powder, although one pale cheek did have a streak of black soot. Strands of limp hair evaded her tortoiseshell combs. Delicate silk flowers crowded her hat, which must have cost a pretty penny. Yet even he could tell the hat was well out of style. It also sat squarely on top of her head, rather than at the jaunty angle most women favored. Her walking suit was expertly tailored in fine fabric, but was as wrinkled as the one she wore the day before. There were moth holes in the lapel.

"Doesn't every woman who lays eyes on me want to . . . you know? Relax, that's a joke."

She stood quickly. "You are a cruel and rude man. I regret coming here."

"Sorry—really, I'm sorry," he said. "Please sit back down."

"No." Her body trembled.

"I thought we were going to work on Lizzie's murder. Doesn't that matter anymore?"

"It does to me. But you do not care if Lizzie's true killer is caught. You do not care about justice."

Jack got up and stepped behind her chair. "I do care. Come on, let's talk a little more."

She hesitated for a bit, then sat. Despite her moralizing, Jack found himself admiring this strange woman. Maybe all her talk about truth and justice was prodding something in him to life. He went back to his seat. "Can we prove Shaw innocent without another autopsy?" he asked.

"I am not certain what can be accomplished absent additional official proof obtained from the corpse." She looked to the right of him and then to left as she repeatedly leaned forward, then back, in her seat. "We would have to gather more physical evidence. We would have to interview a number of individuals. Rigorous analysis would then be needed to support a definitive conclusion—or at least a well-reasoned conjecture. All that calls for a large expenditure of time." She abruptly sat still. "What about payment for our services?"

Jack smiled, glad that she had come down from her high horse about money. "I got a sudden inspiration about that. Don't worry."

"Very well." Her gaze traveled across his face just long enough for him to notice that her limpid brown eyes were flecked with gold. They were her best feature—too bad she spent so little time looking back at people.

"Let's start with the info I got from Clara," he said. "Says her sister talked about some crooked scheme involving Nick Monkton. Probably a blackmail bunco involving one of the guys that Lizzie was . . . fornicating with. She also said Lizzie was scared of Lipp."

"Are you inferring that Adolph Lipp had sexual congress with Lizzie?"

"No, not exactly. Clara was kind of fuzzy about Lipp. Anything's possible. Let's just keep it in mind as a theory."

"You mean a hypothesis. A theory is a hypothesis that has been tested and found plausible. We have yet to form a hypothesis, much less test one."

"Remember that I'm maybe a quarter as smart as you."

"I do not mean to condescend." Her eyes met his again and quickly slid away. "Tell me if you have learned any other useful facts. From that woman or otherwise." She pulled out a notebook and began writing with a pencil.

"Plenty. I went to Lizzie's boardinghouse and didn't see any sign of forced entry. She knew everybody who came and went. I looked through her stuff and found these things." He put the chisel and the sheet music for "Oh! The Suffragettes" on the table. "Maybe Lizzie got hit in the head with this chisel. See the blood?"

She peered at the tool. "You were careless in handling these objects and have compromised any useful fingerprints."

Jack drummed his fingers on the table. Sarah was starting to get under his skin. Couldn't she try to be more sociable?

"I do not believe this tool was used to strike Lizzie on the head," she said. "The narrow blade does not match the wound profile. Neither does the handle, as it has a series of grooves that would have imprinted themselves on her flesh. The tip of the blade, however, is consistent with a laceration I observed on Lizzie's left index finger."

"So maybe it slipped and cut her while she was using it to defend herself."

"That is possible." Sarah looked at the sheet music. "Are we to posit that Lizzie was a supporter of women's suffrage?"

"Don't know, don't care." Jack opened the cover, revealing a sheet of writing paper covered with large, childish handwriting. "This is what I find interesting."

"A manuscript."

"It's an unsent letter." He picked up the paper and read it out loud:

Dearest Bob—Don't worry none about what happened between us. I am fine. I know you did not mean to hurt me. You were just upset. I know that you are truly sweet. I care for you. But I must stand by my true love. He is a better man than you say, so don't be angry with him. I know you are a real good boxer (that is how you got your nice hotel). Please don't hurt Nick.

"It's signed 'Much Love, Lizzie' and dated last Friday—isn't that about when you think she got banged on the head?"

"Yes. This is a critical item of evidence. You will note use of the phrase 'you did not mean to hurt me.' That may implicate the addressee in causing Lizzie's head injury. We must learn the identity of this person."

"Think I know who the guy is. I'll talk with him later today." Jack sucked on a tooth, wondering if Bob Foster beat women—and maybe killed one. "It's a reasonable guess that the 'true love' is Nick Monkton. Nick was also very cozy with Patterson, I hear."

"I have an appointment to speak with Lucas Patterson this afternoon."

"Good. Quiz him about Nick." Jack leaned back and stretched his arms over his head. "We haven't got much time—things are looking bad for Shaw. A detective pal told me last night that the cops found items of his clothing in Lizzie's room. They also got a cabbie who picked up a very agitated Shaw near

Lizzie's boardinghouse about one a.m. Monday morning. That means Shaw's going to get collared after the inquest for sure."

"Mr. Shaw withheld those facts from us during our meeting yesterday." Sarah wrote quickly in her notebook.

"Yep, sure did. I'm going to see Shaw after we finish. It's in his interest to come clean. But I can't force him to play ball."

Sarah blinked rapidly, pencil hovering over a page as if she failed to understand his words. An awkward silence fell between them as he wondered what the problem was. Finally, she spoke. "You will see Mr. Shaw and ask him to be completely forthcoming?"

"Yeah. Like I said. Hey, can I see the crime scene photos again?"

"Of course." She quickly produced the prints.

"That pistol is a Colt Vest Pocket. Real small—even you could use it. Those wiggly, swirly lines are your precious finger-prints, I see. You might want to check in with the city police Bertillon Bureau. They're the ones that took these photographs —see the stamp? They try to identify crooks using all the modern methods."

Her eyes flitted from the photograph, to his chest, and back to the print. "That is an excellent idea, Jack. I will visit with them later this morning."

"Just a piece of advice—take it or leave it. The guy who runs the bureau fancies himself a lady-killer. Goes after anyone in a skirt. A little flirting will get him talking."

"Are you mocking me?" Sarah's fingers wiggled in the air over the table.

"No. What is it with you today?"

"You claimed to approve of my manifest sincerity. Now you tell me to engage in false flirtation with a stranger. I am confused and wonder if you are being intentionally rude to me."

"No need to talk so loud, Sarah. Forget what I said. I wasn't trying to be rude. I'll just keep my trap shut since I keep putting my foot in it." Jack slurped down the rest of his coffee, which was now stone cold. The woman might be without guile, but that didn't mean she made things easy.

Sarah flipped pages in her notebook. "I gathered some details about Adolph Lipp, Horace Shaw, and Lucas Patterson from someone who knows them socially," she said. "They have different backgrounds with a common ambition for elective office. Adolph Lipp is known for his opposition to alcohol and the rights of Negroes and immigrants. Horace Shaw is an unscrupulous businessman with corrupt habits. Lucas Patterson is a wealthy progressive reformer with bohemian tendencies."

"You've been busy," said Jack. "And I'll bet you have a plan of attack all mapped out."

"If you mean I have prepared a schedule for my day's activities, that is correct," she said. "First, I will consult with my mentor at Johns Hopkins. Second, I will attend the coroner's inquest regarding Lizzie's death. Third, I will go to the police Bertillon Bureau and make some inquiries. Fourth, I will meet with Lucas Patterson at the Children's Benevolent and Protective Society."

"What's the point in going to that inquest? You said the coroner rigged the results and that Lipp is bent on getting Shaw arrested. If we could have convinced Clara to demand a second autopsy it would be worth showing up. Now it's pointless. A detective has to use his—or her—time in the smartest way possible."

"You raise a credible point. My inclination is to believe that the inquest will be objective, yet there are substantial grounds to doubt that in this instance." She scribbled in her notebook. "I will cancel my plan to attend the inquest while noting the reason for doing so."

"All right," said Jack as he scratched his neck. "And besides checking in with Shaw, and talking with 'dear Bob,' I'm also going to visit the Gayety Theater—that's where Lizzie was dancing before she died. The manager might know something. Also, I'm going to try to track down Nick. He could be the key to everything."

"We must meet again soon to share our findings and determine our next steps."

"How about dinner? No romance, cross my heart." He gave her a toothy smile.

"No. I need time to myself to compile notes and do background research."

"Okay, then. Let's meet right back here tomorrow morning."

Her nose wrinkled ever so slightly. "No. This establishment smells strongly of sauerkraut and onions, which I do not like. Meet me at my residence tomorrow at eight a.m."

"Do you live with others?"

"I do not."

Jack shuffled his feet, unsure if he had to state the obvious. "Sure that's a good idea, me coming to your place?"

Sarah fixed her gaze over his head. "If you are referring to the propriety of a man visiting a woman alone in her home, I am unconcerned with that consideration at this time. We have agreed that the basis of our interaction does not include romance. You have behaved reasonably, for the most part, and appear to be pursuing our joint investigation in good faith." She ripped a page from her notebook, scribbled her address, and pushed the paper at him.

He scratched behind his ear, wondering how she could recoil from his innocent touch yet expect to entertain him alone. Sarah was unusual, but she was obviously a lady. If any society types saw him coming or going from her house, her reputation would suffer terribly. Yet she didn't seem to care. "Okay by me." He pulled out change to pay the bill, his hands shaking so badly the coins spilled onto the table.

"Jack." She reached out across the table, flexing her fingers. "Do you feel well? A tremor such as your hands display can be indicative of a pending bout of mental distress. There is a medical basis for apprehension."

"I feel great. Steady as steel." As they stood, he had the urge to lightly touch her arm, just to acknowledge appreciation for her attention. He didn't do it and she marched straight to the front door without a backward glance.

He followed her with a wobble that faded by the time he opened the door for her. Good. He needed to be on his best game today. Sarah wouldn't like what he had in mind during his first stop, but what she didn't know wouldn't cause him any problems.

CHAPTER 9

SARAH—TUESDAY, OCTOBER 12, 1909, 10:00 A.M.

*J*ohns Hopkins Hospital sat, along with the medical school, atop Baltimore's eastern heights flanked by the old Hebrew Hospital on one side and a profusion of row houses on the other and to the rear.

The spot provided a commanding view of the city center and its northern environs. Steamships with inky smudges above the smokestacks moved slowly across the harbor waters, while the Continental Building and several smaller skyscrapers dominated the downtown skyline. New buildings were under construction, their soaring iron skeletons appearing impossibly flimsy from this distance.

Directly down Monument Street was the elegant column topped with George Washington's statue. She loved how meticulous green rectangles of parkland flanked the monument on all four sides.

Towering alongside the monument was the spire of the United Methodist Church, pleasing with its green-toned brick. Just north stood the eleven-story Belvedere Hotel, resplendent with its pink and white stonework.

She turned around to look at her favorite structure of all—

the main building of Johns Hopkins Hospital. It was built of warm red brick, creamy sandstone molding, and terra-cotta ornamental panels. Two hospital wards flanked the central structure with its steep-sided dome. Although much smaller, the dome reminded her of the Florence cathedral, as both had raised ribs and a cupola balanced on top.

The visual treat continued as she went up the steps and into the main lobby, where a ten-foot Carrara marble statue of Christ stood in the airy rotunda. Although a religious agnostic, Sarah always found the figure calming, with his arms spread in a gesture she had come to interpret as warm and caring. But she never had interest in rubbing its toes, like many students and even doctors did to encourage good fortune.

The clerk in the administrative office told her that Dr. Anson had finished his paperwork and left. Her mentor's forgetfulness was one aspect she did not admire about the man. Still, as she went back down the central staircase circling the rotunda, she was glad to have had the chance to revisit this marvelous space. It was a welcome, if frivolous, bit of pleasure. She crossed the lobby and entered the long corridor that went past the five general wards, the isolating ward, and the colored ward before ending at the Pathological Building.

As they sat in his office, Dr. Anson apologized for missing their scheduled meeting. "The mayor called," he said with an uneasy laugh. "It seems the medical examiner had his buttocks bruised by a motorcar, and I've been asked to serve as acting today and tomorrow. I didn't have the stomach to say no—even though I've got to develop lecture notes for a new toxicology class. And on top of everything else I cut myself on a cadaver's fractured rib." He held up his bandaged left hand. "Please, Sarah, can I ask you to stay close at hand to assist with any necessary autopsies? We can work here instead of that dreadful city morgue."

She hesitated. He was offering her a chance to do what she

most wanted—apart from analyzing Lizzie's murder. "If I were not engaged in my own work, Doctor, I would eagerly accept your invitation."

"Well." His body slumped. "A student could assist me. He might miss something important that will have consequences for justice. I'll watch him as carefully as I am able." Anson peered at her through his smeary glasses.

Sarah owed too much to this man to disappoint him. "Dr. Anson, I can assist you today and tomorrow as necessary. I request only temporary use of laboratory space. I also must keep some previously scheduled appointments later this morning and early this afternoon."

"That would be wonderful," he said as his face brightened. "I knew I could count on you. There is a spot in the histology lab where you can sit while on call. Are your appointments connected with this investigation of yours? The one you spoke of yesterday?"

"Yes."

"Could you keep me informed of your activities? I am concerned—we have the university's good name to consider." He pursed his lips as his eyes swam back and forth. "And I will also say that I am worried about you. What you are doing is peculiar. Some might even call it downright disturbed. Think about the impact on your career—there is still time to back away with no harm done."

"I acknowledge your concern, Doctor." She stood abruptly and waited while Anson struggled to his feet. "I will return at two p.m. this afternoon then, as we agreed. Good day." Sarah walked off, her resolute footsteps echoing down the hall.

SARAH REVIEWED what passed for her strategy while walking along the creaking hallway floorboards of the city courthouse as fast as her long skirts would allow. She was proceeding with a novel approach for her next appointment: plunge into action without a detailed blueprint. Her only plan was to deal with the head of the Bertillon Bureau as a man of science. A spiky ball of unease sat in her stomach.

The frosted glass door of the Baltimore City Police Bertillon Bureau had a typed sheet of paper taped to it.

ATTENTION PATROLMEN.
ALL arrestees brought here must NOT be:
—Unduly intoxicated or otherwise incapable of
    sitting up straight;
—Beaten to the extent that their facial features are
    distorted (broken noses, swollen eyes, etc.);
—Belligerent, mentally unstable, or otherwise at
    risk of damaging records or equipment.
You will be reported. No exceptions!
—Head Bertillonist, Baltimore City Police

The paper was torn and wrinkled, as if it had been ripped down and reposted more than once. "Bertillonist" was crossed out and "Ass" was crudely scrawled in its place.

Sarah opened the door and stepped into a large room with long rows of wooden file drawers. She closed her eyes and savored the smell of fresh ink and old paper. The odor was less refined than that of her books, but it was not unpleasant. She forced her eyes open and approached a well-groomed young man sitting at a desk and sorting file cards. His shiny black hair was parted in a ruler-straight line exactly down the middle of his scalp.

"I wish to speak with the bureau head."

The man looked up with wide eyes that quickly squinched with annoyance. "What business do you have here, miss?" His long, slender fingers twitched, eager to get back to the cards.

"I want to discuss a recent crime."

"The head is a very busy man." With a smirk, he returned to his solitary labor.

"I insist. I will not leave until I speak with him."

"By 'him' I surely hope you are referring to me, miss." She turned to see a short, plump man with a red rose boutonniere in his jacket and a wolfish grin. His mustache was so thin it was no more than a dark filament over his upper lip.

"If you are the bureau head, then yes. I wish to—"

"I live to make young women's wishes come true." He stepped closer and she flinched at the overwhelming smell of his Bay Rum cologne, which she hated. The olfactory irritation boosted her discomfort as he introduced himself while pressing her right hand between both of his. Fortunately, she was wearing gloves.

"I am Dr. Sarah Kennecott," she said, pulling her hand away. "I attended the autopsy of a recent murder victim by the name of Lizzie Sullivan. I am interested in evidence related to the case."

The little man's smile froze as he stiffened. "Is that so? Well, it's against our rules to discuss ongoing cases. Now if you would be so kind—"

"You are a man with whom I have a strong desire to converse. I therefore request your continuing attention." Jack had suggested she cultivate the man's interest.

He stepped toward her with a fulsome smile, offering his arm. "The least I can do is give you a little tour so that you can get an overview of how we operate. How about that?"

"That would be acceptable." She ignored his arm and walked over to a case showing an array of knives, pistols, and clubs. A grouping of photographs depicted various murder scenes, each with a body flung into a sad, ungraceful pose of sudden death. Except for the bodies, the scenes were jarringly banal, set in bedrooms, barrooms, streets, and alleys. "Do tell me about this display."

"Sarah, my dear, all of that is far too upsetting for a young woman's eyes. Ah, you are engrossed. All of these exhibits relate to our work on criminal methods. We have an assortment of actual murder weapons and crime scene photographs. Our chief work here is to identify criminals. We use all methods—physiological measurements, narrative description, photographs, and fingerprints."

"I admire your robust adoption of criminal science."

The man's wolfish grin returned. "That is music to my ears, of course. You mentioned that you are a doctor? How charming."

Sarah walked briskly over to the long bank of filing cabinets. "Tell me about all of these records. A quick summary will suffice."

"Nothing less than our crown jewels. Some like to call it 'the rogues' gallery,' as we have five thousand photographs on file here. But we have far more than that." He yanked open a cabinet and pulled out a large printed card filled with annotations. Two pictures of a man—one facing forward, the other in profile—were affixed to the top. "We operate the full Bertillon system with five measurements—"

"Head length, head breadth, length of the middle finger, length of the left foot, and length of the forearm from the elbow to the extremity of the middle finger." Sarah had read a book on the system and knew that it was the brainchild of Alphonse Bertillon, a French policeman. Bertillon had come up with something known as anthropometry, based on the idea that no two people shared an identical set of physical measurements. The photographs—also known as "mug shots"—were supplemental.

"Most impressive, Sarah. You are such a clever girl. I wish our police officials knew as much. Over here is where we take photographs and perform computations—"

She held up her hand to quiet him. "Tell me how you use fingerprint science."

"Fingerprints are the latest identification technique, and many old-timers are skeptical." He waved his hand with irritation. "We have a devil of a time getting cooperation from detectives and patrolmen. They complain the courts don't accept prints as evidence of guilt and see the process as a waste of time. I tell them—"

"What of fingerprints associated with Lizzie Sullivan's murder?"

"You have a most direct manner. I like a girl who knows what she wants." He stepped closer.

"I have asked you a question."

"I photographed the crime scene and found the fingerprints on the gun." He frowned. "And how much interest has there been in my work? Zero. Detective O'Toole says he already has enough evidence. The photographs will just sit in our case files and remain unused, my effort wasted. Outrageous that I get so little appreciation."

"You have faith in fingerprint science?"

He nodded sagely. "I think that, in time, fingerprints will prove to be a valuable addition to the Bertillon system. Sir Edward Richard Henry has set us on the right course."

"Who is he?"

Her host chuckled. "My dear, he wrote the book—literally. *Classification and Uses of Finger Prints*. Here, I have an extra copy. I'll give it to you on one condition." He snatched a volume from the bookshelf and held it just out of her reach.

"What condition do you impose?"

"That you join me for dinner at my apartment this Saturday evening."

She swallowed hard. "Very well. I reserve the right to cancel upon my successful determination of the facts in connection with Lizzie Sullivan's murder. I will need time to document my findings."

He was first astonished, then convulsed with laughter. "My sweet, you said that with such a straight face! You are so very droll. Investigating a murder case, indeed." He handed her the book. Then he scribbled something on his calling card and pressed it into her hand. "Sarah, precious one," he said. "I am so looking forward to our private rendezvous."

"Good day, sir. I will see myself out." She quickly moved away from his enveloping cloud of Bay Rum and hurried down the long row of filing cabinets, past the young man at the desk and out into the hallway. She glanced at the card. He had written *"Mon Chères—* You have my heart. I tremble with anticipation for the moment when we can bare our souls before each other. Until then, *Adieux."*

The man could not even distinguish between the plural and the singular in his irksome French. She tore up the card and hurled the pieces into the mouth of a cuspidor. Despite the difficulty of the experience, she had obtained valuable information. Now she had to get to the waterfront as quickly as possible.

LUCAS PATTERSON HAD AGREED to meet with Sarah at the Children's Benevolent and Protective Society, which was on Thames Street in Fells Point, fronting the harbor. Traffic delayed her hansom. Freight wagons, handcarts, and pedestrians—all overloaded with commodities of one sort or another—pressed in from all sides. A torrent of sensory input jostled for her attention: the crude shouts from teamsters, the flinty astringency of the dust billowing from coal yards, the penetrative clanging from iron foundries, the astonishingly putrid smell of chemicals and decaying flesh from tanneries.

When she finally stood outside the address, it looked

nothing like a place where one could find a member of the city's social elite. The three-story brick building sat in a commercial block, nestled between a liquor wholesaler and an employment agency. The Children's Benevolent and Protective Society announced its purpose with a small sign in the window: "We Help the Poor, the Orphaned, the Friendless Child."

Workmen were everywhere around her, rolling barrels, hauling crates, yelling at each other in a foreign language. A row of slouching vendors had rickety tables set up on the sidewalk and were selling everything from garish bolts of cloth to cheap gimcracks. A cluster of small children—barefoot and in ragged clothes—were looking at her with their thin, foxy faces as if she had just stepped out of a storybook. Sarah's heart pounded as they moved toward her with their grimy little hands extended.

"Nickel so I can eat, miss?"

"I ain't got no mama—please help me."

"I'm starving! Can't work 'cause I'm lame."

Their piping little voices filled her with compassion, but also dread because she had no idea how to respond. She had money —how much was enough? How should it be distributed? What if they grabbed at her?

"Clear on out," said a large older woman as she stood in the open door of the society. "All of you had your lunch. Go." The children scattered like startled mice. The woman turned to Sarah. She wore no hat, and her gray hair was pinned in a practical bun. Her long, lumpy nose looked like a fingerling potato. "You must be here to see Mr. Patterson, miss. A high-class girl like you ain't got no other business around here. Come in."

"Yes. I have a one-o'clock appointment. I regret being one minute late." Sarah went to the steps, careful to lift her skirts over the splintered remnants of a wooden crate on the sidewalk. Many rusty nails stuck through the boards. Those children were at serious risk for tetanus. After entering the place, she opened her handbag. "I will give you money to pass on to the children."

The woman pressed her lips together tightly. "It's no good giving them money. They waste it on candy and foolishness."

Sarah pulled out several dollars in change and bills and thrust them forward. "Then please buy them shoes. Or whatever you think is best."

The woman shrugged and took the money. "Come this way, miss." She led Sarah through a large open room with long rows of low wooden tables. Several children were scrubbing the floor and ferrying armloads of dishes to a kitchen toward the back. The room reeked of cheap cleaning powder. Pictures with captions exhorting children to behave, keep clean, and follow instructions covered the walls. Sarah followed her guide down a hallway to a door that opened quickly after a soft knock.

"Mr. Patterson, sir, a lady to see you." The woman nodded curtly and headed back to the main room.

"Dr. Kennecott, how good of you to visit." The man before her was about thirty-five years old with carefully combed dark hair, brown eyes, and a deep olive complexion. Sarah dreaded the physical aspect of introductions, but was relieved when he gave her hand just a quick, gentle touch. "Margaret Bonifant speaks about you in glowing terms."

She flashed quick glances at him and noticed a trimmed mustache that sat between two dimples on his clean-shaven cheeks. His tweed suit was well tailored. Her eyes fixed on his shirt. It was cerulean blue, her favorite color. She had to suppress the urge to touch its perfect starchy sheen.

"Have I spilled something on myself?" He dropped his head to look.

Sarah gazed at the carpeted floor. "Thank you for seeing me, Mr. Lucas Patterson."

After giving his shirtfront a quick brush, he looked up. "Please call me Lucas. And don't think me forward, but do you mind if I call you Sarah? I'm happy to call you 'Doctor' if you wish. It's wonderful to meet such an accomplished young woman—someone who has, I imagine, had to overcome a lot."

Sarah was uncomfortable with his rapid informality. Still, a more familiar approach increased the probability for getting useful information. "Please feel free to use my given name. I only prefer to be called 'Doctor' in a professional context." Since eye contact supposedly put people at ease, she forced herself to stare into her host's eyes.

"All right then, Sarah." Patterson's warm smile faded as he held her unblinking gaze. "Before we get down to the business of your visit, please allow me to present you with a gift." Patterson strode to a sideboard and lifted a published volume from a stack. With a solemn look, he offered her a copy of *Diary from the Shameful Heart of the Rebellion*.

"I do not know this book," she said while flipping to the title page. The author was listed as Alice Monroe Green, described as "wife of Beauregard Green, plantation slave master and aide to the treasonous Jefferson Davis, president of the purported Confederate States of America, 1861–1865." The publication date was 1908.

"I had it printed," said Patterson. "It's the diary of a privileged white woman living in Georgia during the War of the Rebellion. Despite living on a plantation operated on the backs of Negroes, Alice Green hated slavery and wrote many heartfelt observations. Here, listen to this."

He snatched the book from her, opened to a section near the front, and began reading in a loud voice. "'One sees racially mixed children at every plantation, so many with the features of their master. When one converses with the planter's lady, she quickly notes such resemblance with regard to the husbands of others. When it comes to her own domestic domain the same lady is mute.'"

Sarah's throat constricted as she listened to language that was utterly unsuitable for a lady to hear, especially immediately upon introduction. She held up her hand to stop him, but without any effect.

"'One cannot deny that our men enjoy their concubines—'"
She interrupted. "There is no need to recite more."

He stared at her, mouth agape. "As you wish." He gestured to a leather armchair. "I would be thrilled to talk with you more about race matters, but Margaret has told me you want to discuss something almost as sordid—Baltimore city politics."

"Yes." She placed the book in her bag and sat in the chair.

Patterson busied himself at a credenza before presenting her with a small crystal glass of amber liquid. "I hope you find this amontillado acceptable," he said as he sat.

She was very finicky about sherry. Too often she found offerings to have a maritime quality with a smell redolent of a fish market in summer. Just the thought of it made her gag. It would be rude not to take a sip. To her astonishment the smell was exquisite; even better, it tasted bone dry with just the right acidity.

"This is the best amontillado I have ever tasted." She took another sip.

"I see you have a good palate. Please finish your glass, and let me get you another."

"No." Sarah was dizzy from the sensory pleasure. Another glass of that amazing sherry would just be too much. "Please . . . Lucas, tell me why a wealthy, cultured man such as yourself has an office on the waterfront. And why are you interested in politics?"

"I do get those questions quite a bit." Patterson chuckled as he adjusted his red paisley ascot, which he wore wrapped high around his neck with an open-collared shirt. The effect was one of a young English aristocrat relaxing at his country estate. "The simplest answer is that I want to help the less fortunate."

"That is a platitude. Do you have a more substantive

answer?" She had retrieved her notebook and pencil and was scribbling.

A few moments ticked by and Sarah was compelled to glance up at her host. His smile was gone. "Scratch below anyone's surface and you will find complexity," he said. "In my case, I want to improve the lives of people who have been cast aside by the rich and the powerful. Children are the most vulnerable, and that is why I founded this charity. I chose to locate it here, in the heart of the Polish tenement district among the needy, the struggling. You ask why I have an office here. I ask: How can I not?"

"You wish to set a commendable example for your class—"

"I don't want your approval." Patterson's brow was low over his eyes as he set his sherry glass down with a loud clink on a marble-topped table next to his chair. "Or anyone else's. One must live and work among the poor, the shunned, the deprived to know their struggles. Only then can anyone appreciate their nobility."

Sarah looked at a row of colorfully framed illustrations past Patterson's left shoulder while preparing to move the conversation back to topics relevant to the investigation. "Now, what of politics—"

"What are you doing to help the poor, Doctor? You should be fighting tuberculosis and syphilis. Helping men whose bodies are broken from work, women destroyed from prostitution, children suffering from disease. You should be easing their pain. Or are you too busy wasting time and money on the latest fashions like other empty-headed society women?"

"Your argument is fallacious." Sarah was up from her chair, standing rigidly straight, hands clenched into fists. "You are weaving glib generalizations with a baseless personal attack."

"So much needs to be done." Patterson's eyes blazed, and Sarah wondered if he had forgotten she was in the room. "Feeding the poor, clothing the naked. Healing the sick. The children in our city, regardless of race, nationality, or creed, must be our top priority. And there's the money to do it!" He punched the air excitedly as his voice kept getting louder. "All we lack is political will. That's why we need to bring about the revolution."

Sarah reminded herself she was here to get information and sat back down.

"Let's consider getting women the vote—surely something you support," said Patterson, suddenly calmer. "You know the motto of the English suffragette Emmeline Pankhurst: 'deeds, not words.' I only wish we could stir up as much trouble here as she has in London. Wouldn't it be great to see Baltimore women breaking windows, smashing mailboxes, chaining themselves to railings, getting arrested, and going on hunger strikes?" Patterson's eyes were bulging with zeal.

"I support female voting and extension of women's rights, yet the militancy of some British suffragettes is disturbing. Do you believe violence is an acceptable means to an end?"

Patterson leaned back in his chair. "Please excuse me, Sarah. I express my beliefs with passion. I feel called to help the downtrodden of our city and have the arrogance to press for change, even if my views are considered extreme." He noticed her eyes focused on the wall behind him. "Are you interested in ragtime music? Wonderful!"

Patterson jumped up as if launched from a spring and pointed to a framed sheet music cover. The lithograph drawing featured a crude depiction of a Negro man wearing a red polka-dot bow tie against a bright red background. "This is 'The Dusty Rag,'" Patterson said. He began snapping his fingers and singing with gusto. "'I could keep on dancin' all the night / Sets my heart thumpin' playin' tag / Oh! It's the Dus-ty Rag.'"

"I know nothing of that music." A grandfather clock in the corner sounded a chime—it was now one thirty p.m. Every additional minute Sarah stayed here with this erratic man increased the chance that she would be late in returning to the hospital. Still, she had more questions to ask.

"Then there's this one." Patterson pointed to an adjacent framed cover with the title "Ma Ragtime Baby." The drawing pictured a well-dressed, black couple promenading against shades of red and pink. With fingers snapping time, he sang, "'The black four hundred were there right in line / Bad coons from Johnson Street looking mighty fine—'"

"I heard you know Nick Monkton, a musician."

"His fame grows by the day." Patterson's nostrils flared as he crossed his arms. "Nick's a musical genius but wastes his talent on silly pursuits. I've told him again and again to stick close to his true friends and to focus on writing and playing." He leaned close to her, eyes wide. "Nick wants to do things his own way. I can only hope the boy comes to his senses before it's too late."

"And Lizzie Sullivan, Nick's . . . former companion?"

"How on Earth do you know about her?" Patterson's eyes narrowed. "And why do you care?"

"I attended Lizzie's postmortem examination and am curious about the circumstances of her life and death."

"Forgive my earlier outburst. You have more interest in the demimonde than I gave you credit for. Nobody else in your social class would give a second thought about a murdered prostitute." Patterson fussed with his ascot. "I feel compassion for any woman forced to sell herself, although Lizzie was more of a leech than a victim. She sucked at Nick's attention and money. I told him that she stood between him and greatness. I don't want to speak ill of the dead, but Nick is better off without that woman."

"Have you discussed her death with Nick?"

Patterson gave her a hard glare before walking briskly to the door and opening it with a flourish. "Sarah, I must conclude our chat. By all means, please come back again, and we can talk more about music or even politics—I promise to keep my enthusiasm more under control." He smiled, displaying his large white teeth.

Sarah moved so quickly down the steps to her waiting hansom that the ragged children had no opportunity to cajole her. She chewed her thumbnail with quick little chomps in the cab on the way to the hospital while wondering if Lucas Patterson was unstable enough to commit murder.

CHAPTER 10

JACK—TUESDAY, OCTOBER 12, 1909,
10:00 A.M.

*T*he sun hung in a cloudless sky, and the temperature was warm enough to let the flies cluster in force on the horse manure in the streets. Jack continued his brisk pace up Saratoga Street and over the dogleg to Liberty, where the hulking twin towers of the Hotel Rennert dominated the skyline.

The Rennert was one of Baltimore's best hotels. It was even more famous for the Chesapeake seafood delicacies served in its lavish restaurant. The eatery was far too pricey to cater to the likes of Jack, but the lobby was free to enter.

Antsy as he was to conduct business, Jack got a shoeshine before going inside. When the bootblack kid finished, he pulled out a little whisk broom and gave Jack's suit a quick brush. At first, he could only reach up to his chest. Then the kid jumped on top of his box to finish the job. At least now Jack looked as good as he possibly could.

The Rennert lobby made no bones about the class of people it aimed to serve. It had plush carpets, dark wood paneling, glittering crystal chandeliers, and huge stuffed armchairs. Usually when Jack entered a ritzy hotel some uniformed lackey was on him instantly, asking what his business was. Nobody bothered him here because even seedier-looking guys came and went to confer with Horace Shaw, who held court with his political cronies in a nook off the main lobby. True to form, Shaw was jotting notes while conferring with a gangly man in a garish plaid suit.

"Councilman, I don't like those lawless hillbillies moving into your district any more than you do," said Shaw. "Let me get back to you on your concern. Now, if you will excuse me, I see a fellow I must consult with." The scarecrow pol got up and walked off.

"Hello there, Harden!" Shaw roared with hollow enthusiasm. "Take a load off." Jack sat in a chair that sagged from the hundreds of hack butts it had held over the years. Shaw bent down and, after eying the overflowing spittoon by his feet, leaned over and spit a stream of tobacco juice into a crystal ashtray on the table next to him. "You're here to pitch your services directly now that the Pinkertons have dropped me. Going to try and gouge me, no doubt." Brown juice dribbled down the man's chin.

"Here's the deal. I want a thousand dollars right now. I'll do my best to spring you—with no promises." Jack spoke with breezy confidence, even though he had never collected more than three hundred dollars for a single job.

"You've got some crust." Shaw grinned broadly. "I don't have that much cash on me." He pulled out his wallet and thumbed through the bills. "Got forty-six bucks. Maybe a little more in loose change."

"Took a big risk leaving your bankroll at home today, don't you think?"

"I figured this would be more than enough to cover any new problem. I instructed my lawyer to go to that coroner's inquest this morning and do what you couldn't—get me off the hook. My man can grease a palm when he has to."

"You're kidding yourself, Shaw. I got inside dope—the cops are coming for you today no matter what. You need to tell me what really happened with Lizzie."

The man gazed warily at him. "I get it. Lipp hired you to talk to me. You're going to come away with my supposed confession. It don't matter what I say. You'll just parrot what Lipp tells you and lie in court. Everybody knows you private detectives are natural-born perjurers. What a piece of scum won't do for a few dollars."

Jack stabbed a finger at the man. "The cops already got all the evidence they need, sport. They found the cabbie who picked you up outside Lizzie's place early Monday. Guy says you were nervous as a long-tailed cat in a room full of rocking chairs." Shaw's assurance drained away. "And they got plenty besides the cabbie—your gun, your overcoat, your monogrammed drawers. The coroner's going to use that inquest to say Lizzie was killed with your gun. No bribe is going to stop you from getting arrested. Scum or not, I'm all you got."

"Okay, take it." Shaw pulled the wad of bills from his wallet and thrust it out.

"That's short of what I need. Way short."

"You a betting man, Harden?"

"Not when I have my wits about me. Like now. See you later, pal." Jack stood.

"Wait." Shaw tossed the cash into Jack's empty seat and rubbed his chin. "I've got a flunky right over there carrying plenty of kale. I'll give you ten centuries as a flat fee with no assurance of success, just like you asked. Easy money if you want it."

Jack scooped up the loose cash and sat down. "That's more like it."

"But you're selling yourself much too cheap. And I'd like you to have a lot more motivation on my behalf. Pass on the thousand dollars now and I'll give you five thousand if you help me beat this rap—all charges dropped, my name cleared. Quintuple or nothing. What do you say?"

"Why should I bet on a horse everybody thinks is headed for the glue factory?"

"Because there's plenty of life left in this old stallion, that's why. Look, I've done plenty of bad things in my life. But I swear on my dear mother's grave I didn't kill that girl. There's got to be a way to prove it. I'll give you some details that will help."

Jack searched Shaw's fleshy face and saw no tell, no hint of deception. Was the guy really innocent or just a great bluffer? The man did speak the absolute truth about one thing, though: Jack should have asked for more than a grand. He needed at least enough to pay off Knucks after giving half to Sarah. Shaw was offering him a chance he wouldn't get again.

"Okay. Write up a contract that says you'll pay me five grand after everything's settled."

"After you get me cleared of all charges."

"Deal. Write it down. And sign it."

Shaw scribbled on a sheet of paper and gave it to Jack. It looked legit enough.

"Now it's time to cut the bull. Tell me what happened between you and Lizzie."

Some of Shaw's old swagger returned. "Nice girl—knew her real good. Visited her early Monday morning a little after midnight. Had a busy few days down in Newport News and spent most of the day and night Sunday passing cash around Ward 3. Met with dozens and dozens. "

"People will confirm that you were out of town from Thursday to Sunday morning?"

"Only the governor of Maryland, a US senator, and half the Baltimore City Council. They were with me during the whole trip, down and back."

"Tell me what happened the last time you saw Lizzie."

"She wasn't in a great mood. Had a bump on her noggin and

was carping about a headache and feeling dizzy. But she don't get paid for complaining. We got into bed. Everything was wrapping up just dandy when she starts shaking bad. Then she just conked out—not breathing, looked dead. I'm there just half an hour being nice and friendly and she up and died. Just my luck."

"I feel *real* sorry for you."

"Yeah, well it scared the bejesus out of me, so I threw my clothes on and got out of there as fast as I could. Damn well wish I had taken the time to collect all my things though, especially that pistol."

"You didn't bother to call for help before taking off."

"I never claimed to be a saint," said Shaw. "You got to believe me, though—I didn't kill her."

"You go to the Pinkertons to clean up the mess. Too bad you happen to be running for mayor against this particular police commissioner—otherwise the cops would take a bribe to make the problem go away. As per usual."

Shaw nodded and heaved a sigh. "I know what's what in this town. Money's like oil on troubled waters for lots worse than this. But not this time."

"How'd you meet Lizzie?"

"Got pulled in by that pimp of hers, Nick. Real sharp operator. Always ready to squeeze a buck out of a man."

"Nick blackmailing you?"

Shaw looked tired and used up. "No hiding anything from you. Yeah. Creep demanded a hundred dollars out of me early Monday morning. Banged on my front door and said he'd tell the cops about me being with Lizzie when she died. That shook me up. Still, I wasn't ready to pay that kind of money to a guy the cops probably wouldn't believe. Then the rat sweetened the offer."

"Nice concept—sweetening a blackmail threat."

"Nick told me he had written proof that someone else whacked Lizzie on the head a couple of days before and that's probably what killed her. Said he'd turn that evidence over to the cops and get me off the hot seat. Like a chump, I agreed to pay."

"Take it that proof still hasn't turned up," said Jack. "Probably never existed in the first place."

"Probably not."

"Any idea where I can find Nick?"

"Open your wallet and wait for the two-bit grifters to show up." Shaw looked up at the ceiling. "Failing that, all I know is that his aunt or something runs a five-dollar cathouse on Fawn Street. Name's Fanny Suggs. That's where I met the man. Wish I never had."

"I'll check into it."

"You'd better work fast, Harden." Shaw pulled out a tobacco pouch and loaded up his cheek with a fresh wad. "I was a fool for hoping to buy my way out of this jam without admitting I knew the girl. Lipp will use all that evidence you talked about to push me right quick through the wheels of justice, just like a prime side of beef into a grinder."

Jack patted his jacket pocket. "Our contract gives me reason to move lickety-split. I can't collect from a barrel of ground beef."

"I've always said that the right man with the right incentive can do remarkable things."

Jack heard approaching footsteps and turned to see Snake Eyes O'Toole crossing the lobby, flanked on either side by a uniformed cop.

"Horace Shaw," said O'Toole. "You're under arrest for the murder of Lizzie Sullivan. Cuff him."

"Let's not be hasty, boys. What'll it take to leave me be?" Shaw spoke warmly, as if to old friends. The cops pulled him roughly to his feet and handcuffed him.

"Put him in the wagon." O'Toole held Jack with a dead-eyed stare as the cops marched their man away. "Got something for you." The detective held up a small rectangle of paper—a spanking-new Honus Wagner baseball card.

"Gee, thanks. That my reward for keeping him company while you were on your way from that rigged inquest?"

O'Toole struck a match and lit a corner of the card. He let it burn before dropping it on the carpet. Jack stomped on it.

"Stay out of this, Harden. Or I'll hurt you bad."

"What's Lipp's promised you? Captain of Detectives? A bunch of no-show jobs? It's got to be the sweetest graft you've ever dreamed of." O'Toole turned to leave. "Wait, I know. Lipp's hiring Enrico Caruso to sing 'Kiss Me Good Night, Mother.'"

The detective spun around and stepped so close the mothball smell wafting from his jacket was sickening. Jack wondered about the need to protect such a ratty-looking garment as O'Toole pulled out a long piece of sewn leather weighted at the end with lead shot. Getting smacked in the kisser with that would take out teeth and break bone. Quick as a wink, the sap whooshed by, just stinging the end of Jack's nose.

"That smart chin music's going to get you killed, wise guy. Looking forward to the day." O'Toole pocketed the weapon and sauntered off.

Jack's knees were jelly. He took a few deep breaths before bending down to pick up the burned baseball card. Only the bottom half of Wagner's torso was left with "Pittsburg" misspelled across his chest. What a darn shame. He dropped the scrap into his pocket.

THE GAYETY THEATER was a ten-minute walk from the Rennert. As Jack went east on Baltimore Street he passed a slew of retail shops. They worked hard to grab people's money, with awnings stretched over the storefronts to lure customers out of the weather to linger over sidewalk displays. Every foot of merchant space was plastered with come-ons broadcasting the lowest price, best of this or that, biggest selection, newest arrival.

Some joints went all out with new electric signs, including the five-story-high job that spelled out "The New York Clothing House" with dozens of flashing lights. Jack couldn't figure why anyone would go into a place like that—the prices had to be pumped up to pay for all those lightbulbs. Yet salesgirls and office clerks flocked to the place. Buying duds in a store with a gaudy sign must make people feel classier and deserving of a better life.

People also came to this part of town for cheap entertainment. The penny vaudeville halls were big draws with their phonograph booths, punching bag slots, and mechanical fortune-telling Gypsies. Most popular were the peep shows, which offered short glimpses of everything from camels walking in the desert to dreadnoughts firing their big guns out into the ocean. A guy looking for a bigger thrill could go to the curtained section in the back and drop a nickel to look into a box and see images of bare-legged girls frolicking.

The arcades packed them in, but the moving picture parlors were getting ever more popular. People lined up, eager to spend twenty-five cents to sit in the dark and let all kinds of flickering fantasies take over their minds.

In spite of all the automated diversions, the vaudeville and burlesque theaters still packed them in. The joints counted on customers paying for live acts—especially shows with pretty girls in skimpy costumes. A bunch of theaters crowded the block just ahead. The signs were even flashier and the buildings gaudier than the storefronts. The Grand Theater was a real sight, with life-size statues of nude women perched on the windowsills as if ready to jump down and hug any man in sight. Next door, Lubin's Theater looked almost sedate with only one naked statue holding a pair of lights aloft.

The Gayety Theater was directly across the street. Consistent with its occasional claim of "polite vaudeville," the building displayed no naked statues. Still, a poster for the "Big Girlesque Burlesque Revue" displayed a kick line showing off their naked legs and frilly underclothes.

He went around back to the stage door. Unlike the public entrance, this spot was squalid and bleak, with broken whiskey bottles and nasty puddles covered with flies. Inside, the joint was dark, with muffled shouting coming from deep within. Jack barked his shin against something before his eyes adjusted.

As he rubbed away the pain, he recognized the theater manager's voice. Jack had done a job for him a while back— collaring a one-armed acrobat who had cracked the theater's safe and run off with the Saturday night receipts. Stepping closer, he saw a few dim strip lights and one glaring spot hitting two girls onstage wearing the fewest feathers they could get away with and not be arrested for indecency. The manager was waving his arms.

"You two can't dance to save your lives. Take some lessons! Practice! You need more than skin to get on my stage. Yeah, yeah, I know you panicked the house in Altoona, but this ain't there." The girls pleaded for another chance. The manager shook his head. Jack decided to barge in.

"Can I interrupt?"

The manager looked over and dropped his arms. "Yeah, sure. We're done here, girls. Get dressed and get lost." Jack followed the other man's long, quick strides up the theater aisle to the lobby. "Harden, you got great timing. Let's go to my office before those no-talent dames really get me mad."

"Tough job, dealing with undressed girls all day," said Jack.

"They all think they're ready for the Folies Bergère. As if prancing around in ten-twenty-thirty-cent joints out on the Kerosene Circuit in the middle of nowhere makes them ready for the big time. Nine out of ten aren't even good enough for the chorus. After a while it's not even worth fooling around with them—which they're happy to do with any guy who might put them on a stage."

The manager was younger than the lines etched in his face suggested. Maybe he had a naturally nervous disposition, or maybe it was the aggravation of his job. Booze no doubt contributed. The man wasted no time plunking a glass on his desk and filling it with whiskey. "Take it you're still dry, right?" Jack nodded. "Don't know how you get through the day." He downed the glass with a grateful shiver. "Got an open bottle of sarsaparilla around here someplace. Want me to look?"

"Don't worry about it. You knew Lizzie Sullivan, right?"

"Already talked to the cops about it." The man's eyebrows came down in a sharp V, which made the vertical furrow running above his nose and up his forehead look deep enough to plant corn. "Real shame. Nice kid and an okay dancer—she was never going to headline, but didn't embarrass herself either."

"You liked her."

"Like a daughter, believe it or not. She had personality to burn. Real engaging and full of life but with a soft side, too. Most of the girls in this game—even the young ones—get hard quick. Not her. She was still friendly like the girl next door."

"Any idea who might've killed her?"

"Cops said that Horace Shaw croaked her. Bastard."

"What was the deal with her and Shaw?"

The manager shook his head. "The usual. A married man gets a little paid attention from a showgirl."

"Heard Nick Monkton arranged the introduction."

He filled and then drained another glass. "Yeah. I kept telling her Nick was bad news, that he didn't care a lick about her. She was his meal ticket, that's all. Still, you know how skirts are." He folded his hands under his tilted head and said "I love him" in a warbly falsetto.

"Nick found her clients other than Shaw."

"'Course he did. That's the biz."

"They include Lucas Patterson? Or Adolph Lipp?"

The manager laughed and pounded the desk so hard that Jack worried the guy was having apoplexy. "I hear jokes all the time, but that's great—takes the cake." He wiped tears from his eyes as he caught his breath. "Next, you're going to ask if those two have a comedy bit. I wish. Just picture it: 'The Socialist and the Preacher,' trading one-liners about the virtues of free love and the evils of liquor." He drew in a wheezy breath. "And if I could get them to work blue this joint would sell out every night for weeks on end."

"I'll take that to mean neither of those guys hung out with Lizzie. Tell me who else she was with over the last week or so. Could be that Shaw's innocent. If so, I want to find the killer."

"That so?" The manager scratched his chin. "I only catch so much, you know. Did see Nick showing her off to this funny little guy last week. Had these glasses that made his eyes so big he looked like a bug. He also had this little pointy patch of hair sticking up on his bald head. Fellow got her excited, though— she came back and told me he was a doctor who wanted to examine her. Now, imagine that."

"Know anything else about the guy? Like his name?"

"No. And I always take what these guys tell the girls with a chunk of salt."

"Lizzie ever mention her sister, Clara?"

"Oh, yeah, the acclaimed Clara Sullivan. Lizzie loved her, even though Clara gave her a ton of grief."

"Acclaimed?"

"Not a fan of the legitimate theater, are you? Clara Sullivan's a stage actress. Does high-brow stuff. She was in that Ibsen show—*A Doll's House*—that ran at the Academy of Music last week. Had the lead and got good reviews."

I'll bet she did, thought Jack as he stared at the last few drops dripping down the sides of the grimy whiskey glass. "What was Clara badgering Lizzie about?"

"Family dispute. The mother died and Clara ran off and left Lizzie alone with the father, who was sick. When he died, he left the farm to Lizzie. She sold it for a little money and moved here. Being young and foolish, she spent the cash real quick on clothes and whatnot. Ask me, all that money was hers to spend. But Clara showed up with the gall to demand half the inheritance. Lizzie should have told her to take a hike. Instead, she gets all boo-hooey and lets her sister push her around, even when Clara got mean. Guess highbrow acting don't pay all that well."

"Yeah, but it's a skill that comes in handy offstage, too. Did Clara know Nick?"

"No way anyone got to Lizzie without going through Nick."

"I hear Clara's at the Hotel Kernan."

"Yeah, all the Academy of Music acts stay there. Except for them that want more privacy. There's a deal with the Academy Hotel next door, where performers can stay under a fake name."

Jack got up. "Thanks for the information. Just what I needed."

"Hope you find out who killed Lizzie. Like to strangle the guy with my bare hands."

JACK GOT on a trolley going east on Pratt Street toward the Fawn Street cathouse Shaw had mentioned. Clinging to the back of the rattly car as it moved along the harborfront, he got a good view of the old and the new Baltimore. The brand-new Power Plant on Pier 4 was spewing thick black smoke from its four towering stacks while ginning up extra juice for the United Railways and Electric Company streetcars. A handsome array of double-globe electric streetlamps ticked by, the metal posts still showing off their glossy black paint. City boosters touted these lights as providing a "great white way" to blast away the night. Jack knew shady business still took place around here after the sun went down, although some crooks and grifters had reluctantly shifted to darker locations.

Another sign of progress were the trenches ripped into the street paving. One work crew was installing sewers, which offered the promise of flush toilets to this section of town. Another gang was digging cuts for electrical conduits that were supposed to replace the mess of wires now drooping overhead. Good move. Hissing wires routinely slithered off the overloaded poles to kill people like deadly electrified cobras. A drawback to all this worthy work was that traffic had to weave among open ditches, piles of dirt, clouds of dust, and knots of inattentive laborers. As the car rolled past Hollingsworth Street, Jack gaped at an automobile lying upside down in a construction pit.

"Idiot joyrider. Serves him right for racing down the street at twenty miles an hour with no care for anyone else," said a pale young man standing nearby. "Those damn devil wagons should be illegal."

"No turning back from our fine progressive age, my friend," said Jack. "Horses are on the way out. At least the streets will be cleaner and not smell so bad."

"Hope I'm dead before machines outnumber horses."

"Take some comfort that a whole bunch of autoists will croak themselves—like that guy under his big boat in that pit."

Old Baltimore was still alive in the harbor rolling by on the right. Dozens of rake-masted bugeyes and skipjacks crowded the water's edge unloading oysters lugged in from the Chesapeake. Wagons and carts were backed up to the low harbor wall. A parade of men with bushel baskets hauled in the catch from the boats. Both whites and blacks were working together. The urgent need to move fresh oysters overrode the usual practice of separating the races. That maybe meant the blacks earned as much as the white men for their work. All the oyster brokers standing around in their natty suits and bowlers were white, naturally enough.

Jack jumped off the car just across the Jones Falls bridge on the edge of Fells Point. It was a quick jog to Fawn Street, with its worn paving stones and broken curbs. Sunken stretches of roadway held pools of dark, greasy water. Privy stink hung in the air. Rows of modest three-story buildings lined both sides of the street—typical working-class houses.

One place looked different. It sat next to an open alley with a locked gate. The front door was reinforced with iron bands. A neatly lettered sign hung on the brick next to the door handle: "Do not inquire within without prior appointment." Unlike the other houses, every window in the place was covered by thick curtains. All hallmarks of your fancier whorehouse. Jack knocked and stood back from the door, in case he had to dodge something. The door opened a crack to reveal a woman's chubby face with dark bags hanging under surly eyes. "What you want?"

"You Fanny Suggs? I'm a private detective." Jack waved a five-dollar bill. "Just want to talk. That's it."

"You alone?" The door opened a little wider, and the woman stuck her big head out to get a better look.

"Yep. Five bucks for five minutes."

"What else is new. Men." She snatched the money from his hand. "Okay."

She stepped back from the door and Jack went in. The front room smelled like expensive cigars and cheap perfume with an undertone of sticky sweet champagne. There were two big divans covered in plush red velvet with lace doilies on the arms. Ashtrays on stands sprouted from the floor like brass weeds. A massive player piano with a candle sconce set on either side of the keyboard filled one side of the room. A roll of punched paper music sat above the keyboard, and a nearby cabinet was stuffed with more rolls.

"Heard you know Nick Monkton. That true?"

"Man's a low-down weasel. Got no use for him." Fanny turned away, picked up a feather duster, and swiped lazily at an amateurish oil painting of a well-endowed nude woman reclining with what was probably supposed to be a beckoning look on her face. The rough brushstrokes gave the gal a cross-eyed look.

"I need to talk with him. Where's he at?" The annoyed voices of two women bickering drifted down from upstairs.

Fanny moved across the room and flicked the duster at a collection of ceramic figurines arrayed on a side table. She worked on several smirking cherubs poised to let arrows fly and moved on to a girl holding a bunch of flowers. A vigorous flick knocked the girl over. "Nick's a piece of garbage but I ain't peaching on him." She dropped the duster and stood up the fallen figure with tender care.

Jack noticed a moth bumping into the gaslight globes hanging from the ceiling. The thing didn't give up until it found an opening, flew straight into a gas jet, and vanished in an orange burst of flame. "From what I hear, you're right about Nick's character. Thing is, he's got himself tied up in the murder of a soiled dove. That should mean something to you, given your line of work."

Fanny puffed up her big cheeks and blew out a breath. "You best leave, mister." He held up two more five-spots. The woman's baggy eyes fixed on the cash as the argument upstairs escalated. Fanny thrust out a meaty hand and he put the bills into her palm. "Staying in an old stable down on Fell and Ann near the water," she said. "Got a pistol to keep him company."

OUTSIDE, the sunlight was fading fast. Jack jammed his hands into his pockets, thinking it would be safer to visit Nick tomorrow morning in the daylight. The Silverstrike Hotel was close by, and he needed to have another chat with Bob Foster. On the way, Jack heard a newsie yelling about World Series game four. The cagey kid made him buy a paper to get the result: Detroit 5, Pittsburgh 0. The Series was all tied up at two games apiece.

While walking, he thought about the life of a whore. It was pointless to blame any gal for lack of morals because forces outside her control called the shots. Both young men and women came to the city to find work and to escape a dreary farm life. A man could get any number of laboring jobs and, if he managed to save a little, could buy a horse and start hauling stuff for higher pay. Assuming the guy was careful, he could save enough after a while to buy multiple wagon teams or even a store. Given Baltimore's crazy growth, a penniless hick could turn himself into a proper businessman in a few years.

A woman from the sticks faced a different situation. Factories were among the few places to get respectable work, and the wages were a lot less than what men earned. Only those gals who were pretty and clever enough could get work in a department store and earn a little more, or dance in a chorus line for a little more still. None of those jobs paid enough to allow even the thrifty to save much. But few saved a dime, as the social pressure to buy clothes and go out on the town kept them poor. The promise of cash and "having a good time" drew gals into prostitution, but the life could be harsh. Pimps and madams were experts in skimming earnings, and johns dished out abuse, violence, and disease.

Unlike the last time Jack was in the joint, the Silverstrike was packed. It took time to find a spot at the bar, and getting there required a lot of pushing and shoving. His height, along with his sobriety, made the job easier. One guy took a wild swing at him and ended up hitting a big man in the back. Jack didn't bother to turn around to watch them scuffle. He slid cash to the barkeep. "Tell Bob I have something he needs to see." The man left on his mission just as the piano player sat down.

"Good evening, ladies and gents. I'm going to start out with a Nick Monkton tune. You all know Nick—he's a master of the raggedy piano and got a rare talent for writing good-time music. He calls this number 'The Baltimore Riprap Rag.'" The guy started playing fast. His strong voice dipped and soared around the lively piano notes.

> *What's that by the shore?*
> *With all that jumpin' looks like a dance floor*
> *Guys goin' way up and girls step so great*
> *Nobody's steady, nobody's straight*
> *It's a new kind of dance, just for shock*
> *You got to step from rock to rock*
> *It's the Baltimore riprap rag*
> *It's just what you need to feed your jag*
> *Come on now, forget your woes*
> *It sure ain't steady as she goes*

Jack was tapping his finger in time when the bartender leaned over and shouted in his ear.

"Bob." He jerked his thumb.

Jack pushed his way to the back of the bar and opened the office door. He stood across from Foster, who sat stone-faced behind his desk. "You weren't kidding about knowing Lizzie, now were you?" Jack tossed the letter down on the desk. Foster read it silently, his expression unchanged.

"Look, I know you cared for the girl," said Jack. "And I'm inclined to think somebody else killed her. Still, that letter's suspicious, don't you agree?"

Bob got up and stepped within punching distance. "You're as reckless and cracked as everyone says, Harden. What did you think I would do when you showed up at my place and shoved this in my face? Give you a fat reward? Break down and confess? You had to know that I'd lay you out before your hand even touches that gun of yours."

"All I want is answers to two questions. First: Where were you last Friday?"

"You got some big brass balls coming here to play this game." Bob raised his fists.

"Answer the question."

"I was at a boxing exhibition in Washington, DC, from early Thursday morning until late Saturday afternoon. It was in the paper. You can read, can't you?"

"An expert says Lizzie got hit in the head on Friday. That's what eventually killed her early Sunday morning. Not the gunshot."

Bob held his aggressive pose for a second before dropping his hands. "You should be a bloody mess right now. Want to know why you're not?"

"Because I brought the letter here. If I'd gone to the cops they'd come after you. What's that you said about a colored man and a white woman? That letter's enough to get you in big trouble."

"Yeah." Bob dropped back into his chair. "And I respect that you're serious about getting to the bottom of Lizzie's murder. What's your second question?"

"What about Nick—"

"That damn guy." Bob pounded the desk with the flat of his hand. "I got hot at Lizzie, told her to dump the man, that she deserved way better than him. Why are some women so loyal to men who treat them bad? It don't make sense. She stuck with him until it was too late." He hit the desk again, harder.

"Okay—"

Bob waved the letter. "I know what some would say about this. Proof that Foster was so jealous that he smacked the girl. But I didn't. Never laid a hand on her. When she wrote 'you didn't mean to hurt me' she was talking about her hurt feelings, all the rough stuff I yelled about her and Nick." He looked at the letter. "Last time I saw her she was crying. I've got to live with that."

Jack stayed silent for a while before leaning over and putting his hands on the desk. "Let me just spit out my second question. What about Nick's latest con? Got a strong hunch it's tied up with this whole mess."

"I knew something about what Nick was up to. Made me sick."

Jack tilted his head. "I'm listening."

"I'd finally had it with the bastard Sunday night—told him I was letting him go. Laughed and said he didn't need the job because he had something proving a big-deal white man in town was part Negro. Said he was going to make a mint off it and move himself to New York. Wouldn't say anything more—just went over and sat with Lucas Patterson for a while before the cops came and took him off."

"Patterson the mark? Or in on the scam?"

"No idea. But a man making money off someone's secret Negro blood don't deserve to draw breath. Especially Nick, who's passing himself. It's wrong to regret your ancestors. Wrong to let the white man make you ashamed. But I'll level with you—I was scared when the cops dragged Nick away and tore apart his room. Figured the less I let on about what I knew about Nick, the less I had to worry about what that devil O'Toole might do."

"Don't blame you for that. Since we got all the cards on the table, how can I find out more about Nick's shakedown?"

"Go visit Nick in his love nest with Patterson." Bob held a match to Lizzie's letter, then dropped it into a big brass ashtray and stared down at it. "All I got for you apart from that is Nick spends a lot of time consorting with the crowd at Kernan's Rathskeller. He loves to run his mouth, so one of them might know something." Bob's fixed eyes reflected the flame as the letter burned.

"Thanks for that. Promise you I'll do my best to get Lizzie's killer."

"You mean you'll do what it takes to get Shaw off."

"Says he didn't do it."

"Something you should know about Shaw. He's the type that would just as soon kill a woman as swat a bug. Lizzie was scared of him. Far as I'm concerned, the man could be guilty."

"Or maybe he's innocent and I'm the guy who'll find out who really killed her. That would mean something to you, right?"

"Okay, Harden, maybe you've gone and sold your soul to Shaw. You think he really needs you—and he does to stay out of court. But just remember the man is too well connected to spend time in jail. He owns lots of judges. And even if he's convicted, his good pal the governor will pardon him in a flash. Shaw will still be running this city come what may. The only reason he's dangling money at you is that you're the cheapest and cleanest way for him to get out of the mess. Stop pretending to be some damn white savior crusading for justice. I'm not buying it." Bob opened a book with *The Souls of Black Folks* by W.E.B. Dubois stamped on the cover. "You can get on out of here now."

Jack shrugged and walked out. Bob was, of course, dead right. Shaw had managed to claw his way into the heart of the political power structure, and that might make him arrogant enough to kill with no fear of consequences. Which made it all the more remarkable that Lipp had the sand to push for Shaw's arrest. The only question was whether the commissioner's motivation was strictly moral or rooted in something less honorable.

～

IT WAS past 10:00 p.m. and his boardinghouse was six blocks away. Jack was tempted to take a roundabout route out past Patterson Park to work off his nerves. But it was smarter to get into bed as soon as possible. He had only nightmares to look forward to, but he should give himself a shot at some sleep.

Walking down Caroline Street he thought again of Sarah, how she could be so smart about hard stuff and so dumb about straightforward dealings with people. How she could be a blunt pain in the rear one minute and honestly caring the next. How she wanted to be independent while at the same time work as a team. He liked her plenty, but working by himself was less complicated.

The two men were waiting for him behind a wagon parked in a dark stretch. One guy clubbed Jack on the knee from behind, tumbling him into a row of empty ash cans. The men lifted him up, one on each side.

"Knucks has a message for you, pally."

"I'm not late. I got until Saturday to make a payment." He spoke through teeth clenched tight with pain.

A blow to the gut knocked the wind out of him. They dropped him to the street and each gave him a hard kick in the side. A guy bent down and stuck the point of a blade into Jack's cheek. "Situation's changed. Knucks needs your nine hundred plus two hundred vig paid in full by Saturday. Terms ain't negotiable. Got it?"

Jack grunted and heard the men's footsteps fading until it was still again. He laid curled up on the sidewalk, blood trickling down his cheek and into his mouth. After struggling to his feet, he pressed a handkerchief to the wound and limped away.

This was rich. Leave it to him to fall in with a loan shark who wanted cash in full rather than the usual weekly payments. Knucks must be so desperate for cash himself that he had no time to milk the debt. Which meant that Jack either paid off everything in four days or he was a dead man.

CHAPTER 11

SARAH—TUESDAY, OCTOBER 12, 1909, 2:30 P.M.

*F*ortunately, Dr. Anson had not noticed her tardiness and no bodies lay in wait for Sarah's attention at Hopkins Hospital.

She finally had time to analyze evidence. A search of the pathology library turned up an illustrated volume describing the characteristics of plant and animal fibers, and it was a simple matter of putting the material from Lizzie's nails under a microscope and comparing them to the printed examples.

Despite the blood stains, it was clear the fibers were cashmere from a pinkish-colored fabric. Cashmere was an expensive material often used for ladies' garments, including shawls, skirts, and dresses. Lizzie was a burlesque dancer—an occupation presumably involving cheap wool or cotton costumes. Her personal clothing also was likely not of luxury quality.

Could the assailant have been a woman? While men were known to wear cashmere, it was more common in women's clothing. A man would also be expected to batter a woman during a struggle. Lizzie's body, however, showed no damage apart from a minor-appearing head injury, a finger laceration, and the gunshot wound.

Sarah retrieved the photograph of the pistol. It was a handgun that Jack had referred to as a vest pocket model—small enough to fit in a woman's hand. Female murderers were rare, yet Jane Toppan of Boston confessed to thirty-one killings in 1902. More recently, Belle Gunness killed over two dozen men, women, and children in Indiana. There was also Sarah's own experience with her stepmother. No doubt women were more than capable of homicide.

Sarah next turned to the piece of paper found in Lizzie's mouth. Using fine forceps, she carefully opened it into a flat two-by-three-inch sheet of cut newsprint. The ink was still readable. On one side was a list of ocean vessels docking in Baltimore Harbor. The other side had part of a news story dated April 3, 1907. The headline was "Foster Triumphant in Battle Again—Bob a Victor in Romance—Second Love Engagement with Dusky Beauty Promises Ecstasy with a Knockout Punch."

This clipping was odd. Had Lizzie placed it in her mouth to identify who hit her on the head? Or had her assailant put it there for some mad purpose—perhaps to indicate a romantic interest, either fulfilled or not? The name "Bob" jumped out. Lizzie had addressed her draft letter to someone named Bob.

She set aside the clipping and quickly read the book on fingerprinting. The science was basic; the key was that no two people had identical prints. Once finger marks were left on glass, metal, or another smooth surface, a light brushing with fine metallic powder could reveal them. Then it was a matter of matching the skin pattern of arches, loops, and whorls to prints of specific individuals.

It was possible—maybe probable—that the gun in the police photograph showed the prints of the person who last fired the weapon. Obtaining comparison prints from suspects would help identify the shooter. The frustration of the Bertillon Bureau chief was understandable—if the police didn't fingerprint people, there was no way to apply the technique to the prints on the pistol. Sarah considered the suspects while gently squirming in her seat.

There was Horace Shaw. And the men Shaw had suggested: Adolph Lipp and Lucas Patterson. Plus Lizzie's exploitive partner, Nick Monkton, as well as the cryptic "Bob." Who else? Clara Sullivan—the woman who had found the body—had refused to press for a second autopsy and had inserted herself into their investigation. The woman who was so friendly with Jack.

"Dr. Kennecott?" The Scots burr announced the man before she jerked her head up to see his smiling face. "My good friend Anson told me you were down here waiting."

"I am not merely waiting, Dr. Norbert Macdonald. I am reviewing evidence in connection with a criminal investigation."

"Aye—I heard you were working on something like that." The professor of psychiatry pulled up a stool to sit near her. "Please tell me what you have found. And, if you would be so kind, please stop your rocking. Makes it hard to look you in the eye."

Sarah had little interest in recapitulating the case and wished that Dr. Macdonald would leave her alone. Still, she knew it was socially unacceptable to rebuff his attention again so soon. If she was obligated to interact with the man, perhaps she could draw some useful insight from him. She forced herself still. "I am working to investigate the murder of a young woman. It is a curious case where a head injury caused death two days later. Someone then shot her corpse."

"Is that the murder of the showgirl? It's in the papers. They say a gunshot killed her. You seem to have a different view. And I hear you are working with a mysterious private detective."

"There is nothing mysterious about the detective. He and I are gathering evidence. We are the only people committed to uncovering the truth in this case. The authorities most certainly are not."

"I see." Macdonald nodded gently. "And who is this detective?" He looked around the room. "Is he with us now?"

"His name is Jack Harden. Your question about his location is illogical, as he clearly is not present in this space. He is following investigative leads elsewhere in the city." She flicked her gaze to Macdonald's face and saw he was looking at her closely with his warm brown eyes.

He was the type of man described as elegant and handsome, and his calm, deliberate manner put her more at ease than most people. At ease enough to venture a question another would regard as impertinent. "Doctor, could you offer an idea as to the personality of an individual who would shoot a corpse?"

"What a strange question." He pulled his head back. "I don't want to encourage any odd thinking, but I will say that certain disturbed individuals will mutilate corpses."

"Why?"

Macdonald shifted uneasily in his seat. "Some children use bizarre cruelty as a tool for asserting control within the family and, when they are grown, to control others."

"One may then may defile a corpse—even that of a sibling—if the act serves some selfish purpose."

"A sibling?" Macdonald sat his hat on the lab bench and leaned in closer. "You are weaving a strange story here. Is there an episode from your past that you want to talk about?"

"No. I am only considering evidence associated with my investigation."

"Do you have any facts that are not available to the police?"

"Everything I currently am evaluating was available to the authorities. They chose not to consider it, either through incompetence or willful neglect."

Macdonald glanced back at the two students working at the other end of the laboratory before leaning in even closer. "Let me repeat what I am hearing from you." He spoke in a near whisper. "You believe the authorities are conspiring to hide the truth. That belief fuels a compulsion to undertake a mission that only you, with your special knowledge, can perform. You have a supposed helper—this fellow Jack. Do you understand what all of this sounds like, lass?"

"You misconstrue what I have said." Her chest was now uncomfortably tight and her lower back ached with greater discomfort than usual. "Jack is real. I do not understand why you doubt that."

"Sarah, please lower you voice." He had never before used her first name. "Others should not overhear our conversation. Dr. Anson is worried and asked me to check on you. He's concerned about your state of mind. And now, after our talk, I too wonder about your mental soundness. You appear to be in the grip of a delusion. And you have added a rather florid twist with this Jack character. Let me guess—you see him as unlike other men in that he looks past your quirks to appreciate your specialness. This is textbook behavior caused by your unusually neurotic female sexuality."

"Jack is an actual person." Sarah sat completely still, her body numb and her mind swimming against a riptide of panic.

"There may indeed be an actual man, aye. If so, he serves your need for a fantasy to protect your fragile psyche." Macdonald spoke in a calm, steady murmur. "Therapy will help us learn more. Perhaps it is only a bout of hysteria, which is common among fragile young women of the upper class. I must warn you, however, of a more serious possibility. I worked closely with Dr. Eugen Bleuler in Zurich. He identified schizophrenia, a mental condition involving a break with reality. Sufferers undertake strange quests and come to believe in imaginary facts, people, and paranoid conspiracies."

She forced herself to speak. "Do you regard me as insane?"

Macdonald smiled and reached to pat her arm. She dodged his touch, but his smile remained. "No, not necessarily. You need analysis starting as soon as possible. That must be your sole focus now. Fortunately, I have the next two weeks open. We'll get started right away—I'll speak to Anson. He'll understand and release you from duty."

"Leave me now, Doctor. I no longer wish to hear your voice in my ears."

"Sarah, your entire body is trembling. I insist we—"

She held up her hand. "Leave. Immediately." Her loud voice caused one of the students to approach them with a demand for quiet.

Macdonald stood and apologized to the fellow before bending down and speaking softly into her ear. "My dear, think carefully about what I have said. The sooner we start, the better for you." He picked up his hat and left the laboratory.

She had no sensation in her hands or her face. It was happening again—people thought she was mad. After some time, her thoughts began to settle, and she glanced at the clock. It was after 6:00 p.m. and past time for her to return home.

SARAH STEPPED into her entry hall, closed the front door, and felt some of the tension racking her body lift. Home—the familiar, solitary domain where she was safe from the world.

Her father had the house custom built and installed all the modern conveniences, including electricity, telephone, and central furnace. He also filled it with fine artworks and furnishings. Just after her father died, her stepmother had a chandelier dripping with garish red crystal installed in the main entry hall. The only change Sarah made after moving back was to have the chandelier removed.

She mounted the grand staircase and went to her dressing room, where she undid her high-button shoes and stripped off her jacket, skirt, shirtwaist, petticoat, and corset cover. Unpeeling her stockings, she noticed they had holes and runs everywhere, as usual. Sarah's body thanked her as she undid the front laces of her new "long line" corset, which extended awkwardly down the thighs and up the bust. The only good thing about the garment was that it was an improvement over the old swan-bill corset that used steel boning and tight lacing to bend the body into a contorted S profile. Just the thought of it made her back throb even more.

Unpinning her hair, she thought about what Macdonald had said. It was devastating. He was a renowned expert in mental disorders, and his opinion carried great weight.

She knew that she was different, that other people regarded her as odd. But was she slipping into madness? Macdonald had originally shown interest in how her mind worked, but now he believed she had invented an imaginary detective to help her with a deluded investigation. Why? Perhaps the why did not matter. As a well-educated, assertive woman, she was familiar with negative male attention. She had to avoid giving the man any further reason for thinking she was insane.

She slipped out of her drawers and undervest and put on the outfit she always, without exception, wore at home—a flannel nightdress, soft dressing gown, and ankle-high slippers. Then it was down to the library to nibble on the cheese, bread, and fruit her housekeeper had laid out for dinner.

This was the room where she spent her time, reading, writing, and thinking—the one place she felt comfortable, where pleasant childhood memories blended with her adult life. Everything was in exactly the right spot. The wooden bookcases glowed with reassuring oaken warmth; the table had the perfect waxed sheen; the air smelled wonderfully of leather bindings and fine paper pages; even the nymphs carved into the marble fireplace were like old friends.

Sarah ran her hand over the books she'd lined up on the writing table and stopped at *Alice's Adventures in Wonderland*. As a child, the Knave's trial for stealing tarts had fascinated her with its utter absurdity. The more she learned about the world of adults, however, the more piercingly allegorical the story became. While Alice found the trial nonsensical, the other characters behaved as if she were the mad one. Yet Alice had the advantage of knowing that the queen and her followers were merely a pack of cards. And Alice always ended up safe at home, living again in a world she understood.

She set her mind to analyze evidence about the case. Some pieces of the puzzle were in place. According to Jack, there were no signs of a break-in at Lizzie's room, indicating that she knew the last person to see her alive. There were the cashmere fibers under her nails, pointing to a struggle, possibly with a woman who might have been Clara Sullivan. Lizzie's body showed no sign of major trauma apart from the head injury and the bullet wound.

Why would someone shoot a corpse? Sarah considered Macdonald's psychosexual analysis before rejecting it as extreme. Perhaps the shooter merely wanted to ensure Lizzie was truly deceased. On the other hand, the limited bleeding from the gunshot indicated not only that she was dead, but also that she had likely died a while beforehand. Whoever shot Lizzie had done so knowing she was dead. The shooter would have had time to carefully consider their action, which indicated some specific—and practical—motivation. Such as falsely implicating Shaw. Or something else.

So many unanswered questions. Additional evidence—such as fingerprints to compare with those on the pistol—was needed. If she could get prints from the suspects, she could do the analysis herself. That would mean getting close to each person and acquiring an object they had touched. How to do that?

With a start, an idea occurred to her about how to get fingerprints for at least some of the men in question. She called Margaret Bonifant and was quickly put through.

"Margaret, I must go to the Daughters of the Confederacy Oyster Banquet on Thursday."

"That is marvelous, dear. It will be just the diversion you need."

"I must obtain fingerprinted objects from the men we discussed."

Except for the slight crackle of static, the line went quiet. "You are still doing that investigation of yours. I was hoping you had come to your senses."

"I need evidence."

"If that gets you out and about socially—"

"I need a glass held by each man."

"I will help you under one condition. And do not try to talk me out of it because I insist. You must have the proper appearance. Meet me at my dressmaker at nine a.m. tomorrow morning."

"That is acceptable to me. However, Dr. Anson is the acting medical examiner and requests that I assist him tomorrow."

"The good doctor is seeking a donation from me for his department," said Margaret with a fluttery laugh. "I'll call him. He'll be glad to give you as much time as you need tomorrow morning."

"Very well."

"I'm so glad that you are going to the banquet, Sarah. It will be good for you to be around people."

As Sarah hung up the receiver, the full impact of what she had done hit her. Until that moment, she had focused on the narrow objective of obtaining and analyzing evidence. Yet getting the necessary finger marks would involve a fraught process of finding a gown, getting dressed, having her hair fussed with, and applying cosmetics. The preparatory work would take hours. And then the hard part—overcoming her awful nervousness about the event itself.

She stood and ran upstairs to Grace's bedroom, which was unchanged since her death.

Grace had always showered her with love and kindness and never mentioned her sister's quirks. The girls were inseparable, even when Grace played with her friends, whom she insisted never tease or torment her sister. Grace was endlessly patient in explaining social cues and expectations, often using two of her dolls to demonstrate. That helped Sarah enormously, and while still dependent on Grace's support for most social situations, she was eventually able to go to school on her own. Even after she turned sixteen, Sarah loved talking with the dolls—it was a rare chance to feel calm in a social situation. It became a cherished bedtime ritual, with the sisters taking turns brushing the dolls' hair while talking with them about the events of the day. She continued the ritual after Grace's death.

Now, Sarah was especially eager to sit with the dolls—to cry, shout, and talk freely about the big challenges facing her. How to complete the investigation despite hindrance from powerful men. How to cope with her severe anxiety about attending the oyster banquet. What to make of her relationship with Jack.

She could count on the dolls to be good listeners and give her their complete attention while she divided eye contact equally between their painted porcelain faces, which were blessedly free of emotional messages. It was also comforting to know that neither doll would ever doubt her mental health.

CHAPTER 12

JACK—WEDNESDAY, OCTOBER 13, 1909, 7:00 A.M.

*J*ust the ticket—the long walk from his boardinghouse to Sarah's place on the other side of town. His nerves needed settling, big style.

West on Aliceanna took him past the St. Stanislaus Roman Catholic Church, with its nearby school and convent. This was the heart of the Polish tenement district, and the air was full of strange-sounding words. If he focused on the tone of individual voices, though, he could distinguish among arguments, basic transactions, friendly exchanges, and the various shades in between that were common to the language of every population on the planet.

Several blocks farther on he came to the point where multiple spurs of the Philadelphia, Wilmington, and Baltimore Railroad freight yards connected to the main track. To his right were three rows of long wooden warehouses, which were already alive with work gangs moving freight to and from railcars.

Jack turned right and went by the President Street station. A chatty barfly had once told him the first deaths of the Civil War happened near here. A unit of Massachusetts troops pulled into the station in April 1861 and were attacked by a proslavery mob. Both sides had multiple killed and wounded. The story didn't surprise him—Baltimore was a southern city at heart.

The neighborhood past the station was Jewish, filled mostly with recent arrivals from Russia and nearby lands. Tenements lined both sides of the street, and laundry flapped in every courtyard, defying the gritty soot flying everywhere. Children stared at him with dark, blank eyes from stoops and open windows. Like the Polish district, the three-story tenements were crammed with three, four, or five families, each of them packed into two or three rooms. The housing was cheap, but landlords tended not to bother with things such as ventilation, sanitation, or fire safety.

One quiet night in a saloon Jack overheard a building inspector blabbing about a recent survey of tenements in Baltimore. Out of six hundred buildings checked, only nine had indoor toilets. There were only twenty-seven bathtubs, and two were used as kitchen sinks, one for storing clothes, and one as a bed. Most places had no indoor running water, and outdoor privies—most of them overflowing—were the rule. "That's how them immigrant-types want to live," the inspector said. "Breeding brats, vice, and germs around the clock." To Jack the situation seemed more about necessity—no one would live that way if they had a choice.

Moving west on Pratt Street across the Jones Falls bridge was slow going, as two brewery wagons, each harnessed to a six-horse team, stood still in the center of the span opposite each other. The drivers argued about who had the right of way, not caring about the backed-up traffic and chorus of angry shouts. Jack stepped around the jam, careful to avoid the growing piles of manure and rivulets of urine. At least the beasts were enjoying a break.

Once over the bridge a fruity-bright smell smacked him in the nose—pineapples stacked outside the fruit seller storefronts on the edge of the harbor. A right on Market Place and a left on Baltimore Street had him once more surrounded by arcades, moving-picture parlors, and other cheap thrills. There was, however, no fun to be had this early in the morning—the joints around here didn't begin to stir until noon at the earliest.

On Holliday Street he cruised by the fancy city hall, with its marble columns and cast-iron dome, before turning left on Pleasant Street and passing the massive Terminal Warehouse. It was a hulking, six-story brick pile with rail spurs running into cavernous arched entrances. He went inside on a job once and found that it had water-powered elevators, which for some reason didn't scare the devil out of him.

Places like it were, to Jack's mind, a riddle. Sure, there was big cash in the Baltimore warehouse business. But why? How could you earn money without producing raw materials, making something useful, or selling goods to regular people? All you did was unload stuff, pile it under a roof, let it bake in the summer and freeze in the winter, and then hump it back onto a wagon or railcar to go somewhere else. There must be some slick trick behind it, just as there was for so much modern business in the big city.

He turned north on Calvert and passed the Home for Worthy Boys and, a block later, the sprawling yards of the Northern Central Railway. Then it was west on Monument Street and up the hill to Mount Vernon Place, where a statue of George Washington perched on a towering column.

Washington was holding out a rolled shape in his right hand. Jack once imagined the shape was an invoice for services rendered, listing charges for the battles he had won during the Revolutionary War. Heck, the guy could even charge for lost battles. He got the job done. It turned out the statue depicted Washington handing back his military commission without asking for a nickel. Guess George was already a rich guy by that point and didn't need the dough.

Jack continued west on Monument Street past the procession of grand mansions known as Millionaires Row. He closed his eyes and savored the smell of good coffee, the faint sound of a violin, and the feel of a soft breeze blowing over freshly manicured shrubbery.

He was getting closer to Sarah's neighborhood, which he knew little about apart from its location near Druid Hill Park. He went past the Johns Hopkins University campus, turned right on Eutaw, and followed the dogleg to the northwest. The street became Eutaw Place and split in two, with a big grassy median in between. The structures grew progressively bigger and ritzier, as if each block were trying to outdo the previous one.

At the intersection with Lanvale, the Oheb Shalom Synagogue reared three gold domes on top of imposing stone walls. Grand mansions began popping up, some bigger and fancier than those on Mount Vernon Square. This was a world away from the bustle and grime of downtown. The streets were neatly paved, with just the occasional carriage or delivery wagon quietly passing.

Once past North Avenue, open lots were common. There was new construction here and there, but the place still had a country feel. The forests of nearby Druid Hill Park put a nice autumn tang in the air.

Outside Sarah's address near the end of the street, he stood agape. The house had four floors—maybe five if there was a basement—with a massive bow front topped by dormer windows under a slate roof. It was big enough for at least ten people to live in total luxury.

Most houses in Baltimore—even fancy ones—were joined by common sidewalls. This place was freestanding on both sides, with a carriageway to the right that led to a covered entrance with a courtyard and a stable that could manage a dozen horses. The house seemed to keep extending back forever from the street, with different styles of windows, jutting protrusions, and towering chimneys. An ornate wrought-iron fence bounded perfectly kept grounds.

Jack's sore knee wobbled, forcing him to clutch a piece of curlicue iron on the waist-high fence. Maybe he should go around back to the tradesmen's entrance. It felt right and would protect Sarah's reputation from prying eyes. No; forget it. She invited him here.

He pushed open the front gate and slowly mounted the huge marble steps to the pair of eight-foot-high front doors. He imagined a snooty butler opening, then slamming, the door in his face. The big brass knocker felt as smooth as butter.

The door flew open, and there was Sarah in a tightly wrapped dressing gown, hair down over one shoulder. "Jack. Come in." She turned, went through an interior set of doors and into the foyer. He closed the outside door and stood for a second in the carved granite vestibule that reminded him of a fancy bank. The front hall was church-like, with soaring arches of dark wood decorated with carved gingerbread patterns, and the walnut wainscoting and fine dark furniture glowed with a fresh polish. His beat-up shoes sank deep into the plush Turkish carpet. This was by far the most high-class place he had ever set foot in.

He quickly snatched off his hat. An enormous gilt frame mirror hung on the wall next to a row of fancy oil paintings. He looked at his reflection, which was a mistake. He was way past due for a visit to the barber, and his suit was so worn and tattered he looked like a bum.

"We can talk in the library." With her usual determination, Sarah walked down the hallway and into a large, orderly room filled with bookcases. She sat at a table with a row of books standing in a precise line off to her right. Jack sat, eyes fixed on a gleaming silver coffeepot on a silver tray in front of him.

"I have studied fingerprint science and plan to compare the

prints of suspects with the marks documented in the police photograph." Sarah sat bolt upright like a freshly planted fence post.

"Good morning, Sarah. I would love some coffee." Like her, he averted his eyes. He'd never seen a proper lady with her hair down, much less in her nightclothes. Even though she was covered from the top of her neck to the bottoms of her feet, her appearance was unsettling. With any other woman, Jack would take her attire as an invitation for sex.

"I should have offered to serve you." She poured coffee into an impossibly fragile cup set on an equally fragile saucer. "I can ring for milk and sugar, if you need it. I drink coffee black. It tastes much better that way. I like tea, too, as long as it is black and fully oxidized."

His head throbbed as Sarah talked. Eventually she stopped, and they sat in silence for a moment.

"Jack. You have a laceration on your cheek." She was up in a flash and quickly back with a washbasin and a medical bag. "Turn your head so I may inspect and clean the wound."

He flinched as she pressed a washcloth against his cheek. "No big matter," he said. "Just nicked myself with the straight-edge this morning."

"Nonsense. This is a severe puncture wound. It is as yet uninfected, fortunately." She put a few drops from a small bottle of liquid onto a cotton swab and dabbed the skin around the cut.

"Hey, I can't feel my cheek. What'd you put on it?"

"A weak solution of cocaine. It is a local anesthesia. Hold still while I stitch the cut." She pierced his cheek with the needle.

"What the—"

"You will remain still." She deftly worked the needle to place three stitches and sat back down.

"Nice bedside manner, Doc."

"I am pleased to hear that. I had difficulty reassuring patients while in medical training."

"No kidding." Jack touched his cheek gingerly.

"Keep the wound clean. Make an effort to wash it."

"Knock it off." He dropped his hand to the table harder than he meant to. "I wash myself every morning. I've even been known to take a bath or two every year."

"I did not mean to offend you. I am concerned about your well-being."

"Yeah, sure." Jack reached for his coffee, his hand hovering over the delicate-looking china cup. His thick fingers could never manage that tiny thread of a handle. He wrapped his hand around the cup as carefully as he could and took a big gulp. "Nice little place you have here," he said, waving his hand around the room. "Where are all the servants?"

"My late father was a successful businessman. I am his only heir. I live here because it is available and familiar. The only help I require is a housekeeper, who spends most of her time arranging for physical maintenance."

Maintenance of the house only, thought Jack. Any other woman of Sarah's class would at least also have a maid to brush her hair, look after her clothing, and insist that her mistress get dressed before receiving any kind of visitor, most especially a man. That same maid should be hovering nervously in the background, worried to the extreme about the propriety of a guy like himself meeting alone with the lady of the mansion.

Sarah took a careful sip from her cup. "We should dispense with idle talk. I must leave shortly to be fitted for a dress so that I may attend the Daughters of the Confederacy Oyster Banquet tomorrow. After that, I need to assist the acting medical examiner in performing any necessary autopsies."

"Oyster Banquet?" Jack whistled softly. "So hoity-toity. Bet you'll be happy to mingle with your own class." He gulped down the rest of his coffee, picturing her standing around with sweet-smelling folks chitchatting about lofty things. People whose smart, cultured personalities were as different from his as a dollar is to three cents.

"I loathe society events. They cause me great anxiety. I am attending this one strictly to acquire the fingerprints of suspects who will be present."

"I couldn't get within a block of a shindig like that before being told to get lost."

"That speculation is of no consequence at this time. We need to discuss the status of the investigation." She opened a notebook and began writing with a pencil.

"Sure." Jack set his cup noisily down on the saucer. "You need to tell me more about this new autopsy job. I thought we were working together."

"I am only on call for official autopsies this afternoon at Johns Hopkins Hospital. I plan to spend my free time conducting research and studying evidence."

"Did you get to the city Bertillon Bureau? You were going to check on fingerprints, as I recall."

"Yes. I met with the bureau head," said Sarah. "I learned the police are not pursuing any fingerprint evidence. I have educated myself about the science and plan to gather and analyze finger marks from suspects, as I have previously indicated."

Jack reached into his pocket and pulled out the burned half of the Honus Wagner baseball card. "Can you get fingerprints off this?"

"You mean apart from yours. Do not handle potential evidence with your bare hands. It is faulty procedure."

"Yeah, yeah." Jack shrugged, tossing the burned card on the table. "The other guy who touched this was Snake Eyes O'Toole, the city detective who hauled in Nick and collared Shaw. Wouldn't surprise me at all if O'Toole were involved in what happened to Lizzie."

"I see you used your coffee without the handle. I can isolate your fingerprints from the cup."

"Great. I managed to do something half right."

Silence ticked by. "Jack, have I offended you again?"

"Look, Sarah, I'm just a low-rent guy doing his best to grub for some info. I know you're way better than me in every way. Smarter, classier, richer—you name it. You don't have to keep rubbing it in."

More silence passed. "My intent is not to look down upon you." She wrung her hands in her lap. "On the contrary. I worry that you devalue me because of my sex. And because of my eccentricity."

Jack slumped in his chair, feeling like a chump. "Sorry. You're a pip. A peacherino. I like working with you a whole bunch." He had the urge to reach over and touch her arm, maybe her shoulder, but knew she'd jump. "Listen, I've got lots of news," he said. "Horace Shaw's in the clink, for starters. Got him to spill beforehand, though. Says Lizzie died during . . . you know."

"Sexual intercourse. That is consistent with the position of Lizzie's body in the police crime scene photograph."

"I got a hunch Shaw might be innocent, just like he claims."

"We must base our work on empirical observation and analysis. Mere guesses are not scientific."

"The gut plays a big role in detective work." Jack drummed his fingers on the thick white tablecloth. "Anyway, Shaw said Nick squeezed money out of him early Monday morning. Nick threatened to rat on him about Lizzie dying while they were— you know. Nick also said he had written evidence that someone else whacked Lizzie in the head a couple of days before she died. Shaw gave me a lead on where to find Nick. I'm going to go pay him a visit as soon as we're done."

"What is this alleged written evidence?"

"No idea. It might not even exist. I got some other interesting tidbits. Heard that Nick was trying to cash in on some kind of proof that a Baltimore big shot has secret Negro blood. Blackmail. Patterson might be involved."

"What kind of proof pointing to which person? We need hard facts, not vague assertions."

Jack drew in a sharp breath. "All I got is bits and pieces. That's how this game works. It isn't like some big library where you can just pull a book off the shelf and read everything you need to know."

"I did not allude to a library. I am merely pointing out that incomplete information hinders our ability to—"

"Okay, I hear you." Jack held up his hand. "There's another lead for you to consider. The manager of the Gayety told me that Nick linked up Lizzie with some guy who claimed to be a doctor who wanted to 'examine her.' What do you call it when someone uses nice words to mean something not so nice?"

"A euphemism. I am not fond of such usage."

"Yeah. Well, the guy who wanted to do the examining was short with big glasses and a pointy bit of hair sticking up from the top of his bald head. You know any doctors who look like that?"

Sarah jerked her hand across the table, sending her teacup onto its side with a soft plop. "Are you quite sure of that description?" She made no effort to mop up the brown liquid spreading across the snowy tablecloth.

"Manager had no reason to lie. You okay?" She had jumped up and was pacing rapidly from one side of the room to the other, her hands a blur. "Sarah?"

"I believe I know the man you describe. I will see him this afternoon."

"Maybe you can worm something out of him. Look, I've got more to tell you. Sit down." She sat prim. "I spoke to the Bob in Lizzie's letter. He liked Lizzie a lot, probably even fell for her. Says he told her to drop Nick. Bob's a fierce guy, and it's easy to imagine him hurting her feelings. He says he didn't hit her, and my gut wants to believe him. And he has a solid alibi for the day you think Lizzie got whacked in the head."

Sarah leaped from her chair again and pulled a brown paper bag from a shelf. She reached in, pulled out a scrap of newsprint, and dropped it in front of him. "I retrieved this from Lizzie's mouth. It was between her upper lip and gum. Please note the reference to the name 'Bob' as well as references to violence and romantic attachment."

Jack leaned back in his chair, scratching his chin. "Is the 'Bob' you spoke with the Bob Foster mentioned in this clipping?" Sarah asked.

"Yeah."

"I used the evidence to formulate two separate conjectures. One is that Lizzie felt some romantic attachment with Bob Foster, or that someone wished to convey that impression. Another is that someone wanted to implicate Bob Foster in her death."

Jack grinned, then laughed. "At last I get a chance to say you're wrong."

"State how you think my reasoning is invalid." She sat down and stared at the coffee pot.

"That clipping is more than likely a cocaine wrapper. Some dope slingers like to associate their product with famous athletes, so they wrap it in little packets ripped from the sports pages. Bob's a big-time boxer. And he's in the marrying habit— that headline's about his second marriage. Which is already long busted up."

"Even if what you say is true, why would Lizzie have the paper in her mouth?"

"Folks who like coke can't get enough of the stuff. They put the empty wrapper on their gums to draw out the last bit. Let me guess—Lizzie's front teeth were a mess, right? Sure sign of a true coke fiend."

"Your explanation is plausible, yet I will not withdraw my conjectures. More evidence may implicate Bob Foster."

"More evidence will prove you wrong on that count, Miss Smarty. Seems you don't know everything after all." He kicked himself for teasing her. It was like shooting fish in a tub. And who knows? This case had so many twists and turns that maybe Bob really did have a role—the guy had already withheld information at least once. Jack probably should have held on to that letter. "I told you he's got an alibi."

"Did you verify his alleged alibi?"

Jack fidgeted in his seat. "No, but I believe him. He's a decent enough guy."

"Jack." She slashed the air, her hand a blur. "You must not only collect data, you must ensure the data are correct. That is how we formulate a theory. Unsupported assumptions have no basis in the scientific method."

"And I'll tell you again, Sarah, that the gut is as important as the brain in detective work. Give me a little credit—I might be a dummy but I've done this work a little longer than you." She was staring at the floor as if she spotted a gold nugget. "Found out something else that you should find interesting," said Jack, hoping Sarah would loosen up a little. "Clara Sullivan was pestering her sister for cash—wanted a cut of a piddly family inheritance. And Clara's a sneaky little liar—turns out she's a classy actress who just finished a run at the Maryland Academy of Music doing a show called *Doll House* or something."

"Do you mean she acted in *A Doll's House* by Henrik Ibsen?"

"Guess so."

"Which character did she portray?"

"The lead."

Sarah sprung up again and went to a distant shelf, where she ran her fingers along book spines before pulling one out. She read in silence until Jack got antsy. "Anyway, that's what I dug up. How about you—how'd things go with Patterson?"

She didn't respond until he called to her again. She marched back to her seat, where she opened a small notebook. "Lucas Patterson is a study in contrasts. He is wealthy and yet keeps his office in a poor section of town. He is well educated but is also a ragtime music enthusiast. He can speak rationally one moment and slip into emotional speech the next. He is mercurial—that it to say, he has sudden changes in temperament."

"He say anything about Lizzie or Nick?"

She set the notebook down. "He claimed Nick as a close friend and praised his musical ability."

"That's not all Patterson likes about Nick."

"What do you mean?"

"I hear that the two of them are lovers. Patterson seems to be more emotionally involved than Nick."

Sarah blinked rapidly. "Patterson indicated great frustration with Nick's nonmusical activities, most especially in connection with Lizzie. In his view, Lizzie was a distraction of great magnitude."

"I heard Patterson hated the girl."

"He did not speak well of Lizzie."

Jack whistled softly. "Nick's got one temperamental, frustrated friend. Maybe Patterson killed the competition."

"I agree that Patterson is elevated as a suspect." Sarah quickly turned pages in her notebook. "I wish, however, to focus on another suspect. Clara Sullivan may have murdered Lizzie. Or fired the bullet into her corpse."

"Come on—you think she'd do that to her own sister?"

"Clara Sullivan had the means and the opportunity. You heard she wanted money from Lizzie, which points to motive." Sarah hugged herself tightly with both arms. "Have you seen her naked body since we last talked?"

Jack dropped his hand on the table hard enough to make the cups dance. "No."

Sarah flinched, her pale face pinkening. "I ask because Lizzie

169

might have struggled with her attacker and scratched them. The fibers under Lizzie's fingernails were cashmere, which is a woman's luxury material. If you observed such scratches on Clara Sullivan—her neck, arm, perhaps even leg or torso—it would be an important clue."

"I got the same look at Clara as you did."

"The dress she wore at the lunchroom may have contained cashmere. I request that you obtain a sample of fibers from that dress when you see her next. You may need to use subterfuge to accomplish the task."

Jack knew Sarah was on to something about Clara, but was irritated with the way she was pushing it. "Are you encouraging me to have sex with Clara to help the investigation?" She glanced down at the table and then over at the far wall and then back at the table. "Sarah, look at me. Answer the question."

Her eyes locked on his for three seconds before shifting to a spot beyond his left ear. "I do not enjoy prolonged eye contact with any person. It is extremely uncomfortable for me."

All the anger flooded away, leaving Jack feeling like an idiot once again. What was it about this woman that stirred him up? "Sorry. I was way out of line. Got a short fuse these days."

"I accept your apology. I apologize as well." She clasped her hands tightly in her lap. "I often offend people with my speech and manner. I do not intend to do so."

"Let's just say that you don't beat around the bush."

"I assume that is an idiom."

"I don't know what that means. What I'm saying is that you get right to the point without worrying about politeness. I like it —most of the time." He grinned and then stood. "I need to shove off. Let's meet back here tomorrow morning to compare notes."

"That will be satisfactory." She got to her feet and strode off.

He followed, eyeing her from behind until they reached the door. "Bet you'll look like a million bucks for your banquet."

"Jack." She put both hands in front of her, palms up, and flexed her fingers. The veins in her thin wrists were like violet threads running under a layer of fine white tulle. "Please be careful to avoid further injury."

"Don't worry—last thing I want is getting stuck with that needle of yours again."

One corner of her upper lip barely lifted—possibly the first hint of a smile he had seen from her—before the door closed.

CHAPTER 13

SARAH—WEDNESDAY, OCTOBER 13, 1909,
9:00 A.M.

The only thing that came close to the agony of a formal social engagement was getting ready for one—as she was now doing with Margaret's retinue of seamstresses dedicated to improving Sarah's appearance.

Wearing a strapless chemise, she stood on a raised wooden box in front of a full-length mirror. All she could think about was the White Queen in *Through the Looking-Glass*, who was wholly inept in dressing herself and relied on Alice to set things right.

"Let us see the ivory silk charmeuse with the square neckline and crisscross beaded bodice," said the chief dressmaker, who sat with Margaret. "Your friend is somewhat deficient in natural development. Fortunately, slim hips have just come into fashion. She clearly needs a well-padded bust improver. That, along with some artful dress alterations, should bring out her womanliness."

"Let us find something quickly," said Sarah as an attendant helped her step into a pile of couture pooled at her feet. After the gown came up, she apprised the bodice with its sparkly green beads set against a white satin fabric as predictably garish.

"Lovely, lovely," said the chief. "I would recommend three strings of pearls with that gown. Either that or a ruby pendant on a diamond necklace. I'm assuming something is to be done with the unfortunate hair, yes?"

"Sarah, what do you think?" asked Margaret.

"The dress is fine. Can we leave? I have urgent matters to attend to."

"Do you have something a little less busy on top?" Margaret asked. "And in something other than white? Her gown should have some color."

"Of course, madam." The chief motioned to one of the attendants. "We have a most striking gown right here. It is a medium-weight burgundy silk dress with lace sleeves and some discreet beading on the shoulders and neckline. Observe the unique embroidery pattern that runs from top to bottom. A lady certainly makes a statement in this."

After the attendants put the dress on her, Sarah couldn't take her eyes off the embroidery. It looked like a string of lilies coming into bloom. The topmost lily was about two inches wide, with a succession of gradually smaller lilies running all the way to the fabric bunched on the floor.

"Good heavens," said Margaret. "That dress is stunning— perhaps a bit too vivid for your taste, Sarah?"

"I favor the embroidery, which looks to be a perfectly expressed arithmetic progression with a common difference of minus two." She ran a finger along the pattern and thrilled to the thick, ribbed texture.

"The color is a striking contrast with mademoiselle's pale skin," said the chief.

"Sarah, please look at yourself in the mirror."

Sarah pulled her gaze away from the descending pattern of lilies and gasped at her reflection. The woman staring back at her looked like a character from a novel—someone who couldn't possibly be awkward little Sarah. Could she? Just as Sarah was about to start pulling the dress off, she noticed the lily pattern continued under the bust. Craning her neck behind, she saw the pattern running the length of the train until it disappeared under a plump roll of fabric.

"Well, what do you think?"

This astonishing article of clothing was confounding. She had never worn anything remotely like it, and her resistance to novelty argued for rejection. But there was something strangely compelling about how the woman in the mirror looked in this dress. After a long pause she managed to respond. "I like it more than not."

"Wonderful, dear. You had better be prepared to turn heads and break hearts at the banquet."

"Why is that?"

"Darling, in that dress you will attract the interest of any man with a pulse."

Sarah blinked back at the reflection, which still looked like someone else—even as the woman copied her hand gestures. It took an eternity to have the dress pinned for alteration. Then there was the tedious matter of getting shoes, earrings, and a boxful of cosmetic powders. She was exhausted, but Margaret insisted on having tea. Sarah repeated chunks of the Baltimore and Ohio train schedule to herself while the waiters fussed over them.

"This is such fun," said Margaret.

"I appreciate your efforts to alter and adorn my body, face, and hair."

"You're more than welcome. It is so wonderful to spend time with you in this way. We must do it more often."

"We should discuss how to obtain the glasses I require for evidentiary purposes."

Margaret's lips pressed tightly as she patted Sarah's arm. "I've been thinking—you relied on school for many years to focus your powerful mind. Are you perhaps now desperate for some other distraction?"

"I do not understand your question."

"Is that unknown man still helping with your . . . investigation?"

"If you are referring to Jack Harden, the answer is yes."

Margaret reached over the table and took hold of Sarah's hands. "If you insist on working with this man, I would like to meet him. Perhaps he could visit later this afternoon?"

"Jack is not familiar with society etiquette. In any event, he is engaged in gathering information."

"I am willing to suspend the formal rules in his case. How about if we meet after the banquet? Even a brief encounter outside the hotel would satisfy my curiosity."

Sarah considered Jack's professed sensitivity regarding class and knew that he would bridle at being summoned to meet with Margaret in her evening gown on the sidewalk amid other well-dressed society people. "No. As I said, Jack is far too busy."

Margaret sighed deeply. "You are too absorbed in this detective story of yours, dear. You need to ground yourself in the world as it is, rather than as you pretend it is. Perhaps we could take a shopping trip to New York? Or even Paris. Wouldn't that be nice?"

Sarah pulled her hands free. "Margaret, I have given you no reason to suspect that I am deluded. And I assure you that Jack is a tangible human being upon whom I do not project fantastic thoughts. My mind is clear and my thoughts rational." She arranged her silverware while pondering why yet another person thought she was losing her mind. Dr. Anson must have passed on concern about Sarah's mental health when Margaret telephoned him. A headache building since the early morning now blossomed.

"There is no need to feel any shame," said Margaret. "You have every right to your emotional distress after such a difficult life. Your mother deserted you. Your father and Grace died horribly—"

"You do not need to keep reminding me about my family. I have not forgotten them."

Margaret got up, walked behind Sarah, and embraced her. "I know. Forgive my dwelling on those awful facts. You have been under such a terrible emotional strain for so long. I worry so much about you."

As much as she was enjoying the embrace, Sarah pulled away and stood. "I acknowledge your concern. I must now return to my duties at the hospital."

Margaret reached for her but then pulled her arm back. "You are in danger, dear. Remember your time in that place."

"It remains firmly in my memory." Sarah wanted to say something to allay her friend's worry and struggled to form the right words. They did not come. All she could manage before departing was "I shall appear at your residence tomorrow morning to complete preparations for my appearance at the banquet. Good day, Margaret."

SARAH TRIED to suppress her thoughts during the cab ride to the hospital. It was unwise to fixate on the deaths of her father and sister, but Margaret had brought the memories back to life.

When she was sixteen, her father introduced a new wife: Marie, a widow with social ambition. Marie insisted that Sarah formally enter Baltimore high society, and her father reluctantly agreed, despite his long-standing empathy for Sarah's social difficulties. The calendar was cruel, as Marie demanded that Sarah come out at a grand charity ball just six months away.

Margaret was appalled and lectured her parents about the hardheartedness of expecting Sarah to dance gracefully, display exquisite manners, sparkle with charm, and otherwise meet the expectations of a debutante. Marie was unmoved.

At Margaret's direction, an extremely patient ballet master worked to teach Sarah dance. Margaret also spent hours tutoring the young woman about how to pass as a proper young lady. Eventually Sarah learned enough to get by and even managed a semblance of charm through memorization of stock phrases such as "Your hat suits you," and "Do tell me where you got your dress." Sarah successfully navigated her debutante ball despite spilling grape punch on her white silk dress and long white gloves.

After graduating from Vassar, Sarah met with her father to discuss her financial future. He had a new will that left all his assets to his second wife, with the understanding that his daughters would have all their expenses covered. Sarah was unconcerned, as her need for money was minimal. Inspired by the work of Marie Curie, she planned to pursue an advanced degree in physics, which her father promised to support.

A couple of weeks later Sarah, Grace, and her father fell ill. Doctors diagnosed typhoid and ordered bed rest. Her step-mother, usually cold and aloof with the girls, tended to them with copious amounts of tea and soup. Sarah refused much of it —her finicky taste buds could not tolerate the liquids.

When her father and sister died within hours of each other, Sarah had a breakdown, switching between catatonia and nonstop wailing. Marie convinced the doctors that Sarah had lost her mind and had the girl packed off to an insane asylum selected for its low cost and distance from Baltimore.

Sarah recalled nothing of her first hours in the place, but found herself in a small closed room with an iron-barred window and a dozen other women. Her bedding was a straw pallet, a dingy sheet, and a foul-smelling blanket. She found it difficult to sleep, as her roommates variously shrieked or babbled at all hours.

Attendants regularly clomped into the room, one holding a lantern and another using a stick to poke inmates to make sure they were still alive. In the morning Sarah put on a worn woolen dress and was marched with the others into a cold dining hall for a breakfast of lumpy porridge and weak tea. Afterward she was taken to see a well-dressed young man, who asked her name and other personal details. She rationally answered all his questions as he leisurely wrote in a large notebook.

"Who are you and why am I here?" she asked.

"I am Dr. Grant. You are here because you are hopelessly demented."

"I am not demented." Sarah squirmed uncomfortably as the coarse wool dug into various parts of her body. "I recall hearing about the deaths of my father and sister before waking up in this place. I must have suffered a temporary nervous reaction. I wish to leave immediately."

Dr. Grant smiled. "I know your type of madness. You can act normal for a while, but sooner or later you'll snap back into a fully deranged state. We need to stop your playacting. Let's start with some hydrotherapy."

She was taken to a room with a tub of water. Three large matrons emptied buckets of ice into the tub, forced her to undress, and lifted her into the water. A matron held her in the tub until her teeth chattered uncontrollably. Then she was plunked into a near-scalding bath and scrubbed with coarse brushes until her skin was raw. After a rough toweling and redressing, she was moved to a large room filled with wooden benches. A bin by the door held a sad assortment of broken dolls, torn children's primers, wooden spoons, and other objects. An old woman in front of her was told to pick something and go sit down. When she refused, an attendant knocked her to the floor. After time on the benches, Sarah and the others were back in the dining hall for a lunch of bread and watery mashed potatoes.

Next came occupational rehabilitation, which included tasks such as scouring floors, emptying privies, and grinding wet laundry against a washboard. After a dinner of dry cornbread, overcooked vegetables, and gristly meat, it was back to the barred room for a few hours of fitful sleep. Weeks passed with only slight variation in this routine.

Then Dr. Grant said she needed more intensive treatment and prescribed something known as "counter-irritation." The idea was to refocus the mind through physical pain. A caustic ointment was smeared on the back of her neck to raise a huge, oozing blister that hurt more than anything she had ever known. Sarah continued to insist she was sane, and the ointment became a regular part of her day.

In the midst of this terrible ordeal, Sarah found she could ease the suffering of some inmates with a careful touch and a few moments of positive attention. Soon she had an assortment of wretches seeking her help at all hours. Never had so many people needed and accepted her, and she benefitted so much from the experience that she was able to endure her treatment.

Then it was suddenly over. The Bonifants, who had searched for her without pause during the five weeks since she had been whisked away, found the asylum and got her released. After a month under Margaret's care, Sarah was well enough to review the official findings for the deaths of her father and sister. She learned that arsenic, if carefully administered, can mimic typhoid. She noted also that arsenic was also known as "inheritance powder," the full meaning of which she took care to understand.

A thorough search of the Kennecott home turned up a large canister of arsenic hidden in the pantry along with a record of doses, written in Marie's hand, that matched the dates for the family's illness. Sarah convinced Margaret to arrange, through her husband, for the bodies of her family to be exhumed and tested. Both had lethal doses of arsenic in their remains. That led to the arrest, trial, and imprisonment of her stepmother.

The experience with her stepmother caused Sarah to switch her career plans to medicine. She would use the science of pathology to identify victims of foul play and bring their murderers to justice.

Just one ambition eclipsed her passion for catching killers—avoiding placement in a lunatic asylum ever again.

CHAPTER 14

JACK—WEDNESDAY, OCTOBER 13, 1909,
9:00 A.M.

*T*his part of the waterfront had seen better days. The stable on the corner of Ann and Fell Streets abutted two crumbling brick structures, and all three leaned together as if they longed to lie down in the rubble-strewn vacant lot to their right. The stable looked abandoned, yet this was where Nick was supposedly holed up.

Jack ground his teeth at the sight of teamsters lashing an eight-horse team pulling a railroad freight car up a spur to the main line. Citing safety, the city government didn't allow locomotives this close to the wharves. The city cared much less about cruelty to horses.

The stable doors were closed and locked, so he walked around and saw a rickety shed tacked onto the back of the place. The wood siding on the shed was rotted and saggy. He gave one of the boards a quick kick, and it fell off. He waited for a guy to pass by with a handcart filled with caged chickens before ripping out enough boards to crawl inside.

Thick dust swirled around in the bars of sunlight coming through cracks in the walls. There was a dry, musty smell of old hay and horse manure that grew as he walked into the blackness

of the main stable building. The place was cold in the perma-
nent way that abandoned buildings get. He walked to within a
couple of feet of a partially open door marked by a thin slant of
light.

It was quiet except for a faint rumbling from the street and
rustling of mice in the walls. Pulling out the Colt, he softly
pushed the door open to a room dimly lit by two filthy windows.
A man's body, wearing a flashy yellow suit, was slumped over a
table. Dead as a mackerel.

Jack glanced around—the room was a dump, with junk
tossed everywhere. Jack used the Colt to lift the head from a
sticky pool of blood on the table just far enough to see the stiff's
pretty boy face and a bullet hole in the right temple. He smelled
whiskey from the open mouth and noticed an Iver-Johnson .32
revolver on the floor under the dangling right arm. As he
stepped closer to the table, something crunched. Lifting his foot,
he saw a small lump of bone and gristle—a pig's foot with the
meat freshly chewed away. Well, how about that.

Two chipped glass tumblers and a pile of musical compositions tied with red cloth tape sat in the center of the table. A
single sheet of paper had I'M SORRY—NICK written in crude
block letters. The body had nothing of interest in its pockets
other than forty bucks in mixed bills and a bank draft for fifty
dollars from Lucas Patterson made payable to Nick Monkton.
Jack left the dough alone. Someone would lift the cash before
the body reached the morgue, but he'd give the cops a chance to
use the draft to identify the body.

He looked back at the tumblers and thought of fingerprints.
Definitely a long shot that the cops cared about that—but Sarah
would. He wrapped the glasses in old newspapers and stuck
them in a grain sack. There was the note—the cops really would
want that—still, he had no reason to do them any favors. He
picked up the paper with his handkerchief and pushed it into
the grain sack with the glasses.

After ensuring no one was around, Jack stepped outside. He turned north on Broadway, grain bag in hand. He had to jump, tumblers clinking, to avoid getting bowled over by a young woman coming straight at him behind a baby carriage. "I got a kid here, you stinking bum!" she yelled over her shoulder without slowing down. The gal was making the most of her time with a baby. Then again, maybe she was cracky and trotting around with no kid in the stroller at all.

A column of black smoke rose into the sky just ahead. A fire engine charged past, its horses frothing and steam pump hissing like a tub of snakes. Another engine followed, siren cycling from a low groan to an earsplitting wail with each hand crank. At the intersection with Fairmont fire engines were busy spraying water onto a fire raging in a storefront across the street from the Church Home and Infirmary.

Dozens of people were gawking at the scene, with more pressing in all the time. Jack slowly elbowed his way through the crowd and took a detour west toward Bethel, the next street north, until a cop blocked his way. "Keep going," he said, gesturing with his nightstick. "New policy says we got to keep streets clear for six blocks around any building fire."

Jack heaved a sigh and kept walking. He didn't care much for city rules and regulations, but he had missed the 1904 fire that razed downtown right to the edge of the harbor. The city big shots had to keep demonstrating their concern to citizens who remembered the fire—even if it meant doing things more for show than prevention.

Finding Sarah at the Hopkins Hospital turned out to be a drawn-out chore that involved questioning a series of bored clerks and harried nurses in two different buildings. He eventually arrived at a brick structure behind the hospital at the corner of Wolfe and Monument Streets. Inside, the place was all done up in fancy marble, carved wainscoting, and shiny wood floors. A row of distinguished old guys stared out from

paintings on the wall. None of them looked pleased to
see him.

"The boiler is downstairs."

Jack turned around to see a sharp-featured young man with
slick black hair. He wore a crisp white jacket and had a monocle
stuck in one eye socket.

"Boiler?"

"Do you speak English? I swear you tradesmen are getting
more bothersome every day." The man spoke loudly while
pointing down. "The. Boiler. Is. Downstairs."

"Listen, pal, I'm not here to fix your damn boiler." Blood was
hammering in Jack's ears as he stepped to within inches of
the guy.

"Oh. Well." The man somehow managed to seem arrogant
and afraid at the same time.

"I'm looking for Sarah Kennecott."

"Really, now. That is so *very* interesting." He smiled tightly
as he pointed a droopy finger attached to a limp hand. "She is
downstairs in the histology laboratory."

As Jack walked off, he heard the guy release a high titter.
How could Sarah stand to be around characters like that? A
stream of young people came rushing up the stairs as he went
down. Students. Out of two dozen, Jack saw one woman,
walking alone with her head lowered. Jack wondered if she got
better treatment in this place than he did. Different, probably,
but not necessarily better.

The laboratory was a long room with two rows of work-
benches. Eight round stools—the adjustable kind with seats
attached to long screws—were evenly spaced along each row.
Glass bottles of different shapes and sizes, along with some
complicated-looking instruments, clustered in spots along the
benches. A woman was at the far end, hunched over and examining something with a big magnifying glass. He recognized
Sarah from her mussed hair. She remained completely absorbed

in whatever she was inspecting and didn't look up as he
approached.

"Finding anything good?" Her whole body flinched before
she looked up, eyes big as saucers. "Sorry to have startled you."

She had a hand on her chest and was blinking rapidly. "Jack.
What are you doing here?"

"I brought you a present. Three, actually." Jack set the bag
with the glasses on the table next to her. "Found Nick, shot in
the head as if he killed himself. That doesn't make sense—
don't think he was the type. I smelled booze and thought it
was possible someone gave him a drink, got the drop, and shot
him. Found two glasses and a note. Didn't touch anything
with my bare hands because I figured you could check for
fingerprints—this stuff could be linked to what happened to
Lizzie."

"Have you reported the death to the police?"

"Why should I? They'll find him eventually."

"Jack. You must report the death immediately." She stood
and leaned within inches of him, talking with energy, hands
chopping the air like pale little hatchets. "The quicker the body
is brought in for an autopsy, the better chance we have for
obtaining evidence. It does not matter if the death is related to
our investigation or not."

"You're welcome, Sarah."

"I told you that I am assisting the acting medical examiner
today. It is my responsibility to assist with autopsies in connection with suspicious deaths."

"No need to bite my head off. Don't forget I'm just a simple
private dick, not a highfalutin bone carpenter like you."

"You are not simple." She raised both fists, shook them, and
took a deep breath. "Stop making that assertion. I find it
vexing." A student glared at them while making a loud shushing
sound.

Jack put his finger to his lips. "You're going to bring the cops

here yourself if you don't lower your voice. I'll call it in—
where's the telephone?"

Sarah sat down on the very edge of the stool. "There is a
telephone booth in the hall." She spoke in a labored whisper. "I
will alert Dr. Anson to expect the body."

"Don't you think he's going to be suspicious if you tell him
before the cops do?"

"You are correct. I must remain here until officially alerted."

"I'll be right back." Jack went into the empty hallway and
dialed the telephone. The police operator answered with dull
annoyance. When told of the dead body on Ann Street, the operator's tone ticked up to mild boredom. Jack left the booth and
went back to the lab. "I called, but there is no saying when the
cops will collect the cold meat, so you could have a wait."

"That is acceptable, as I have work to do," she said. "Did I
speak too harshly to you earlier?"

"You were pretty intense. I'm getting used to it."

"I value working with you." Her eyes flicked up to his and
then her head abruptly lowered.

"Yeah," said Jack. "I like you, too."

"You made a reasonable judgment in suspecting there may
be more to Nick Monkton's death than is readily apparent," said
Sarah, addressing the bench top. "And it may be that his death
relates to Lizzie's murder. Strictly speaking, you should have left
the evidence for the police to analyze. The degree to which the
police would have used the evidence in this instance is,
however, questionable, as you likely understood. You also did
well to keep the evidence intact."

"Thanks for the pep talk, but let's focus on how these
murders are linked."

"They may be associated, but proving that assertion requires
conclusive evidence."

"You still have that baseball card I gave you? Okay." Jack
smiled with a tinge of satisfaction. "Compare the prints on it to

those on the glasses. You might find a match to the bull who burned the card."

"Is your thought that Detective O'Toole killed Nick? That is possible." She began rooting among bagged objects near her.

"I'm going to the Rathskeller in the Hotel Kernan. Heard that Nick was always shooting his mouth off down there and somebody might have heard something useful." Sarah ignored him as she carefully opened a bag, one of her legs bouncing up and down like a steam triphammer.

Jack felt pretty good about pointing her to O'Toole as he left the building. It wasn't until he got on a streetcar that he felt a sudden, stabbing regret for not warning her to keep mum about it. Sarah was no blabbermouth, but if word got back to Snake Eyes, she would be in big time danger.

CHAPTER 15

SARAH—WEDNESDAY, OCTOBER 13, 1909, 2:00 P.M.

ab space in the Pathological Building had room to lay out several objects for comparison along with a tray, jars of metallic powder, a fine brush, and a large magnifying glass.

Wearing rubber surgical gloves, she carefully sprinkled dark powder on one side of the burned half of Jack's baseball card. Then she lightly twirled the brush over the powder to reveal many fingerprints, most of which were smudged or overlapping. She repeated the same process for the flip side of the card and found several clear prints. The next step was to dust Jack's china cup from his visit to her house earlier in the day. Brushing revealed his prints along the cup's side.

Comparing prints from both objects allowed her to identify thumb and forefinger marks from the card that were from Detective O'Toole. She turned to the repellent burlap containing the tumblers from Nick's death scene. Both glasses had separate finger marks from two different people, neither of them O'Toole. Presumably one set of prints would match Nick's. The other set of prints belonged to someone who was with Nick shortly before—and perhaps during—his death.

She was nearly finished writing up her observations when Dr. Anson's assistant strutted into the lab and carefully inserted his monocle before addressing her. "Doctor. Your presence is required in the dissection amphitheater. It is a most urgent matter. Come immediately, if you please."

The amphitheater was the largest room in the Pathological Building. A semicircular tier of seats ascended from a small, well-lit stage dominated by a large metal table holding a sheet-draped body. An assortment of people stood chatting among themselves in the well. "Sarah." Anson looked at her closely, eyes bulging under the bright lights. "The police just brought in a fellow who committed suicide. It is a simple case. Are you capable of taking the lead in conducting the autopsy?"

Sarah kept her gaze on his pointy tuft of hair for a long moment, wondering why her mentor had incited Dr. Macdonald to question her mental health. Why he—or someone who very much looked like him—was in a burlesque hall consorting with Nick and Lizzie. Looking at his bandaged hand, she recalled the bloody chisel Jack had found in Lizzie's room. Maybe Lizzie used it to cut Anson's hand before he hit her in the head. It was difficult to think of her mentor in this way even though his behavior was suspicious.

"If you are not feeling well, Doctor, I can bring in someone else." Anson shuffled his feet. "It's quite all right. Really. I know your nerves are unsettled of late."

"No. I am quite well and ready to examine the body." She turned to face the knot of people milling around. "Attention all!" Sarah called loudly and the talking stopped. "Everyone but Dr. Anson must leave the well."

No one moved. A rough-looking man in an ill-fitting suit poked at Anson. "Doc, you mean to say this little girl here is going to slice him open? Is that all proper and fitting?"

"Yes, Detective, yes. Dr. Kennecott appears well enough, I

189

suppose . . ." Anson paused ever so slightly. "In any event, this is not a hard case."

"Yeah, guess it don't matter since the guy blew his brains out. I want to get this off the books fast as possible." The detective hawked up phlegm, looked around, and spit into a stained handkerchief. "First time in fifteen years on the force I seen a broad cut into a carcass. Modern times are getting crazy, tell you what." He gave Sarah a look before walking off.

The two doctors put on white surgical gowns. Sarah washed her hands and put on surgical gloves while Anson stood by the sink. "Doctor," she said, "how did you hurt your hand?"

"Oh, didn't I tell you?" He laughed and rubbed the gauze around his wound. "Perhaps not. I cut it on a cadaver's cracked rib. I suppose I should wear those new gloves to lessen the chance of hurting myself again." She made a mental note that, at the very least, his story about the hand injury remained consistent.

The body was on the dissecting table, covered with a sheet. Anson pulled the drape back and drew a quick breath before looking away. A stout older nurse with a commanding air stood by with a clipboard. "Do you know the deceased, Doctor?" The nurse spoke in a high, dramatic voice.

"No." Anson removed his glasses and pinched his nose hard enough to leave angry red spots. "I have never seen this man before in my life. I swear."

Sarah scanned the body. The only sign of recent injury was a blackened hole in the right temple.

"I suppose, sweetie, elephants stampeded the man to death?" She could barely make out the coroner sitting in the darkened amphitheater. "Let me state that I distinctly object to this woman's involvement here."

"The way you're slurring you ain't in any condition to distinctly state a damn thing," said the city detective, who was sitting nearby. "And by the way, that's the carcass of Nick Monkton. I've run him into the station more than once."

"We have a white male, approximately twenty-five years of age, presenting with an apparent bullet wound to the right temple," said Sarah.

"Dr. Anson, may we please follow the proper procedure?" said the nurse while giving Sarah a baleful look.

Anson nodded vigorously. "Oh, yes. We are in the habit of having the head nurse start autopsies by presenting known details about the decedent."

The nurse slowly lifted her pince-nez and put the lenses on her nose. She cleared her throat with her hand to her chest and moved the clipboard back and forth numerous times as she sought the best focus. Sarah clenched her fists and looked at the body until the nurse finally began reading in a mannered falsetto.

"An anonymous telephone call received at the Eastern District police station at approximately one forty-five p.m. this afternoon reported the body of a deceased male—identified as Mr. Nick Monkton—located in a stable on Ann Street, in Fells Point, city of Baltimore. Responding officers found the body seated in a chair, expired. A pistol, thirty-two-caliber, was found under his right hand. One gunshot wound to the brain, fired at close range, is present on the right side of the deceased's skull. This appears to be an obvious case of suicide."

"I insist upon holding all judgments as to cause of death in abeyance until the examination is complete." Sarah didn't look up from the body. "What other evidence was at the scene?"

"Dr. Anson." The nurse glared at Sarah. "If I may be allowed to continue without these rude interruptions." She raised her chin, a hand on hip. With more nods from Anson, she slowly moved her gaze to the clipboard and cleared her throat with a series of audible hums.

"For God's sake, woman, you ain't delivering the Gettysburg

Address," said the detective. "Spit it out." The nurse shot an icy glare into the darkness of the amphitheater.

"Nurse, please proceed," said Anson in a pleading tone.

"The police recovered no additional evidence at the scene," said the nurse.

"Wait—what about the suicide note?" Anson asked with a quaver in his voice. "Are you quite sure such a note was not found with the body?"

"Doctor, did I not make myself clear?" The nurse glared over her pince-nez.

"Well, yes, yes. But perhaps the police should recheck the scene? Suicides often leave a message behind."

"Forget it, Doc," said the detective. "I've already wasted enough time on this riffraff. He did a gun croak, clear as day."

Anson twisted his hands together while mumbling under his breath.

"If there is nothing else, then, Doctor." The head nurse slowly removed her pince-nez, stood regally erect, and strutted away.

"You heard what I said," said the detective to Sarah. "We see lots of suicides every month and most of them don't bother writing no farewell postcard. Let's wrap this up."

"He's right," said the coroner. "Just cut him open if you need to and get this finished. I want to round up a jury and get the inquest form signed as quickly as possible."

"I will now proceed to examine the front and back of the body." Sarah found nothing unusual apart from the gunshot wound. There were no major cuts or bruises. The limited lividity indicated a recent death. The fingernails held no blood or fibers. She opened the mouth and smelled whiskey. She made the abdominal incision and saw that the stomach was irritated and its contents limited—the man had not eaten recently. She emptied what there was in the stomach into a sample jar, noting a distinctive melon-like odor. Sarah cut the chest and cracked open the rib cage. The heart and lungs were normal. After sawing the skull and dissecting the brain tissue she declared that Nick had died from the gunshot. The amphitheater greeted her statement with derisive snorts.

"I am not, however, prepared to declare this a suicide," said Sarah. "I noticed something about the stomach contents that compels further testing."

"Yeah, he could've eaten a bad oyster that gave him such a headache he had no choice but to shoot himself. Manslaughter by seafood." The coroner and the detective laughed.

"Are you sure about the need for further testing?" Anson fidgeted with his glasses and caused them to slip down to the tip of his nose before ramming them back into place.

"It is possible this man was drugged, immobilized, and then shot. That would make the case a homicide."

"Yes, yes—I suppose that's possible." Anson thrust his hands into his trouser pockets and jingled coins energetically. "Unlikely, however."

"I will also need to obtain fingerprints from the deceased. I can do it myself with the ink pad and sheets of notepaper I brought with me."

Anson blinked rapidly with his mouth silently opening and closing before walking off. As she listened to the coin-clinking recede, Sarah suppressed an urge to chase after and confront him about Nick, about Lizzie. The man would offer no useful information. He might even retaliate by telling Dr. Macdonald that she was growing more unstable. She must gather information about him in secret.

As she lifted the body's left hand to take fingerprints, she noticed the fingers and palm were heavily stained with what looked like dried India ink. The top knuckle of the middle finger also had a pronounced callus—the type produced by a pen or pencil—on the side next to the index finger. The right hand had no ink stains and no similar callus. Nick Monkton likely was left-handed. He would have written his music with that hand. More than likely he would have shot himself with his left hand —not the right, under which the pistol was found.

Rushing back to her lab space, Sarah put a sample of Nick's stomach fluid into a test tube. She added a single drop of ammonium sulfate. The solution turned a cloudy yellow, indicating the presence of chloral hydrate, commonly known as knockout drops. Since it wasn't necessary to heat the tube to get this result, the amount of chloral hydrate was high—more than enough to render the man unconscious prior to the gunshot. She hurriedly wrote up her findings and took them to Dr. Anson. She presented the case for murder while he nervously shuffled papers on his desk and said little.

Sarah wanted to do more work with the fingerprint evidence, but it was almost 9:00 p.m. She had to endure the Oyster Banquet tomorrow—and she needed rest to muster the necessary stamina. In addition, she needed to get to the hospital library before they closed. The librarian had promised to get her the writings of Dr. Eugen Bleuler on mental illness.

Lizzie's—and now Nick's—deaths presented a puzzle that was far from solved. She tapped the workbench with her finger, wondering what to do. The more she worked on this case, the more people around her thought she was deranged. But she was determined to solve Lizzie's—and now Nick's—murder. The only option left was to work fast. Very fast.

CHAPTER 16

JACK—WEDNESDAY, OCTOBER 13, 1909, 5:00 P.M.

*L*eaving Johns Hopkins Hospital, Jack jumped onto a westbound streetcar.

He was headed to Kernan's Rathskeller, a place where dancers, musicians, and other self-styled bohemians liked to congregate. They rolled out of bed in the afternoon and ambled into the place for their first drink or first dose of whatever drug they preferred. Jack was comfortable with the crowd, for the most part. They didn't like rules and they didn't like cops.

Soon he was on the Charles Street trolley headed north. The late afternoon sun brightly lit buildings on one side of the street and cast the other side into shadow. His eye kept falling on churches. Carvings of Christ and Moses—both looking far too otherworldly to notice traffic—sat on either side of the cloudy stained-glass window of St. Paul's on Saratoga Street.

Crossing Mulberry, he got a view of the massive Catholic cathedral. The cross-topped cathedral dome blocked out the sky behind the luxurious archbishop's mansion, which ran the length of the block to his left.

Stepping off the car at the corner of Franklin, the first thing that caught his attention was the blocky, blinding whiteness of the First Independent Christian Church. A carved angel holding a scroll stood out on the wall near the top. The scroll had writing in some foreign language—it probably said something like "fat chance you got without Jesus, pal."

A little farther down Franklin Street he passed the Maryland Academy of Sciences and then its next-door neighbor, Hazazer's Hall. A block farther west across Howard put him on Kernan's Corner, named after the guy who owned nearly all the property on the northwestern slice of the intersection.

Kernan's newest venture was a "million-dollar triple enterprise" featuring the hotel bearing his name, along with two nearby theaters. The Maryland Theater devoted itself to "classy vaudeville attractions," while the Auditorium Theater offered "the best musical comedies and extravaganzas." The old Academy Hotel sat square on the corner's tip. A few doors north from that was the Maryland Academy of Music, where Clara had performed in her highbrow play.

The entrance to the rathskeller was down a flight of stairs and through a dark wooden door studded with iron nails. Inside, the space was huge—easily more than eighty feet wide and a hundred feet deep. The ceiling was low and held up by four massive columns clustered in the center, making the place look like a hard-rock mine. The floor was a showy mix of colored stones set in mortar, and the walls held old-time engravings of famous politicians alongside chintzy chromolithographs of prancing circus animals. Big round tables and clusters of chairs filled the room. The most dominant feature was a sixty-foot-long bar carved from solid white marble.

Jack spent a minute scanning the depths of the joint before heading to a table in a far corner where a dozen men and a couple of women were laughing it up. They had the right look—the men a mix of black and white, all dressed in flashy shirts and ties and wearing expensive hats. The women's faces were bright with paint and powder. One gal had her legs across the lap of a guy who was massaging her calves. Most everyone had a cigarette in one hand and a glass in the other.

"Hey, I'm looking for anyone who's talked with Nick Monkton lately." The chatter stopped. Jack looked at the guy rubbing the girl's legs. "What about you, Romeo—know the guy?"

"Sheesh, you fly cops don't fool anyone."

"I'm not an undercover cop. I'm a private dick looking into Lizzie Sullivan's murder. And the murder of Nick, too."

That brought out gasps. "Nick's dead?" asked a young woman with an enormous green feather in her hat.

"Yeah. Bumped off a couple of hours ago." The girl ran a hand over her mouth, smudging her blazing red lip paint.

"Look. If any of you give a hoot about Nick or Lizzie, you need to talk with me. Otherwise you can bet nobody's ever going to know who killed them. And, you know, that's really just okay." Jack pointed at the red-lipped girl. "Just have another drink and don't bother wondering who's going to give a rat's ass after you get knocked off."

"What do you want me to say?" She pulled out a small mirror from her bag and inspected her mouth with disapproval. "Nick was always flapping his gums. I can't hardly remember everything he said."

"I'm most interested in what he talked about within the past few days. Especially about a con or a get-rich-quick racket."

"Man, Nick got what was coming to him," said a black man wearing a fancy fedora.

"I'm listening."

The man stood up. "Let's have a seat at the bar. You can buy me a highball."

They sat at the far end of the marble bar. "Always wondered about the point of a highball," said Jack after managing, with some trouble, to get branch water. "Why thin your whiskey?"

"I'm a buck and wing man with three shows to do tonight. Can't dance if I'm all liquored up." The man grinned. "And if you want to charm the ladies it pays to nurse a drink and stay on your game."

"Yeah? Water does the job even better. Why'd you say Nick had it coming?"

"Saw him before dawn on Sunday. Hit me up for some cash —said he had to hide out for a while. Promised to pay me back soon."

"What else did he say?"

"He was jagged as anything—flying on coke, yammering nonstop. Tells me he's worked up because something got stolen that Lizzie was keeping for him. In the next breath he says Lizzie croaked under a john and that he planned to blackmail the man. I said something like, that's hard-handed, cashing in on Lizzie's death. Nick laughs like a maniac and says no, what's hard is him putting a bullet into Lizzie's dead body because some other guy will pay him for it big time. Evil dude."

"You willing to testify in court about that?"

The man took a long sip of his drink. "Ridiculous question. 'Course not."

"Okay—what about Nick's plans to get money from the two guys he mentioned?"

"Didn't want to hear any more from the man, so I walked away. What I can tell you is that a day earlier Nick was going on about how his slave great-granny died and left him proof that was going to make him a rich man. Maybe that's what Lizzie was holding for him that got stolen. Just speculating."

"Proof? What kind of proof?"

"Got no idea."

"Maybe evidence about some big shot with secret Negro blood?"

The guy lit up a cigarette and spit out little pieces of tobacco. "Brother, you've got no idea how sore a subject that is. Every time you, a white man, walk around downtown you get respect. People treat you like you belong there. Like you're a man. Now try and see it from my point of view. When I walk downtown, it's a different story. Nobody wants me there. I either get avoided, or I get too much attention, especially from the cops. The whole idea is to treat me less than a man, less than human. It's built into the system."

"Sure." Jack shrugged. "I'm hep."

"I'm not calling you a liar, exactly. I'll just say that I've never met a white man who really is hep to what I'm talking about." He shook his head. "Nick was like a lot of light-skinned people. He passed as white because he wanted respect. He wanted a better shake. Don't blame him for making that choice. But it takes a toll. You got to lie, got to reject your family, got to deny who you are. Eats away at your soul. And the whole time you're worried that someone's going to find out the truth and kick you in the ass. Personally, that's why I think Nick turned bad. Nerves got to him."

Jack took a gulp of water. "You got any more ideas about what Nick was up to?"

"Nope. How'd the man die?"

"Made to look like he blew his brains out."

The man shook his head. "No way he'd do that. Nick was way too vain about his looks."

"What about Lizzie? Know anything more about her or any of her other gentlemen friends? She chummy with any of the girls over there?" Jack gestured back toward the table.

"Naw. But there's another gal who was tight with Lizzie. Name's Lulu LaRue."

"Come on."

"That's what she calls herself. Lots of personality. Former high-kicker—was a headliner in burlesque theaters around town until she got herself in a little too deep with dope. Reduced now to whoring at Macy's cabaret down on North Paca

Street." The man stepped away from the bar. "That's it for me, sport."

"One more thing—know who won the Series this afternoon?"

"Pirates, eight to four. Now it's back to Detroit for game six. And game seven, if need be."

"Thanks."

Jack crossed the vast space and threw open the door to the stairs. He was ready to squint against the daylight, but it was getting dark outside. On the sidewalk he rubbed his chin, wondering how much cash it would take to convince the buck and wing man to testify. Right now, that looked like the only way to get the charges against Shaw dropped. And collect those five Gs.

He asked for the time and learned it was 6:10 p.m.—late to meet Clara. Shady Clara who knew a whole lot more than she let on. Lucky the Hotel Kernan was right next door. Jack started going up the hotel steps two at a time when a gunshot sounded behind him on the street.

He froze, anger and fear boiling as the spirits wailed all around him. There was that bloody little brown woman again, right in front of him holding out her hollering baby. He grabbed her brightly patterned jacket. "I'm sorry, sorry, sorry—but you got to leave me alone!"

"Come on now, son. Ease up. Cast off the demon." The ghosts vanished, leaving him holding a thin old guy by his preacher lapels. Jack let go, and the guy edged away while smoothing the front of his come-to-Jesus frock coat. "Son, I was just asking you to join us at our next meeting at the Men's Abstinence Tabernacle Mission. You got to renounce alcohol, and I mean now. Take this literature. Go on, take it. Come pray with us. Fill yourself with the love of God rather than whiskey."

Jack stared at the pamphlet. "Gunshots. Heard them."

"Just an automobile backfire. You're in a real bad way, boy—I can tell because I've been there myself. Hearing things, seeing things. The barroom does that to a man. The devil enters you through the bottle and won't leave until you quit. Or die."

"Sorry, padre. Had you confused with someone else. Got to run." *This thing with the ghosts is getting bad,* Jack thought as he continued up the steps. He took a quick look behind and saw the preacher buttonholing another sinner on the sidewalk.

The Kernan lobby did a good job looking swank without being too stuffy. Big marble columns hit the high ceiling with flowery golden spreads. The furniture was made of highly polished mahogany. The massive reception desk was a quarter circle chunk of gleaming white marble.

He didn't have much of a chance to look around before Clara was on his arm. "Hello, Jack. Golly gracious, I'm hungry enough to eat a darned horse. Hey, what happened to your cheek?" She was still using that phony hick accent while flashing a killer smile with dimples on both cheeks. Her eyes seemed bigger and more hypnotic than ever—she had little black lines drawn around them. Her eyebrows were as sleek and russet-shiny as fox fur. She was dressed to the nines, with a big hat loaded up with feathers to set off her orange hair, which was styled in fiery swirls. She wore a flashy, low cut dress made of shimmering pale-blue fabric trimmed in lace. The woman was so stunning he decided to play along with her act for a while.

"Farm accident—cut myself with a sickle. Let's go to a restaurant just down the street. They serve a good country supper that'll remind you of back home. And by the way, you look like a real dish. Did your Pa have to sell another couple of cows or something?"

"Oh, gee whiz, thanks for noticing my silly little outfit. My cousin lent it to me." As they stepped outside, Clara moved close to him. "Oh, it's chilly, and I didn't bring my wrap." Jack took off his suit jacket and put it around her shoulders. She pressed close enough for him to feel her body heat as they walked the short distance to the restaurant.

Once in the place, he put the jacket back on. Her hands lingered on him as she smoothed the garment, all the while beaming a big, happy smile. Her vanilla-maraschino smell was strong and sweet. As they went to their table, Jack noticed everyone openly gawking at Clara. Several men shot him an awestruck look as if to say, "Buddy, you've got to have something real special going for you." There's nothing like squiring a beautiful woman to give a guy a cheap boost of self-worth.

Before sitting down, Clara ran both her hands lightly down his arm, causing him to shiver involuntarily. "I'm tingling all over, too," she said, her voice a low purr.

She was good. Like any accomplished performer, she knew exactly how to play to her audience. "Just hoping to clear some stuff up with you," he said.

"Sure. Ask me anything. Just don't get me too tipsy—I might say something naughty." He held her chair while she sat. The first thing she did was pick up a butter knife and check her reflection, turning her head one way, then another. "Be a dear and get me a Jamaica rum cocktail, will you, Jack?" The drink didn't last long, and Clara got another. Dinner then arrived—a bowl of soup and a rib-eye steak for him and lamb chops for her. Clara kept nattering about how dirty and unsafe the city was compared to the country, making occasional teary references to her poor dead sister. Jack finally had enough.

"Knock off the act, Clara. You're not playing to the peanut gallery while doing *House of Dolls*."

The fork loaded with chop paused briefly before continuing to her mouth. She chewed daintily for a moment. "Well, it seems you're a decent private detective after all." Shorn of its rube affect, her voice was deep and cultured, with each word pronounced clearly and forcefully. "And, by the way, it's *A Doll's House*. I played Nora Helmer, a woman who leaves her

husband to seek freedom and see the world. It's a natural part
for me."

"As natural as you demanding a slice of the family inheritance from your sister?"

"Ah, yes. Filthy lucre." She swept out her arm dramatically.
"'If money go before, all ways do lie open.' That's Shakespeare."

Her slipperiness was getting under his skin. "Cut the crap."
He leaned in close over the table, and her simpering smile faded.
"You killed Lizzie, didn't you?"

"Don't be a fool. We argued, but I loved her. She was the
only family I had."

"All you care about is coin. Here's what I think happened."
Jack gripped the sides of the table and made it shake. "You
dropped in on Lizzie to demand your cut of the family cash. She
tells you it's gone and laughs in your face. Then to rub it in, she
tells you her man Nick has a line on a ton of dough—and you're
not getting any of that, either. You gave her a shove, she fell,
and—"

"No!" Clara slammed her hand down on the table. Heads
swiveled to look at them. She leaned in, leaving their faces
inches apart. Jack had never seen such a fierce glare from a
woman. She looked ready to tear him apart.

"Impressive," he said. "When do you switch on the tears?"

She leaned back and drained her second cocktail. "Look, I
don't blame you for doubting me. Pretending is what I do.
Whatever it takes to put on a good show. And I'll admit I can be
a teeny bit deceptive offstage, too. Lizzie wasn't like that. She
couldn't help but to be sweet and honest all the time. She liked
everybody—just the nicest person you could ever hope to meet.
I could never hurt her. Can't believe anyone could."

"You want money. That matters more than anything to you."

"You talk like money's better than sex. Phooey—cash is just
a means to an end. I'm going to California." She tilted her long,
milky neck and struck a pose worthy of a theater poster. "I'm a

howling success onstage, darling. I've done Molière, Strindberg, Chekhov. But the future's onscreen—in motion pictures, or as some fuddy-duddies call them, plays without words. They're getting longer and more sophisticated all the time—Vitagraph is rolling out a four-reel version of *Les Misérables* as we speak. That kind of stuff's a cinch for me to play. And the censors will eventually stop getting their knickers in a twist and let the talented directors show powerful, artistic pictures all around the country. There's this fellow Griffith I know who's making a picture at Biograph called *A Corner in Wheat*. It's a dramatic story about how a tycoon forces up the price of bread and sends farmers into poverty. Griffith's the guy who told me to move out to Los Angeles—he's sure that's the place where the best moving pictures are going to be made. And I want to do more than act. I'm going to direct, maybe even start my own production company."

"Stop gassing on about yourself and let's get back to Lizzie."

"Get me another cocktail first." Clara leaned back and regarded him with a cool look until her drink arrived. "I went to see Lizzie twice recently." She took a long pull from the glass. "First time was last Friday. And yeah, I pushed for my share of the family inheritance. She's all guilty because she spent it. I yell, and she starts apologizing, crying—then says they have a book worth a king's ransom. She's busy promising me money when Nick walks in and shuts her up. I tell him to leave her alone, and he takes a swing at me. Lucky he was drunk and missed. Then I left."

"What book? What was in it that was so valuable?"

"I stew for a while and worry that Nick's going to run off himself with all the money and leave Lizzie high and dry. I go back early Monday morning, hoping to find Lizzie and warn her. The door's cracked open, and I find her shot dead." Clara's eyes filled, and a single tear rolled down her cheek before she lifted her glass and finished her cocktail. "I tell the landlord, and the cops show up. I went back to my hotel and got an idea—what if Lizzie kept a diary about some bigwig lover? Perhaps I can find out who the guy is and, just maybe, I can scare him into giving me some cash to blow town. I didn't know what else to do. My show's over and I'm broke. So, I put on my farm-girl outfit and went to the cop station to find out whatever I could. Then you showed up and started asking about Nick and Lizzie. Figured I'd get friendly and maybe you'd give me some leads. Pretty smart, huh? No, Clara, it sure didn't turn out that way." She lit up a cigarette and inhaled deeply.

"Lizzie's room was tossed pretty good," said Jack. "Seems like someone was looking hard for something—like that book. Maybe you found the thing."

"Her room was already torn apart when I found her. Anyway, you don't know Lizzie. She's not dopey enough to leave something valuable in plain sight. And if I had that book, why would I still be here? Believe me, I'd cash in quick and catch a train west." Clara set her smoke in an ashtray and poked at her food. "You aren't the only one who thinks I might have it. A man's been following me all day. Don't think he's one of my theater fans."

"I know," said Jack, eyeing the city dick sitting nearby. "He's right behind you. Don't look."

"Great, just great." She dropped her fork. "Tell me, Jack. Do you know who killed my sister?"

"I'm afraid your work to rope me in has gone for nothing, sweetheart. All I know is the guy they arrested is probably innocent. And I bet you know a lot more about that book than you say."

"No, I swear I don't." She dabbed at her lips with a napkin, careful not to smudge her lip paint. "Hey, you ever act? Like on a stage?"

"Think you can change the subject that easily?"

"I'm serious. You look like John Barrymore, the famous

actor. Dark hair, nice eyes, roman nose, big chin. Actually, you look better than him because you're taller."

"Don't waste your breath." Her gall was really something. She'd have him curled around her finger if he had an ounce of vanity.

"You've got the perfect looks for moving pictures and maybe ought to come to Los Angeles, too. Picture acting's easy—no lines to recite or anything. All you'd have to do with that face of yours is flash three big expressions: anger, joy, and lust. Got the first one down pat. I can help you work on the last two." She tapped the ash off her cigarette, took a puff, and blew smoke at him playfully.

"I'll bet you've helped more than one guy act like a perfect sap."

She looked hurt for a moment before drilling him with a dead-level gaze. "Maybe you prefer the company of that lady doctor. Your funny little friend."

"Leave her out of this."

"Touched a nerve, I see." Clara's face went blank as she sat straight and stiff in her chair. "I am Jack's mechanical automaton. I am dull as ditchwater. I do, however, have the ability to operate in the dark so that my imperfect approximation of a womanly appearance does not distract Jack from his unpleasant human desires." It was an uncanny imitation of Sarah, right down to her flat, inflectionless voice.

"Knock that off right now or we're done."

Clara snapped back to herself in an eye blink. "Serves you right for that crack about me playing men for saps. I'm not a monster. I'm human. I've got feelings."

Jack looked into her huge eyes, which were pools of awesome beauty. The sight was breathtaking—like the Pacific meeting the cliffs at Big Sur in California or the turtles swimming across the Hinatuan Enchanted River in the Philippines.

Or maybe it was like staring down into a gorge with a mighty urge to jump into the void. He shifted his gaze away.

"Can you walk me back to my hotel?"

He wasn't going to get any more useful information out of her. "Yeah, sure."

They walked in silence to the hotel and then into the lobby. He wasn't surprised when she stepped close, her breath hot on his neck. "Jack. I know you think I'm a schemer. But right now, I'm just a girl who feels sad and lonely. Not to mention scared to death of the guy who's following me. I'm leaving tomorrow." Clara pressed her body into him, rubbing an ankle against his lower leg. "Will you stay with me tonight? Please?"

Despite his better judgment, excitement ripped through him. Clara was the kind of woman a man dreams about. The kind of woman a guy would die to have and, afterward, leave a smiling corpse. And here she was, all ready to go. "Sorry, Clara. I've got an urgent appointment at a cabaret down the block." She gave a little gasp and put a knuckle in her mouth, body trembling. "I don't think you have much to worry about with that shadow of yours. He's a city detective. Probably just interested in who you're talking to. And I'm strictly a small fry who nobody cares about."

"Well, aren't you a hard-boiled egg. I'd accuse you of not liking girls, but it's pretty obvious that you do." She pushed off against him, stood back, and applauded softly. "Bravo for your own little performance. Good-bye, Jack."

He knew it wasn't good-bye. She hadn't strung him along this far to give up just yet.

JACK WASN'T in a good frame of mind to visit a fleshpot. Clara's invitation left him wildly stirred up. But mixing business and pleasure where he was headed was a sure-fire plan for disaster.

Macy's cabaret was close by, just blocks down Howard Street from St. Mary's Seminary. Jack always got a kick out of how the sinful and the virtuous were jammed together in the city. It was the time of evening when the crowds were changing from respectable-seeming to shady-looking. People one might see in the daylight as laborers, clerks, or businessmen now could be taken as thieves, strong-arm men, even killers. There was something about nighttime in the city that brought home that anyone —including himself—could be a victim or a criminal, depending on fate and circumstance.

A rowdy gaggle crowded the sidewalk outside Macy's. Macy himself was long dead, but the guy who ran the place continued the founder's willingness to pay big bribes to the authorities. Employment of off-duty cops further sealed the deal. Their supposed job was to maintain order. Mainly they were there to bless the liquor and vice violations. He passed a short, broad-chested guy in a dirty slouch hat who was yelling at another man while waving his arms around. The arm-waver lurched backward and bumped into Jack.

"Excuse me, bub," said Jack, continuing on his way. He was ready when the guy threw a sucker punch, and easily dodged it. "Sorry, little casino. I got no time for a fight." The man roared and charged. Jack stepped aside like some kind of freak show bullfighter and the guy crashed into a group of toughs. Fists flew as he made his way inside.

The place made it easy to separate a customer from his money. Straight ahead was a bar backed by a long mirror, which made the liquor bottles lined up in front of it shimmer like a desert mirage. Next to the bar was an iron door that led to a gambling hell where, rumor had it, a high-stakes poker game had been going on continuously for three years. Off to the left was a small stage where a band made up of a cornet, piano, and fiddle banged out a hot song while a couple of underclothed women danced a halfhearted hootchy-cootchy in front of leering drunks parked at rickety tables. To the right was a row of curtained cubicles into which women led men.

Jack went straight to the bar and put his foot on the rail. He didn't get anything to drink. This was the kind of place that served stuff worse than the usual coffin varnish—they used cheap chemicals to stretch their liquor and give customers a special kick. The glasses were rarely washed, so even getting water came with a risk of some nasty additive. It didn't matter because he had company less than five minutes after walking into the joint.

"Honey, how about we go someplace private?" He turned to see a rangy woman in a sparkly, low-cut top and flimsy skirt that barely made it to her knees. The gal was on the downside of her career—whatever freshness she'd started with was long gone. She pressed up against him, a sad substitute for Clara.

"Looking for Lulu LaRue," said Jack. "She around?"

"Well, ain't you the picky one." She put two fingers in her mouth and gave an earsplitting whistle. "Hey, Lou. You got a command performance." The woman took her charms to the next guy hunched over the bar.

"Hello, baby." A woman came rushing over, skirt bunched around her thighs. "You got great timing. Little Lulu just chucked her crummy old tights and shoes." She lifted a bare foot for his inspection, wiggling toes with a chipped coat of blood-red paint on the nails. "Let's go." She scurried into one of the cubicles and yanked the curtain shut after him. The only furniture was a cot with a filthy sheet stained various shades of brown and a rickety bentwood chair. Jack took the chair.

"Don't get many customers as handsome as you, baby." Lulu was painfully thin with dry bottle-blond hair and dark circles under bulging, hophead eyes. Her cheekbones stuck out like bright pink doorknobs. She was fidgety and kept scratching her arms. "That'll be two dollars for the basic, in advance. You want anything else, got to pay up first, too." She held out a shaky hand. Needle marks, some oozing pus, covered her forearm. Jack gave her two fives.

"Woo-hoo!" She jumped up and down with the money held in front of her like a kid with a lollipop. "Baby's going around the world tonight." She did a quick high-step dance, spun about gracefully, and kicked a leg straight over her head. She wore nothing under her skirt.

"Sit down, Lulu. Just want to talk."

Her manic smile didn't fade as she dropped her leg and glided onto the cot. "You want me to tell you that you're a naughty boy, right? About how much you need spanking." She shook a scolding finger at him. "Tell Momma just how bad a boy you are and I'll whoop your bare bottom as hard as you need."

Jack sighed, feeling exhausted. "I want to talk about Lizzie Sullivan. About some crooked plan she and Nick Monkton had, maybe for blackmail. A plan that looks to have gotten them both killed."

Her smile disappeared and her intensity drained away. "You ain't a cop. Too nice."

"Private detective. I'm investigating Lizzie's murder."

"Poor Lizzie. I hoped she was going to make it. Really wanted to see someone get out of the game and live a decent life." She scratched an armpit.

"You're injecting dope," said Jack. "Looks like you've been doing it awhile."

"Started with jabbing coke. Added morphine shots to keep me on the ground. Smoke opium, hashish, and whatever else, too." She fished in a pocket and came out with a marijuana cigarette and a match. "When I'm on the hop, it's the best thing that ever happened to me. Different story when I ain't, of course." She looked up at him. "Met Lizzie before I got kicked out of burlesque. She was wonderful nice. Stood by me after I ended up here. Kept telling me I still had my looks, that I should get back on the big stage." She gave a humorless laugh.

"You know anything about her cashing in on a lover?"

"She had plenty of lovers, sweetie. Got to make hay while the sun shines, as my daddy used to say. That son of a bitch." The cigarette glowed as she took a drag, filling the cubicle with sweet smoke. "Last time I saw Lizzie she talked about coming into serious money, it's true. Seems her pimp got a Bible from his great-granny that spilled some dirt on some big shot. I told her she was nuts if she thought that creep Nick was going to give her a dime. The girl was so darn sweet and trusting."

"She say anything more about that Bible?"

"Nick didn't want to have it on him when guys came looking. He gave it to Lizzie for safekeeping. Bastard knew she would guard it with her life even though he treated her bad." She swung her legs up onto the cot and effortlessly bent in half to lay her cheek on her shins. The woman still had the flexibility of a gifted dancer. "Lizzie was just that kind of person."

"I keep hearing what a swell gal Lizzie was. Makes me sad."

"Yeah." Lulu popped up to a sitting position and took another drag off her smoke. "She was good and kind, always had nice things to say. And so funny—couldn't help laughing when she was around. Like how she used to say words made her see colors. Swore up and down that every time she heard 'love' she saw sky blue. Hearing 'dance' made her see the same kind of green as the new leaves on a potted palm. Said she was that way since she was a kid. Yeah, and she used to tell this blue joke— how did it go . . . ." She scrunched her face and tapped the side of her head lightly with a finger.

"That's okay. I've got to run."

"Hey, wait, I got it. "How can you be sure a preacher man doesn't look at naked girls"? She looked at him while trying to suppress a giggle.

"I give up."

211

"Because he always blows the lamp out first thing!" She gave a silly, high-pitched laugh while pounding the cot. "Lizzie said she thought of it herself after she got involved with some real serious Holy Joe guy recently."

"She say anything else about the guy, like his name?"

"No—just that he was big deal. That's all I know."

"Thanks for everything, Lulu. You're a real doll."

Her big smile came back. "Hey, thanks." She put a hand on his thigh. "You want a little something? Still got time for you."

"I'm tempted but got to run."

"Okay, baby."

Jack took a last look at her. The woman's vigor had kept her going longer than most in her situation. Drugs and whoring were now dragging her down fast. Soon she would get kicked out of this dump and have to solicit on the street. It was only a matter of time before she shot up the wrong dose, picked the wrong john, or found some other way to die. Poor gal. There was nothing he could do but feel twice as sad as before.

He left the place with a plan to go home and sleep so that he could be in better shape to visit Sarah at her swank house tomorrow morning. He'd get a haircut and try to swing a slightly classier look for their meeting.

After a block, his mood darkened further. Drunks were relieving themselves in doorways or sprawling in the gutter. A well-dressed guy—a prime target for lush rollers—staggered past, shouting incoherently. A rat-faced pimp worked hard to pull Jack into a dance hall—an even sleazier joint than Macy's—with promises of little girls in pigtails. When Jack kept walking, the guy shouted about the freshest, youngest boys available anywhere.

And fear not them which kill the body, but are not able to kill the soul: but rather fear him which is able to destroy both soul and body in hell. The thundering Bible voice stopped him in his tracks. This wasn't the voice of God calling. At least Jack wasn't bughouse enough to think that just yet.

No, the voice was a reminder of his older sister. She had been a bad combination—brilliant, manipulative, and stone crazy. His parents thought of her as filled with the Holy Spirit and stayed out of her way.

His sister told him at age five that God had made them superior to other people because the two of them had a divine mission to preach the Bible. When he lagged in that mission, she spent all day and most of the night calling out chapter names and verse numbers and judging how well Jack could recite the text. Any mistake led to the switch, the belt, or worse. He was so desperate to get things right he would lay awake at night listening to a voice repeat the Good Book from cover to cover repeatedly. He eventually learned the Bible word for word, but also came to despise hypocrisy and reject the idea that he was better than anyone else.

The Bible voice stopped after he ran away at eleven. He was big for his age and able to get work as a farm laborer. At sixteen a stable owner in Pittsburgh hired him to take care of the horses, and two years later he was managing the whole operation. Then the owner died, the property was sold, and Jack was back on the street.

The army cavalry looked like a good bet, so he joined up and spent a number of years out west chasing rustlers and the occasional group of Indians who dared wander off their reservations. Then his unit shipped out to the Philippines to suppress a revolt of the native Moro people on the island of Jolo. There he witnessed the army massacre a thousand people in a volcano crater known as Bud Dajo. When he complained to the brass about the bloodbath, he was kicked out of the service. And now, for whatever reason, the Bible voice was back along with ghosts from the massacre.

Jack went to a speakeasy over on Saratoga Street. He thought hard about buying a bottle of whiskey before a whole separate load of bad memories about booze and craziness scared him off. He ended up parked at a table with a warm jug of celery tonic, thinking of Sarah. Despite her aloof, formal manner, he knew she had strong currents of emotion flowing within her. She cared about the problems in his head, for sure. That she never would get gushy-gushy about it only made him like her more.

After a sad succession of hookers, two guys sat down, uninvited, with a half-starved mutt on a leash. Jack knew this was the old bunco act about a rare pedigree dog stolen from some rich guy who would pay a big reward to get the animal back. The con men would claim they were so desperate for cash they'd part with the dog for just a few bucks. Jack got up during their patter and dumped one guy out of his seat onto the grimy sawdust floor. The dog came over and licked the guy's face while the other grifter ran off.

"Take care of that mutt, mac, or I'll give you the lacing of your life," said Jack. "And be glad some living creature cares about your worthless ass."

CHAPTER 17

SARAH—THURSDAY, OCTOBER 14, 1909,
4:00 A.M.

*A*s dawn broke, she was studying two papers written by
Dr. Eugen Bleuler, whom Dr. Norbert Macdonald had
mentioned in connection with her supposed mental illness.

One paper discussed people who perceived color when they
heard spoken words. The condition was known as synesthesia,
and she recalled that Bleuler was among the first to study it.
Interesting, but irrelevant. She skimmed it quickly.

The second paper drew her full attention. It was from a
conference proceeding of the German Psychiatric Association
just last year. Bleuler had some new ideas about a serious category of mental illness known as "precocious madness." It
featured swift mental disintegration, typically beginning
between ages sixteen and thirty. Those stricken experienced a
break with reality, and most doctors believed the condition was
hopeless—little could be done except to lock sufferers away in
asylums.

Bleuler had a more optimistic view. He coined a new name
for the illness: schizophrenia, to highlight the split, or fractured,
thinking of the afflicted. He urged individual attention for each
patient, as each had their own particular type of delusion.

Sarah liked Bleuler's method. He based his ideas on data gathered directly from patients, and his primary concern was compassionate treatment. The man held out hope for people whom most everyone else assumed were hopeless. Dr. Macdonald said he believed the same thing, which should mean his offer to help her was rooted in sincere kindness.

But she did not have schizophrenia. Now, it was true that people had long said she was unusual, even outlandish. But she was, and always had been, firmly grounded in reality. Why did Drs. Anson and Macdonald think she was slipping into insanity?

Dawn crept around the edges of the window coverings as she finished reading. She stood and pulled back a drape just enough to make out her white marble steps glowing against the faint outline of the surrounding sidewalk. Jack would arrive soon. He had been uncomfortable the last time they met. She developed a checklist to remind herself to avoid any mention of the banquet or anything else that might offend his attention to money and class distinctions.

Sarah pushed away those thoughts only to confront anxiety about the banquet that afternoon. The ordeal would start hours before, as she had to be at Margaret's at 9:00 a.m. for help getting dressed, coiffured, powdered, and all the rest of it. She didn't want to dwell on that, either.

She thought instead about her future, which at the moment appeared bleak. She held out faint hope for work as a pathologist in a traditional setting. That had long been her goal in life—and why she had put up with so much hardship during medical school.

Trouble started early in her second year during a lecture by one of the most renowned members of the faculty. He raised the topic of female doctors and asked for questions. The overwhelmingly male students peppered him with queries such as "Are women too unstable, talkative, and soft-minded to be good doctors?" and "Is it true that studying anatomy confuses and distresses girls?"

The professor said nothing to discourage such ideas. He recounted how a friend preferred a third-rate male doctor to a first-rate woman doctor, which drew laughs from the crowd and then a question as to whether it was even possible for a woman to achieve first-rate status.

"There may be among you a woman who beats the men in class," he said. "While bully for her, consider what happens to the poor fellows she trounces." Nervous laughter flitted around the room. "Female success may force men to lose their confidence and their vitality. High-achieving females could drag medicine away from manly progress and toward useless womanly frivolity." The professor stared directly at her. "So yes, we can have first-rate women doctors—at great cost to the medical profession. Think of it—the physician of tomorrow might prefer mindless chatter rather than aggressive combat against disease."

After that, some treated her with open contempt. Fellow students sabotaged her work and circulated gossip. Instructors went out of their way to make her work harder. The stress was terrible, although only Grace's dolls ever saw her cry. Still, she questioned her competence as a would-be doctor. Was she too odd? Too assertive? Too out of touch with other people?

Under great strain, Sarah still excelled. She even got top marks from the professor who started the antagonism against her. She asked to meet with him after the final class. "I merely bring into the open what everyone thinks about women students," he said. "If a girl can't handle it in class, she shouldn't be a doctor."

"Is your intent to drive female students away?" she asked.

"Not at all. I am a believer in coeducation. Yet I have found the more intelligent the woman, the more anxiety she has about success. As well she should. It's hard enough working in a man's profession without being obviously smarter than the men on top of it."

"You only wish to discourage the top females."

"I want all our graduates prepared to deal with the world. You have a first-class mind with an exceptional ability to focus on a problem without distraction. But you are also socially clumsy and quite obviously peculiar. As a brilliant, odd woman doctor, you will face enormous difficulty. I was certain your nerves would make you drop out. As you may still. In the meantime, congratulations."

Sarah pulled in a deep breath and thought again about what she faced at today's banquet. Her last social outing—a luncheon with Margaret and some middle-aged friends a few weeks back —had been trying. All the ladies could talk about was the marital chances of various young women. A matron carried on for some time about the bad prospects of one girl who had obtained a master's degree. "She has limited her possibilities because no man will marry someone more educated than he," the woman said. "Men already think a wife will try to dominate him. I do wish that poor child had invested her time in getting a husband rather than in all that schooling." A sharp look from Margaret finally quieted the woman.

Not only did those lunching ladies dismiss the value of education, they also rejected the possibility of an unmarried woman living a fulfilled life. Sarah knew marriage was out of the question. Even worse was the prospect of having children—a man totally conquering her through biology. It was just as well that no man would ever find her attractive enough to even think of launching a courtship.

The copy of Ibsen's A Doll's House lay on the table where she had left it earlier. It was an impressive work. The main character progresses from a childish wife to a woman determined to claim her independence. Sarah knew the play stoked controversy because of the heroine's rejection of family life. Critics called the work immoral, scandalous, and a terrible influence on young women.

To play the role, Clara Sullivan must be worldly and intelligent enough to see the need for a second autopsy for Lizzie—but had refused. Why? Perhaps the autopsy would clarify something inconvenient for her. Maybe Clara's pink cashmere dress matched the samples under Lizzie's fingernails?

She forced her attention to the need to get dressed. It seemed absurd to struggle into all those layers—corset, petticoat, skirt, and the rest—just to travel the short distance to Margaret's, where she would have to pull everything off again before getting jammed into a whole different costume for the banquet. It would be a horrible process, as Margaret's maids would have to touch her skin as they helped her into tight-fitting undergarments and then the gown.

A cold shiver ran down her neck with the anticipation of the women brushing her hair and then attending to the laborious business of styling and setting. She arched her back, savoring the unconstricted freedom of her nightdress and dressing gown. If only she could wear this all the time. She ordered her anxiety to recede as she forged up the stairs.

Margaret's carriage would arrive soon, yet Jack had not appeared. Was he angry with her? Had he finally had enough of her difficult behavior? Was he injured? Was he still with Clara Sullivan from the night before? The possibilities were endlessly horrible.

She wanted to wait for him but it was too late.

CHAPTER 18

JACK—THURSDAY, OCTOBER 14, 1909, 6:30 A.M.

*P*ain kept him staring at the ceiling all night. The lack of sleep was a mixed blessing—there were no nightmares but also no refreshment. When he got up, the shaving mirror revealed a grim sight—puffy eyes, pasty complexion, discolored cut on his cheek.

One thing was certain: he needed lots of black coffee before he met Sarah. Walking outside cleared his head a little and he snapped to attention when he heard a newsboy hawking a morning paper with the headline about Horace Shaw getting released on bail.

Bailed out right after getting arrested for murder? Jack bought the paper and read quotes from the governor and other muck-a-mucks defending Shaw. The article also quoted Commissioner Lipp opposing the release but expressing confidence that Shaw would be convicted at trial. Yeah, sure. Bob Foster was right: Shaw was too well connected for the system to corral him.

When he made it to the Monumental Lunchroom the place was packed, with some little kids banging silverware at a nearby table. He was turning to leave when a woman called.

"Jack! Over here!"

It was Clara, sitting alone. He didn't want to deal with her, but she had a full cup of coffee ready at the empty place at her table. That was enough to seal the deal. She took a long look at him after he sat down. "Honey, you're a mess."

Jack took several gulps of coffee before looking up. Clara had a bruise on her cheek—it was small, with two different shades of purple. "You look a little rough yourself."

She covered the bruise with her hand. "Do you think I'm horribly ugly? Be honest."

"You've got to be kidding." He picked up the coffee, sloshing much of it on the table.

She mopped it up with a napkin. "I would've done anything to have you with me last night. I knew something bad was going to happen. And it did. That horrible city detective burst into my room and tore it apart. I tried to stop him. He hit me." She sniffled softly. "You had more important things to do than to protect me."

"Did he find what he was looking for?"

"Jack, I usually get what I want. But believe me—not here, not now. First Lizzie hasn't got my cash, and then she gets killed. Then you give me the cold shake. Now I can't even sell something juicy to Horace Shaw. I was stupid to even try."

"You found what Lizzie had after all. Should have known you lied about that."

Clara dabbed her eyes with a handkerchief. "Heck, it's just easier for me to lie than to tell the truth. I admit it—I'm selfish and rotten. When I found Lizzie dead, I checked a special hiding place we used when we lived at home together. I found this." She yanked out a black book and set it on the table.

"A Bible? The one Nick's great-granny gave him?" Jack put his hands over his eyes and rubbed hard.

"It's what's written in the back that matters," said Clara. "It's from Nick Monkton's great-grandma, Annie. She was a slave, and some reverend wrote down notes on the blank pages about her relations. Guess who the slave owner was."

"No more guessing games."

"Horace Shaw's great-grandpa. The notes say he got Annie pregnant. Then old master Shaw raised the kid as his only white heir."

"You're saying Shaw's got Negro blood and is passing as white. And that Shaw's related to Nick."

"Yes. The Bible makes it all clear." Clara spoke in a low voice while shuffling her feet. "I figure when Nick got the book, he wanted to blackmail Shaw before the election. So Nick gave Lizzie the Bible to hide. Then Nick shook down Shaw. Shaw didn't play. Instead, he hurt Lizzie and paid somebody to kill Nick."

"We're back to Shaw killing your sister." Jack pushed his derby back and ran his fingers through his matted hair, trying to figure out just how much she was lying. "Where did Lizzie hide the Bible?"

"She'd pried up a floorboard and then hammered the board back down. We learned that trick living with our Pa. Nick couldn't find it, which must have driven him up a tree."

"That's why she had that chisel in her room. Bet you have one, too. You hid the book under a floorboard so the detective couldn't find it in your room last night." Jack drained his coffee and waved for more. "Why can't you sell it to Shaw?"

"After what he did to Nick? Come on."

"Okay—why not give the Bible to the cops?"

"Because they already suspect I stole the thing. They'll toss me in jail if I turn it in now. If they don't kill me." Clara tilted her head back and closed her eyes. "I'm so thick. I should have left right after Shaw was arrested. But I needed money so badly I thought I could still get something for it. No dice. Now I'm just plain scared." She put her head down and looked at him. "I'm going twenty-three skidoo—catching a train west in an hour. And look, I really do want Lizzie's killer caught. You're the only one who can do that." She pushed the black book at him. "Here—take it."

Jack was suddenly seven years old with his older sister hovering above him. "Do you know every word of the Bible?"

"Yes, ma'am."

The switch hit his back with three stinging thwacks.

"Yes, really I do, ma'am." He forced enthusiasm into his voice.

"Do you swear to use the Bible to educate all those inferior to you?"

"I swear I will, ma'am. Always."

"Take the Good Book. Hold it tight in your hands. Never let it go."

Jack's hand automatically grasped the book and pulled it toward him while two thoughts clashed in his brain. *This Bible can crack the case. But Clara is probably pulling something for the benefit of her city detective shadow.* Before he could resolve the conflict, Clara rose and stepped away from the table.

"Good luck, Jack. Hope you get the guy."

"'For the love of money is the root of all evil: which while some coveted after, they have erred from the faith, and pierced themselves through with many sorrows.'" Jack's voice quaked as he spoke scripture out loud for the first time in almost twenty years.

"Never would have taken you for a religious man. Guess it's a sign from heaven." Clara shot him a tense smile. "Got to catch a train. If I knew how to pray for you, I would." She turned and walked out.

Jack looked around and didn't spot Clara's tail—but that didn't mean the detective hadn't already seen them. He opened the Bible to the title page, which proclaimed *The Holy Bible Containing the Old and New Testaments,* along with a bunch of other stuff. One phrase set in fancy type caught his eye: *Newly Edited by the American Revision Committee.*

He shook his head, uncertain why it was necessary to edit a message that was supposed to be straight from God. He flipped to the back pages, which bore a neat inked script.

The account was basic. Annie didn't know what year she was born on the Maryland plantation of Thomas Shaw but guessed it was between 1812 and 1814. She said Shaw got her with child about 1838. Shaw's wife got pregnant around the same time, and the children were born within hours of each other. Mrs. Shaw and her baby died during the delivery. Master Shaw then took Annie's fair-skinned baby boy and switched it for his dead child.

According to Annie, Shaw got her pregnant again two years later, and this time she raised the child as her own. The family tree showed the current Horace Shaw as both the great-grandson of Annie and the second cousin of Nick Monkton.

Horace Shaw was one eighth black. If that got out, prejudice would ruin all his connections. Shaw surely would be convicted of murder and hanged. Jack stuck the Bible under his jacket, next to the Colt in his belt. As he walked out of the lunchroom, the book rubbed painfully against his side, reminding him that holding onto the thing really put his ass in a sling.

After looking left and right, Jack saw no cops. Heading toward Charles Street, he came upon a crowd rubbernecking at two blue boys yelling at a wagon driver for carting an unsafe load of bananas piled at least six feet high. Jack had seen far worse violations—the cops were either new on the beat or angling for a bribe. Three men darted from the gaggle. Jack dodged one and was reaching for the Colt when a sap hit him in the left kidney. When the pain cleared he was against a wall in a piss-smelling alley. Snake Eyes O'Toole stood close by with two other city detectives.

"Nice one, Snake." He grinned. "Cops usually have no imagination, but anything's possible if the payoff is big enough."

Snake Eyes nodded, and Jack howled as a club hit him on the elbow. "The book." O'Toole held his face inches away. "Give it."

"You know," said Jack as he breathed through the pain, "those charcoal lozenges do wonders for bad breath. You got to give them a try."

O'Toole put on a set of brass knuckles with dried blood and hair stuck all over them. Jack saw the arm cock, a concussive flash, then blackness.

CHAPTER 19

SARAH—THURSDAY, OCTOBER 14, 1909,
1:00 P.M.

*M*argaret's carriage sat near the main entrance of the Hotel Belvedere. They had been waiting in line for ten minutes as the other carriages unloaded. Sarah would have been pleased to wait even longer, but the hotel staff worked efficiently to move the well-dressed passengers from their vehicles.

All too soon, a man took her hand as she stepped from the carriage, only to stumble headlong over the hem of her gown. The attendant caught her deftly and escorted her through the mammoth brass and glass revolving door into the lobby. Another attendant took her wool wrap.

Margaret, escorted by her husband, lost no time button-holing the mayor. After a few stilted words of greeting, Sarah stood silently alone, repeating to herself the mad tea party chapter from *Alice's Adventures in Wonderland*. She could only hope to navigate this event as coolly as Alice did hers.

Sarah caught sight of herself in a floor-to-ceiling mirror. While she had glimpsed views of herself dressing at the hands of Margaret and her wardrobe assistants, this was the first time she saw the finished result. The person she saw in the glass was a complete stranger. Her hair was parted in the middle and care-fully combed and lifted away from the sides and back of her head to form a sculpted, gravity-defying mass.

The most shocking thing of all was the dress. The material clung tightly, giving a clear outline of her body before pooling on the floor in a four-foot train. She looked away while trying to adjust the bodice into a more comfortable position.

"Sarah, are you feeling well?" Margaret had dismissed the mayor and was standing close by. "Do you need to rest?"

"I have objectives to accomplish."

"You look wonderful." Margaret smiled more broadly than usual. "Two young men with the mayor asked about you. I had better escort you into the ballroom before one of them tries to take your arm. And please do remember to gather the front of your dress in your hand before walking."

It took a couple of tries before Sarah could bunch enough of the flowing fabric to keep her feet clear. Even so, the drag of the train made walking difficult. Falling on her face was a definite possibility.

The ballroom was an enormous space with twenty-foot-high coffered ceilings trimmed with gilt dentil molding. Three crystal chandeliers floated above thick carpets upon which guests stood mingling in clusters. "I'll arrange to get one glass each from Commissioner Lipp and Lucas Patterson." Margaret made a dour face, although she had given up trying to force Sarah to abandon her plan.

"As we discussed, I must witness the removals. I need to know the provenance of each glass. Also, ensure the servants do not contribute their finger marks. That will complicate my work."

"I'll arrange things with that waiter." Margaret nodded at a middle-aged black man dispensing champagne with gloved hands from a bottle wrapped in a linen napkin. "He'll collect the glasses while you're conversing with each of your—well, your targets." Margaret swept her arm over the room. "I must circulate before the food is served and all the boring speeches begin. Will you be all right by yourself?"

She nodded, and Margaret glided off to chat quietly with the waiter. Sarah moved to a corner to stand by herself next to a wilted palm potted in an ugly iron urn. It was one of those offensive faux-Roman things covered with a mishmash of beads and wreaths. She looked over the rim and wrinkled her nose at the fork, cigar butt, and ancient dinner roll lying on top of the potting soil.

She scanned the crowd and noted the men's faces were red from alcohol and their mouths wide with conversation or laughter. The women's faces were powder-white, their mouths fixed with tight smiles. There was a lot of loud conviviality, with voices layered on top of one another. She could not imagine what these people could be talking about. *Try to appear normal,* she told herself.

"A crime, an absolute crime—a pretty girl all by herself. Allow me to join you."

She jumped and glanced up at a young man slightly older than herself. His black hair was slicked back from a forehead that glistened with a sweaty sheen, and his eyes were bloodshot and unfocused. Sarah recognized him as the boy who had given her a ham-handed grope at one of the few society events she had attended after coming out. He had put one hand on the back of her neck, the other on her rear end, pulled her close, and was going in for a wet kiss when she bit his lip.

"What's a gorgeous apparition like you doing in a place like Baltimore? Waiting for me, I hope. Been wishing for a magical girl like you to appear and rescue me for a long, long time." He stared at her chest.

"Go away. You are a louche man with whom I am, unfortunately, already acquainted."

The man backed away rapidly. "That voice—Sarah

Kennecott." He walked away as quickly as his unsteady legs could carry him.

She had to complete her task and get out of this place as soon as possible. She saw Lucas Patterson holding forth nearby with several men she did not know. A series of deep breaths helped calm her a bit as she approached them. "Mr. Lucas Patterson, I see you are present at this social event," she said. The men ran their gaze over her as Patterson did introductions. She felt like a bug before a group of entomologists just before getting stuck with a pin.

Patterson broke into a smile, his brilliant white teeth contrasting with his dark complexion. "My dear Sarah. What a pleasant surprise to see you at this dreary affair. You look—well, smashing." His clothing was more extravagant than the last time they met, with a jet-black jacket framing a white shirt with glossy ebony studs and a high wing collar. A silk bow tie rode under his chin.

As Patterson introduced her, each man tried to outdo the other with compliments on her appearance. Sarah wished her intellect could elicit a fraction of this reaction. "I was just saying this city needs to restrict child labor," said Patterson. "Six-year-olds must be in school, not dulling their minds packing oysters or vegetables. This election must be about the future of our youth—"

"We must drink alcohol," said Sarah. "The purpose is to ritu-alistically acknowledge Mr. Lucas Patterson's candidacy for mayor of Baltimore." The waiter appeared on cue with a fresh bottle and a tray of clean glasses. Murmurs of approval sounded all around.

"See, gentlemen? She is both lovely and a supporter of my quixotic candidacy. The perfect combination." Patterson raised his glass.

"Sir, I must inform you that this bottle here is our best vintage." The waiter spoke smoothly. "And I will be scolded if I return to the kitchen with any remaining." *However much Margaret is paying this man,* thought Sarah, *it isn't enough.*

The waiter took Patterson's glass and presented him with one freshly filled. "I want a fair election," Sarah said, offering a toast. She had hoped to come up with something cleverer, but that would have to do.

"Most appropriate, Sarah, as my entire campaign is about bringing fairness to all of Baltimore's citizens," said Patterson. "Let us drink up—and leave no heel taps in the glass."

"Speaking of fairness, how about that rascal Shaw getting bail after a murder," said one of the men after emptying his drink. "The corruption in this city is outrageous. Everyone knows he's as guilty as a whore in church. I hope that a jury sees that and he dangles at the end of rope." All the men laughed except Patterson.

"Let us not joke about corruption or capital punishment," he said. "And Horace Shaw is innocent until proven guilty. We must respect the rule of law, which applies equally to all men, despite their race, nationality, or circumstance." Patterson's sober look slid into a sly smile. "The voters may feel differently."

"The commissioner was a brave man to take on Shaw—but Lipp now appears to have the election in hand," said a man. "No offense, Patterson."

"Just remember the election has yet to occur," said Patterson. "Don't underestimate the good citizens of Baltimore. More of them wish to advance Negro rights, help the poor, and improve public health than you think. Many also favor my support for giving women the vote."

"Thanks for reminding me not to vote for you," said a man as he chuckled and slapped Patterson on the back. "Women don't want the vote. All they want to do is shop, gossip, and boss us around."

"That is untrue." Sarah crossed her arms tightly. "Even in

the face of prejudice, women have done great things. Consider Clara Barton, Jane Addams, and Margaret Sanger, just to name some. Broadly speaking—"

"Speaking of broads, you mean," said one of the men, stirring great guffaws.

Her chest constricted as she prepared to continue the attack, but she remained silent as Patterson darted off to place his arm warmly around the shoulders of Dr. Anson, who had just arrived. Sarah was surprised to see her mentor, as he was not a habitué of high society events. Patterson leaned down and spoke into Anson's ear while the other man nodded gravely. Sarah had no idea the two men knew each other, much less were on such familiar terms. She was about to leave when the duo approached.

"Is that you, Sarah? You look so . . . different." Dr. Anson's eyes were red under his filmy glasses. His complexion had a green cast, which his spinach-colored jacket enhanced.

"Sarah here is the life of the party—she's shed her somber ways and is even forcing champagne on us," said Patterson. "Is there any left?" The waiter provided a glass, which Anson drained in one slurping gulp while reaching for another.

"Well, well. How nice." Anson spoke in the slow, deliberate manner of someone who knew they'd had too much to drink. "How are you feeling, poor dear?"

"I am in acceptable health." She began edging away.

"She looks fine," Patterson said, cocking his head.

"What of your quest to reveal the secret truth that only you can know?" Anson spread his arms and held the pose, looking at her like a wobbly lawyer questioning a hostile witness in court. "Or have you moved on from a murder investigation to a search for unicorns? I have pressed Macdonald to help you, but the man's too polite. Him and his European manners."

Sarah felt a livid blush rise up her neck to her face. Anger and hurt crashed wildly within her. How could her mentor speak to her this way, and in public no less? She swayed erratically, wondering how she could possibly endure this shock.

"Murder investigation?" Patterson turned to her with his brow raised. "Whatever are you up to, Sarah?"

"Pure folly," said Anson as his glasses slipped down his nose. "The girl has mental problems." He shot a finger up to adjust his eyewear but missed the frame, his digit skidding across his sweaty cheek.

Sarah turned and walked away as quickly as the trailing fabric of her dress would permit. She stumbled and had to clutch a man's arm to stay upright. Ignoring his words of concern, she advanced before abruptly stopping with the realization that she could also get Dr. Anson's fingerprints—if the waiter could capture his glass. As luck would have it, the man was nearby and agreed to the request. She observed him smoothly exchange the doctor's empty glass for one newly refreshed.

She had a final objective. Standing on her tiptoes, she spotted Adolph Lipp in conversation with two matrons and headed for the group. *Do not speak too loudly. Do not be argumentative. Do observe the glass going into custody.*

A plump matron dressed in gathered yards of patterned white silk stood to Lipp's right. Another woman, wrapped in a pale-yellow brocade and chiffon that matched the tint of her white hair, stood to his left. The commissioner's suit was cheap and shiny, and with his deep frown and downturned mouth, he appeared as ill at ease as Sarah felt.

"Good afternoon, Mrs. Abigail McHenry. Good afternoon, Mrs. Martha Chase. Good afternoon, Police Commissioner Adolph Lipp."

Lipp's scowl deepened as he looked back at her. "Miss."

"I do so love your dress, Sarah," said Mrs. Chase. "I'm so envious—whose creation is it?"

"A team of seamstresses assembled the garment. I do not know their names."

"Well. You look so glamorous and sophisticated—I do so hope we will continue to see this side of you in the future."

"I find your dress pleasing. You are charming." Sarah turned to Mrs. McHenry. "Your dress is also pleasing and you are equally charming."

"Let us return to our conversation before the interruption," said Lipp. "I was detailing the decline of our once great civilization."

"Oh, yes. I was treated so very rudely by a store clerk the other day," said Mrs. Chase. "The girl had the sauciness to refer to me as 'you' rather than 'madam.' In my day all the clerks were properly trained men. Now, even in the finest department stores, half the staff are uncouth girls from the hinterlands. It is beyond outrageous."

Lipp nodded with great solemnity. "You raise a critical issue, madam. Those girls not only lack manners—they are in the city alone, without parental guidance, leaving them free to indulge in the basest forms of behavior possible. Wearing dresses well above their ankles. Attending moving pictures and sitting in the dark with strange men. It is but a short step to smoking cigarettes, consuming alcohol, and throwing away any scrap of virtue they retain." Lipp's scratchy voice rose and fell with the cadence of a sermon. "Mark my words—this moral decay is only going to get worse. The values we cherish are trampled underfoot by a new generation that cares nothing for decency. Today's youth are under the sway of a scandalous popular culture that nourishes wickedness."

"The awful slang young people use," said Mrs. McHenry. "I mentioned an eligible bachelor to a debutante of my acquaintance. Do you know what she said? 'He's crackerjack. And such an awful swell dresser.' I had no idea if she cared for him or not. The girl sounded like a scullery maid."

Sarah galloped past the warning flags waving from her mental checklist. "Henry David Thoreau equated slang with vitality. He wrote, 'It is too late to be studying Hebrew; it is more important to understand the slang of today.'" The matrons exchanged looks.

Lipp pointed at Sarah, his eyes smoldering. "This young woman is a perfect example of what is wrong with our country today. She has been made hysterical by too much education and from trying to do a man's work. She has lost sight of a woman's place. She quotes godless decadents when she should be looking after a husband and children. Not that any decent man would have her, mind you."

"Excuse me, sir. Your beverage." The waiter stood with his head down and tray extended within Lipp's grasp. The tray had a bottle of water and a partially filled tumbler. Lipp sniffed and peered carefully at the glass before taking a sip. He screwed up his face as if concentrating on the flavor of a vintage wine before guzzling the entire thing, holding on to the tumbler.

"Coloreds make for good servants, but it pays to be careful. You never know if they might mix up your water with their gin." Lipp held on to his glass and gestured to the waiter to leave. The waiter hesitated for a second, glanced at Sarah, and edged away.

"Commissioner, I worry terribly about beastly criminals," said Mrs. Chase. "What can be done to keep us safe?"

"I have a plan to attack the problem." said Lipp. "We need to free the police to do their jobs. Right now they are constrained by do-gooders and the press, who question everything the patrolman does on the beat."

A city detective in a rumpled suit approached and asked Lipp in a rough whisper to step away. The men walked off with the commissioner still clutching his glass.

Sarah followed them through the open double doors and into the hallway. Lipp stopped to set his empty glass on a marble-topped credenza so abruptly that she almost collided with him. Fortunately, they had their backs to her and she was able to slip behind a nearby column. She noticed the servant unobtrusively remove the commissioner's glass.

"The notes in the Bible are fake, sir," said the detective to Lipp in a low voice. "Book was published in 1906 but the writing's dated 1899. Another thing: Harden's beat good. Got him in lockup—just clinging to life, he is."

"I demand to see Jack Harden," Sarah said, stepping around the column to within inches of Lipp. "I am a physician. Take me to him immediately."

Lipp gave a violent start before backing away and then waving a fist at her. "Get away from me, you contemptible woman."

"Commissioner. That is no way to speak to a lady." Margaret's voice was regally calm.

"I overheard that the police have injured Jack Harden." Sarah was talking very loudly. "I must attend to him medically. There is not a moment to spare."

Margaret looked first at Sarah and then at Lipp, who had turned an alarming shade of red. "Is there a Mr. Harden in your custody, Commissioner? Is he injured?"

"The man is a lowlife thief who resisted arrest."

"Dr. Kennecott knows this man and vouches for his character. Why not allow her to examine him?"

"Out of the question," said Lipp, pounding his walking stick on the marble floor.

"I agree with Mrs. Bonifant, Commissioner." Blaine Bonifant had joined her along with several leading citizens who, while plainly uncomfortable with the scene, did not offer the commissioner any aid. "I urge you to allow Dr. Kennecott to visit the man," said Blaine in his booming courtroom voice. "Immediately."

"I may need to take him to the hospital." Sarah's vision was getting foggy around the edges and her breath was coming in short bursts.

"Sarah," said Margaret, "use our carriage. The detective will accompany you to the police station. You have the authority to move Mr. Harden to the hospital if you deem it necessary. Isn't that so, Commissioner?" She nodded once at Lipp to indicate the discussion was over.

Lipp gave his walking stick a feeble tap as he looked away from Margaret. "Do it, Detective."

"Yes, sir." The detective answered hurriedly as Sarah was already running for the door with two bunched handfuls of her dress lifted to the top of her shins.

CHAPTER 20

JACK—THURSDAY, OCTOBER 14, 1909,
3:00 P.M.

*B*lood and puke. The pain came a second later. The
agony squeezed out everything, and it took a long
time to grasp that he was stretched out on a slimy stone floor.
He made a faint slurping sound as he worked his lips.

"Not dead after all, eh? Police surgeon wasn't sure you'd
make it. Man was a complete incompetent. I had to roll you over
myself after he left so you wouldn't choke to death on your own
vomit."

Jack pulled himself up on one arm to see a man kneeling
next to him. He was older, with a shock of white hair flowing
over his forehead, and a couple of days' worth of white stubble
on his chin. "Where?" His tongue felt like a slab of wood. Black
spots blurred his vision as he propped himself against a wall.

"This is district lockup." The man put a cracked cup to Jack's
lips. At first, the water sloshed around in his mouth as if he had
forgotten how to swallow. Jack touched his face. The left side
was bloody and pulpy with torn tissue. There was no sight in his
left eye.

"Thanks for the drink."

"Glad to do it. It's my job to help people." The man stood and stretched.

"Why you here?"

"Good question. I'm just a businessman and an honest citizen. I run a family pharmacy."

"Coke peddler." Forming the words and pushing them out was hard, but Jack sensed it was important to try to talk, try to stay awake.

"If that's how you want to put it, sure. I'm just like every other druggist." The man sat on a rough wooden bench. "The trouble is that I—allegedly—sold cocaine to Negroes. Now, over the years, I sold more cocaine than German aspirin to white customers. Plenty of opium, morphine, and chloral, too. Had a whole product line of patent medicines to fix everything from indigestion to toothache. Everything changed when I expanded my business to black customers. Cops came down hard on me."

"Drugs mess up everyone."

"Yes, sir. And that's any man's free choice. Can't stand the phonies who turn a blind eye to one group of people using drugs and get frantic when another group does the same darn thing. Did you see that article in the paper the other day?"

Jack knew about the cocaine hysteria that had recently burst upon the city. The drug used to be legal and widely used, but lurid—and wildly exaggerated—reports of blacks misbehaving while using the stuff had the authorities cracking down on the major distributors, nearly all of whom were pharmacists reaping fat profits.

"It was all wrong." The man was now pacing. "Going on about how colored washerwomen are dying out in Baltimore. All those Negro women who walked with clothes baskets on their heads. Gone! Paper says those women started drinking beer, then five-cent whiskey, then taking cocaine—and it was the coke that finally made them stop working. Now, any fool knows the steam laundry is what put washerwomen out of business." Jack grunted. He was tired and wished this gent would shut up.

"Then there was that story with that idiotic headline 'Baltimore Negroes Run Wild on Cocaine,'" continued the druggist. "Says that dope arouses their worst instincts. Complete nonsense, but who gets blamed? Honest businessmen such as myself. All for just helping people restore their vitality."

Jack shut his good eye and invited blackness to seep around the edges of the pain.

"What about you, sir? I'll wager you know about the invigorating benefits of cocaine and are against its prohibition." The man pulled up Jack's sleeve. "Looks like you haven't started injecting. Wish I could give you a shot right now. Snap you right out of your funk." Heavy footsteps came down the corridor. "Sorry, brother," said the man, "they aren't done with you yet."

A key rattled in the cell door, and two sets of hands yanked Jack to his feet. His eye fluttered as he was half dragged down the corridor and dropped into a chair in an interview room. O'Toole sat across the table. "Taking your time killing me, aren't you, Snake," said Jack.

"Need to talk with your redheaded whore. Where's she at?"

"I'm flattered, but she's out of my league. And out of town by now."

"She's still in town. Hiding."

"So what? You got the Bible."

"Need to tie up some loose ends."

"Got no idea where she is."

O'Toole pulled out his .38 Special and scratched the side of his chin with the iron sight at the end of the barrel. "Way I see it, you got no reason to live if you don't tell me."

"Screw you, Snake. I'm half dead already. Do me a favor and finish the job."

The detective scratched the other side of his chin while looking at the rear wall, no doubt weighing the pleasure of shooting Jack against the mess from splattering his blood and brains all over the place. He put the gun away. "Nah. I'll let you rot in that cell until you squeal or die. Makes no difference to me." He stood up. "By the way, Detroit whipped Pittsburgh today, five to four. Series is tied at three games each. The Pirates are finished, just like you."

Another detective walked in. "Snake, commissioner says some skirt doctor has to look at this guy. No joke."

O'Toole's mouth twitched once before he stalked out of the room. The other detective followed, and things were quiet for a moment until he heard the rustle of fabric along with a light tap-tap of footsteps.

"Jack!"

Squinting with his one eye, he thought he saw Sarah, wearing a very fancy red dress. She dropped to her knees next to him and held a cloth to the left side of his face. "Press this as tightly as you can to the injury." Sarah rustled back out the door, and the sound of her shrill voice ordering the cops around was enough to make him think about smiling. Two cops came and dragged him out of the station and put him in a fancy carriage. Sarah got in next to him and told the driver to go to Johns Hopkins Hospital.

"No," Jack said. "Let me die someplace else."

"You are disoriented." She was sitting very close, and his head lolled against the fine cloth of her dress. This couldn't be real. "Sarah. That really you? You're so close. So nice."

"Jack. You are going into shock. Please try to remain conscious."

He faded in and out of awareness as the carriage bounced and swerved. This was it—he was going to die. The thought didn't bother him much. He'd already lived longer than he'd expected. And he'd seen so many people killed, so many bodies ripped apart and piled on top of one another, that death was no stranger. The Grim Reaper had always been close by, whiling away his time like a spectral hoodlum leaning against a wall, smoking a cigarette. The villain was about to flick away his cig and take care of business.

A FAN TURNED SLOWLY on the ceiling. Thick bandages wrapped the left side of his head. The rest of his body was a lump under a long white sheet. He tried to sit up but couldn't move.

"Keep still." He rolled his head and saw Sarah sitting on a chair next to his bed.

"What happened?"

"We are at Johns Hopkins Hospital. You needed emergency surgery to relieve the swelling in your left eye." She set aside a book and stood over him.

"Thanks."

"You were lucky to have an excellent surgeon."

"Yeah, I always catch the breaks." He rubbed his good eye. "Did I dream about seeing you in a fancy dress?" She was now wearing a long white gown over a plain black skirt and a shirt-waist with a lace collar that covered her neck.

"I was wearing such a dress. I came directly from the banquet." Her eyebrow trembled faintly.

"Did I bleed or slobber on your fancy duds? I'll pay for the damage."

"That is of no consequence."

"I remember laying my head on your chest. You must have hated that."

The eyebrow shuddered. "I was preoccupied with tending to your injury. And trying to quiet your semiconscious ravings about me. And about Clara Sullivan."

"Drawing a blank on that—sorry. Hope I didn't say anything too idiotic."

"I did not record your . . . spontaneous remarks regarding myself." She blushed deeply as she fumbled for the notebook in her bag. "But your comments about Clara Sullivan are relevant to our case, I believe." She flipped to a page. "You spoke in fragments, such as 'Clara set me up,' 'still in town,' 'cops looking for her,' and 'lying bitch.'" Sarah spoke in her deadpan voice, although Jack wondered if he heard a slight emphasis on the final bit.

"I wasn't at my best this morning," said Jack. "Clara shows me this Bible supposedly from Nick's slave great-granny. Had a handwritten family tree in it—seems Great-Grandpa Shaw got her pregnant, then took the baby and raised it as his only heir. Bottom line is that Horace Shaw is one-eighth black. Like an idiot, I took the thing from her. She wanted to take the attention away from herself and put the cops on me."

"How did she obtain the Bible?"

"Nick gave Lizzie the Bible to hold. Lizzie used that chisel I found to stash it under a floorboard. It was how Lizzie and Clara hid things at home."

"That would explain the laceration on Lizzie's finger and the blood on the tool," Sarah said. "She may have injured herself accidentally."

"Yep. She did such a good job hiding the Bible that Nick couldn't find it after she died. Clara knew just where to look when she found her sister's body."

Sarah kept her arms tight across her chest. "I overheard a detective tell Police Commissioner Adolph Lipp the Bible was counterfeit."

"Yeah, figured as much. Clara probably copied the family stuff into another Bible, hoping that it would distract the cops long enough for them to think I had what they wanted. And long enough for her to drop out of sight." Sarah moved over to a table next to the bed and reached for something. "Clara probably wanted to shake the cops so she would be free to sell the real Bible for a boatload of money to Shaw." He lifted his blanket and tried to swing his legs down to the floor, but they barely budged.

"You must stay in bed." Sarah was filling a big hypodermic needle.

"Can't—got to track down Clara. I'm starting to think you're right—she could have killed Lizzie. Woman's bad to the bone."

"It is time for your morphine." Sarah bent down with the needle ready.

Jack knew dodging that thing was impossible. "Wait—we have to keep working."

"I will examine new fingerprint evidence in the Pathological Building, which is nearby. I expect that work will advance the investigation."

"What about—" She jabbed him with the needle. Warm pleasure spread from his arm to his entire body in seconds. Everything seemed impossibly wonderful as he watched her walk away.

"WAKE UP, Jack. Come on now, wake up." He heard the voice from far away, as if he were in the basement and the caller upstairs. It was a woman's voice, full of authority yet caring. A sharp smell jolted him awake in his bed in the Hopkins Hospital ward. Jack still felt a lingering euphoria from the morphine, although his body was starting to hurt again.

"Time to change your bandages and give you a bath, Jack." A young woman dressed all in white—including a pointy little hat —stood over him holding a bottle of smelling salts. She took his wrist and felt his pulse.

"I've got the prettiest nurse in the whole place," he said in a woozy slur.

"Aren't you the charmer." She let go of his wrist and began to unwind the bandages on his head. "I'll bet you say that to all the girls who wrap gauze around that thick head of yours."

"What time is it, anyway?"

"It's about midnight. Your wounds are looking as good as can be, but don't plan to sit for a photograph anytime soon. Hope your girl already has your picture."

"Don't have a girl." He winced as she tugged the last bit of bloody bandage stuck to his face.

She began wrapping fresh gauze around his head. "You seem close to Dr. Kennecott—don't tell me she's just your physician."

"Sarah . . . Dr. Kennecott . . . is my . . ." Jack wasn't sure how to describe the relationship.

"Friend?" asked the nurse with a coy look.

"Yes. She's a good chum who's helping me with a business matter."

"I see. Well, your friend left a while ago. She asked for directions to the Academy Hotel. Funny, I didn't picture her as the type who would want to go to that part of town. You smell awful. Here, sit up so I can remove your dressing gown and sponge you down."

Jack sprang upright, ignoring his throbbing skull. "You're sure she said the Academy Hotel?"

The nurse pressed a hand to his chest and pushed him back down. "You can't leave bed—don't even try." Jack was too weak to do more. "I'll have to calm you down with morphine if you keep causing trouble."

Jack wondered why Sarah would go to the Academy Hotel. It was the kind of place where acts stayed when they played nearby stages, such as the Maryland Theater. Or the Academy of Music —the joint where Clara performed her play. But Clara stayed in the ritzy Kernan Hotel. Then he remembered what the Gayety manager had said—performers who wanted privacy could check into the Academy under an assumed name. Jack must have raved about that after he blacked out. Sarah had decided to confront Clara by herself.

"Okay, then. Get ready for the stick." The nurse loomed over him with another one of those awful needles.

"Don't need it—I feel jake." His head now felt like a guy was going at it with a pickaxe.

"Sorry." She stuck him in the arm.

Sarah was in danger. He managed to toss off the bed covers just before the soothing warmth of the morphine hit him full force, leaving his body feeling like warm jelly. His physical pain faded, but his mind remained a mess, racked with worry and regret.

CHAPTER 21

SARAH—THURSDAY, OCTOBER 14, 1909, 7:00 P.M.

*T*heatrical performances were unpleasant. All the human behaviors that baffled Sarah were magnified on stage, leaving her with an even greater sense of separation from other people.

Yet here she was, stepping from a hansom at Howard and Franklin Streets, near three of the city's largest theaters. People moved past her with their boisterous faces, and the mix of shouts and laughter was almost as unbearable as the awful odor of cut-rate perfume, rotting garbage, and unappealing food. She clutched her handbag tightly and began walking, paper wrappers and other trash swirling around her feet.

"Get your pretzels right over here, got your salt, got your mustard, your yap wants it, come on over." The whiny, nasal voice came from a short, bearded man with pretzels stacked on a stick. He was one of many peddlers lined up on the sidewalk selling snacks and cheap novelties. The competing appeals faded from her awareness when Sarah noticed the rich, earthy smell of autumn and early winter: roasted chestnuts. She spotted the chestnut seller and walked over to him. He was older, with a cloth cap pulled low over a lined, stubbled face.

"I am fond of roasted chestnuts," Sarah said. "This is the first time I have seen them this season. I do wonder if they smell better than they taste or even if it's fair to compare them in that way."

"Want some, miss?"

"Yes."

"That's a nickel, miss." He handed her a small brown bag filled with warm, almost hot nuts. She paid and walked slowly to the hotel while popping one of the cross-cut treats into her mouth. It was cooked just right and tasted delightful. She wanted another but pushed the bag into her purse. The time for indulgence was over.

The lobby of the Academy Hotel was small and smelled of mildew and cigar smoke. The carpet, originally fine, was worn and stained. There was a scattering of armchairs, some of which were leaking stuffing.

Garish posters covered the walls. One picture featured a grotesque, grinning man with lettering that proclaimed, "Do Spirits Return? Houdini says NO and PROVES IT." Another poster declared, "The High Rollers Extravaganza Co., Nettie Barton!" The prancing woman pictured—presumably Miss Barton—at first glance appeared nude. On closer examination she was revealed to be wearing tan tights and a leotard. Sarah turned her attention to the battered reception desk and approached the woman behind it.

"I am looking for a young woman who is checked into this establishment under an assumed name. She has red hair—"

"Sorry, miss. Against policy to ask for any guest except by name." The belligerent cast of the woman's face deepened.

"I have reason to believe that she has registered under a false name."

"Can't help you." The clerk's attention switched to two young women standing behind Sarah, both snapping gum between bouts of raucous giggles. "Help you, girls?"

"Just a moment." Sarah stood even stiffer and straighter. "It is urgent that I find this woman. She is an actress who appeared in the recent production of *A Doll's House* at the Maryland Academy of Music. I know your establishment has provision to accommodate performers under assumed names."

The two young women behind Sarah stopped laughing. "Come on, sister, we got two dance shows tonight," one of them said. "Hit the bricks."

"Look, hon, forget it." The desk woman swept her hand inches from Sarah's face. "Step aside."

"I refuse to leave until I receive cooperation."

"Ooh—Miss Vanderbilt's in a tizzy," said one of the dancers in a mocking imitation of an upper-class accent. "Indeed," said the other in the same manner. "The rabble are so unpleasant. I must return to my golden coach and draw my velvet shades."

Sarah was seconds away from failure. The only thing she could do was give a name and hope it struck home with the reception clerk. "The person I am looking for is Nora Helmer."

The clerk's face didn't change. "Why didn't you just spit it out in the first place? Like making a scene, do you?"

"I do not." Sarah held her breath.

"Room thirty-three. Next!"

As Sarah went up the stairs, her sense of good fortune rapidly cooled. The truly hard part was next. Rapping on the door of room thirty-three brought no response. She knocked again, louder and with insistence.

"Who is it?" It was a woman's voice, muffled behind the door.

"Clara Sullivan. This is Sarah Kennecott. I wish to speak with you."

"Go away."

"I will stand here until you admit me."

After a moment, the door cracked an inch. "You alone?"

"Yes."

Clara opened the door and quickly closed it once Sarah entered. "How the heck did you find me?" Her breath smelled strongly of alcohol.

"I knew you recently performed the role of Nora Helmer onstage and guessed that as your false name for registration in this hotel."

"Clever girl. Does anyone else know where I am?" Clara had her hair down and was wearing a long red silk kimono knotted at the waist with a clear view of her neck. There was no sign of any scratches from a struggle.

"Jack nearly died because of your deception. He is now in critical condition at Johns Hopkins Hospital."

Clara's hand flittered at her throat. "Gosh, how horrible. What do you want from me?" She walked unsteadily to a small table holding a bottle of champagne in an ice bucket as well as a large plate of raw oysters on the half shell. She took a sloppy gulp from her glass and sat down.

"I am here to demand the truth from you about Lizzie's death." Sarah looked directly at the woman, but Clara's eyes were intense emotional whirlpools. Sarah quickly looked away and grabbed a chair to steady herself.

"Not great with people, are you?" Clara lit a cigarette and exhaled twin jets of smoke through her nostrils. "Anybody else would try to break the ice a bit. Not little old you. Bet you're not even human—you're a mechanical puppet." Clara laughed harshly as she made a cranking motion with one hand. "They must wind you up with a big key before turning you loose."

"You may insult me however you wish as long as you reveal the truth." Sarah gripped the chair harder.

Still smiling, Clara reached under a napkin and pulled out a small handgun identical to the one found with Lizzie's body. "Hey—look at me, Sarah. See this gun? What's to stop me from shooting you?" Her hand was so unsteady that it was likely she would miss any target farther away than a foot or two.

"That would cause you undue complication."

Clara sniggered and tossed the gun on the bed. "Lady, you're a piece of work. Here, you're looking a little peaked. Sit down and have some bubbles. Relax. If that's possible." She found another glass and poured the rest of the bottle into it with an unsteady hand. "Look. I'm impressed that you care about who killed Lizzie. Lord knows nobody else does. Like I told your boyfriend, Jack, I didn't do it. She was the only person I loved in the whole world."

"If you did not kill Lizzie, whom do you suspect committed the crime?" Sarah eyed the chair seat, gave it a quick brush with her palm, and sat.

"I'm guessing it was that loser Nick. He was the type to knock a girl around and shoot her dead body for kicks. May he not rest in peace."

"Did you have anything to do with Nick's death?"

"Who do you think I am, Lady Macbeth? I'm not involved in any murder."

"You told Jack you were leaving today. Yet you remain here. Under an assumed name."

"So many nosy questions. Hey, I'm starved for conversation, so I'll play along. Fact is that I've got to stick around until this little show's over. One more visit with the guttersnipes, then it's time for me to skedaddle off to the big time."

"Your theatrical engagement ended days ago."

Clara rolled her eyes. "For a doctor, you can be pretty darn slow. I'm talking about my one-woman performance that's going to get me the money I need to get set up in moving pictures out in California. It takes big money to do it right. I need a nice place to live, lots of new clothes, and the means to show myself around town. And I aim to get into the directing side of the business. A girl needs cash—a lot of cash. Otherwise, the men treat you like a slab of meat. Not this broad. I'm going to set the place on its ear." She gave a big, loopy smile.

Sarah's hands flapped wildly until she abruptly balled her fists and jammed them between her thighs. "You do not care about the harm you cause."

"It's a shame about Jack. But I needed to get that cop off my tail." Clara aimed to snuff out her cigarette in a butt-filled oyster shell but hit the edge and flipped the mess all over the table, causing her to laugh uproariously. "Whoops. Well, all of you will be rid of me soon, cross my heart." She reached across the table and picked up a railroad ticket for a westbound train leaving at 12:35 p.m. tomorrow on the Baltimore and Ohio St. Louis Express. "It's bye-bye for real." She gave a tiny wave.

"You plan to exchange the original Bible documenting Horace Shaw's mixed heritage for a substantial amount of money."

"Why should that darn Bible matter to you? Thought you were interested in who killed my sister—keep your eye on the ball. I'm bored with this topic." Clara pushed the plate of oysters at Sarah. "Long as you're here, sweetie, have some of these oysters—they're scrumptious. Only good thing about this lousy dump of a town is the seafood."

"No. Those oysters appear excessively briny."

"Suit yourself."

As Clara noisily gulped down more oysters, Sarah knew her time was running out. "You have many items of clothing. Do you own any items made of cashmere?"

"Oh, yeah, do I!" Clara said. "Let me show you." She jumped up, staggered to the wardrobe, and came back with the same pink dress she had worn the day before. "Here—stand up." Sarah stood stiffly as Clara draped the dress over her. "You know, you might not look so bad if you wore something like this."

While Clara was holding the dress against her, Sarah plucked some of its fibers and stowed them when Clara turned to put the dress away. "Do you own anything else made of cashmere? A skirt? Stockings?" Sarah followed and looked over Clara's shoulder into the wardrobe. There was no sign of any other cashmere garment.

"Nope. Too expensive. You just wait—when I hit it big, I'm going to have fancy everything. Even cashmere drawers." Clara giggled as she kept rooting among her clothing in the wardrobe. "Now, here's a possibility for you." Clara turned and thrust a silver and black dress with a low neckline against Sarah. "Well—no. You're just too flat-chested. You've got to find yourself a way to show some skin if you want to hook a half-decent man."

As Clara put the second dress away Sarah grabbed the woman's empty glass with her gloved hand and stuffed it into her purse. "I must depart," she said.

"Yeah, sure. Just one more thing." Clara pointed toward the pistol on her bed. "Don't want to see you again. I might not be so friendly the next time. And don't tell anyone about finding me here. Got it?"

Sarah chewed on her lip. She knew the easiest thing to do was just to agree, regardless of her true intent. But she had exhausted her ability to lie. "The only person I will speak to in the immediate future is Jack."

"Jack." Clara smiled widely, eyes sparkling. "Of course. He's some good-looking hunk of man, isn't he? The kind you just want to"—she bared her teeth and gave a little bite—"eat all up, nice and slow. Am I right?"

"What do you mean by 'eat'?"

Clara giggled madly. "So cute and innocent. Guess you haven't slept with him yet, huh? Don't know how you hold yourself back—that man is sex on a stick. Still, it's good to wait if you're playing the long game. Give him just enough to keep him eating out of your hand." She cocked her head with an off-kilter grin. "Oh, gosh, what am I saying? You couldn't vamp a man to save your life. Too pushy, too smart, too strange. I'd love to be a fly on the ceiling and see you try to seduce Jack. He'd think you want to play chess."

Clara let loose a snickering laugh. "Seriously"—the word came out slowly and sounded like "sheerrisshly"—"you're lucky I know you're a harmless oddball that nobody pays attention to. And you're lucky that I know Jack's too beat up to do anything." She opened the door. "Nightie-night, Sarah."

Sarah marched down the stairs quickly. The hotel lobby was crowded full of people. Their harsh laughter echoed in the small space so loudly she was nearly unnerved. Things were slightly quieter on the sidewalk, but there was still too much commotion to think properly. She hailed a cab and told the driver to take her to Johns Hopkins Hospital.

ATTENDING to Jack and confronting Clara Sullivan had kept Sarah from further analyzing the physical evidence. She hurried to her lab workspace and was relieved to see a note from Margaret. After pleading with Sarah to telephone her immediately, the message explained that the glasses from the banquet were in an accompanying bag. A slip of paper in each glass identified which man had held it.

She began with the evidence obtained from Clara Sullivan. Sarah set Clara's glass on its side on top of a sheet of paper and carefully applied fine powder. She dusted with a brush to reveal many individual prints. Over the course of an hour, she compared the prints on the glass to those in the police photograph of the pistol. At any moment, she expected to find a match. But none of Clara's prints matched. Using a microscope, Sarah compared the cashmere from Clara's dress to the fibers found under Lizzie's nails. The two samples were obviously different.

The clock bonged 10:00 p.m. but Sarah paid no attention to her leaden body as she looked over the inked prints she had lifted from Nick's body. They were familiar. A comparison quickly revealed the marks matched those in the pistol photograph, including a partial print on the trigger. Nick had shot Lizzie's corpse—perhaps Clara was right in assuming that Nick had also caused the fatal head injury.

Sarah dusted the two glasses and the note Jack had found with Nick Monkton's body. The first glass was a match for Nick. The second glass and the putative suicide note each had different prints that didn't match any person yet identified.

She turned her attention to the glasses from the banquet. The finger marks for Lipp and Dr. Anson matched nothing. As the clock ticked 2:30 a.m., she was working on the last piece of evidence she had—Lucas Patterson's glass from the banquet. Hovering over the exposed prints with the magnifying glass, Sarah's eyes were so bleary she began to question their efficacy. Doubt vanished the instant she saw the match. She checked again, and then one more time.

It was clear that Lucas Patterson had left his fingerprints on the second glass found at Nick Monkton's murder scene. Sarah sat up straight and stretched her aching back, thinking about what motive Patterson might have. The man admitted to feeling frustration with Nick regarding the direction of their relationship. Perhaps Patterson had gone to collect the Bible to use against Shaw in the mayor's race. And Patterson could have become even angrier with Nick after learning the book was lost. Angry enough to kill.

Even if Patterson had killed Nick, who'd killed Lizzie? Sarah had found little evidence thus far to confirm Jack's hunch about the connection between the two murders. But there was still more to learn about Dr. Anson, whose involvement with Nick and Lizzie remained unexplored.

The Pathological Building was empty at this hour. Sarah went upstairs to Dr. Anson's office, which was unlocked. She stepped inside, switched on the lights, and closed the door. Prowling around her mentor's office was a terrible transgression. With memories of his appalling behavior toward her at the banquet still fresh, she decided to proceed.

The only thing of interest on his desk and bookshelves was a copy of Eugen Bleuler's 1908 paper. Many passages were underlined in the text, along with penciled notations reading "fit this symptom to SK." The only place left to check was a small safe with a combination lock. She recalled that the man was terribly absent-minded, which meant he probably kept the combination in written form somewhere nearby. She found it in the first place she looked: under a plaster bust of Rudolf Virchow, the father of microscopic pathology.

The safe held a small amount of cash, lecture notes, and a stack of photographic prints. Sarah was shocked to find the prints depicted naked young women tied up while a short man wearing a hooded mask wielded a riding crop, walking stick, or some other object. Welts were visible on the women's bodies. No faces were shown, although the masked man's form did bear a strong resemblance to Dr. Anson.

Sarah debated what to do. If she gave the photographs to the police, Anson could deny owning them, or perhaps claim the images were related to a medical study. It would also be clear to the police that she had conducted an illegal break-in. The only option was to return the prints and close the safe.

Dr. Anson had allegedly been seen with Lizzie, and he had purportedly offered to examine her. Did such an examination involve striking her head? Is that how Lizzie received her head injury? Did Nick learn about it, and try to blackmail Anson? If so, her mentor would have a motive to murder Nick and perhaps to shoot Lizzie.

That scenario would also explain why Anson wanted to keep Sarah close over the last couple of days. And why he was trying to make her appear mad—he needed to discredit her before she finished the investigation.

If all this was true, she had just one course of action: prove him a murderer before he had her locked away.

*W*ailing, soul-wrenching, and terrible. The keening cut through Jack's drowsy brain like a freshly stropped razor.

From his half-open eye, he saw a middle-aged woman sobbing at the next bedside. "He can't be dead!" she shouted in a thick brogue. "You fixed him! All you doctors! He can't be dead!" Grief is grief, but Jack always thought the Irish had a way of pouring it out that made them sound like the unhappiest people in the world.

Two nurses were nearby. One put her hand on the crying woman's arm. "Mrs. O'Dowd, please try to be quiet. The other patients need their rest." The other nurse bent over the body in the bed.

"Tell me my husband ain't dead!" Mrs. O'Dowd was in no mood to worry about anyone else.

The second nurse pulled a sheet over the body and turned to the woman. "I'm sorry, Mrs. O'Dowd." The woman bawled even louder as the nurses escorted her out of the ward.

Jack looked away. This joint was an efficient death house for the modern age—instead of picking up dead bodies off the street, the authorities arranged for the doomed to get hauled to this central place before croaking.

The ward looked deceptively healthy. It was thirty feet by eighty feet of bright whiteness, and a row of sun-lit windows reached from the floor to the top of the eighteen-foot ceiling. Electrical lights enclosed in white globes hung from above like ever-vigilant eyeballs. Two rows of beds filled the room from one end to the other. Each of the beds was identical, with white metal frames and white linens. Clusters of nurses and visitors stood over patients.

A young doctor approached. "Hey Doc," called Jack, "where're my clothes? You can have your bed back."

"You're in no condition to go anywhere." The doctor lifted the sheet off the departed Mr. O'Dowd.

"Your guy?" Jack asked.

"He had an accident unloading tobacco hogsheads on the docks—got a compound fracture of the femur. We operated and reset the bone, and he was doing well." The doctor spoke in a cool, confident tone, yet there was a hint of unease about him. He was like someone walking around in a new pair of shoes that looked good but pinched. "An infection killed him. There was nothing we could do."

"Definitely not your fault, then. No way, no how."

"I've saved dozens of patients, my friend. My father's a doctor, and he told me there used to be signs in hospitals warning patients to 'Prepare to meet your God.' You don't see any of those signs around here now. People come to this hospital to meet their healer, not their Maker."

This guy was as earnest and know-it-all as Sarah. What was it these doctors believed in that gave them such certainty? "Unless God has other plans, like for your patient here," said Jack.

The doctor looked a little more uneasy and a lot more irritated as he yanked the sheet back over the stiff. "Mister, we've cut infections dramatically in the past few years. But infection is always possible, and once it occurs deep in a patient's body, no human intervention can save them."

"Ever think about putting those signs back, just as a reminder that things can still go wrong?"

"Judging from those bandages, it appears that a doctor saved your life. Think about that—it might help reduce your uninformed cynicism."

"Yeah, you medico types are one hundred percent right all the time." The doctor stepped away, and the nice nurse took his place.

"I like thankful patients," she said.

"Any patient who doesn't die in this dump should be thankful."

"Your condition clearly is improving. How about another shot of morphine?" She had the needle in hand.

"No thanks. Feel calm as a clam."

She gave him a bright smile that faded as she looked up. "Oh, look who's coming. Your chum."

Jack heard a familiar set of purposeful footsteps approaching.

"Good morning, Dr. Kennecott," said the nurse. "Our patient is doing well. He doesn't even want morphine."

Sarah ignored the nurse as she lifted Jack's chart from a hook on the bed over his head. While focusing on the chart, her palm went to his forehead. Her touch was warm and made his skin tingle. For a second, Jack thought Sarah was going to be friendly, but she was her typical self. "No sign of fever," she said as she scribbled on the chart and banged it back on its hook. "Are fresh bandages available?"

"Yes, Doctor," said the nurse. "They are in a sterile wrapper on the bedside table. I was just about to change them."

"My hands are clean, and I am more familiar with the wound. You may go."

Jack cringed. It seemed as if Sarah was speaking even more brusquely than usual.

"Yes, Doctor," said the nurse, who then walked away.

"Heard you went to the Academy Hotel last night," he said.

"I met with Clara Sullivan. I—"

"Sarah, Clara's capable of anything. She could have hurt you." Jack tried to sound scolding, but it was difficult to manage with her yanking off the gauze stuck around his eye.

"Given the urgency of the situation, I judged the risk worth taking. What I found—"

"You're a respectable lady. You just can't go rushing unescorted into police stations and hotels to order rough people around. Especially at night. Someone's going to knock you on your sweet little—it's dangerous."

"This may sting." Sarah dabbed disinfectant over his eye and on the big gash next to it. Jack drew in a sharp breath as he waited for the fiery hurt to fade. Without any show of sympathy, she deftly replaced the gauze over his eye and the side of his face and secured them with a large eye patch. "I am not as help-less as you think. My intervention was necessary for our investigation."

Jack was all too aware of that. And the fact that she had saved his life. "Yeah, maybe."

"Be quiet and listen to what I have to say." Sarah sat in a chair next to his bed. "My primary reason for visiting Clara Sullivan was to obtain her fingerprints and a sample of fibers from her cashmere dress. I did so successfully. Neither matched evidence from Lizzie's murder."

"Okay, so she—"

"Do not interrupt. Clara Sullivan admitted to deceiving you with the Bible so as to distract the police. She likely still has the original and plans to exchange it for a substantial amount of money before leaving town later today. She showed me her ticket on this afternoon's twelve thirty-five westbound St. Louis Express."

"Okay. Sounds like she's getting out of town for real this time."

"I also found fingerprint evidence pointing to Nick Monkton as the person who shot Lizzie's body," said Sarah.

"Yeah, heard Nick confessed to that before he got croaked." Jack sat up. "Do you know more about Nick's death?"

"I identified finger marks matching those of Lucas Patterson on one of the glasses you retrieved at the stable with Nick's body. One hypothesis is that Patterson flew into a murderous rage at the stable when Nick revealed he had lost the Bible."

"Maybe. But Patterson cared a whole lot about Nick. Now, it could be that Nick demanded a payoff for shooting Lizzie to frame Shaw. But that's no reason for Patterson to kill the guy. And why would Patterson just happen to have knockout drops to use after losing his temper? They're not exactly the kind of weapon a guy turns to in the heat of anger."

"We must also consider Adolph Lipp's interest in the Bible," said Sarah. "And why Clara Sullivan expects to collect a large sum of money for the object."

Jack ran his hand over his stubbly chin. "It figures that Lipp is hot to get the Bible. He needs it to sink Shaw—the man's prejudiced connections would drop him like a hot turnip and he'd land in jail and probably get hung. But Lipp hasn't got money, so it's got to be Shaw. The only question is where Clara will collect the cash."

"Clara Sullivan told me that she needed 'one more visit with the guttersnipes' before she could leave town. What does that term refer to?"

"Guttersnipes are street urchins."

"Such as those with whom Lucas Patterson works."

"She's not selling to Shaw." Jack sat up. "She wants to get the biggest payout possible, and Patterson's got the most money along with a burning desire for reform. Clara goes to him and demands a big price for the Bible. So big that it took a couple of days for him to pull the cash together, which explains why she had to hang around. Still—what does that have to do with our murders? Unless you still want to pin them on Clara."

"I have more information about who might have killed Lizzie."

Jack shuddered as he sat up on the bed. "You've been one busy gal while I've been laid up in this joint."

"The description of the man seen speaking with Nick and Lizzie at the Gayety Theater matches my mentor, Dr. Frederick Anson. I found a disturbing cache of photographs in his safe last night. The images depict a masked man beating naked young women with various instruments. It is possible Dr. Anson hired Lizzie for this purpose and delivered a fatal blow during their session."

Jack gave a low whistle. "You're a safecracker on top of all your other talents. Sarah, you are one amazing woman."

"Perhaps we should call the police." Sarah was now rocking with her arms wrapped tightly around her body. "They could obtain a search warrant, find the photographs, and compel Dr. Anson to confess."

"Forget it. Things never go that smoothly with the cops, especially when a well-known guy like your doctor friend is involved. Besides, Lipp's mixed up in this some way himself, which means we truly can't trust the cops. But there *is* something I can do." Jack swung his legs onto the floor.

"You are in no condition to leave this bed."

"Have to. You said Clara's cashing in on the Bible and got a ticket out of town a little past noon. Knowing her, she's got everything planned to the minute. It's almost nine o'clock now. If I hurry, I can trail her to the meet-up with Patterson."

"What good will that do?" Sarah rocked so hard in her chair that it was slowly moving across the floor with little squeaks.

"Maybe nothing. But it's the last chance to learn what she knows before she's gone for good. Where are my clothes?"

"You propose confronting two people, neither of whom have an incentive to reveal anything incriminating. One or both of these people may also be murderers and inclined to use extreme violence. Your plan is illogical and reckless."

"Do you have a better idea?" Knowing her, she probably did.

She stared off into space for a moment, then reached under the bed and pulled out a box containing new clothes, his old derby, and the Colt. "I instructed the nurse to get you a new suit of clothing, as your previous articles were beyond repair. I also demanded the police return your firearm." She lifted the pistol with both hands and clutched it tightly. "I will only relinquish this weapon if you agree to take me with you."

"Okay, come on. I'll need that darn gun."

*T*he black medical bag bounced on the seat between them as the taxicab crossed one set of rail tracks after another.

Sarah was not in the habit of carrying the bag, but she worried about Jack's injuries. She forced herself to ponder the case evidence instead, wondering why the details refused to fit into a logical whole. Dr. Anson had a sexual perversion that might link him to Lizzie's head injury. Nick framed Horace Shaw for Lizzie's murder. Lucas Patterson might have murdered Nick. Clara Sullivan had a family Bible with an explosive secret. What did all of this add up to?

"Hope the rain holds off," said Jack. "I'm ready to see the sun."

Sarah's attention snapped back to the present. For the first time, she noticed the morning was dull and gray. Patches of mist hovered over the ground. There was a chill dampness in the air that made her wish she had worn something over her walking suit jacket. It was difficult for her to switch her routine as the seasons changed—she sweated under an overcoat well into summer and shivered without one sometimes as late as Christmas. "I prefer to consider the facts of our investigation rather than speculate on the weather, which is out of our control."

"Sometimes people talk about the weather to take a break from the hard stuff. It's called small talk."

"I do not appreciate idle conversation." Sarah spoke with force, thinking of all the occasions during which she stood silent amidst mindless chatter. "I am speaking in general terms. I did not intend to single you out for criticism."

"Don't worry about it. You're right—I should know you better by now."

Her heart raced as she considered his remark. Apart from her father, no man had ever tried to understand her, much less blamed himself for not doing so. She came out of her reverie when Jack told the hansom driver to stop half a block down from the Academy Hotel. From West Franklin Street, they had a clear view of the front entrance.

Jack checked his watch. "It's nine forty-five a.m. I hope she's still there."

"I called the Academy Hotel after requesting our taxicab. The clerk told me that Miss Nora Helmer—that is Clara Sullivan's pseudonym—is planning to check out at ten a.m."

"You're good, Sarah."

She blinked rapidly. "Do you truly regard me as capable at detecting?"

"You bet. You're a natural. And with all that autopsy and science stuff—cripes, you put me to shame."

"I am aware of my limitations. I lack your intuitive talent. And your ability to easily interact with people."

"Everybody's friend. That's me." Jack had a hand over his bandage.

"Is your injury causing you pain?"

"Missing my coffee. That's all."

"Remove your hat."

"Why?"

"I wish to check for fever. Getting out of bed so quickly after surgery puts you at risk." Sarah extended her hand partway toward him.

"Sarah, your thumb is bleeding. 'Physician, heal thyself.'" He gave her a weak smile. "Sorry. New bad habit of mine, spouting the Bible out loud."

She glanced at her thumbnail and saw that blood was dripping from the well-chewed cuticle. "How terrible." Casting about in her medical bag, she found a piece of gauze and pressed it to the finger. "I cannot say your biblical reference is unwarranted. I, too, have bad habits."

Jack removed his hat, and she placed her uninjured hand on his forehead. He was slightly clammy with no sign of fever.

"Let me see your thumb," he said.

Looking down at the battered digit, she saw that the gauze had come loose and more blood had oozed out of the cuticle. Reflexively, she jerked her hand away.

"Come on. I won't bite it. That's your job."

Slowly, she extended her right hand. Jack held it gently in a calloused palm as he dabbed at the end of her thumb gently with the gauze. Her entire arm shivered with an odd combination of fear and pleasure. Motion off to the side, in the direction of the hotel, drew her attention away from his touch.

"Jack. Clara Sullivan is departing."

A parade of bellmen lugged trunks, hatboxes, and smaller cases out to a four-wheel hackney carriage under Clara's unsmiling direction. She wore a green traveling suit trimmed in dark blue silk. Her huge hat was wrapped in pink chiffon and decorated with a profusion of silk peaches, complete with leaves.

"She looks like a darn tree," said Jack.

"I do not like figures of speech." Sarah pulled her hand away. "If I did, I would use a less flattering construction to describe that woman."

"There's sweet fruit on her surface, but everything underneath's rotten."

"That is more agreeable."

Jack told the driver to follow Clara's carriage at a distance. As they bounced their way along, Sarah's anxiety spiked. She had no idea how Jack was going to resolve this matter. If Clara Sullivan was meeting Lucas Patterson, it meant accosting two potential killers. Killers who had no intention of peacefully yielding to moral authority. She wanted to question Jack about his strategy but decided to keep quiet. Any plan conceived by a one-eyed man who was near death a day ago would not sound convincing in any case.

Clara's carriage headed southeast, toward the waterfront. While Sarah appreciated the motorized efficiency of the taxi, she regretted that the landaulet roof was down as the streets grew increasingly crowded with wheelbarrow and pushcart traffic. Men yelled at each other demanding the right of way, horses snorted, and wheels skidded into and out of ruts among the paving stones.

Every so often, all traffic lurched to a stop at freight train crossings, where everything was subsumed under the shriek of the locomotive and the earthquake rumble of steel wheels. Thick dust raised from tearing up nearby streets rolled across them with every gust of wind.

As they got closer to the water, a succession of powerful smells appeared: ground coffee, raw sulfur, putrid meat, rotting produce. Turning onto Thames Street, Sarah almost swooned at the overpowering smells of coconut, chocolate, and burned sugar coming from the candy factory on the corner.

"You may be correct about a meeting with Lucas Patterson," Sarah said. "The carriage is stopping in the vicinity of the Children's Benevolent and Protective Society."

Jack told their driver to stop. He flipped open the door and got out. "Whatever happens, stay here," he said. "If worse comes to worst, flag down a cop."

"You said the police are of no use in this matter."

"They're the only option if shooting starts." He pointed to her thumb. "Take care of that, hear?"

"I refuse to be left behind." She tried to leave the carriage but couldn't get past him at the door. "Your ability to act physically is limited. You need my help. Let me pass."

"Yeah, I'm bushed. But I've got enough energy to keep you pinned in this buggy long enough for the bad guys to get away."

She eased back into the cab. "Very well."

"You sit tight. This will all be over in half a jiffy."

Sarah stared straight ahead, a lump rising in her throat, as Jack walked away. She was confident that "half a jiffy" did not mean safely, as it was obvious the encounter would end violently.

CHAPTER 24

JACK—FRIDAY, OCTOBER 15, 1909,
10:00 A.M.

*C*lara's cab stopped half a block from the Children's Benevolent and Protective Society. She got out and spoke with a swarm of street kids before handing over some coins. As soon as the money dropped into their hands, the children ran and threw rocks at two uniformed cops lounging across the way from Patterson's building. The kids scattered, with the cops lumbering in pursuit. Once they were out of sight, Clara continued down the street and went into the building.

"Mister! Mister! My baby sister's real sick. Got a penny?" The commotion had alerted another pack of children, who ran up to Jack and began working their cons. Jack looked at a small girl holding the hand of another kid about two years old. Both had thin, tubercular chests, ragged clothing, and filthy bare feet. When the older kid stopped wheedling, the younger one stuck out her lower lip and began crying right on cue.

"You two got a good sympathy racket going." He held out a dime to the older one. "Keep that kid quiet, and this is yours." The crying stopped, and Jack handed over the coin.

The rest of the kids crowded around, and he pulled out all his change, which was about a dollar's worth. He pointed at a shifty-eyed boy. "I'll give this to you to spread evenly, all right?" The kid nodded, and Jack forked over the change into his grubby hands. The whole cluster of kids disappeared into an alley. Better they got his change than the cops or morgue flunkies if this went bad.

"Don't you be giving them money." A big foreign-sounding woman stood in the open doorway of the Children's Benevolent and Protective Society. "Handouts hurt their character, mister."

"Can't help it. Just a natural sucker, I guess." He mounted the steps. "I'm with that red-headed gal who just came in."

"Are you now." She didn't sound the least bit convinced.

Jack stepped inside and looked around at the big tables that filled the front room. A couple of small boys were lugging baskets of foodstuffs into a rear kitchen. "Just point me to where she and Patterson are at and I'll announce myself."

The woman pointed a thick finger at a closed side door. He opened it without knocking. Clara and a well-dressed guy stood over a satchel full of money. A black Bible sat on the table next to the bag. Two pistols were leveled at his chest.

"Jack," said Clara, "you look like a mummy with that stuff wrapped around your head. How can you even see? You should have stayed in your hospital bed, poor man."

"You're such a caring soul, Clara. Patterson, let me introduce myself. Jack Harden. Private dick."

Patterson grinned. "I heard you've been snooping around. Put your gun on the table, real slow."

Jack complied. "You're a cool customer. If I were you, I'd be scared to death that Clara and I were going to take your money and that Bible. You don't trust her any, do you?"

"Not in the least," he said. "But Clara's too smart to hang onto that Bible and too greedy to split her cash. That leaves you all by your lonesome, friend."

Clara finished counting the money. "It's all here." She looked at Patterson. "What're you going to do with him?"

Patterson ordered Jack to his knees. Jack didn't move.
Patterson cocked the hammer of his gun. "Get down. Otherwise
I'll shoot and tell the police that you came at me with that big
pistol of yours. It's clear from that bandage that you aren't in
your right mind."

"Yeah, you got experience getting away with shooting guys
in the head, don't you?" A firm knock sounded at the door.
Clara and Patterson exchanged a look as the door opened and
Sarah joined them.

"Well, the gang's all here. Hello, Dr. Goody-Goody," said
Clara as she closed the satchel.

"Lucas Patterson," said Sarah, "there is evidence tying you to
the murder of Nick Monkton. There is also reason to suspect
you murdered Lizzie Sullivan."

"That's absurd." The pistol shook in Patterson's hand. "I
haven't hurt anyone. And you have no idea how much I cared
for Nick. I did everything I could to help him, to promote his
talent. Nick had his stubborn pride and wanted to make it on
his own. He pushed me away—even though he still wanted my
money."

"Nick offered to sell you that Bible, right?" Jack nodded at
the table, careful not to move his hands.

"He knew how much it would help me in the mayor's race."
Patterson laughed softly. "Nick wanted cash for the Bible so he
could move to New York. I'd hoped to talk him out of it."

"I identified your fingerprints on a glass at the scene of
Nick's death." Jack marveled at Sarah's fearlessness. Her analyt-
ical mind kept right on going even with two guns trained on her.

"After I had Nick released from the police he sent me a
message." Patterson's face relaxed as he looked off into the
middle distance. "He told me the Bible was missing, but that he
still had great news. Like a fool I hoped he wanted to reconcile,
so I dashed over to that grubby stable where he was hiding. I
brought a fine brandy to toast our love, but he laughed in my

face after we drank. It was still just about money for Nick. He told me he'd found Lizzie's dead body and shot her to set up Horace Shaw—as a favor to me. Then he had the nerve to demand a thousand dollars for the favor so he could go to New York. That was it for me. I wrote him a bank draft for fifty dollars and said I never wanted to hear from him again."

"You gave that man fifty bucks for shooting Lizzie?" Clara turned to Patterson.

"I suppose I could have given him more," he said with a shrug. "I was upset."

In a single fluid motion Clara stomped on Patterson's instep and kneed him in the groin, sending the man to the floor. She stepped to the door, leaning to one side from the weight of the bag of cash. "Jack, thanks for caring about what happened to Lizzie. I'm sorry you got hurt." Her big eyes were full of sincerity. "Read the back of that Bible. It'll make up for things. I promise."

"That look from you makes me think that a safe's about to fall on my head."

Clara gazed at him for a second, then left.

Jack picked up the Colt and walked over to where Patterson was gasping on the floor. Although the guy looked down for the count, Jack kicked his pistol across the room.

"What do we do now?" Sarah was moving like a cornstalk in a windstorm.

"Let's look at the Bible. That's what this whole mess has been about." He flipped the battered book open to the title page. "Sarah, is it legit?"

She hovered over the book. "The American Bible Society published this volume in 1870." She flipped to the back, where the notes were dated 1899. "There is no obvious reason to suspect forgery, as with the earlier book."

They read the account, which began: "I, Rev. Charles Lombard, have recorded these words from the lips of Annie

Monkton, former slave, according to her wishes in the year 1899." The handwriting was neat, the story clear.

"The real Bible has nothing to do with Shaw," said Jack. "Clara lied about that, too."

The door swung open and banged against the wall. A small girl with stringy blond hair and bright blue eyes charged into the room. She was about seven years old and wearing an ill-fitting, washed-out blue dress. Little legs churned under the billowy frock as she waved a handful of envelopes in her hand. "Mr. Patterson, here's your mail."

Patterson raised himself to his knees and retrieved a small derringer pistol from his jacket pocket. The girl slowed as she approached him, but Patterson reached with his free hand and pulled her close as mail scattered to the floor. His carefully combed hair spilled down his forehead. "Put the Bible on the table and leave," he said. "I have great things to accomplish."

"Let her go," said Sarah. "You cannot achieve good through evil means."

Patterson put the pistol to the girl's head, a smirk on his lips. "Despite your education, Sarah, you are a simpleton. There is no hope for justice without blood. The corrupt forces of the rich ensure that. When I release this Bible, I will be elected mayor. I will make Baltimore a shining example of social justice. Think of it—Negro rights, child labor laws, votes for women. An end to police graft and violence. It's worth any price. Even that of little Laurie here." He pushed the gun barrel even harder into the girl's scalp.

"Oww—that hurts," Laurie said with a whine. "I don't like this game."

"Release the child." Sarah took a step toward him.

"You have far too much bourgeois sentimentality to risk her life, dear. We both know that." Patterson used one arm to press his hostage across her windpipe while keeping the gun nestled in her lank hair. Laurie's bony arms and legs flailed as she gasped for air.

"Pal, there's no skating away from this." Jack raised the Colt, hoping his one good eye would permit a decent shot. Patterson's kneeling form was blurry—it was difficult to separate his shape from that of the girl. Still, Jack had no trouble sensing the spiky ripple of unstable energy flowing from the man.

"Sarah, call off your barbarian. Do it now. I've got all the leverage." Laurie's eyes bulged as the full terror of the situation dawned on her. She clawed at Patterson's arm, which led him to tighten his grip even more. The girl made a gurgling sound as her face began to turn blue.

"Jack, we have no realistic option other than to do as he instructs. We must leave." Sarah set the Bible on the table and slowly backed toward the door.

"What, we're going to let him get away with this?" Jack had to ask although he already knew the answer. He lowered the Colt.

"Good. Now get out of here. I'm going to hang on to this child for a while to make sure you don't come back." Patterson relaxed his arm. Laurie squirmed like an eel and almost broke free, but Patterson managed to grab a wrist. The girl screamed.

Jack experienced the next series of events as happening very slowly. The scream brought forth a bunch of ghostly brown children, all of whom were wailing. Then a new variation on the supernatural: Sarah leaping past the spirits with skirts billowing, right foot extended. *So many people need my help.* Jack stood frozen and watched Patterson's mouth drop open as Sarah's flying form came closer. *Do something.*

Patterson let go of Laurie, who scrambled away just before Sarah's foot glanced off his upper arm. *I'm letting it happen again.* Sarah tumbled to the floor and Patterson stood, carefully aiming his pistol at her. *She's going to be killed.* A thunderclap as the Colt bucked in Jack's hand. Patterson jerked, looked in disbelief at the blood blooming across his crisp white shirt, and collapsed. The ghostly children stared at him for a brief moment through the gun smoke and vanished.

Sarah jumped up, grabbed her medical bag, and ripped open Patterson's shirt. "Jack, press this gauze on the wound."

Jack rushed instead to Laurie, who was sobbing in the arms of the big woman who had appeared in the doorway. "Are you all right?" he asked the back of the girl's torn dress.

"What happened here?" The woman gave Jack an accusing look. "What happened to Mr. Patterson?"

"Get the cops. Patterson's been shot." Jack walked over and pocketed the derringer.

"Jack." Sarah's voice was very loud. "I need you. Right now." She was pressing a bandage over Patterson, who looked at her glassy-eyed. "Place as much pressure on this as you can."

Patterson yelped as Jack pushed down on the wad of gauze over his right shoulder. "I can pay you," he said between gritted teeth. "Pay you a lot."

"Shut up." Jack put his back into it, and Patterson uttered a piteous groan.

"Now lift him so I may apply this bandage behind the exit wound." Sarah presented a clean bandage bundle. "Raise him gently."

"What's the point? Isn't he a goner?"

"The wound is likely nonfatal," Sarah said in her matter-of-fact voice. "It appears the bullet passed cleanly through while missing the bones of the coracoid process and scapula."

"Too bad my aim was off." After she placed the second bandage, Jack pointed out the door. "Now go check on the kid." Sarah left just as a terrible dizziness forced him to sit on the floor, head between his knees. *The other guy's shot, and I'm the one about to pass out,* he thought with a punchy grin.

Sarah returned. "Jack. You are pale. This exertion has been excessive, considering the seriousness of your head injury."

"I'm fine. How's the girl?"

"She has some bruises but is otherwise uninjured. She talked with the woman about what happened, and appears largely recovered from the trauma." Sarah flexed her fingers while looking over his head. "I am grateful for your action to save us, Jack."

"That was some chance you took, jumping at a guy holding a gun."

"I used ballet: grand jeté—a horizontal jump. It was inelegant, as I have always been too clumsy to perfect the steps."

"Looked dandy to me." A wave of nausea was rolling in. "Look, we got to get our story straight before the cops get here."

"Story? We must tell the truth, Jack. I insist."

"We need to package the truth carefully. I'm not saying we lie, exactly. More like we just don't tell the cops everything we know."

"Lying by omission is still lying."

"Sarah, just put the Bible in your bag and don't say anything about it. Say nix about Clara. Just say we were having a friendly chat with Patterson. My gun went off by mistake and he got winged. I'll talk to him before the cops get here—got a feeling he'll be happy to chalk all this up to an innocent accident."

"No. I intend to reveal the evidence connecting him to Nick's murder. And I will provide details about what he did to that child."

"Not a good idea. First off, the detectives won't care about your fingerprint work—but they'd be happy to arrest us for tampering with evidence about Nick's death." Jack loosened his tie as clammy sweat ran down his face. "Second, if we rat on Patterson, he'll turn around and accuse us of charging in and attacking him. He's got money—the cops are bound to like his story better. Don't worry, though. That Bible's going to come in real handy."

"Are you planning to use the Bible for corrupt purposes? I am extremely disappointed with you, Jack."

"Skip the righteous lecture. That book's going to get Shaw cleared of murder."

"You want to collect your fee. That is all you care about—not justice."

"You're getting a cut, don't forget. Suppose you'll donate your dough to charity. Or give all your servants a raise." The room spun like a roulette wheel.

"Under no circumstance will I subvert justice." She turned to minister again to Patterson.

"It so happens I do care about justice," said Jack. "And we just might squeeze out a little bit of it in this case. But you know what makes me happy? You and me are almost finished." The last thing he remembered was how soft the carpet was when his head hit it.

CHAPTER 25

SARAH—FRIDAY, OCTOBER 15, 1909,
1:00 P.M.

*T*elling less than the complete truth grew harder each time the authorities questioned her. First were the uniformed policemen. They made few inquiries, most of which she let Jack answer—fortunately he regained consciousness quickly. Then the same city detective she had seen at Nick's autopsy showed up. He sauntered over while she was replacing Patterson's bandage.

"Criminy, sweetheart, what have you got yourself mixed up in this time? Never saw a gal who liked blood and guts as much as you." The detective turned to Jack, who was propped in a chair. "Why'd you plug Mr. Patterson, snooper?"

"Accident," said Jack. "Patterson told us he was dropping out of the mayor's race because he wants to take up target shooting full-time. He asked to see my Colt, so I pulled it out. The guy suddenly grabbed for it, and it just went off. Man needs to learn a lot more about handling a big pistol."

"That true, Mr. Patterson, sir?" the detective asked.

"Yes, the whole thing was just an unfortunate mishap." Patterson was on the floor with a gold silk pillow under his head and his hands pressed over a pile of bloody gauze. "I'm just so grateful no children were nearby when it happened. My interest in firearms was clearly misplaced. I'm going to quit politics and redouble my efforts to serve poverty-stricken youth."

Sarah clenched her fists tightly as she listened to the man lie without any apparent compunction. Her body trembled with the effort to keep quiet.

"Well. How about that, now." The detective turned to Sarah. "The boys were just playing with a gun and then it went bang, all innocent-like?"

She gave a stiff nod.

"Can't hear you, sugar pie."

She crossed her arms. "The pistol was displayed and then discharged. Fortunately, I was able to stanch the resulting wound. Detective, Mr. Patterson must be transported to a hospital in short order so that surgeons may examine his injury."

"Got a meat wagon on the way." The detective snorted and turned to Jack. "I know something fishy's going on here. You can bet I'm going to tell Snake Eyes all about it. He'll be wanting to pay you another visit. Keep that one peeper peeled while you still got it, hear?"

"Tell O'Toole to take a bath before he shows his ugly mug again." Jack put his handkerchief to his nose and blew. The detective tromped off.

Sarah went to Jack, fingers waggling in a blur. "You need a change of dressing and immediate bed rest."

"No more hospital for me. And my landlady don't permit female visitors. Not sure she's ever heard of a lady doctor. Or a lady detective." He gave her a half-witted smile. "I like sitting here. Getting cold, though."

"You are slipping into shock. I will take you to my residence and have my housekeeper prepare a room for you."

"Take me—I'm all yours." Jack tried to stand without success. Sarah checked his pulse. It was alarmingly weak.

"Ambulance is here!" called the large woman as two attendants walked in with a stretcher.

"Take this man to my residence," said Sarah, pointing to Jack. "I will accompany him."

"What about Mr. Patterson?" asked the woman.

"He can wait. Call another wagon." She supervised Jack's placement onto the stretcher and walked with the attendants to the ambulance, providing directions to her home. He was babbling nonsense and blood was trickling freely from the gauze over his eye.

Sarah knew it was a serious risk to take him to her house rather than to Hopkins, yet she was afraid to go to the hospital. Not of the facility itself—but of one of its most eminent doctors.

CHAPTER 26

JACK—SATURDAY, OCTOBER 16, 1909, 9:00 A.M.

A clobbering headache kept him company as he sat with Sarah outside Commissioner Lipp's office.

Thanks to her, he was in the best shape possible. He'd rested at her house, eaten well, and had a clean bandage put over his eye. While passed out, someone had shaved and bathed him. Even though the housekeeper was an old woman with a withered arm, Jack told himself that she must have been the one to scrub and put him in a new union suit. At least he would leave a clean corpse if he couldn't pay Knucks later that afternoon. Everything depended on how their meeting with Lipp went.

Sarah pulled strings to get the appointment. Lipp wasn't happy about seeing them, a fact made clear by the presence of Snake Eyes O'Toole in a nearby chair.

The dick was there for intimidation, maybe worse. At the moment he was thumbing through a *National Police Gazette*. A beautiful woman showing lots of skin looked out with a smoldering gaze from the cover. The caption was "Fatal Beauty's Husband on Trial for Killing Her Wealthy Lover." Now, that was a story that had everything going for it.

"Snake," said Jack, "game seven's later today in Detroit. Last chance for your man Cobb to prove he's a winner."

"Got his spikes sharpened and ready to plant in krauthead Wagner's shin." O'Toole didn't look up.

Sarah was reading a medical journal, leaving Jack to wish there was another issue of the *Gazette* handy. All he could do was look around the office at the lounging clerks, beat-up furniture, and framed pictures of bygone cops.

There was a potted palm in a corner. Somebody had been taking decent care of it, and some new leaves were sprouting. "Heard something funny about Lizzie," he said to Sarah, who seemed to ignore him. "A friend of hers told me she saw colors when she heard words. Like when someone said 'dance' she saw the same color green as those new palm leaves."

Sarah stared at his forehead with the most intense look he had ever seen from her. "Do you know if it was common for Lizzie to see colors when hearing words?"

Jack sat up a little straighter. "The friend said Lizzie talked about hearing colors since she was a kid. Strange, huh?"

"This is highly significant. It likely indicates that—"

Lipp appeared at his door, eyes shooting daggers. "I will give you five minutes to explain yourselves. You are lucky I can spare that much time." They went into his office. Lipp sat in an expensive-looking leather chair behind an enormous oak desk with a mirrorlike finish. The only things on it were a fancy clock and a gilt-framed portrait of a light-haired girl standing next to an older woman.

"The wife and daughter?" Jack asked, pointing to the portrait. "Handsome pair."

"My family has nothing to do with you." Lipp leaned forward on his elbows with his brow low over his small eyes. "Tell me what you have to say and get out."

Jack heard Sarah's hands tapping against the underside of

the desk. One of her legs was jiggling so hard the fabric of her long skirts rustled like a sail in a fair wind. "I know you're a busy man, Commissioner. And given you're now running unopposed in the election, you'll be our next mayor. Both Dr. Kennecott and I are grateful for your time."

"Enough. I insist that you—"

Jack held up his hand. "After all, why should you bother with us? I'm a nobody, and you're not a fan of Dr. Kennecott. Could it be that you wonder if we have a certain Bible in our possession?"

Lipp sat back in his chair and steepled his fingers. "I live my life according to the Bible. I have naught to fear from the Good Book." His mouth flattened into a diagonal white slash as a vein in his forehead began throbbing.

Jack dropped Annie Monkton's Bible on the desk. "You know this is your great-granny's, don't you?" Lipp stared at the book for a while before pulling it toward him and flipping to the handwritten pages in the back. The vein on his forehead pulsed like a snake in a sack. "I'm guessing you've known for a long time that your great-grandma was black," said Jack. "That makes you one-eighth Negro, or as some put it, an octoroon. The law says you're passing as a white man. Your pull with the white supremacist crowd will take a hit when this gets out."

Lipp snorted. "This proves nothing. An old colored woman makes up a story. Who's going to believe it?"

"Most everyone if it's backed up by the big casino Reverend Charles Lombard, who wrote down what Annie told him. He took it as the gospel truth." Jack pushed the Bible closer to Lipp. "I'm sure Lombard will confirm this if push comes to shove."

The commissioner raised a finger as if he were about to call down divine wrath, but said nothing. Slowly, he dropped his hand as his jaw quivered. "My father told me the secret when I announced my engagement, just as his father told him. About the chance of having children with Negro features. In the end, we put our faith in God and He rewarded us."

Sarah slammed her hand down on the desk. "It has nothing to do with religious faith. You have no excuse whatsoever for your appalling hate and hypocrisy."

"I have prayed so hard," said Lipp in a shaky voice. "And, for a long time, the sin was hidden. My great-grandfather had his only living heir with his slave. The child was fair enough to substitute for the son who died with his mother in childbirth. There was talk, but that was common on plantations. One learned to evade, to deny, to believe what one wanted to be true. My grandfather and father both had children that, for all appearances, were white. I also have a child, and as you see, she is as pale as snow."

"Not according to your racial belief system," said Jack. "Imagine how shocked your daughter would be to know she's mixed race. That's not all—according to the law your marriage to a white woman was illegal and you could get tossed in jail."

"Stop!" Lipp shook his raised fists.

"You thought your secret was safe," said Jack. "You didn't know that your black great-granny got that preacher to write what she knew about her family in the Bible. Then she dies, and the Bible gets sent to her favorite great-grandson, Nick. He reads the family tree, sees your name, and figures out you two are cousins. Since Nick was a natural sleaze, he tries to blackmail you. The guy was no genius, yet he was bright enough not to keep the Bible on him. You had O'Toole pick up Nick to make him talk, but Patterson's lawyer interfered. O'Toole finds Lizzie's place tossed and suspects Clara got the Bible. Cops tail her until she slips me the fake book."

"That woman."

"I hear you. Anyway, you discover she gave me a fake—it was pretty clever on her part to substitute Shaw's name for yours, by the way. You needed to find her again, but she's dropped out of sight. Since Patterson's still in the mayor's race, and since he's loaded, it makes sense to you that Clara plans to sell the Bible to him. Problem is that he's too rich and important for you to intimidate directly. So, you have cops watching Patterson's office with orders to snare Clara before she gets to him. She's too smart for you. Again."

Lipp sank even lower in his chair. Jack stood and leaned over the desk. "You know what's too bad, Lipp? If your boys had done a competent investigation of Lizzie's murder you would have found out that Nick shot her. Then you could have cut an easy deal with the guy—no muss, no fuss."

Lipp's sour look returned. "What do you want?"

"Let's talk about what you're not going to do. You're not going to have us bumped off or arrested—I assume that's why O'Toole's waiting outside. I've made photographs of your family tree here and left instructions that they go to the press if anything happens to us."

"I'm not a rich man, but I can offer you some money."

"Don't want your money."

"You want a city job. Just name it."

"Here's what we want: you drop charges against Horace Shaw. Immediately."

"Agreed."

"And you let Dr. Kennecott write up the official cause of death for both Lizzie and Nick. You'll have both reports accepted as official."

"All right." His voice was faint.

"Also, the cops will use Dr. Kennecott's evidence to investigate Lucas Patterson for killing Nick and Lizzie."

"No," said Sarah.

"I beg your pardon?" Lipp shot her a cranky look.

"I strongly suspect that Lucas Patterson did not kill Nick," said Sarah. "Or Lizzie."

Jack leaned over to her. "Wait a minute. What about your evidence on the guy?"

"I have reason to believe someone else killed Nick. That same person also likely inflicted Lizzie's fatal head injury."

"Who?"

"This a matter requiring discretion. Ensure no one is listening at the door."

Jack sat with his mouth open for a bit before going to the door and looking back into the waiting area. O'Toole still had his nose in the pink sheets of the *Gazette*. "All clear."

"Very well," she said. "Let us now have further discussion with Police Commissioner Adolph Lipp."

THE REST of the morning and early afternoon went great. Jack met with Horace Shaw at the Rennert Hotel and never saw a guy happier to fork over a fat bankroll.

"Fine work, Harden." Shaw was back in his throne-like chair, chewing a big wad of tobacco and surrounded by men who were again eager for his approval. "You can bet I'm going to tell everyone what a good detective you are. Should get some work out of that. And when I get elected mayor in four years—the good citizens of Baltimore will have long forgotten my involvement in this little dustup by then—you'll have more business than you can handle."

Next came a visit to Knucks Vogel at his saloon over in the Butchers Hill neighborhood. The loan shark took his eleven hundred dollars and graciously invited Jack to sit at his table along with four pretty girls. Jack politely declined.

Walking out of the joint, he saw a newsie hawking papers with the World Series results. Two cents bought more happiness —Pittsburgh won game seven, 8–0, to take the Series. Wagner hit a triple and knocked in two runs while Cobb did zilch. Jack wished he could needle Snake Eyes about that, but the city detective had a bigger problem to deal with.

Jack knew he had plenty of time to walk across town to Johns Hopkins Hospital. He'd rather go almost anywhere else. The place represented sickness and death—never more so than right now.

CHAPTER 27

SARAH—SATURDAY, OCTOBER 16, 1909, 3:45 P.M.

*A*voiding Dr. Anson in the Pathological Building was easy—she hid in an alcove when he passed by, a book open inches from his nose.

Gathering her long skirts, she rushed up the stairs to the landing outside Dr. Macdonald's office. He had agreed to meet at a time set for ten minutes later. Anxiety drove Sarah to arrive early—but she did not want to see him just yet. She turned to go back downstairs and froze when Macdonald called to her.

"You're eager to meet," he said. "Excellent."

She followed him into his office, and when he began to close the door she asked him to leave it slightly ajar, stating a fear of closed space.

He agreed with a smile and gestured to a couch raised at one end and covered in a spread featuring colorful geometric shapes set against a bright coral background. A blue-green patterned pillow with a head-shaped dimple in the middle sat on the elevation. A small Smyrna rug with a red and gold floral pattern lay at the opposite end to protect from patient shoes.

Sarah perched on a chair opposite while Macdonald sat in a

massive wooden armchair set just behind the couch's lifted section. "Laying on the couch helps," he said in his soft, soothing voice. "Want to try it?"

"No. I prefer to sit where I am."

"Fine. I am just pleased to have you here at last, lass." He opened a thick notebook and lifted a pencil.

Sarah noticed two small ceramic creatures displayed on a nearby table. "Those are curious figures," she said, pointing. "A hedgehog and a snake."

"They were given to me by a friend, Professor Carl Jung, after we worked on a case together. The patient was a woman struggling with nightmares about those two animals. Her problem was sexual repression—the hole-forming hedgehog and the phallic snake represented her forbidden desires. Casting off restraint and relishing sex is the key to good mental health."

Sarah looked around the room, wanting to move their conversation to a subject other than sex. She considered asking him about a collection of antique bronze amulets hung from strings on a nearby wall, but noticed the objects were all shaped like phalluses.

"You're here to discuss your illness," said Macdonald. "Correct?"

"You say Dr. Anson first alerted you to the seriousness of my supposed condition?"

"He was worried about your deluded investigation. I told him you showed signs of mental illness, we compared notes, and I suggested that Bleuler's concept of schizophrenia might possibly apply. He urged me to visit you in the lab."

"Did Dr. Anson first come to you with his concern after I spoke with him on Monday afternoon? That was when I told him of my investigation into Lizzie Sullivan's murder."

"Aye." Macdonald pressed his fingertips together. "Anson came to me that afternoon. He cares for you and was worried that you were having a break with reality. And when I visited you in the lab I agreed—your condition had gotten much worse since we first met."

"I have read Dr. Bleuler's paper on schizophrenia and disagree that I have the disorder. My mind is not fragmented, nor am I in any way broken with reality."

Macdonald wrote in silence after she finished. "My dear, denial of the condition is a cardinal sign of the illness." He spoke calmly and slowly. "I once had a patient who believed she was Marie Antoinette. When I didn't believe her, she pointed to her paper crown and asked if I was blind. When I said her crown was not real she ordered me guillotined. Now, your illness is just emerging. You are quite lucky—you may have periods of lucidity."

"You are well acquainted with Dr. Anson, are you not?"

"Aye. He is a good friend." Macdonald continued to write.

"When you worked with Dr. Bleuler, I assume you shared his interest in synesthesia—known colloquially as 'hearing colors'?"

Macdonald's pencil hovered over his notebook. "Aye. Dr. Bleuler is a leading authority and we had many discussions on the topic. Synesthesia is fascinating, and anyone writing about it is assured of a large audience. Sarah, your questions make no sense."

"When Dr. Anson told you he had found a subject presenting with robust synesthesia you arranged for her to come here for an interview. Correct?"

"You are now paranoid, my dear." Macdonald lowered his pencil. "Your condition is even farther along than I suspected."

"I have a hypothesis about how events unfolded when you met with Lizzie Sullivan in this office last Friday. She laid upon this couch while you asked about her synesthesia. She was very happy that a man was interested in her mind—that was likely a unique and thrilling experience for her. You took notes with the

idea of compiling a case study and found Lizzie to be a cooperative subject. But she was an attractive young woman and you
found yourself aroused. You demanded sex, she refused. A
struggle ensued, and she scratched you through the pinkish
cashmere throw on the couch. You retaliated and threw her to
the floor. She hit her head—likely on the leg of the chair in
which you now sit."

"A remarkable fantasy."

"Lizzie lay unconscious," Sarah said. "And instead of seeking
help, you first recorded what happened in your notebook. The
key to effective self-analysis is keeping an immediate and
scrupulously honest record of one's behavior, is it not? Then
you went to ask Dr. Anson for his assistance with Lizzie. When
you returned, she was gone. Along with your notebook. It was
her way of revoking consent to participate in your research."

Macdonald slowly stroked his beard.

"Nick Monkton then got in touch with you two days later,
saying Lizzie had died and that he had your notebook—which
now amounted to a confession of murder. He demanded money
in return for the notebook and instructed you to meet him
Tuesday at a stable in Fells Point. You went there with alcohol,
which Nick believed to be a gesture of goodwill—not suspecting
that you put chloral hydrate in his drink. Once Nick was unconscious, you shot him, wrote a fraudulent suicide note, reclaimed
your notebook, and removed all traces of your visit. It was clever
of you to leave the glass remaining from an earlier visitor."

"They told me you were smart. Strange but smart."
Macdonald smiled broadly. "Poor dear, it is your brain that will
be your undoing."

He stood and brushed the wrinkles from his trousers. "I
merely have to file with the court for your involuntary commitment to the asylum. Anson will concur. Soon—what is the
popular phrase?—the men in the white coats will come for you.

That will make your story nothing more than the ravings of a hysterical woman lashing out at colleagues because of her own professional failure. And even if the police did pay any attention to your claims, there is no evidence of my involvement in those deaths."

"You overlook a piece of physical evidence that is conclusive. Your fingerprints on the suicide note, which is in my possession. That was a serious flaw in your method. If you had worn gloves no one could ever associate you with the murder."

She was conjecturing that the unidentified prints on the note were Macdonald's. This was a guess—what Jack would call a bluff, since even if the prints did belong to Macdonald there was no assurance the police would consider them. And there was little chance that the police could gain access to a doctor's private notebook even if they tried. If Macdonald chose to laugh at her he could get away with his crimes.

Macdonald did not laugh. Instead, he strolled over to his desk. "Impressive—you are a female Sherlock Holmes who has unmasked the killer. Yes, it's true—I caused Lizzie's death and shot that criminal Nick. Not that anyone else will ever know."

He picked up a letter opener shaped like a dagger. "Some schizophrenics are known to have violent, unprovoked rages—such as you did when you attacked me with this weapon. Look what you did to me." He ripped his shirt open to reveal three deep scratches down his neck. "During our struggle the blade accidentally plunged into you. So very tragic." Macdonald stepped toward her.

Then there was Jack, yanking Macdonald away. A second man—Detective O'Toole—smashed the doctor in the head with a large revolver. Macdonald fell to the floor as the detective kept raining blows on him.

"Stop this brutality! Stop!" Sarah shouted.

"Keep that frail under control, Harden." The detective gave

the doctor a final kick in the face before handcuffing him and hauling him to his feet.

"Detective," said Sarah, "you will find an autobiographical account of the man's malfeasance in this volume." She handed over Macdonald's notebook.

"Snake," said Jack, "she's saying you got the goods on the guy on those pages."

O'Toole shrugged, took the notebook, and frog-marched the doctor away.

"Sorry we were a little late coming in. The guy seemed harmless right up until the end. You okay?"

"Everything resolved satisfactorily," said Sarah. Her heart was pounding furiously. "I am pleased that we have revealed the truth about Lizzie."

"Yeah. Too bad Lizzie had to die for us to understand what a rare kid she was."

"Jack, I have a request."

"Sure. Name it."

"Embrace me." She extended her arms stiffly. He stood rooted to the floor, causing her an awful moment wondering if he was going to reject her with some cruel remark. Then he took her lightly in his arms. She pressed her body tightly against him and buried her face in his shirtfront. His leather-in-the-sun smell was strong and intoxicating. A desire flowed through her: *Let me stay here forever and ever.* She squeezed her arms as hard as she could around him, causing a cry that forced her to pull away.

"I forgot about your injured ribs. Please accept my apology."

"Not a problem," he said, patting his side.

"I have not been in a man's arms voluntarily since my father died. He used to comfort me in that manner."

"What about me? Did I manage the trick?"

"I am quite well, thank you." She jammed her thumb in her

mouth and furiously chomped on its nail. How stupid she had been to give in to that impulse, which would drive him away. And she had been so pleased with the relationship she had established with this man. Now yet another social blunder had ruined everything.

"Now I have a request," said Jack. "You can tell me to jump in the lake—I mean, you can say no and I won't mind."

She dropped her hands to her sides, baffled at what he might want. "What is your request?"

"I want to kiss you. On the cheek."

She stood motionless for long time before slowly, very slowly, offering her cheek. Jack gently brushed her face with his lips. Bright patches of light swam in her vision and for a moment she thought she would faint. She was desperate to be alone, to escape this confounding man, to get herself under control.

"Hey," said Jack, "here's something that'll give you a thrill." He reached into his pocket and offered her a roll of cash. "This is half what Shaw gave me."

"Leave me now." She blinked at the money.

"Take it. We're partners."

She snatched the roll. "Go."

"Let's meet Monday morning. Your place?"

"No!"

Jack flinched. "Jeez, you don't have to yell. Where then?"

She had not cried in front of anyone but the dolls for many years, but found herself alarmingly close at this moment. "Lunchroom."

"But the smell—" He looked at her carefully. "All right. See you there at nine a.m." He left quickly and closed the door behind him.

Sarah sat in Macdonald's big armchair and sobbed until her nose dripped onto her skirt. There was a neat pile of folded handkerchiefs on the table, and she used one to clean her face.

Then she took several deep breaths with her head between her knees. Mind aswirl, she wanted nothing more than to go home and pour her heart out to the dolls.

But more tears could wait. She still had one difficult—and dangerous—task left.

CHAPTER 28

JACK—MONDAY, OCTOBER 18, 1909, 9:00 A.M.

"*T*ell me exactly what happened. Keep it simple and don't worry—I'll keep my mouth shut."

Jack leaned forward in his chair at the Monumental Lunchroom and gestured for the waitress to sit down. She refused but twirled her finger to get him talking.

Jack checked that nobody was nearby and motioned her close. "It all started when a sleazy con man named Nick found a family Bible that had notes about how Commissioner Lipp and himself had the same great-granny. According to the law, that meant Lipp is colored—which is a problem, since the guy preaches white supremacy and is running for mayor. Nick tries to blackmail Lipp, who hasn't got the money.

"Nick then offers to sell the Bible to his rich boyfriend Lucas Patterson, who's also running for mayor. Things really get interesting when Nick finds his girlfriend Lizzie dead after sex with Horace Shaw—the third man in the mayor's race. There're two pieces of good news for Nick here: one, Shaw left his pistol behind; two, Nick finds a Scottish doctor's notebook that describes how he gave Lizzie the knock on her head two days earlier that ended up killing her. The bad news is Nick gave

Lizzie the Bible to hide and he doesn't know where she put it. Change of plan—Nick decides to blackmail the doctor. He also shoots Lizzie's corpse with Shaw's pistol, figuring the guy will get arrested and knocked out of the race, which will help Patterson and get him to cough up money."

"You ain't nearly smart enough to solve that kind of case, boy. Don't be fibbing now."

"You're darn right. Wouldn't have had a chance if it weren't for a special woman—who I'm going to be meeting here in a bit."

"How about that. Been hoping a nice gal would settle you down."

"Not so fast." Jack grinned. "Anyway, Nick's scheme fell apart pretty quick. Lipp gets Snake Eyes O'Toole to go after Nick and find the Bible. Nick goes into hiding and demands cash from Patterson and the doctor. Patterson goes to see him but gets fed up and tells the guy to get lost. The doctor goes later, drugs Nick, and kills him in a way that looks like suicide. He also fetches back his notebook."

"What's the connection between Lizzie and that Scottish doctor guy?" The waitress had a puzzled look on her face.

"Get this: Lizzie had some condition where she saw colors when she heard words. The doctor is interested in that same condition. When a pal tells him about Lizzie, she gets invited to the doctor's office. The doc decides he wants sex, Lizzie says no, they struggle, and she hits her head. He writes it all down and goes to get help, but she wakes up and runs off with the notebook.

"It gets better. Lizzie has a sister, Clara, who's a highbrow actress. She finds Lizzie dead, checks a special hiding place, finds the Bible, and knows she can sell it for a barrel of coin to rich man Patterson, which she does. Then Sarah and I convince Patterson to give us the Bible, which we use to get Shaw cleared."

"Heard you got a ton of money for that."

"I did okay. It was Sarah who figured out that the Scottish doctor whacked Lizzie on the head and also killed Nick. Then she led the cops to him. A real swell lady."

"And plenty smart." The waitress cocked her head. "You sound like you want to marry her."

"You said she's smart, so why the heck would she want that?"

"Hon, can't argue with that." She cracked a rare smile and ambled off.

Sarah appeared at his table a few minutes later, exactly on time. She looked the same as always—wan face, droopy hair, out-of-date hat as well as a dowdy jacket and skirt. Her shirt-waist buttons were misaligned, with the uppermost buttonhole peeking over her collar like a tiny, sleepy eye. He stood and held her chair. "Sarah, you look lovely this morning."

"Dispense with the idle and disingenuous talk." She dropped into her seat.

"Just as blunt as ever. What can I get you?"

"Tea. I assume it is indifferent, at best, yet I will sample it."

Jack motion to the waitress, who gave him a big burlesque wink. "How was the rest of your weekend?" He returned to his greasy plate of bacon, eggs, and fried potatoes.

"I will provide a summary. After you departed, I confronted Dr. Anson about referring Lizzie to Dr. Macdonald and then conspiring to cover up her death. He was unpleasant and even somewhat aggressive. I informed him that Dr. Macdonald was in custody and that the police had his detailed notes. Dr. Anson then apologized to me and attempted to reestablish our previous relationship. I spurned his overtures and departed."

"You're the bravest woman I ever met. Suppose he'd tried to brain you? You should have had me come along."

"He was my mentor." Sarah lifted the bulky cup and sniffed its contents carefully before taking a small sip. "And, until recently, he was the only living man with whom I felt a degree of trust. I felt it necessary to express my grave disappointment to him directly. And alone."

"Is that 'until recently' a roundabout way of saying you like me?" Jack began the question as a tease, but found himself oddly giddy waiting for her reply.

A tremor ran through her body, causing some tea to spill over the side of her cup. "That is a most forward and rude question. Are you making a joke at my expense?" Her cheeks were bright crimson.

"Sorry. Poor choice of words on my part." He was pretty sure he had stirred a reaction that was hard for her to manage, so hard that she was close to bolting. She wanted to keep her feelings about him in the private place where she kept all her other emotions. His own feelings were plenty strong, and he was glad to keep them in check—for now, anyway. "Tell me more about what you did after we caught Macdonald."

Sarah set down the cup and straightened the silverware on either side of it. "After finishing my conversation with Dr. Anson, I visited the medical school dean and provided a full report concerning his two errant faculty members. He vowed to fire them." She took another sip of tea. "The dean also offered me a junior faculty position in the Pathology Department."

"Good for you. That's right up your alley."

"I refused the offer. I no longer wish to have my autonomy curtailed through employment in a male-dominated institution."

"Yeah? Well, what do you plan to do?"

"I will work as a detective." She was staring into her cup with one eyebrow twitching every so often.

"Really. All by yourself?"

"I am accustomed to working alone. I prefer it."

"Seems to me that we make a pretty good team. Why don't we work together?" She looked at him and quickly dropped her eyes back to the cup. "For a little while, I mean. No commitment."

"I shall consider your offer." She glanced up him again. "I see your hands are still shaking. Your color is better. There is no sign of blood on your bandages. Are you in significant physical pain?"

"Nope."

"How is your nervous condition? Do you still have intrusive memories of your traumatic experience? Have you had any recent seizures or fits of aggression? What of your hallucinations?"

Jack grimaced and put a finger to his lips. "Please keep it down. People around here think I'm peculiar, but it's not a good idea to shout about it."

"You should now be well aware of what some consider peculiar behavior on my part, as well."

"Maybe that's why we get on so well. We're both odd ducks." He laughed. "I haven't gone nuts lately. Can't make any promises about the future. I'm jumpy as anything, and my ghosts still haunt me. I expect they always will."

"You must talk to me at length about your trauma. I will provide whatever help I can to ease your suffering."

"Well, a doctor who really wants to help people, you don't say."

"But I just did say that."

"Yeah, okay, you did." Jack smiled but she didn't notice, as she had pulled out a book, opened it, and jammed her nose deep inside the pages. "You want to read. I do, too—there's a great summary of the World Series in the paper."

She kept the book pressed against her face while inhaling deeply for several seconds before lowering it. "I have brought *The Principles of Psychology*, by William James, with me. I am uncomfortable with the author's interest in spiritualism and mystical experience, but feel it best to further acquaint myself with the man's ideas."

They sat in comfortable silence reading for about forty-five minutes until a well-dressed older man approached their table. "Excuse me, sir, miss. My wife is missing, and I'm sick with worry. I've got it on good authority that the two of you are the best detectives in Baltimore, and I sure could use your help."

"Best in the city, how about that." Jack looked at Sarah. "What do you say?"

Sarah blinked rapidly while gazing at the man's shirtfront. "Please sit down, sir, and describe the circumstances of your case. It is possible that it might benefit from the joint efforts of Jack and myself."

AUTHOR'S NOTE

SARAH AND THE AUTISM SPECTRUM

I have tried to present Sarah Kennecott as a person on the autism spectrum. She could not, of course, have been diagnosed as such in 1909 because the concept didn't exist. Still, I am confident people like Sarah—not identical in all ways, but similar—lived during that time.

The American Psychiatric Association's Diagnostic and Statistical Manual of Mental Disorders identified Autism Spectrum Disorder in 2013. This is the latest of many (often, in hindsight, ludicrously inept) attempts by the medical profession to categorize a particular set of physical and mental traits. What follows is a non-exhaustive list of such traits.

Children and adults with autism have difficulty with verbal and non-verbal communication. For example, they may not understand or appropriately use:

- Eye contact
- Facial expressions

- Tone of voice
- Expressions not meant to be taken literally

Additional social challenges can include difficulty with:

- Recognizing emotions in others
- Expressing one's own emotions
- Seeking emotional comfort
- Understanding social cues
- Feeling overwhelmed in social situations
- Gauging personal space (appropriate distance between people)
- Repetitive body movements (e.g. rocking, flapping, spinning, running back and forth)

Many clinicians and advocates hail use of the term "spectrum" because an autistic person is like any other—they are a unique individual with their own way of being in the world. As Dr. Stephen Shore has noted, "If you've met one person with autism, you've met one person with autism." Those with autism range from people who are fully disabled to those who are highly functional and have great success in life.

While many, perhaps most, people diagnosed with ASD have lower than average intelligence (as measured by tests), there is evidence that some with autism have exceptional intellects, including "increased sensory and visual-spatial abilities, enhanced synaptic functions, increased attentional focus, high socioeconomic status, more deliberative decision-making, [and] professional and occupational interests in engineering and physical sciences."

Broad public awareness of autism dates to the 1988 film *Rain Main*, which starred Dustin Hoffman as an intensely awkward savant who could perform amazing, but highly selective, mental tasks. The film was useful for educating the public about autism, but also led to a general assumption that every autistic person was just like the Hoffman character.

What we now call autism was largely unknown among the public prior to 1988. The first mention of autism appeared in the 1980 edition of the DSM; during the 1960s and 1970s autism was blamed on "refrigerator mothers" who failed to love their kids enough. Autism was also linked to schizophrenia as late as the 1970s. Leo Kanner in 1943 described a group of largely intelligent children who craved aloneness and "persistent sameness;" he called this "infantile autism." During the late 1930s and 1940s Hans Asperger used autism in reference to people with a perceived milder form of the condition that came to be known as Asperger's syndrome. Eugen Bleuler coined the term autism sometime between 1908 and 1911 (there is disagreement as to exactly when) as a symptom of schizophrenia, another term that Bleuler invented (more on that below). Bleuler derived autism from the Greek word meaning self, and used it in reference to people who lived in a world that was not accessible to others.

But autistic-like behavior was noted long before the term itself came into use. As Kanner noted, "I never discovered autism—it was there before." Samuel Gridley Howe gets credit for first noticing, prior to the American Civil War, that some people considered "idiots" had a combination of skills and strengths that set them apart from others with intellectual disabilities. Looking back into history, it is arguable that many people, including Michelangelo, Emily Dickinson, Leonardo da Vinci, Isaac Newton, and Thomas Jefferson, were autistic.

The modern neurodiversity movement urges replacement of the term "disorder" with "diversity" to account for neurological strengths and weaknesses and to suggest that variations in brain wiring—such as autism—can be a net positive for individuals and for society as a whole. Neurodiversity and autism advocacy groups share an even more important goal: insisting that people whose minds work differently are treated with respect and compassion.

For more information, see:

1. *Autism Speaks* website, What are the DSM-5 diagnostic criteria for autism?
2. Autism as a Disorder of High Intelligence, *frontiers in Neuroscience*, 2016 Jun 30.
3. *Spectrum* website, The evolution of 'autism' as a diagnosis, explained.
4. *Autism Independent UK* website, History of Autism.
5. How autism became autism: The radical transformation of a central concept of child development in Britain, *History of the Human Sciences*, 2013 July.
6. The Early History of Autism in America, *Smithsonian Magazine*, January 2016.
7. The Myth of the Normal Brain: Embracing Neurodiversity, *AMA Journal of Ethics*, 2015;17(4).

INSTITUTIONALIZED RACISM

During the early years of the twentieth century, Maryland, along with many other states, enshrined racism in a framework of law and social convention. A cornerstone was prohibition of "miscegenation"—the inbreeding of people considered to be of different racial types. Maryland had America's first law criminalizing marriages between black men and white women (1661). The state had a statute on the books forbidding marriage between a black and a white person until 1967 (see the Epigraph), when it was the last state to repeal its law after the Loving v. Virginia case. In addition, there was a law punishing "Any white woman who shall suffer or permit herself to be got with child by a negro or mulatto," as well as a law requiring railroad cars "to provide separate cars or coaches for the travel and transportation of the white and colored passengers."

When a black lawyer bought a house in a posh Baltimore neighborhood in 1910, whites were so upset the city was officially divided into black and white blocks: No black could live on a block where more than half the people were white, and no white could live where more than half the residents were black. *The New York Times* contemporaneously declared this "the most pronounced 'Jim Crow' measure on record."

A coalition of powerful forces tried during the first decade of the twentieth century in Maryland to prevent blacks from voting. Voters, however, defeated proposed amendments to the state constitution in 1904, 1908, and 1910. The principal reason for defeat seems to have been a fear among immigrants that they, too, would be kept from voting; that concern was well-founded, as immigrants were also often the object of scorn and discrimination at the time.

A more fine-grained depiction of racism is evident in the pages of newspapers from the era, including *The Baltimore Sun*. Articles from 1909 are rife with racial stereotypes and explicit bias against people of color. All the headlines and news stories recounted by the pharmacist in the jail cell with Jack in Chapter 20 are drawn from pages of *The Sun*. The same bias can, of course, be found in scores of other newspapers across the nation dating from that time.

For more information, see:

1. *Evoking the Mulatto* website, Timeline.
2. How Racism Doomed Baltimore, *The New York Times*, May 9, 2015.
3. *Here Lies Jim Crow: Civil Rights in Maryland*, C. Fraser Smith, 2008.

BLEULER: SCHIZOPHRENIA AND SYNESTHESIA

Norbert Macdonald's suggestion in Chapter 11 that Sarah suffered from schizophrenia would have been at cutting-edge of medicine in 1909. Eugen Bleuler coined the term in a seminal 1908 paper, which as far as I can tell, has not been made available in an English translation from its original German. Many of the paper's main points are outlined in the Maatz and Hoff article noted below.

Bleuler's ideas about schizophrenia challenged prevailing ideas about severe mental illness and were not broadly accepted at first. But over time psychiatry embraced his concept as the profession moved toward addressing individual suffering rather than treating seriously ill people as a homogeneous category. Bleuler emphasized use of Freudian psychoanalysis as a principal therapy, and while that has proved less effective than originally hoped, it was a vast improvement over earlier treatment methods, which included hydrotherapy and counter-irritation, as depicted in Sarah's asylum experience in Chapter 13.

Before Bleuler developed his ideas about schizophrenia, he studied the phenomenon where some people experienced a sensation of color in association with specific words, letters, or numbers. He called this "double sensations," which was also known as synesthesia. It is defined today as an unusual neurological trait involving cross-sensory experiences. Bleuler's paper with Karl Lehmann in 1881, "Compulsory light sensations through sound and related phenomena in the domain of other sensations," was the first survey and analysis of synesthetes, as those who experienced the sensation are known.

Despite Bleuler's pioneering work, no one has yet written a comprehensive biography of the man. I hope someone undertakes that worthy project.

For more information, see:

1. The birth of schizophrenia or a very modern Bleuler: a close reading of Eugen Bleuler's 'Die Prognose der Dementia praecox' and a re-consideration of his contribution to psychiatry, A. Maatz and P. Hoff, *History of Psychiatry*, 2014 Dec; 25(4) (paywall protected).
2. The "golden age" of synesthesia inquiry in the late nineteenth century (1876–1895), *Journal of the History of the Neurosciences*, DOI: 10.1080/0964704X.2019.1636348.

JACK AND PTSD-LIKE SYMPTOMS

Jack Harden's recurring emotional trouble from his memories of the 1906 Bud Dajo massacre during the Moro War would today likely be diagnosed as Post Traumatic Stress Disorder. The concept was unknown at the time, and the understanding that people could suffer enduring problems after trauma was embryonic at best. As Sarah mentions in Chapter 5, there were scattered studies in connection with Civil War veterans (soldier's, or irritable, heart) and rail accidents (railway spine). By the first decade of the twentieth century, Sigmund Freud and others were speculating about the lingering effect of trauma in the subconscious, but broad public acceptance of what we now call PTSD would take decades.

Few men during this era would accept that any trauma, from battle or otherwise, could impair them. During the Civil War, newspapers reinforced the notion that men had to be tough and strong. "Commiseration felt for these unfortunate individuals [soldiers] is modified by the fact that they are men – men with strong hands, high hearts and hardened nerves – men, consequently, who will know how to battle successfully with the difficulties of their lot." Another wrote: "To win [the battle of life] without a struggle is, perhaps, to win it without honor . . . .

Difficulties may intimidate the weak, but they act only as a stimulus to a man of pluck and resolution ... stand up manfully against misfortune."

For more information, see:

1. Irritable heart syndrome in Anglo-American medical thought at the end of the nineteenth century, Yuri C. Vilarinho, *História, Ciências, Saúde-Manguinhos*, vol.21 no.4 Rio de Janeiro Oct./Dec. 2014.
2. *Brainline: All About Brain Injury and PTSD* website, History of PTSD in Veterans: Civil War to DSM-5.
3. Posttraumatic stress disorder and the nature of trauma, Bessel van der Kolk, *Dialogues in Clinical Neuroscience*, 2000 Mar; 2(1).
4. *The Moro War: How America Battled a Muslim Insurgency in the Philippine Jungle, 1902-1913*, James R. Arnold, 2011.

Note that all website citations were last accessed on December 29, 2019

ABOUT THE AUTHOR

Bill LeFurgy is a professional historian and archivist who has studied the seamy underbelly of urban life, including drugs, crime, and prostitution, as well as more workaday matters such as streets, buildings, wires, and wharves. He has put his many years of research experience into writing gritty historical fiction about Baltimore, where he lived for over a decade. It remains his favorite city.

Bill has graduate degrees from the University of Maryland and has worked at the Maryland Historical Society, Baltimore City Archives, National Archives and Records Administration, and the Library of Congress. He has learned much from his family, including patience, emotional connection, and the need to appreciate different perspectives from those on the autism spectrum and with other personality traits that are undiagnosed, misdiagnosed, or unexplained.

Subscribe to my newsletter: http://eepurl.com/gUf6CD

BillLeFurgy.com

facebook.com/billlefurgy.author
twitter.com/blefurgy
amazon.com/Bill-LeFurgy/e/B083D7HG9K
bookbub.com/profile/bill-lefurgy

Made in the USA
Middletown, DE
22 September 2021